"Kat Wallace, wife, mother, pirate. The order probably should be mother, pirate, wife. Kat's a strong woman who knows her priorities. Her marriage is faltering, her attempts at destroying the man who kept her in captivity for many years keep falling short, and now she has someone living with her family to watch her children thanks to threats. Even then … well, you know something has to happen. The anticipation kept me turning the pages.

Burn the Ship is as action-packed and entertaining as the first two books in the series, but in the third novel we see Kat growing as a person, actually feeling her feelings—yikes—and this deepens her personality and increases the stakes in her relationships. *The Pirates of New Earth* novels are fast-paced, engaging, other world creative, and leave you cheering for Kat at every turn."

– Jacqueline Boulden, Author of *Her Past Can't Wait*

"This is Kat's third outing, and each book has gotten better and better. Branson writes her heart and soul into these astonishing novels, bringing the reader joy and heartbreak in equal measure. [Kat is] the most imperfect heroine that I've ever had the pleasure to read, and it's what makes her so compelling. It's a brilliant narrative on how you can never really know who someone is behind closed doors. I only hope Kat's story is to continue. The snippets that were revealed about her past life were so heart wrenching – and with enough left unsaid that leaves you thirsting for more. Bravo, Sarah."

– Sally Altass, The Indie Book Nook and Author of *The Witch Laws*

Praise for Pirates of New Earth

"The author's Kat Wallace is one of the best heroines you'll find in contemporary sci-fi. We recognize Kat's flaws but admire her emotional depth and strength of character as well as her burning desire to do what's right — even if it means breaking conventional rules. Her passion is palpable."

— David Aretha, award-winning author and book editor

"A fantastically fast-paced page-turner, with a dark streak. Sarah Branson plunges readers into the action and doesn't let us catch our breath until the very last page. You won't be able to put it down!"

— Debby Applegate, author of *Madam: The Biography of Polly Adler, Icon of the Jazz Age*

"*A Merry Life* starts as an adventure tale but quickly becomes something richer — Kat Wallace gains far more than her freedom when she flees to the New Earth pirate nation Bosch. Branson shines at depicting the nuanced familial bonds which form the heart of this story. Watching Kat develop from hot-headed revenge seeker to a competent, mature, powerful woman is deeply satisfying."

— R. L. Olvitt, author of *The Feathered Serpent*

"Sarah Branson's novel, *A Merry Life,* is a rousing page-turner. Her tough-as-nails heroine is relatable and genuine, and the plot is action-packed from start to end. Great for any reader ready to buckle in for a lightning fast ride of a book!"

— Andrea Vanryken, author

"Swashbuckling, vengeance and heart - all wrapped up in one heck of a strong woman."

— Sally Altass, author of *The Witch Laws* and Reedsy.com reviewer

"Readers who enjoy a rollicking adventure firmly rooted in family interactions ... will find that *Navigating the Storm* comes steeped in a battle between love and loyalty in which Kat reconsiders her ultimate goals."

—Diane Donovan, Senior Reviewer, *Midwest Book Review*

"I absolutely adored *A Merry Life*.... If possible, *Navigating the Storm* is even better than the first instalment in Kat's tale. Branson isn't afraid to rip your heart out or to make you laugh."

—Sally Altass, author of *The Witch Laws* and reviewer, Reedsy.com

"This is an incredibly impactful, emotional, entertaining, funny, heart-tugging book."

—Martha Bullen, author and owner, Bullen Publishing Services

"*Navigating the Storm* is not your typical pirate book. Rather, it is a blend of science fiction with steampunk and cyberpunk interlaced with realistic human emotions and experiences set in the twenty-fourth century. Action is high paced and riveting. Kat matures as the book progresses; hitting rock-bottom makes her stronger and savvier, and puts her on firmer ground to face whatever lies in the future."

—Cindy Vallar, editor, *Pirates & Privateers*

BURN THE SHIP

Pirates of New Earth

Book 3

SARAH BRANSON

Pirates of New Earth:
Book 3: Burn the Ship

Published by Sooner Started Press
For more information, visit www.sarahbranson.com
Edited by David Aretha and Andrea Vanryken
Cover design by The Book Designers:
Ian Koviak and Alan Dino Hebel

ISBN (paperback): 978-1-957774-06-0
ISBN (ebook):978-1-957774-07-7

Printed in the United States of America

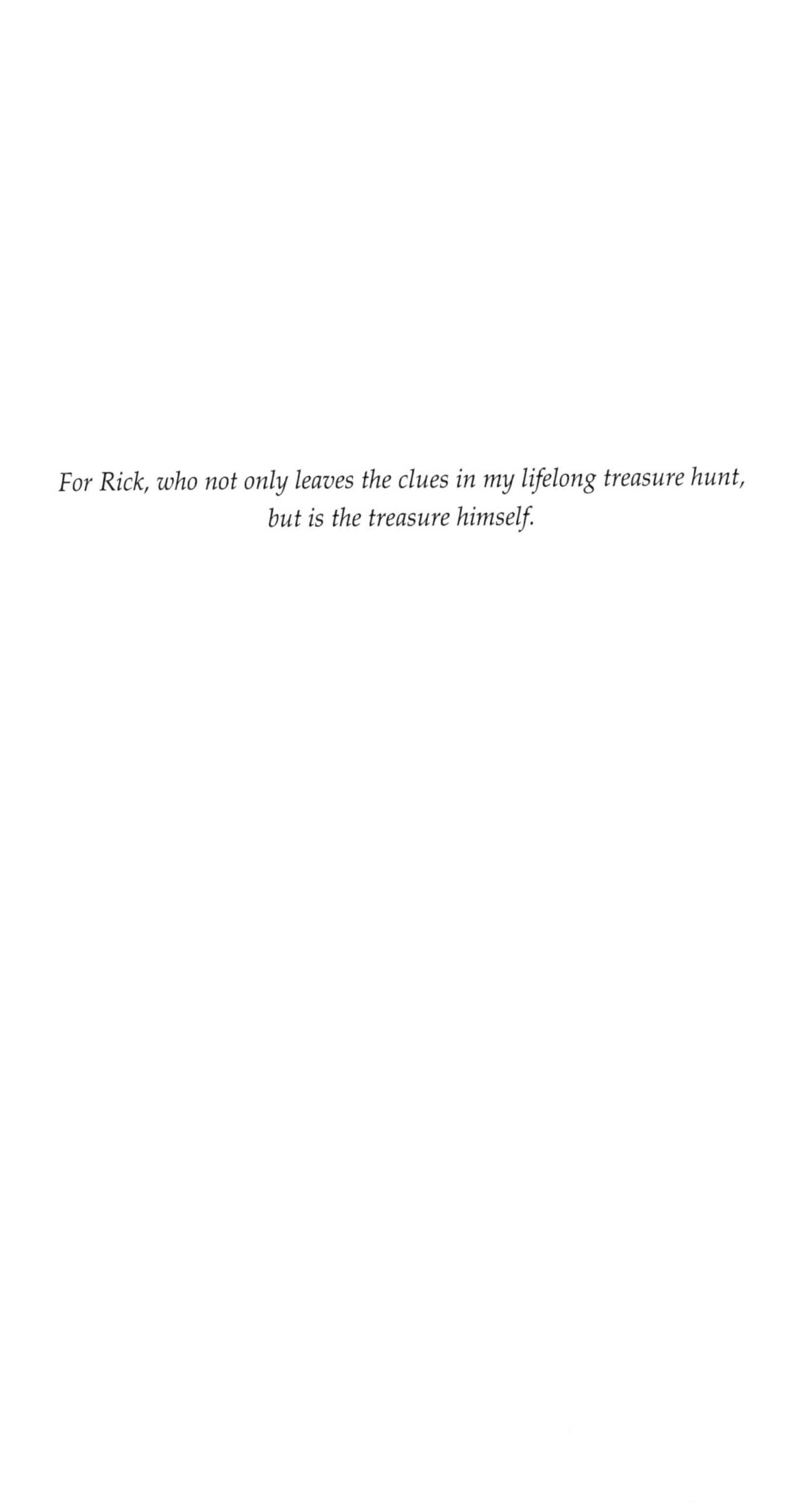

For Rick, who not only leaves the clues in my lifelong treasure hunt,
but is the treasure himself.

The function of freedom is to free someone else.

–Toni Morrison

North Country
Dobarri
Arania
Fairneau
Toronto
Tabonne
Bosch
New Detroit
Haida
Ohlone Bay
State of Eternia
Truvale
New Lisbon
Bellcoast
New Caribbean
Mynia
Parida
Seething Swamp
Dakal
District (I) Banking, Financial, Theater
Distract (II) Light Industry, Business
District (III) Mining (Clay & Glitter)
District (IV) Harbor
District (V) Mining, Manufacturing (Bricks & Glitter) also a developing artist community
District (VI) Agricultural (Grains, Livestock)
District (VII) Agricultural (Vineyards, Orchards)

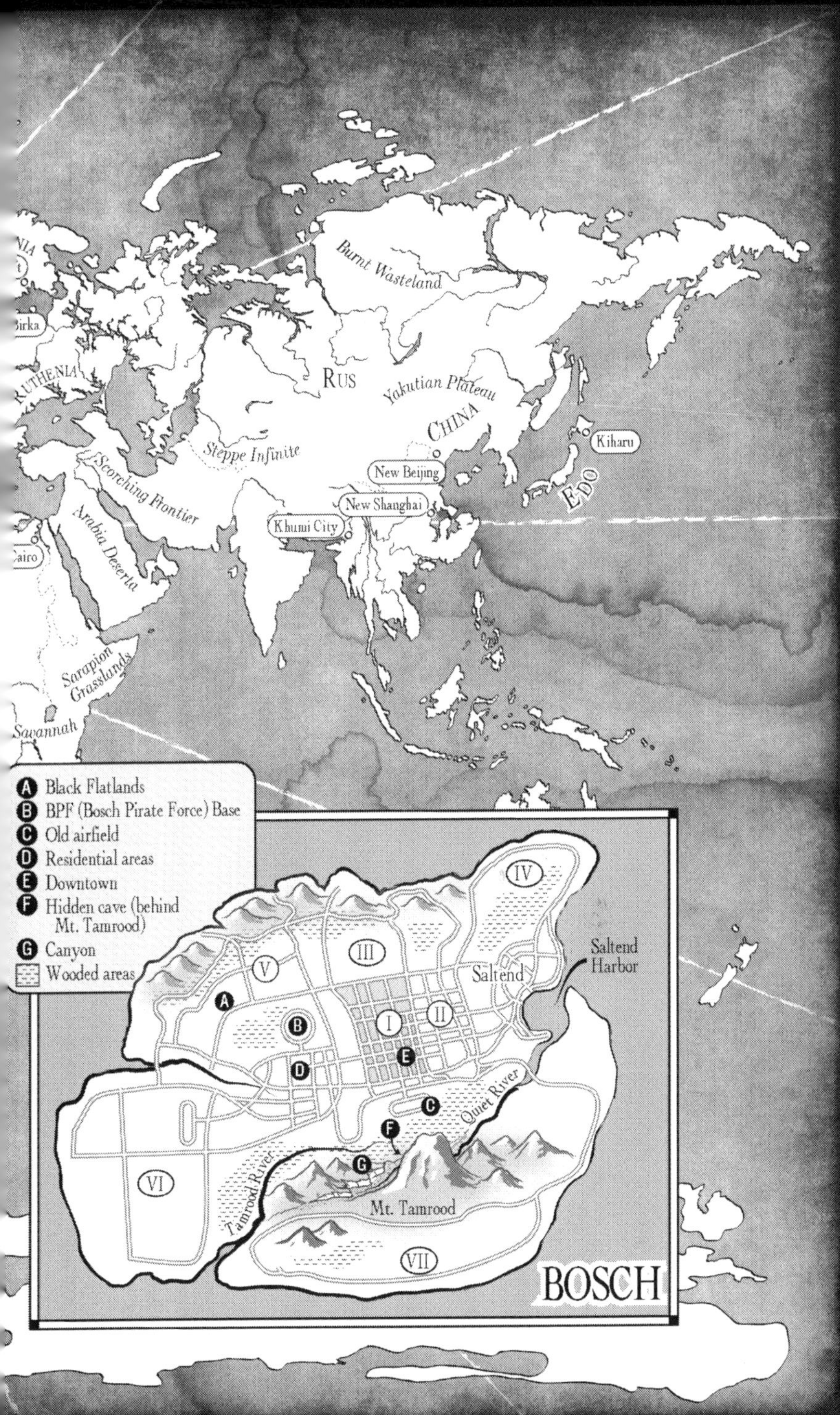

Burnt Wasteland
RUS
Yakutian Plateau
CHINA
Kiharu
EDO
Steppe Infinite
Scorching Frontier
New Beijing
New Shanghai
Khumi City
Arabia Deserta
Birka
RUTHENIA
Cairo
Sarapion Grasslands
Savannah
A Black Flatlands
B BPF (Bosch Pirate Force) Base
C Old airfield
D Residential areas
E Downtown
F Hidden cave (behind Mt. Tamrood)
G Canyon
Wooded areas
IV
III
V
I
II
Saltend
Saltend Harbor
Quiet River
Tamrood River
VI
Mt. Tamrood
VII
BOSCH

Contents

Prologue 1

Part I

1. Revenge Denied 7
Safehaven Point & Bosch, July 2365
2. Nice Shoes 13
Bosch, July 2365 (that afternoon)
3. Say What? 23
Bosch, July 2365
4. Matt Warner 30
Bosch, July 2365
5. Q&A 37
Bosch, Late August 2365
6. Meanwhile 48
Truvale, Sobayton Bay, and Jorge Montt, Patagonia; September 2365
7. New Vest 57
Bosch, October 2365
8. Awilda Unit: First Mission 68
Bosch and Orkneys, November 4, 2365
9. Repercussions 75
Toft, Scania, November 5, 2365
10. Dinner Out 81
Bosch, November 5, 2365
11. Butler Unit: Second Mission 88
Bosch and Far North, November 11, 2365
12. Pirate's Revenge 104
Bosch and Outside Mynia, November 11—12, 2365

Part II

13. What's Next? 133
Bosch and Truvale, November 12—13, 2365
14. Burn the Ship 142
Bosch, November 19, 2365

15. Lydia 148
Bosch, Early December 2365

16. New Plans 155
Bosch, Early January 2366

17. Dominoes 160
Bosch and Edo, Late January 2366

18. X Marks the Spot 186
Bosch, Late January 2366

19. Rats on the Ship 196
Sobayton Bay; Jorge Montt, Patagonia; and Bosch, January 2366

20. The Smoker 205
Bosch, January 28, 2366

21. Graduation Day 216
Bosch, January 29, 2366

22. This Thursday 223
Bosch, February 3, 2365

23. Pasta Thing 230
Seven, February 5, 2366

24. Okay, So Therapy Is an Ongoing Process 244
Bosch, mid-February 2366

25. Another Thursday 249
Bosch, March 3, 2366

26. The Proposal 257
Bosch, March 7, 2366

27. Commitment 262
Bosch, March 10-11, 2366

28. It Pays to Listen 272
Saltend, Bosch March 11—14, 2366

29. It's for the Best 285
Bosch March 14, 2366—Later That Monday Evening

Part III

30. Information 291
Bosch, April 2366

31. Mission 296
Bosch and an Equatorial Jungle, May 2366

32. Best Laid Plans 322
Bosch, Late-May and Early June 2366

33. Politics and Scheming 329
Truvale, June 2366
34. Finally 333
Bosch, June 2366

Acknowledgments 341
About the Author 343
Coming Soon: 345
Blow the Man Down 347
Also by Sarah Branson 355

Prologue

SOBAYTON BAY, FAIRNEAU; SEPTEMBER 2362

Sergeant Demery Ludlow stepped into the Tilted Sip, intent on getting a quick one before flying back to Bosch. The bar was busy, and Demery had to use his broad shoulders to muscle his way to the bar, though he murmured "'Scuse me" as he did so just to avoid a fight. Sobayton Bay, on the windward side of the island of Fairneau, was not known for its culture and manners, especially this close to the docks. It was, however, known for being a great place to move liberated goods without questions being asked. And now, with the unit breaking up and his steady income disrupted, Demery had done just that. Now there were not only markers in his account but also some actual gold coins jingling in his pockets. He may never be on par with Tom Pikari or Kat Wallace, but he was planning to get the spoils that were due him.

"Gimme a shot and a stout." Demery raised his red-brown arm and called to the bartender as he listened to the band start a piece that had some merengue rhythms that could barely be heard over the rumble of conversations in the place. The tune made him think of his childhood in the New Caribbean before his parents had immigrated to Bosch. He turned with his beer and leaned back, elbows on the bar as he watched the drummer on the congas and listened to the brass pick up the melody. "Huzzah!" He lifted his beer and nodded in time with the music, his brown hair flipping slightly with each bob.

"You like the tune?" a voice asked at his shoulder. Demery turned to see a fairly tall man wearing a short-sleeved blue shirt that accentuated his well-formed, suntanned biceps but also did not quite camouflage his overly developed belly. He looked like a powerful man going to seed, but his face was pleasant enough.

"Aye, I do. Reminds me of where I grew up," Demery responded.

At this, the bigger man turned toward Demery and grinned. "New Caribbean, huh? I spent some years there as a young man. Great spot. It's got the best music, the safest banks, and the most beautiful women!" Here he laughed and Demery joined in because it was all very true.

"How about we share a spot of rum? It fits—for your heritage and your job." The man gestured to Demery's Bosch Pirate Force belt. "Name's Owen, Owen Patricks." The man reached out a hand to shake in the fashion of the people of the North Central Continent Federal Alliance, and Demery good-naturedly took it. He was by nature a friendly man as well as a man always on the lookout for contacts that could help make him some markers.

"I'll go you one better. I just made a deal selling some family…" At this last word, he gave an exaggerated wink. "…heirlooms, and I came out a tiny bit ahead. You buy the rum, and I'll buy us some dinner."

"Is that right?" Owen Patrick asked. "Interesting. I'm a man who likes to buy heirlooms, family or otherwise." And here, both men began to laugh. "Why don't you get a table, and I'll bring a bottle?" Demery nodded and headed toward a recently vacated table.

Owen Patrick signaled to the darker-skinned barkeep. "A bottle of your finest rum, Nate."

The man brought it over and handed it across the bar, picking up the markers that sat on the shiny bar top and setting them on the till. "Since when are you drinking rum, Paddy Owens?"

Paddy surreptitiously pulled out five additional markers and slid them over to Nate. "Since I started running a grift on the Bosch. Let's keep it between us, eh, Nate?" Paddy winked. "And Nate, the name is Owen. Owen Patrick."

"Whatever you say…Owen." Nate grinned and slid the new markers directly into his pocket.

Part I

ONE

Revenge Denied

SAFEHAVEN POINT & BOSCH, JULY 2365

I didn't kill today, and that means I failed.

The sky that surrounds the Coupe and me is a deep and peaceful July blue, with only a few puffs of clouds off to the east. The engines purr contentedly as I return from Safehaven Point, a small city just south of Truvale, and a block of sunshine falls onto my left forearm; even now, the little bit of heat causes my thrall brand a twinge of pain. I swing the Coupe around to complete my base leg before coming into my final approach of the old airstrip. The Coupe, both cockpit and cabin, is silent and seemingly serene. But it belies the cacophony in my brain: *Dammit, dammit, dammit, Kat Wallace! Half a bell late. You couldn't have flown faster? Bet Papa never was late because the kids were sick. Kik had to pick this morning to wake up vomiting and crying? So like a six-year-old. Not his fault, poor kiddo, but still. Dammit! And you know Mac will be right behind him: Twins share everything. Fuck! I was within arm's reach of that bastard.*

My brain continues its enraged rant; my victory playlist remains unused, and my mouth is set in a tight line. As I come in toward the runway, "Pilot Kat" takes over, quieting the noise in my head in order to negotiate a small bit of crosswind. I sideslip to touchdown and then roll and brake until I am near the end of the strip closest to the cave. Then I allow the racket of my anger to return.

"Sweet New Earth! Not again!!" I slam my hands onto my armrests and let my head loll back against the headrest, but my neck muscles remain taut, and I continue to feel the adrenaline flow through me from my momentary confrontation with Senator Rob Abernathy. How could I have missed him this time? The plan was flawless. I had collected all the details, just as Teddy had taught me. And I was set to orchestrate my revenge.

The senator was scheduled for a campaign speech to the Bluest, the informal name of the CNE: Chosen of New Earth, a group of religious fanatics who wore blue, hooded robes of varying hues depending on their position in the church. Everyone actually calls them the Bluies, though not to their hooded faces. To my way of thinking, it is a real waste of a palette of a beautiful color. The Bluies' influence in the upcoming Federal Alliance presidential election had escalated as the Abernathy campaign embraced their stance on mandatory population increase: more workers, yes, but especially more employers—or rather enslavers, as well— and, in turn, the Bluies had championed the key plank in his platform on "the economic necessity and humanitarian benefit of thralldom." They were all bastards as far as I was concerned, but having an easy disguise like a blue cloak was too good an opportunity to pass up.

By the time I had wheedled Mama to come over to the house this morning to tend to my sick boy and his likely soon-to-follow brother, I was three-quarters of a bell late. I made up a quarter-bell in flight, but I was still behind. As I flew, I slurped down my hastily prepared coffee, the beans for which

I had liberated on my last extraction campaign, and ran over the plan:

Get to Abernathy's office before his meeting with the Bluie Patrician of Doctrine. Stroll in, bedecked in my lovely blue cloak styled appropriately out of rough fabric to demonstrate humility. This concept was ludicrous given the expensive shoes on the feet and the exquisite hand jewelry that adorned the mostly pale hands and arms that extended from the "humble" coverings. Nonetheless, my humility cloak was the proper shade for a mid-level assistant who might be verifying details before the event and was to be my ticket to my past enslaver's office. I'd be let in after showing my properly pilfered ID, and then I'd kill Senator Rob Abernathy, foiling his plan to be FA president once again and this time for good. And as a bonus, the blame would be pinned on the Bluies.

Except I was late. And the event had already begun by the time I water-landed off Safehaven Point and then maneuvered my small, inflatable boat quietly to shore and moored it there. But I had to see if I could still achieve my goal, though I had no intention of cutting it too close. I had to get safely home. I had commitments.

I planned to pick up some of my sick boys' favorite frozen juice slushies on the way home. In addition, Grey was singing, a talent that she surely had not inherited from me, on stage for the first time this afternoon at Bonnet camp, an on-base program for children ten and up to learn a bit of Bosch Pirate Force, or BPF: boxing, marksmanship, and flight simulator use as well as singing, dancing, playing instruments, and theater. Ever popular, it always closed in late August with a full pirate musical that drew spectators from all over Bosch. This was Grey's first year attending, and today was the first showcase leading up to the big event. Takai was scheduled to arrive home from Edo, where he was ministering to his supposedly ill father, in time to attend as well. So, no cutting it close. Either I would get my target, or I wouldn't.

I am not nearly so phlegmatic now, however. I throw open the Coupe door and leap to the ground, not even waiting to drop the ramp. I grab the first rock I find and lob it at the rocky bank nearest the edge of the runway with a "Fuck!" It lands with a satisfying crack. Five more rocks, curses, and cracks later, and I am breathing hard and not even slightly mollified. I stand and blow an angry breath out.

Once I arrived at the event enrobed in my cloak, I had been jostled through the crowd of Bluies and ended up in the section closest to the hopeful candidate. The almost-late senator, tall, blond and handsome, was greeting the fortunate members, pressing his knuckles together and then clasping his fingers in the CNE gesture of the joining of forces for strength. As he moved along the margins of the crowd, he took care to charm every believer with his charisma, making sure to speak softly to each person, demonstrating his indisputable compassion for each member of his constituency. Fools. One moment I was watching this charade, and the next, he was in front of me, so close I could have shanked him, and I seriously considered that move. But I would never have gotten away. Our eyes met, and the old fury rose in me as I saw him smirk.

"You get to continue to draw breath today, Senator." My voice was low as I hissed this through my teeth.

His smug smile broadened, and he leaned in to murmur in my ear, "And you have failed. Again. Mary. Tsk-tsk. Not much of a pirate after all, are you, Captain Wallace? At least you don't have anyone with you that's going to die this time."

I felt my jaw clench, and my right hand clutched at the bone handle of my blade strapped on my thigh as his taunts hit their mark. Even after more than three years, the pain of Will's death was razor-sharp and caused my old friend,

Remorse, to remind me why I ran these missions solo. I pulled back and met his blue eyes in a steely glare. I gave a slight growl, pulled phlegm into the back of my throat, and spat it in his face.

Time spiraled to a stop for an instant as I watched his expression shift from shock to revulsion and then toward dangerous anger. But neither he nor his anger frightened me any longer. When time restarted, he turned to order his surprised bodyguards to take me into custody, but I had already melted back into the pool of blue, my face covered with my hood as I began to echo the murmurs of dismay of the other Bluies. I shuffled along the perimeter of the crowd, staying just deep enough to be obscured. My eyes darted about as I assessed my best path for exfil.

After a few minutes, I saw my opening: A large vehicle with a logo of a massive black obelisk and the words *Obi: We Cover Your Life* written in block letters on its side was parked near the congregation. The red-headed cameraperson had his video camera focused on a young, dark-skinned woman costumed in a butter-colored dress as she spoke earnestly to the lens in front of her as the sea of blue ebbed and flowed behind her. I slipped to the edge of the mass of fanatics and then stepped a meter or so away from them, seeming to lean down to fix my shoe.

A quick glance at the Obi reporter and then I dodged to the back door of the vehicle and was rewarded when it opened easily. There I shed my blue cloak and sat on the floor, eyeing the various electronic contraptions and cursing my failure for a good half-bell before the rumble of the Bluies slowly subsided into silence, and the door swung open. I stood and nodded at the astonished cameraperson, who looked to be about twenty years old and stood, with his mouth agape.

“Thanks for the haven.” I patted his cheek as I hopped out.

He recovered enough to start to protest, but by the time he had set his heavy gear down and turned to confront me, I was far down the street making my way to the bay and my waiting inflatable.

Now, back home in Bosch, there are no more rocks in the vicinity to throw. I sigh, shake my head, climb back into the Coupe, pull out my purple pen from my sling bag, and reluctantly put a fourth mark in the Failure column of the tally sheet I have posted just above my primary display. Four attempts to end him in three years, and none successful. Teddy used to say, "Don't matter how often you fall, girl. As long as you can get up, you'll make it."

I stroke the area under the word Success. I will make my mark there. One day.

TWO

Nice Shoes

BOSCH, JULY 2365 (THAT AFTERNOON)

"Where's your music? Aren't you supposed to have that?" I am warming up some broth on the stove as I call to Grey. As predicted, Mac's stomach bug started about two bells after I left this morning. The blueberry slushies brought smiles to their peaked little faces when I arrived home. And wonder of wonders, they stayed down, but I am not going to try giving them anything significantly solid until after we get back from the show. Mama headed home to "scrub the toxins from her." She will meet me at the show. I owe her big time. I had missed the messiest part of the day.

My plan is to create a smorgasbord of twin-friendly, easily digested snacks, set up the Obi with a couple of hours' worth of cartoons, tuck the boys onto the sofa with towels and a couple of light blankets, and pay Liara, the neighbor girl who is home from uni, an exorbitant amount to sit quietly, read, and simply be sure the boys survive and don't argue too much.

"Grey, are you dressed?"

"Yes, Mama. I'm not a baby." Grey's voice rolls down the stairs and carries a distinct tone of irritation. Recently, there have been some eye rolls and deep sighs when I ask things of her. Not so much with Takai, nor with Mama. Just with me. I suppose that is part of being a ten-year-old daughter. She comes into the kitchen, and I look at her and can't help but grin. She has on a green summer dress that brings out the green in her eyes with a blue belt. Her legs, now coltishly long, extend from the dress and are finished with a rather attractive pair of blue shoes. With tiny heels. Where did she get those?

"Are those your shoes? I've never seen them before." I am making an effort to keep my voice casual.

I am rewarded with a beaming smile and an adorable toss of her shoulder-length, brown waves, which she has loosely fastened with a green headband. "They were Liara's a few years ago. She said I could have them!"

She looks so pleased that I shift from my intended comment about my hatred of heels to a gentler, "They look lovely with that dress. It all works, Grey." She smiles again and gazes down at them adoringly. "Do you have your sheet music?" I ask again.

Her face loses its smile, and she looks at me and sighs. "Mama, I told you. Mr. Matthieu has it."

"Oh, right. Mr. Matthews, the music counselor you told me about." I am slicing some just-right bananas that Bailey brought for the kids from their last mission to the banana belt and am a bit distracted.

"No, Mama: Mr. Matthieu."

"That's what I said: Mr. Matthews."

"Mama!" Grey stomps her foot hard.

"What?"

"There's no *s*!'"

I look at my girl's frustrated expression. "So, Mr. Matthew."

"Yes. And he is so much more than a counselor. He knows

loads, and he plays guitar and piano and has his own band, and he is going to be my accompanist tonight, so he has the music." Her voice has gotten louder with each phrase, and I stare at her, surprised by her intensity. She looks away from me. I decide to de-escalate. I realize that under the volume, I can hear both nervousness and admiration in her tone.

"He sounds very talented and I am sure very nice. I'm glad he is accompanying you." I wipe my hands and walk over to her. "Grey…" I lift her chin up to look at me. "…you are going to have a fine time this afternoon. Focus on enjoying it. Your papa and I and Mama M certainly will. You are doing something I have never done, nor am likely to!" I add the last part with a laugh that makes her smile return. My lovely babies adored me singing to them as infants, but upon realizing that there were voices far more capable of carrying a tune in the world, they have since branched out, and my singing is now limited to my showers, company sing-a-longs, and long solo runs.

"Let's get pulled together, and we will head to the base as soon as the boys are settled and Liara arrives." I lean in and give Grey a kiss on her forehead, which causes her eyes to roll, but she smiles nevertheless and does not wipe it off. I turn back to the stove, pour the hot broth into their favorite mugs, and take it and the tray of snacks to the sofa. The boys, while slightly disappointed to miss an outing, are mollified by the snacks and cartoons.

A quarter-bell later, Liara is ensconced across the room from the twins with a book of her own, and we are out the door and headed to Ms. Aika Grey Shima's debut performance at the Bonnet Pirate Theater.

~

There's a hubbub at the doors to the theater. I look up from where I have been a bit dozy since convincing the lighting person to let me sit in the quiet, dark theater and relax pre-show. I peer over my shoulder to see who is creating the buzz. Mama is here. I see the silver waves of her hair as she moves into the hall. She is totally an island celebrity: all the people who loved Papa and all the families whose births she attended want to chat with her. I hop up to run interference, putting on my best smile and moving Mama through the crowd that has gathered near her.

"You do that quite deftly, dear." Mama pats my arm as we get seated.

I grin and lean over to whisper, "I think they all are still a bit afraid of me, post-Papa." I make an exaggerated glowering face and put my fists up. But really, I do like this possibility and am glad I can keep most of them at arm's length.

"Kat, really..." Mama deep brown face crinkles into a smile and she giggles. The family and I now can crack jokes about Papa and his Teddy-in-the-Sky choice. Of course, there are still some tears but more laughter and smiles these days. "Nonetheless, you handled getting me to my seat quite diplomatically."

I groan. "Ugh, that word. Spare me that fate." I see Mama's eyebrows come up, and she turns to look at me as I glance impatiently at the doors, waiting for Takai, my occasionally present husband. He said he would be here. Grey isn't slated to perform until just before intermission, so hopefully, her papa will arrive on time. I glance next to me as Mama settles in at my right elbow at the empty seat beyond her, and it makes me relax a bit. I didn't really want to sit next to him. Things have been tense over the half a year since he has been home from *The Venturer.*

Though, I correct myself, *it's not like he has actually been home that much*. Takai attended some six-week diplomatic workshop on something like "Land Use Agreements Between Re-Emerging Peoples" in Truvale just after his captaincy ended and has been in Edo almost every other week since Shigeo, his father, took "ill" three months ago. I was very sympathetic initially until I heard from the old priestess and my friend, Aiko, that Shigeo and Yumiko, my reluctant in-laws, had been the key sponsors at a fundraiser for The Way's Children's Fund and were, according to her, looking hale and hearty. Well, I added the "hale and hearty" part. She just said they looked well enough. That was five weeks ago, just after Takai had returned from "helping with his father's recovery." I shake my head. I decide to focus on the present moment instead of the possible what-ifs. RTT, the woman I talk to regularly about my issues—okay, she's my therapist—says I need to stop denying events and emotions that are painful, but when it is too hard, I should try to stay in the present moment. I choose the present moment ninety-nine times out of a hundred. I take a breath and think about how this is Grey's day. I consider how I started today and find I am a little glad for her day to go un-shadowed by Abernathy. The lights go down, and the head counselor of Bonnet Camp comes out to welcome us. And the show begins, just like much of my life, whether I'm ready or not.

Takai and I sit at one of the umbrellaed patio tables outside of Barton's on a cloudless Saturday afternoon not long after Grey's showcase. The oppressive heat is typical for July, but it's also uncomfortably humid today. I imagine there will be storms rolling in tonight, but there isn't even the hint of a breeze right now. We could use the rain. Of course, between droughts and flooding, it is always a toss-up. But today, we need it. Pleasantly, D'Angelo, the owner of Barton's, has installed some large stand-up fans, and I have positioned myself to catch their breeze if I lean back just right. I tend to wilt in the intense heat, and so the cooling air is a boon for me. Takai is leaning back in his seat with his brown eyes shut, a faint sheen of sweat on his summer-bronzed brow, drumming his fingers on the table ever so quietly. I doubt he is even aware of the motion. Or of me. This "weekend afternoon out" thing was suggested by RTT. It's the third time we have attempted it, and I don't see it creating any... What was the phrase Ruth used? "Significant channels of communication." The rules are: no work or kid talk. Apparently, when those are eliminated, it leaves things pretty quiet between the two of us.

I look around. There's a family with a little one in a high-chair several tables away from us, and I watch as the parents alternately dote on the baby and try to get a few words in with each other. Standard stuff, but the part I notice is that under the table, their feet are entwined, and every now and again they look at each other and smile and wiggle their feet and legs together as first one, then the other gives bites of their meals to their child.

As I scan the patio, I see a man in a blue suit walk up and engage the host several meters away from our table. After what looks like an intense conversation, he is escorted inside. I can't place why the exchange makes me uncomfortable. Then a few minutes later, the man steps back out, and two reasons become clear. One, it's Howard Archer, the nasty little man who has made a career of being a pain in the ass on the Council. He has been contemptuous of me ever since the tribunal after Papa died. And two, his suit is the exact shade of blue the upper echelon of the Bluies wear. That's not good. As he leaves, I file this encounter away to be discussed with Cal

Greene, my friend at the BI—Bosch Intelligence. I return to my visual sweep of my surroundings.

The only other occupied table outside holds five people I think I have seen around on base. There are two women and three men. While they are not in uniform, they still act like a unit. I watch as they laugh, talk together, and joke with Tricia, the server. A smile creeps onto my face as I remember similar times with my old unit. It's something I haven't been part of for any length of time since my old one broke three years earlier, just before I went to Officer Training School and Gia ran for commander. I miss the camaraderie. I've been moving from short-term assignment to short-term assignment since graduating.

Miles and I made the plan so I could learn all the different branches the BPF covers. I had learned during my oft-repeated recruitment lessons that troops can specialize in anything from finances in the quartermaster's office to medic work to Glitter mining and production, which is far more complicated than I originally thought, and lots of engineers are funneled there. There are dozens of other subdivisions as well. I had only ever worked as a pilot doing extractions and Glitter negotiations. It's been eye-opening to actually work in the other sections. While I have yet to find a position that I would enjoy more than flying missions, I have developed an appreciation for how dedicated most of these troops are to their assignments.

A burst of raucous laughter comes from the unit, and I can't help but chuckle to myself as I listen to them hit the table and sputter and cough with glee. The noise brings Takai out of his reverie, and he frowns as his dark-haired head swivels to discover what disturbed his deep thoughts.

I start to ask him what he was thinking of when I see a movement out of the corner of my eye; two people are coming up the small set of wooden stairs to the patio.

I turn, see familiar faces, and grin. Gia Ka'ne and Bailey Alexander are making a beeline for our table. I feel myself come out of the torpor I didn't realize I was in. I am delighted to see my friends. That's another thing I haven't done as much of as I've wanted to in the past couple of years: spend time with Gia and Bailey, Demery, and Tom of the old unit. Well, the surviving members of the old unit.

Tom is busy with the W-Mech business and his new daughter. Bailey and Demery are still gunning together. I see Bailey more often for a drink than I do Demery. They say he has been busy with what he refers to as "side jobs." It's always some get-rich-quick plan with him. Both have been with Matt Warner's unit for the last year and have great things to say about the unit. I have to imagine it is weird since that had been Will's unit before he was assigned to ours. I spend a moment picturing Will with his unruly shock of hair, his steel-blue eyes and that smile. I give my head a little shake to clear the image. I really hate to think what his old unit members must think of me.

Guilt pipes up in my head. *They think you got their friend killed after you broke his heart.* I take a breath. *Hush. His death was Abernathy's doing, not mine.* I see Guilt shrug. *If you say so.* Unfortunately, Heartbreak is a constant companion. Just to be clear, Ruth approves of my personification of my emotions, which is good, because they sure as hell aren't going to shut up.

Gia's time is taken up as a commander, and her girls are as busy as my kids. We do get the kids together when we can, and Gia and her husband, Red, have come to our home for dinner and have hosted us as well. Though not so much lately. I recall the argument Takai and I had after our last time visiting them.

"I think your friends were very rude tonight." It had been

an uncomfortably silent walk home, and Takai had started the moment after he affably walked Mama to the door with a kiss on the cheek goodbye after babysitting. The door clicked shut, and he didn't even wait to fully hang up his coat.

"Ha! I think they—no, we—were extremely patient with someone who was being pedantic and overbearing." I glared at him as I said this, and his eyes flashed at me as he shut the coat closet with more intensity than the door, or I, deserved. Then the two of us padded upstairs into first the boys' room, and then Grey's, moving stray flotsam off the floor, tucking blankets in more snugly, and giving each sleeping child kisses from both of us.

We moved wordlessly into our room, and the minute our door clicked: "I was not being pedantic and overbearing, Kat." Takai pulled his shirt off over his head, folded it, and set it fastidiously onto the red oak bedroom bench that my brother, Peter, had made for me.

I grimaced at him as I dropped my top and pants and then my underclothes in a heap on the floor. "You started pontificating on and practically celebrating the various ends of piracy throughout Old Earth history. While having dinner at a commander in the Bosch Pirate Force's home. With your wife: a pirate. Seems pretty damn overbearing to me." My hands were on my naked hips.

I watched as his eyes took me in from head to toe. A part of me had hoped the conversation would go a different direction. But as that hadn't happened for weeks, I was not optimistic. I saw his jaw work for a moment. Then he took a breath and said, "I was not being pedantic."

I stared at him pointedly. "If you can use 'pedantic' correctly in a sentence, then you were too." I turned to my night clothes pile, selected my oldest and least attractive pair of pajamas, and pulled them on. I then crawled onto my side of the bed, pulled up the covers, and turned the light out. Not surprisingly, we hadn't socialized with Gia and Red since.

"Gia. Bailey!" As I pivot to push my chair back and stand to greet these people I love, I see my husband roll his eyes ever so slightly, his mouth in a thin line. I don't take the bait, choosing to enjoy my friends instead.

THREE

Say What?

BOSCH, JULY 2365

I pour a second round of beers from the pitcher into the three glasses. I look at Takai. "More iced tea?" He shakes his head slightly and lifts a hand in a no-thanks maneuver. I am sweating, and I lean back in my seat and rock my chair to catch any air movement now that the fans have been turned off for a bell due to power rationing. "So, what is it that is so pressing, you came looking for me?" I wipe a trickle of perspiration from my cheek and look questioningly at my friends.

When they walked up, Bailey embraced me and said, "We tracked you down. We have things we need to discuss." Their gentle, brown, eyes twinkling as they brushed their braids back from their brown slender face. Gia was rocking back and forth, patting the soft, gray, stingray leather case I gave her for her last birthday. A tall, strongly built woman, her long, thick, black hair was in a bun as usual. She usually only carries her case for work papers. I narrowed my eyes as I considered this and watched her black eyes dart as her dark expressive eyebrows moved practically independent of each other, while the muscles in her face twitched as if she was bursting with some news.

I looked at both of them curiously; their eyes looked serious, but there was that play of a smile on each of their mouths, so I knew there wasn't trouble but something else. Before they could tell me what, Tricia came up to take orders, and we had a few moments of beer and food discussion as we decided what to order. Takai looked at me in surprise as we had just finished lunch before they arrived. I had said I wasn't very hungry and just had a small Bosch summer salad; now I was talking bean burgers and fries. *So, shoot me. It's more fun eating with friendly company.* A round or two of small talk and catch-up took place and was pleasant, but I was ready for the full story.

Now Gia and Bailey glance at one another with odd expressions, and Bailey bites their lower lip and then looks at me. "Well, there's a few parts." They pause and are starting to grin maniacally.

Gia looks at them and then me and takes up the thread. "Rainey is retiring next month."

Now I start to grin. General Henry "Hank" Rainey had served in the BPF since…who the fuck knows? He was old when I started and is ancient now. I suspect he was old when Teddy came up through the ranks. This is momentous.

"Finally! He should have done that years ago. I mean, hell, wasn't he the last survivor of Sam Bellamy's *Whydah*?" As the three of us laugh at the old joke, the meaning of this change finally dawns on me—slow study that I am, I guess—and I look at both friends, my eyes settling on Gia. "There'll be a space at the Generals' Table! Gia, it's what you've been waiting for!" I feel a delightful spread of joy through my chest. She has worked so hard her whole career to get this chance. "What can I do to help?" I smile and reach over and grasp her arm and hand, but I see her look at me and then look down.

"Well, you know what his position is, right?" Bailey leans in toward me, elbows on the table, their chin resting on their hands. Gia looks back at me as both of them watch as I answer.

"Special Projects. And given that he probably naps three times a day, it kinda explains why there haven't been any significant projects for the last several years." I shake my head in dismay. "What project are you thinking about implementing, General Ka'ne?" I wink at Gia, who flushes at the title.

Then Bailey and Gia exchange the same odd glance as earlier, and I see Gia take a deep breath as Bailey's eyes urge her on.

Gia looks at me and presses her lips together. Then all in one breath says, "The special project has to be anti-trafficking, but I'm not running for general, Kat. You are."

In the stunned silence that follows, there is only a small beat, then Takai utters his first words since my friends arrived. "Not a chance."

Gia glanced over at Bailey and the two of them watched, as surreptitiously as they could, the argument between the couple taking place on the sidewalk. Their voices were not raised, but as Gia observed Kat step into a fighting stance and watched the rapid and furious gesticulation of both of her hands, she knew that her friend was making herself heard. She also recognized Takai's intractable stance: feet set, arms folded, and an expression of angry boredom on his otherwise handsome Edoan face. She glanced again at Bailey, and they both saw Kat's hands and arms shoot up above her head, fingers spread as she turned back toward Barton's and their table. She came toward them, her strong body practically stomping, her blue-green eyes flashing with her brows drawn together. Her usual pale and pretty face was now both darkened and flushed with anger. Kat was a good half-a-head shorter than Gia, with the roundness on both her top and bottom halves that came from having babies, but Gia knew that along with that roundness was a fighter body that Kat kept fit and ready. Behind her they saw Takai watch her, shake his head, and turn to walk in the direction of their family home.

Bailey murmured. "I will never figure out why she stays with him."

Gia shrugged in equal confusion but made a shushing sound as Kat approached the table and pulled out her chair, plopping angrily down.

"Ugh. The nerve of the man." Kat blew out an angry breath. The table sat silently for a few moments. Then Kat shook her head and seemed to refocus on Gia and Bailey. "You want me to run for general?" She shook her head again and snorted. "That's not my dream. It's yours, Gia. And even though I'd love to mount an anti-trafficking campaign, I'm a mere captain. Can't exactly make that kind of jump in rank. I'll just be a willing participant under your command."

Now Gia smiled and considered how she had arrived here. She had intended to run initially. When she had heard the news of Rainey's retirement two evenings ago in a casual conversation with Miles Baldwin-Bosch, her Master Commander and recently developed friend, she was over the moon. It was her dream—Kat was right. But the next day she ran into Bailey and shared the news. They had gone to celebrate, and that's when the kernel of this plan had begun to grow.

"Kat, here's the thing." Gia began in her rich, full voice as she pulled her lovely bag to the table and turned the small silver latch, drawing out a document. "Bailey and I got to talking about what the special project had to be, and we both said, 'Anti-trafficking, absolutely' and then I said, 'Damn.'"

"Darling, you said 'fuck,'" Bailey chimed in, correcting Gia.

Gia nodded and shrugged. "Okay, I said, 'Fuck, I wish Kat was further along in rank and could get elected.' Then Bailey went real quiet and said, 'I gotta go. Let's meet for breakfast at the mess, seven bells,' and was gone."

Bailey picked up the conversation, their bright voice edged with excitement. "I had vaguely remembered something I had read ages ago and wanted to check it out. So, I went to the university library—there's a lovely young woman there I dated last year. And she and I searched until we found this." Bailey pointed at the document in Gia's hand.

Gia looked at Bailey and grinned. "You didn't mention the 'lovely young woman' before. Is that why you were late?"

Bailey shrugged and winked. "The document?"

Gia handed it to Kat. "It's old. So right up your alley." She beamed as she watched her friend read and saw her face move from studious to confused to astonished.

I can't believe what I'm reading. I mean, I do believe it, but I'm not sure what to do with the information.

Gia and Bailey have handed me a copy of the original charter of Bosch. Written over a hundred years earlier when the Bosch were still part sea-marauders and part on-island Glitter miners and country-builders, it detailed the electoral process. The pirating Bosch all held rank when they first arrived island-side with the Master Commander as the historical leader of the fleet and now the island. His position had to be approved by a council of the non-ranked crew, which became today's civilian Council. The positions of the quartermaster of the fleet and the captains of each of the five ships, now the generals, were to be determined by full BPF election, and anyone could throw their hat in. Anyone, regardless—and this was stated specifically—of rank.

I look at them, dumbfounded. There's no way. But what if I could run an anti-trafficking project with all the resources Bosch could provide? My conversation with Miles and Teddy from years before rings in my ears. They said I needed strength, power, and allies to move on my dream to take on traffickers. And as a general, I'd have all of that and more. I let my brain consider the possibility, and then I remember my friend. I shake my head. No. I look at the two faces anxiously peering at me. "But Gia, this rank is what you want, what you have worked for your whole career."

I see her close her eyes. She takes a slow breath, and I know I am right. She smiles and looks at me. "Kat, this position is meant for you, I can feel it. You also have been working toward this—almost your whole life." She taps the space on her arm where a thrall brand would go. Where a thrall brand is on me. Her face is earnest and open. "There will be other retirements. Other chances. I'm not giving up my dream, but what is most important here, a chance to really end the trafficking of humans on the planet or my advancement schedule?"

Bailey reaches out, grabs Gia's hand, and brings it to their lips for a kiss. Then they look at me. "So, Kat. This is it. You in?"

I look at each of their faces in turn. Then I look down at the table and think. *Could I? Should I?* I rub my hands and fingers together, crack my knuckles, and then look back up at their expectant, seemingly hopeful faces. Then I consider Takai's immediate negative response and his subsequent comment that "Wasn't I already in deep enough with the Force?" I narrow my eyes. *Not a chance, my ass.*

"Hell, yes." I bring both my fists to the table, rocking it enough to spill a bit of beer from the full glasses. "Let's get this done. I'm in."

FOUR

Matt Warner

BOSCH, JULY 2365

Monday lunch, and I am about to embark on my first political meeting.

After the initial elation and excitement on Saturday when I agreed to run for the Generals' Table spot, with anti-trafficking as my focused special project, I had turned to Gia and Bailey. "You both know, I know nothing about running a campaign of any sort. I barely even want to talk to most people."

My friends both grinned, and Bailey had said, "Honey, that will have to change. You now love everyone. Except your running opponents who you respect but disagree with."

"Are you fucking kidding me?" I gave them a marked askance look.

Gia tilted her head. "And that potty mouth has got to go." She gestured with a thumb toward the street.

"Potty-mouth? How old are you?" The idea that I may need to tone down my colorful and, frankly, deeply expressive use of certain words in an election didn't surprise me, but still…potty-mouth? I watch as Gia laughs and shrugs.

Bailey was practically bouncing in their seat. "Okay, influencers. We'll need to set up meetings and run-ins with some of the biggest movers and shakers on base: the MC, of course."

"I think I can manage that one." I grinned. "He'll be all in on the notion. Guaranteed."

Both Gia and Bailey nodded agreement as Bailey continued the list, ticking off on their fingers, "The quartermaster, someone in Intelligence, and at least one general, I think Woolcot. You know Helen Woolcot, don't you, Gia?"

"Yep. She would love to see more women serving as generals." Gia had pulled out her device and tapped it a few times. "Let's plan a meeting with her later next week."

Bailey had their own device out. "Good. How about the QM, Etienne Winter?"

I couldn't help but grin as I watched my two friends with their heads together creating a battle plan. I could do my part. "I worked with him a few months ago when I was learning BPF finances. I can go see him Tuesday. It's his lightest day. And I can talk with Cal Greene in Intelligence. He and I go way back."

Bailey had looked delighted and then dropped the bomb on me. "We may as well start you with the head of the Pilot's Coalition, Matt Warner."

Bailey has been after me to meet their unit leader almost since Demery and they started working with the new unit. But I have sidestepped the offer every time. I don't want to deal with the guy who used to fly with Will. I knit my brows and frown. "How is he an influencer?"

Bailey shakes their head and laughs. "Girl, you heard what I said: He is the head of the Pilot's Coalition. Every pilot looks to him for guidance on any issue, and his opinion carries weight with just about every trooper."

I shrugged. "Never had much use for the whole 'Pilot's Coalition' back in the day. Too much politics." I stopped when

I heard myself say that and then put a hand to my face. "Aw, Sweet New Earth."

Bailey shook their head but still smiled. "You've been so caught up in being a solo act, you never bothered to read the room."

I finally said what my real concern was. "Bailey, he's bound to hate me for what happened to Will. I hardly think he'll support me for a jump to general."

Bailey paused and gave me a stricken look, then reached out and grasped my forearm. "Kat, Dem and I have been flying with his unit for a year. He's a decent person. He kinda reminds me of you."

I scoffed and shook my head as Bailey continued, "I can guarantee you he doesn't hold a grudge. You need him, Kat. Meeting: Monday lunch."

So here I am, hanging a distance from the food trucks, about to have an audience with Major Matt Warner. Should be a real treat. After all, pilots are pretty renowned for their egotism. I may know something about that personally. The head of the Pilot's Coalition has got to have a pretty inflated view of themself. Sure, I have heard that Warner is an above-average pilot, and I've seen him around base. With his copper-skinned, stunning looks, it's hard not to notice him. And, as it turns out, he was Grey's and everyone else's accompanist at the showcase. Plus, I have heard him play with a band at Barton's once or twice. Clearly, the man has time on his hands and likes to be in the spotlight. But I have never officially met him, just the brief encounter the morning Will was forced to join our unit.

I hear Bailey call out and look up. They are walking toward me with Gia and the major, waving. I can't help but appreciate his appearance. If nothing else, this meeting will be easy on the eyes. They come up and Gia, Bailey, and I exchange brief hugs.

Bailey makes the introductions. "Captain Katrina Wallace, this is Major Matthieu Warner. Matt, this is Kat, our future newest general." The two of us formally salute, clapping our right fists to our hearts and then snapping them smartly down.

The major gives me an appraising look, raises a single eyebrow, then cuts to the point. "Bailey and Commander Ka'ne told me how you plan to leapfrog to the Table. Seems a bit of a stretch. You think you've got the chops for the work?" His dark eyes are calm, but there is a challenge in them. He doesn't think I can do it.

One thing I certainly can do is recognize a pissing contest, especially when I am in one. "Major, I can do any damn thing I put my mind to. So, I suggest you get used to calling me General." I hold his gaze and give him the slightest smile.

Now both his full eyebrows go up, and he looks vaguely skeptical. "Mmm. Easy to say. Harder to implement. So that remains to be seen." What amazing audacity. He and I have squared up as we face each other. This is someone used to getting his own way. But he holds no authority over me. However...

I continue to look at him, holding my gaze steady and lifting my chin ever so slightly. "I want your support."

I see Gia's eyes widen at my frankness, but I know what I'm doing. For people like him (and me), a person has to present as strong and confident. Anything less indicates a weak spot. And weak spots can be exploited. That's just negotiation basics.

He looks at me, and his face is pleasant but clearly unconvinced. "The pilots and their units trust me to give them good guidance. And anti-trafficking will undoubtedly require our skills and could possibly put troops in harm's way. So, I'm going to want to know more about the program you envision."

Not an unreasonable ask, and I like that he takes his influence seriously. I nod, considering. What is his weak spot? I let my eyes flick over him as I construct my response. He is tall with broad shoulders and well-defined muscles that are actually visible through the white shirt of his summer uniform. His vest is casually unbuttoned, a smart move in this heat and an attractive one. His face is flat-out gorgeous, with those deep, dark eyes that look like they can twinkle with humor or flash with anger as needed. I look a little longer, taking in his dark, tight curls, closely cropped, showing the hint of a widow's peak, and a stubble beard barely covering an angular jaw that is set off by high cheekbones and full lips.

"So, the program, Captain Who-Thinks-She-Can-Be-General?" His query is meant as a prompt, but it interrupts my happy visual tour.

I startle just a bit. "Sorry. I got a bit lost looking at all this." I move my forefinger in a large squiggle to indicate Major Warner's striking self. "I bet you don't spend too many Saturday nights alone." I raise my eyebrows and continue with a small smirk, "Or Sunday mornings."

I watch his eyebrows come together in consternation, and he leans toward me, a finger coming up toward my face. "Excuse me? Captain, I'll have you know I was top of my class in secondary, graduated with honors from both uni and OTS, and have incredibly honed skills, both as an electrical engineer and as one of the best pilots in the Force."

Well, there's the soft spot. I laugh to myself. I've got him on the ropes. "Yeah?" I wrinkle my nose. "I guess I'll have to take your word for it."

As he starts to take in my looks, I decide to go for the win. "I certainly can't compete with you in looks, flyboy, but I can out-pilot you in any vessel." I see that statement land like a lead hook as his eyes narrow, and he starts to open his handsome mouth to respond, but I keep talking over the opportunity. "My skills are honed as well and, frankly, resplendent with talent." I bite my lower lip and raise my brows while looking directly at him.

Bailey, who, along with Gia, has been watching this encounter. They jump in before Warner can say anything, their voice a bit high and nervous. "So, maybe we should decide on lunch before we go sit and talk more about the program. What does everybody want?"

I know exactly what I plan to have, so without breaking my gaze, I quickly say, "Empanadas." But as the word comes out of my mouth, I hear it echoed in a deep, rich tone as the tall major voices the same lunch plan.

We both blink and regard each other. While I don't say it, I am impressed as I believe Dario and his empanada truck do not get the love they deserve.

He looks at me and seems less confrontational. "Your skills are 'resplendent,' huh? And what are you ordering specifically?"

I open my hands and arms. 'Obviously, the combo."

He nods his concurrence.

We turn as one and head for Empanadas Everywhere. As we start our walk, he throws out a tantalizing piece of news. "I heard Dario got in a shipment of beef. Thoughts?"

I pause and my eyes go wide. "Beef? Fuck. With those spices he has? That would be special." I consider my lunch budget. "I could afford two. With chimichurri."

I hear him say with the casual privilege of a man who has always had things go his way, "The beef is likely in short supply. I outrank you, so I fucking get to order mine first."

I pause in my walk, and he stops with me. We turn slightly toward each other and look each other in the eyes. There is definitely a smile playing on those full lips. I tilt my head and say equably, "You aren't wrong, Major. You do outrank me...."

I watch as the smile starts to spread across his face before I continue. "...for about two more months, until you help get me elected to general." He pauses, then nods like a monarch granting a boon and looks very self-satisfied until I give him a small shove backward and take off running, yelling, "But beef empanadas know no rank, so first there, first served!"

I hear him holler in dismay, and the sound of his feet pounding the ground behind me begins. He is quickly getting closer, but I see Dario in the truck waving at me, getting larger as I rapidly arrive under the awning. I slide to a stop in front of the counter, gasping for breath as I spread my arms wide, protecting my prize position.

"Four with chimichurri, please." I say between breaths.

Matty skids to a stop next to me and unsuccessfully tries to unseat my position. "Hey, General, make it five, and can we get spicy sofrito sauce too?" He is out of breath as well, but his deep voice has a hopeful tone, like when I take the kids for frozen ices.

I put on my indulgent mama voice to match, "Well, of course, Major Matty."

"Matty? Am I five?" the major asks.

I decide to answer the question with a question. "Do you want the sofrito?"

He nods vigorously.

I turn and pat his cheek. "Well, then, Matty…" He looks annoyed and then shrugs. "You shall have sofrito. And if you behave, we can even get some tostones." Now his warm laugh rumbles out to join mine as together, we claim our prized beef empanadas, sauces, and tostones on the side and make our way to lunch.

FIVE

Q&A

BOSCH, LATE AUGUST 2365

"Kat, are you ready to go on?" Bailey's voice sounds in my head, and my dream of a quiet beach evaporates.

My head pops up from the table, where it had drifted down for a few precious moments of sleep. I am seated off in a corner backstage at the BPF theater. It is the same one Grey and about two dozen other children had performed on in the musical *Pirates of New Earth* a couple of weeks earlier.

It has been a helluva several weeks. Campaigning is not for the faint of heart. Which is good since I feel that I can be bold when needed. However, it also is not for people who are used to speaking their minds. Unfortunately, I also fall into this category.

My ally game started strong. After my empanada meeting with Major Warner, who I will now and forever call Matty because of the initial dismay it provoked, I garnered his support that same day after a really long and substantive discussion of how to structure an anti-trafficking project, to which Major Matty contributed several excellent ideas. I then approached my friend and Master Commander, Miles Baldwin-Bosch. Miles was beside himself with excitement when I showed him the document Gia and Bailey had given me and told him our plan.

He held the paper in both hands and looked at me across the large, mahogany desk inlaid with Bosch symbols and a map of New Earth. "I had forgotten about this clause in the charter. I don't remember the last time a general didn't come from the commander ranks. But it is definitely legitimate." He grinned. "Sweet New Earth, Kat. There hasn't been a decent special project for years. It is perfect for you. Can't believe I didn't think of it."

Etienne Winter, the quartermaster, pronounced me "fiscally prudent" and threw his support behind me as well, though without as much of the effusiveness Miles provided. Cal Greene turned positively pink and said he would rally his compatriots in Intelligence. General Helen Wolcott was a bit of a harder sell. She expressed some initial reservations during her meeting with Gia and me about experience and perception, but after a quiet lunch with Mama, she publicly gave me her backing at the Women Leaders of Bosch meeting two weeks later. Apparently, Mama was a bit prescient, no surprise there, when she encouraged me to join the WLB and faithfully attend all meetings with her after I finished OTS a couple of years ago. Shortly after General Wolcott gave me her support, Gia recused herself from my campaign as she didn't want there to be any sniff of favoritism, though I knew she was working the ranks for me.

Things went well for the first couple of weeks as I was running unopposed, and the campaigning seemed to be limited to shaking arms and having lunches. Then, right around the time of the musical, General Baradash, the general in charge of external relations, came forward with his personal choice: Commander Eliot Conrad, a commander for five years who had risen through the ranks as a financial analyst and then had taken over resource management when Jace Richmond retired two years before. He was a smooth talker and seemed to know all the right people. He stood a few inches taller than me, and his black hair was well-coiffed and his light-brown skin was perfectly clean-shaven. I saw him as a right tool since one of the people he seemed to be tight with was none other than Howard Archer, the littlest shit of the civilian Council and the closest person I had on Bosch to an archenemy, a term I had gleaned from Old Days superhero movies. I occasionally like to fancy myself as one of the superheroes, though I far prefer the superhero men's costumes to the teeny superhero women's garb. But I digress.

So, suffice it to say, the last few weeks have been a bit rockier. Tonight is the third in a series of three question-and-answer sessions with representatives from each BPF specialty as well as the five generals and Miles. My mission: to repair the damage done from the first two Q&A sessions.

In the first one, which took questions from any officer other than the commanders and the generals, I came across as what Bailey gently called "wooden and dull." Bailey, who has become my self-appointed campaign manager, had prepped me exhaustively, and I had carefully memorized the answers they had given me. The Pilot's Coalition was represented and threw me some softballs—thank you very much, Matty Warner. And Master Sergeant Fred Driscoll showed up with a couple of ground crew folk; he made my original enlistment look pretty rosy with his questions. Fred even gave me a wink and thumbs-up after I finished answering their queries.

Then both Eliot Conrad and I were asked basic questions about our plans for the special project section and our personal history. The problem was, I dutifully recited my answers to the handful of other officers who actually showed up and then stopped. Commander Conrad, on the other hand, took the opportunity to "answer the questions he wanted to be asked," a technique that had not occurred to me until Bailey mentioned it in the debrief we had after the session. So, the night definitely went to Conrad.

At the second session, I was ready to really talk; however, I let my mouth run before my brain. But, hey, I was provoked.

The second Q&A took questions from the commanders only. It had started well enough. The fifteen commanders sat spread through the house with one or two other officers with them. The generals and Miles sat listening in the front row. I remember thinking: *Sweet New Earth, do I have to start sitting up front if I win*? There were only a handful of other troopers present as these events were always pretty dry, and neither my previous performance nor Conrad's did anything to disabuse any potential audience members of this fact.

But then a small group of the old guard, the three Commanders from logistics, transpo, and construction, started peppering me with questions, which were really criticisms, and then throwing creampuff questions to Commander Tool that he turned into pointed "concerns about my abilities and experience."

The logistics commander, who could "trace his lineage back to the original vessels that landed on Bosch" (*Big fucking deal; so could 80 percent of Bosch's population)* said, "While I respect the charter, you seem to be flouting our revered Bosch traditions of movement through the ranks by trotting out some arcane point of law because it suits your needs." This prompted some scattered murmurs in the auditorium.

"And given your sordid, yet admittedly tragic, history, I have to imagine you see Bosch as some haven for these thralls you intend to free. How is our economy going to absorb these uneducated, unskilled refugees?" transportation commander chimed in immediately after.

As I was starting to talk about plans for freed thralls and that most would be returned to their homeland, the construction commander jumped in and said, "That's all well and good, but you seem to have a tendency to dabble and disappear. After all, you left Bosch to live in a foreign country for eight years. How do we know you will actually see the project through?" Unsurprisingly, when I responded that I was raising my young children with their Edoan father during those years, the follow-up from Commander Eliot "The Tool" Conrad became pointed.

"But we all know that one of those years was spent in banishment for robbing our beloved Master Commander of his final years with his family." This statement created a mild hubbub, which admittedly was not unexpected, but then he went on. "So, my opponent wants to take one of the highest and most powerful positions in Bosch, by questionable means, it seems, yet she is foreign-born, married a foreigner, and has those foreign-born children. I wonder if she has Bosch's best interests at heart." The mention of first Teddy and then my children flooded my brain with a red miasma. And so, I constructed a response that had far more to do with the commanders' immediate parentage and various below-the-belt body parts than it did any of the issues at hand. The last thing I remember was saying something like, "You fucking assholes better not mention my children again, or you'll be going the way of your precious Bosch ancestors—to the bottom of the sea!" At that point, I had seen Miles with one hand over his eyes and Bailey who was holding handfuls of their braids and had gone a rather distressing pale-gray shade. At this, I snapped my mouth shut and sat down in the chair provided. But the damage was done, and Conrad had definitely carried the day and perhaps the campaign unless I could fully regroup.

So, now I need to fix the shit I broke. I'm still furious at myself for getting angry, but RTT said that I "got angry in defense of family," and that was appropriate. It was just my response that was not. *Thanks for that astute insight, Ruth.* Bailey, once they finally decided to speak to me again, suggested several different ways to "build bridges" and even suggested I have lunch with the three commanders. I plan to build bridges but declined the lunch recommendation, especially after Mama had retiring General "Hank" Rainey over for tea with me, and he told me a story that I am now holding as the card up my sleeve. I can't do much about not being born in Bosch, but I apparently am upholding some "family" traditions.

As I peek out at the audience from the right wing of the stage, I see a far bigger turnout than the first time. Every seat is filled, even the balcony, and there are people standing in the aisles and around the sides. I turn, wide-eyed, to Bailey, who looks as stunned as I am.

From behind us, Major Matty's voice suddenly sounds in a low tone. "There's nowhere to sit out front. I'm going to watch from here."

"What the fuck are all these people doing here?" I whisper-ask this question to no one in particular. I don't anticipate any response, so I am surprised to hear Matty's warm laugh.

"They've all come to see if you are going to take any prisoners tonight. You might have pissed off the commanders, but the troops were delighted to hear that someone didn't let the LTC commanders push them around. Those three are renowned for their bullying."

I turn my head slightly but still give him a clear side-eye. "That would have been a helpful bit of info before last week's debacle. Why didn't I know this?"

Matty's eyes stay focused on the audience, but he grins.

"Because as I understand it, you didn't start paying attention and listening to other people until a couple months ago."

Now I fully turn my face to him. "You, sir, are an ass."

His grin only gets bigger. "But I'm the ass in your corner, General. Go give 'em hell—nicely."

General Helen Wolcott poses the first question to Commander Conrad, who tonight sports a small, blue ribbon pinned on his vest. *That's not regulation.* "Last week, there was some discussion about Bosch traditions. Please discuss your views on Bosch traditions and how you plan to uphold them if indeed you plan to." Commander Tool takes his place at the podium in the center spotlight that catches and glints off the many medals on his vest. He alternately holds both sides of his pulpit and pounds on it for emphasis while he proceeds to go on and on about the vital importance of holding to the old ways and how vital it is to keep Bosch for the Bosch. He reminds everyone we live on an island (*No shit, Toolie*), and we have limited resources (*Again, a stunning revelation*).

He continues for almost half a bell, and I can hear the audience getting antsy as whispers increase and the sounds of fidgeting rise while I stand quietly nearby with a pleasant smile as I take in every word but still appraise the audience. Eventually, he stops and receives a polite applause, though the dull thrum of audience members talking among themselves continues. General Wolcott looks at me as I stand off to the side of the podium. "The same question, Captain Wallace."

Okay, Teddy, hope this goes well, but if it doesn't, then this isn't for me. I do not take the podium, but instead, step toward the front of the stage, and Masie, up in lighting, scrambles to follow me with the beam. I look up toward the booth and shade my eyes, squinting. "Masie, can you please tone it down a bit? I'm just going to sit here, and I want to see who I'm talking to." I sit down at the front of the stage, and my legs dangle like a child's off it.

Masie kindly drops the light off me and turns the house lights up a bit, and the sea of faces comes into focus for me. I give a thumbs-up toward the lighting booth and receive a small wave in reply. The thrum drops lower and lower as I scan quietly across the auditorium and up into the balcony, raising my hand and acknowledging some of the familiar and the not-familiar faces that raise their hands to me in greeting. Slowly, the theater becomes silent. I wait a beat more.

Finally, I speak. "Well, this is quite the turnout. I'm awfully glad to see all you troopers here because this decision is for all of you to make, not just the heavy vests." Several guffaws are voiced at this Bosch colloquialism. I pause again and feel the anticipation in the audience.

"So, let's get to know Kat Wallace: Yes, I was born in the North Country. You can still hear that in my voice. And yes, I was a thrall. I don't need to tell any of you that. You can read the transcripts, and you can see it on my arm. Maisie?" Here, I raise my left arm and point, and Maisie points a small spotlight on my brand. The hush in the audience is striking. I smile, drop my arm, and Maisie expertly drops the light at the same time, and I continue, "But I escaped that life. I could have ended up stowed away on anyone's vessel that was on Bellcoast that day, but I just so happened to end up on Teddy's." Now I see Mama sitting in her favorite spot, audience-left, toward the middle of the center section near, but not on, the aisle. My mouth curves up even more because I know that, and I see her gentle smile as she nods at me.

"Teddy and Miriam never wavered in their support of me or in their belief that I was meant to be Bosch. And they showed me what that meant, even as I screwed up time after time after time as some of you can remember." A ripple of laughter goes through the audience, and I chuckle along with them. I glance at the front row, and the four generals are even giving in to a few titters. Miles is simply sitting with a politically correct smile on his narrow brown face, but his eyes are shining as he looks at me.

"So how do I feel about the traditions of Bosch?" I entwine my fingers on top of my head and look up, considering, "Who are we? We are pirates descended from the diverse thralls that were forced onto ships to do their masters' bidding. That was the 'tradition' we sprang from. Then we became marauders, freeing other thralls and taking from other ships and seaports —that, too, is one of our distant 'traditions.' And then we arrived here and made this island our home. We became Bosch. We no longer do a master's bidding, and we are no longer marauders unless something begs to be liberated and come with us on our missions…." I wink at the audience, and the ripple of laughter returns and includes the generals.

"We are a young country of a New Earth, and we make the traditions we choose to make. I, in fact, am upholding one of my family's traditions: my papa, Master Commander Emeritus Theodore Bosch, became general almost forty years ago." I glance down at General Rainey, whose rheumy eyes now seem much less rheumy and much savvier. He gives me a thumbs-up and a wink as I continue. "Seems that Papa really wanted the tactical general's position when it opened. Trouble was, he was only …" I let the pause settle as I can almost hear the audience stop breathing. "… a captain. A captain who knew the history of his beloved Bosch, down to every line of its original charter." There is a rush of air as everyone gives a small gasp, and chatter begins to spread. I simply wait for calm to return. I don't look over at Commander Conrad, but boy, do I want to. *Nice work not sticking your tongue out at him, Kat.*

"Apparently, this *is* a tradition in my family. So be prepared to see Grey or Kik or Mac, my Bosch-doan children, up here one day spinning the same story." Laughter returns, and I see someone lean over to one of the LTC commanders (I can't tell one from the other) and whisper something, to which the commander nods and then looks at me and actually smiles.

I give a small nod in response but put my face into a sober place. "So, to be clear: Traditions are important, and the most important one to me is the Bosch tradition of loyalty. I served Teddy Bosch loyally but not blindly. I serve Miles Baldwin-Bosch loyally but not blindly." I give a small nod to my friend in the front. "And I am, as you may have heard from the previous Q&A, fiercely loyal and protective of my family. Even when they ask the unthinkable of me." I suddenly hear my voice shake as I tear up. I am about to be as honest as I ever have been about Papa. I close my eyes. "I long to have Papa here, whole and hale and hearty. I did not rob him of life. I followed his dictates, and I helped him find his peace. He liked the idea of being part of the sky he so loved above the land and the people he also loved." I open my eyes and quickly wipe the tears away, and I see I am not the only one moved as I hear several coughs and throats clearing and see many hands wiping eyes in the audience.

"If you choose to select me for the Generals' Table, I will give the same fierce loyalty to all of you and to Bosch. But Papa always said, 'The best way to lead is to listen.' So, let's change this up." I hop up and go to the podium and take the microphone, nodding pleasantly at Commander Conrad, who looks distinctly uncomfortable. I lean down to hand it to Bailey, who waits, as we had quickly discussed and planned just before I went onstage, at the front of the house. Then I sit back on my spot at the front of the stage. "I'd like to hear from you all. What do you think about our traditions and the special project I am suggesting? And you don't have to agree with me, but just be civil—something I, too, am working on mastering." Again, light laughter. "Colonel Alexander will bring you the mic."

And for the next bell, I listen to the troops, taking in support, concerns, and disagreement and adding my perspective briefly on each part. And no one moves to return to the original format.

SIX

Meanwhile

TRUVALE, SOBAYTON BAY, AND JORGE MONTT, PATAGONIA; SEPTEMBER 2365

Rob Abernathy stepped up to the podium of the outdoor stage, smiling and waving to the crowd cheering his welcome. As he waited for them to calm, he considered them. The throng that stretched before him was not made up of the important and influential people he wined and dined for support. No, these were his base: people hungry for someone to tell them they were special and that there were others below them who they could blame for any difficulties they faced. He watched as the mass of humanity shifted and eddied as if one immense entity. He could see several Bluies carefully interspersed throughout. It was quite a large assemblage, not as large as he'd like, but still significant. *Larger than the ones that woman is drawing, I'm sure.* He stepped up to the podium and began to speak to his followers.

We have the privilege to be part of Eternia, the wealthiest and strongest nation in the Federal Alliance.

Cheers.

And we owe it to the marginalized peoples of New Earth to relocate and provide for them—a home, a job, a place where their families are safe—not only because it is economically the right thing, but it is morally the right thing.

More cheers. Rob no longer had to work to hide his disgust at the masses. Their loud cheers and chants for him more than made up for their stupidity.

Thralldom allows people who are scraping by, starved for not only food but culture and learning to be brought into our world: We can protect them and give them opportunity as well.

Thralls need us. Thralls need us. The chant grew loud. Rob Abernathy waited patiently until it began to subside. It was taking a little longer each time, which delighted him, and he gifted his multitude with a smile.

Yes. They do. And we need them. He showed both hands and then interlaced them symbolically.

Wild cheers.

Now, to add the fear. He let his face become serious and concerned.

But there are those both within the Federal Alliance and beyond it that would rob both us and the people who need us of this opportunity. My opponent…

Boos echoed and several nasty comments about his opponent could be heard.

My opponent does not understand the necessity of legalizing thralldom throughout the FA, thus keeping the advantages of the enterprise away from those of us who could provide the most to the neglected of New Earth. And why? What kind of profit is she gaining from this stance and from where? And will she be able to keep you and your families safe from the rogue states that exist in the world? Some that even call themselves pirates outright.

A few voices yelled out: *She's a traitor. Get rid of the phony.* And Rob's favorite, *Kill the pirates.*

I will keep you and your families safe. I will bring the less privi-

leged into our circle of safety. I will bring a hard line down on those that pillage our world.

The crowd erupted in cheers. *Rob. Rob. Rob.*

He smiled and waved to the crowd. His moment had come.

The young woman watched as her father's most recent assistant brought a tray of drinks into the room. *Lloyd...Porter?* she thought with a creased brow and then nodded to herself, pleased she remembered his name. Casually leaning back on the white leather settee, the white and gold brocade-covered pillow clutched against her belly, she watched him move through the room as he cautiously negotiated around the white grand piano that had never been played and carefully set two glasses of sparkling water on the table near where she and her brother sat. He smiled at her, but his eyes were anxious. "Here you are, Miss Farris."

She smiled back at him. "Thanks, Lloyd."

Her brother, however, frowned at his glass of effervescence and said, "Dad, I'm twenty-five years old. Surely that's old enough to have a brandy with you."

Their father, Senator Rob Abernathy, looked over at his son and raised his eyebrows. Farris tried to subtly look for any indication of emotion in her father's eyes, but as usual, saw none. Then she looked at her brother. He was handsome and broad-shouldered. He looked so much like the pictures she had seen of her father from years before. But Ashton's eyes were alive with emotion. First, the dismay he gave the glass of water and then the fawning hopefulness he had when he spoke to his father.

"We'll see how the night progresses, Ashton. I will consider your proposal." The Senator, which was what Farris had taken to calling her father over the past few years, held his crystal glass of deep amber liquor up and looked at it appraisingly. Farris knew The Senator was admiring his own drink because it held a thing that was very rare and very expensive: two essential qualities to signify value. "And remember, Ashton. It's cognac, not brandy."

Ashton's face crumpled slightly, and Farris knew he was cursing himself for making a mistake. But he bobbed his head with its expensively coiffed deep-brown hair. "Yes, sir. Cognac." He said the word as if committing it to memory. *And he probably is,* she thought disdainfully.

She turned her head and watched Sandra Abernathy take a deep drink of the special flat water Lloyd had served her, which Farris knew was actually vodka that her mother had imported from Rus, but never mentioned to The Senator. Mother, a title Farris used less and less these days, sat silently in the white tufted chair across from The Senator, looking out the large floor-to-ceiling windows of their Truvale penthouse. Her mother was a tiny, perfectly groomed woman with deep, dark hair and a pale complexion kept rosy with products and facials. Farris could never remember seeing Sandra without her hair properly done or not dressed in a tasteful outfit with expensive shoes. She could also never remember seeing her happy.

She followed her mother's eyes out the windows at the gray mist that had gathered around the city as night fell. The tall buildings all around them gleamed with dozens of small sparks, top to bottom, showing people at home and some in late-night offices. Farris liked imagining the lives going on in each brightly lit window she could see. Sometimes she made up stories about them. She gave a small sigh as she gazed at them now.

Lloyd Porter pulled her out of her reverie as he picked up

the Obi remote, looking at his timepiece, and said to The Senator, "Voting is now complete. Would you like to watch the counts, sir?"

Her father turned his head toward his assistant and nodded. Farris considered what it would be like to move into the grand mansion in the center of the park with all those people in it if The Senator won the election. *He'd probably have them paint it blue,* she thought scornfully as she considered the blue-draped sycophants, a word she had recently learned and thought applied to many of the people in The Senator's circle, who were always flattering and doting on him. *He'd probably send me off to some fitness farm before he allowed me to move in as well.* This was an ongoing issue between her father and her. The Senator did not like her body, nor how it looked. But Farris did. It was soft and round and did all the things she wanted it to. She could use it to shop, to walk along the river, to go to lunch with her friends. She had no trouble finding dates, either male or female, though she really wasn't particularly interested in either at this juncture. All she was really interested in was getting away from this family and living a life that felt real. Take this body and person that The Senator despised and go somewhere far, far away.

"Well, that about settles it." Phil Reston, the attorney general of the Federal Alliance, clicked off the Obi and turned to look at the woman who sat on the couch. He smiled. Alyssa Russell had only just sat down after spending the past hour on the running machine in the corner. Her dark, curly hair was pulled casually back in a ponytail, tendrils of it loose and sweaty around her sepia-brown face that had a post-exercise glow. She tipped her water bottle up to her lips for a long drink and then laughed as she spilled some on Phil's ratty T-shirt that she always wore over her exercise top and shorts after she worked out.

Alyssa's comm began to vibrate, and she looked at it. In his pocket, Phil could feel his buzz as well. "Well, Madame President..." Phil came over to the blue-checked sofa and reached out a hand to a smiling Alyssa, pulling her to him. "...I expect you need to shower and get out to meet your people. Lauren is going to be beside herself that we are still sequestered up here."

"Lauren is always beside herself. She can wait a few minutes." Alyssa laughed and then wrapped her arms around Phil. They spent the next several seconds enjoying her first kiss as president of the Federal Alliance. They pulled their heads back to smile at each other, and Alyssa ran her fingers through Phil's sandy-brown hair that was starting to show a bit of gray. "One more kiss before I shower." Phil happily obliged.

As they moved apart and Alyssa headed to get cleaned up and dressed, Phil commented, "You're still going to have to deal with that fucker, Rob Abernathy. I can't believe he'll be vice president."

She shrugged. "I've been dealing with him in the Senate for years. And he is a piece of work. But you know, he's the only one that makes you use that kind of language. Though I get it: If that old testimony you took—what, ten years ago?—is to be believed, he is one nasty individual." She began tapping out a message, likely to her assistant Lauren.

Phil opened the small bar cooler near the stairs, pulling out a ginger drink. "Oh, it was real, and he is the worst. Man, I'd like to have another shot at him."

Now Alyssa's voice was muffled as she shut the washroom door. "Let me at least get into the office before you create a political incident, will you?"

Phil chuckled and replied, "Anything for you, my sweet" as he pulled the small red velvet ring box out of his pocket and grinned.

"What do you have for me today?" Paddy Owens, who was presently going under the name Owen Patrick, leaned onto the window and peered into the vehicle Demery sat in.

"A couple of nice art pieces and some Old Days books," Demery said with a grin. "And they're in great shape."

Owen paused. "Nice. Anything else?"

Demery nodded. "Anything else is stashed in the hold. Several bricks of anything else, to be exact."

"Well, then..." Owen's big grin spread as he opened the passenger door and slid into the seat. "...let's go stash this ride, and we can get a drink and get you paid."

"Now you're talking my talk." Demery laughed. "Price is the same for the 'anything else,' and we can negotiate the goods."

Paddy Owens could care less about the other goods, though over the years, he had made a tidy profit from the pinched items that Demery Ludlow had brought him. It wasn't even the small amount of Glitter that Ludlow filched and fenced to Paddy's alter ego, Owen Patrick, that was of value. Paddy knew that far larger amounts of Glitter were being diverted to Alejandro DeLeon through the Archer contact in Bosch. No, Demery Ludlow's worth was his ability to spin a story and the looseness of his tongue after a few rums.

Alejandro DeLeon looked at his agenda and sighed heavily as he picked up his comm and punched in the number from his contact list. He didn't like dealing with the petty little man from Bosch, but Abernathy was still insistent that they make inroads into the pirate nation. Three years of wheeling and dealing with Howard Archer had certainly created a funnel for Glitter, but DeLeon knew it was but a trace amount compared to what the official Bosch Pirate Force was delivering throughout New Earth.

"You are late." The petulant, slightly high-pitched voice came through the comm.

DeLeon rolled his eyes. "Please forgive me, Mr. Archer. I had another comm that ran long."

"Mmmm. I have business to conduct, too, you know." The voice was taking on a distinct whine. DeLeon knew that any "business" Archer was trying to conduct was one of three things: self-serving, extralegal, or failing.

"What are you wanting to discuss, Archer? You scheduled this call." DeLeon decided to simply jump in and get the distasteful task over with.

A small "humph" came from the other side of the comm. "I asked for a meeting. Face-to-face. But was told that was not possible."

"Is this about our Glitter arrangement, Howard?" Alejandro knew the informality of a first name would offend and used it intentionally.

DeLeon was rewarded with an annoyed breath and a resentful tone. "Yes. Additional checks have been put in place by the Force. They must have started to notice some Glitter production and distribution discrepancies. I won't be able to provide any more until I have had my people discover how to bypass the checks."

"I see. Well, it was inevitable that the missing product

would be noted. We will simply freeze our payment to your New Caribbean account until you notify us the exchange will resume." Alejandro really couldn't care less about this relationship. They didn't even sell the Glitter they received to his knowledge. Abernathy simply had him send it to the storage facility a distance from the mountain estate in Eternia, where DeLeon had first become enmeshed in this business.

Howard Archer quickly replied, "Oh, no. I must have those payments to keep up my payroll. It should only be a few months."

A grin spread over Alejandro's handsome face. This was a trifecta for Archer: self-serving, extralegal, and definitely failing. "I'm sorry, Howard. In three years, you haven't provided even one Bosch pilot to move our thrall cargo, and now your Glitter supply has dried up as well. If you want any markers, perhaps you can beg some of those little, blue-draped people that seem to be popping up all over the place. You have been seen doing some kind of business with them. I have another meeting. Please contact me when you have something to negotiate with." DeLeon turned off his comm and sat back. That felt good.

SEVEN

New Vest

BOSCH, OCTOBER 2365

I am reveling in the colors of the trees as I walk to work this morning. There is a tiny nip to the air, unusual for the first day of October, and I feel it in my nose and throat as I take in a deep breath of the fresh fall air. As I arrive at the Bosch Central building, two small potted plants protruding from my bag, I take a moment to look at the blue sky that seems to go on forever, interrupted by only a few white streaks of clouds. It's a good day.

I step into the foyer and show my new ID to Trooper Moreno, who gives me a grin and a salute, both of which I return, and then make my way to the second floor. I pull out the piece of paper I wrote my note on and head to room 237. A young woman stands on a footstool in front of the door that holds the numbers 237 above it. She is carefully painting the window in gold script: "General Katrina Wallace." My stomach flops over, and I stand staring as she completes her meticulous work. She leans back, surveys her creation, and then pulls a small utility knife from a pocket, scraping at loose gold spatters on the window before she even notices me.

"Oh, I'm sorry, ma'am. Did you need to get into the general's office?" She seems sincere in her apology.

I stare for a millisecond longer at the lettering and shake my head in awe. "Hi. What's your name?"

"Trooper Nia Price, ma'am." I watch as she notes my uniform and then shakes and stands at attention with a salute. "General, ma'am."

I laugh. "Nia, I am not in the least bit used to that title. But I am in awe of your skill with a brush doing those letters. Where did you learn that?"

Nia relaxes a touch, and a warm smile covers her face and glows in her eyes. "My mom taught script in primary. So, she gave me special lessons."

I smile and nod. "Well, good for her and for you. I hope my tenure as general lives up to such lovely lettering."

She relaxes a bit more. "If I may say so, I am sure it will." She leans forward toward me. "I voted for you, ma'am." She says this in a whisper.

My heart overflows. "Well, then, all the more reason for me to live up to the name you have emblazoned so beautifully, Nia."

At this, Nia opens the door and motions me into my newest job of the Bosch Pirate Force.

"Congratulations on your election." Ruth sits down in her usual spot in the comfy blue chair and settles in.

I grin. "Thanks. I don't know if I'm elated, astonished, or alarmed." I walk over to the oversized gray chair that is tucked in between the brick wall and the small wooden table and sit down, curling my legs up. I pull the loose-weave blue throw over me because even though it is still summer-warm outside this afternoon, it's October, and I want to imagine the autumn coolness is fast approaching.

"I see you've been accessing the list of emotions I gave you in the spring," Ruth says, her face pleasant and her hands comfortably in her lap, fingers intertwined. "Still giving them their own personas?"

"I am. I had a small bout with Doubt this morning, which I won. Which works out as I couldn't include him in this list since I wanted to add an alliterative spin to it." I smile proudly.

Ruth wrinkles her brow. "That's not really the point of the list. But also, doesn't *elated* begin with an *e*?'"

I shrug. "Well, yes, but if I pronounce it with a bit of North Country, it sounds like an *a*, and so it works alliteratively."

"Sounds like you really want to use the word," she says, her face neutral.

"You trying to therapize me, Ruth?" I close one eye and peer at her with the other.

The dark-haired woman, who is always immaculately but unpretentiously dressed, slowly shakes her head, her small, gold ear hoops moving in time with her head. "That's not even a word. But if it was, then yes, you are paying me to 'therapize' you." She smiles.

"Well, then, get on with it. Fix me, RTT." I lean my cheek and chin on my palm with my elbow resting on the chair arm and look at this woman I have been seeing almost every week for three years this month.

She starts to laugh. "Oh, you are in a good mood, Kat. I think 'elated' is the accurate descriptor." She looks at me. "You mentioned using your North Country accent. Maybe we should talk some about the language you used before you were taken as a thrall. It might help unblock some of those memories, and you seem to be in a strong enough place to do that. What words are similar to Bosch words?"

I shut my eyes and consider, then nod. "A lot of verbs: plow, bake, cut, harvest, shoot, trip …" I shake my head. "I remember when I first learned to plow. My dad had loaned me out to the Brobergs to get their plowing done. I had never done it before and did a crap job, so Mr. Broberg said he was only going to pay half. My dad took me home and beat me and told me to go back the next day and make sure I did the job right. So, I did. And I redid the parts I screwed up. And he got the markers he was after and then the cheap-ass whiskey and Glitter to celebrate." I tuck the throw around my legs more securely. This is one of the few places outside of home I feel comfortable curling up and being small and cozy. I glance at the table and see the box of tissues next to a broad-leafed potted plant. "Grandma Rina fixed me up with her herbs and gave me a little box with a jar of salve in it. She said that I should put any coins I ever got in there and not ever let Dad know about it." I work my jaw to relieve the tension and blink quickly.

"How old were you?" Ruth's voice is gentle.

"Ten."

"Isn't that the same age as your daughter?" The question comes softly.

I nod. "Yep." I reach for the tissues.

Major Matty Warner sits in front of my desk, an Obi processor on his lap with a unit roster pulled up. Over the last week, I have been prepping my anti-trafficking project, collecting information and recommendations during meetings with representatives from the quartermaster's office, Bosch Intelligence, tactical and weaponry, and now, for the past three bells, the Pilot's Coalition. I am looking at the units that have excelled at extraction missions, and Matty's experience and expertise have been crucial, giving insight into both individual and unit strengths and weaknesses. I watch as he moves some data around on his processor and then gives an approving nod. "Okay, that gives us four units to make the raids and an alternate unit in case of any complications. Aleyn Unit..."

I sigh. While the BPF does utilize the FA's standard phonetic alphabet for ease of communication during flights similar to the old alpha-bravo-charlie from Old Days, we have also implemented one for use internally using pirate names from ancient times to the fall of Old Earth. Unsurprisingly, most of the names are men's. "I like Awilda better as a title," I quip.

"Yeah, you would." Matty peers up at me briefly from where he sits and goes on, saying before he rattles off a list of names, "But that isn't standard." I roll my eyes at the male standard and murmur under my breath about making changes as Matty continues, wearing a smile, "So Aleyn Unit: Tony Diaz, Kajetan Rivers, Isaac Cowan, Stefanie Ratliff, Elina Taylor.

"Butler Unit: Matt Warner, Aaron Morton, Demery Ludlow, Bailey Alexander, Rash Holloway.

"Cavendish Unit: Rylee Banks, Tomas Firth, Hugh Davis, Elissa Suarez, Layla-Rose Collins.

"Drake Unit: Ocean Booker, Darren Beattie, Salim Carr, Angela Livingstone, Kaitlin Pruitt.

"Alternate—Easton Unit: Asmara Cardenas, Lily Sanchez, Guy McCann, Gadisa Kone, Devin Kidd."

I am typing as well and nod my approval at the names that are now very familiar. We ranked the units, rating each one based on qualities essential for rescue work, looking for the right combination of training, leadership, teamwork, initiative, and versatility.

"I think we have formed a good company here for the project. I think the qualities you and I set out are fair and measurable, and I really like the training program you have outlined." Matty has his feet resting on my desk, his long legs bent to support his device as he taps away on it.

"Glad you approve, Major." I smile saucily at him as he rolls his eyes and laughs. His input has been invaluable, and I can't help but think that I am so glad Bailey pushed me and brought him in early on. He is turning out to be a great asset and a potential friend.

He shifts the topic. "We need to decide on training times. Let's check calendars."

I dutifully pull mine up and let out a breath as I peruse the crazy number of meetings on it that my new assistant, Olivia, has put in place. I scan for openings. "How about Tuesday…?"

"Tuesday… Seventeen bells?" Matty queries. "It's late but looks like it would work for most everyone."

I am quick to respond. "Nope. I have a standing appointment with my therapist then."

There is silence, and I prepare myself for the typical Bosch derisive response to therapy.

"You see a head doc?" Matty's voice holds concern. The Bosch are so ego-forward that they assume that anyone who admits to dealing with and working on difficult feelings must be ready to be shipped to Crazy Island. I know this because I thought that, too, before I started seeing Ruth.

"I do. RTT." I decide to use simple, declarative sentences. I like Matty, and I am intrigued how he will take this news, given that he needs heavy machinery to tote his ego around.

"RT…what?" His eyes narrow at the term, but his voice retains its warmth.

I smile. "RTT: Ruth the Therapist."

I see him process this and nod. "Okay. How long?"

My eyes shift down and to the left. "Oh…years." I grin. "Honestly, she struck paydirt when she met me. I think I singlehandedly paid for her place on the beach in District Four." I see Matty tip his head back in a chuckle as I continue. "I am, to her, what a wood-framed home from the Old Days is to a builder: fucking job security." Now I laugh as I delve deeper into the analogy. "Just when you think you've got a repair managed and smoothed over, you lean back on another wall to admire your handiwork, and boom, your arm goes through, and you see you have to deal with dry rot all the way to the floorboards."

Matty is sitting forward now, listening with his hand rubbing his stubble beard. He looks at me quizzically but kindly. "So, you're the house, and you have dry rot?"

I nod. I'm going all in…. He asked, after all. "Yep. Loads."

Matty leans back, puts his feet back on my desk, and looks at the ceiling. "Okay. Now, this is something I get. I'm fixing up a place in Seven. Dry rot: Well, that's salvageable in my experience. Once it's dug out, you may just have to replace a beam or two." He looks at me, and there's a twinkle in his eyes. "How's your wiring?"

I grin and give a laugh. "Not up to code. I'm a fire hazard, just waiting for a spark."

"Aren't we all." He laughs and begins to tap on his device. "Good to know, then. Let's be sure to keep Tuesdays, seventeen bells, open for you and…RTT, right?"

I step into the empty anteroom of Mile's office and look at Betsy's desk. I'm a little surprised she isn't sitting there and a whole lot surprised by how nervous I am. I've been here hundreds of times over the years under dozens of circumstances, but now, the familiarity has waned as I am about to participate in my first Generals' Table meeting. Typically, the Master Commander meets with all five generals each week to receive reports on what is referred to as DIETS, which involves reviews on D: districts, I: internal relations, E: external relations, T: tactical issues, and my area, S: special projects. It is also a time for the five generals to gain information from the MC and make their own suggestions about any issue involving the BPF. However, since my election just took place, the interval was extended to two weeks to "let her get her feet under her" as General Philip Patel had said. At first, I felt like they were doubting what I could do, but now, I'm glad. After two weeks, I actually have something to report on.

The big wooden door opens, and I jump slightly until I see Betsy come bustling out. She sees me and her face breaks into a wide smile. "There's our newest general."

I can't help but grin. "You make it sound like it's my first day of primary."

"Well, honestly, there's not a wide divergence." Her eyes twinkle at me.

I think of my children's favorite parts of school. "Do we get recess and a snack?"

Betsy nods. "Actually, you do. There's always refreshments and a break every half-bell."

"Seriously, Bets? Every half-bell? Why?" I am perplexed, though I also am wondering why I didn't make this jump before if that was the schedule.

"Well, you may be able to convince the table to stretch the break to a bell. It was Hank who always needed several toilet breaks. MC referred to it as the Rainey Rule." Betsy smiles and takes her seat at her desk, busying herself with the tasks of the day.

I grin, unsure if she is putting me on. I hear conversation in the hall, and generals Helen Wolcott, Steve Baradash, and Philip Patel all turn into the office, laughing and talking. General Baradash looks at me. His smile broadens, and he calls out, "Look, everyone—it's the new baby!" which evokes another round of laughter.

I run through all the possible responses, discarding those that involve violence or the threat of violence, and raise my eyebrows. "Not sure if I should be honored or offended by that name, Generals."

General Patel grins. "Well, it could cut either way, so it really depends on what you do with it."

The other two laugh, and General Wolcott opens the big wooden doors, calling, "Good morning, Miles." I consider the challenge and follow them into our Master Commander's office. *Let's get this done.*

The meeting is over, and Jamal, Helen, Steve, and Phil, the other four generals, say their goodbyes and return to their offices for a day of work. I am staying as Miles requested a debrief from my first table. As the wooden door closes, and the room quiets, he stands and goes to the bar, pouring us each a very small measure of bourbon, then returning to hand mine to me.

"So, General Wallace…" Miles' face breaks out into a grin. "I really can't believe I am saying that." He starts to quietly laugh.

I wrinkle my brow good-naturedly. "You said it several

times during the meeting without devolving into laughter, Miles."

"Yeah, but it was a helluva lot of work not to, Kat." Miles is still chuckling. He takes a sip of his drink and looks at me. "So, what did you think?"

"Of the table or your vague attempt at self-control?" I quip and then nod. "I know what you are asking." I look at my friend thoughtfully. "I think you and the table are making the best of a pretty antiquated system. And, I think, there are deeply embedded issues crying for change."

Now Miles bobs his head up and down. "You'll get no argument from me on either point. And you should feel that way. I mean, hell, you've dragged down our average age by at least a decade." We both grin at this. "But look at you, taking the lead on rescinding the Rainey Rule."

I close my eyes and lean back in my chair. "Sweet New Earth, I hope that's not what I'll be remembered for. After all, the project..." I sit up and smile, and then my smile drops as Miles is looking at me with a sober and worried expression. "Miles, what's wrong? Is it the project?"

"Is it the project? No." As he says this, I relax my shoulders that I didn't realize I had tensed. He continues, "And yes. The project ... The project is sound, Kat, and we all agreed that it fits the Bosch moral compass without creating waves with our current customers—a win for everyone. But your teams will be flying..."

"With me...," I am quick to remind him.

Miles sighs. "With you, though I don't like it." He pauses and looks at me over the half-spectacles he has begun wearing to do paperwork. "You all will be flying into risky situations outside our borders and removing people who are seen as valuable property that sells for thousands, sometimes tens of thousands of markers, from an exceedingly well-organized affiliation of cartels that has been growing stronger over the past several years."

"Yes, Miles. That is exactly what we will be doing." I pause to hear the rest of his concern.

He looks at me, and his face is serious. "You are going to war with the traffickers, Kat. So be prepared: When you go to war, you lose people."

EIGHT

Awilda Unit: First Mission

BOSCH AND ORKNEYS, NOVEMBER 4, 2365

It's early on a beautifully clear, deliciously chill Thursday morning, and I am in the jump seat with Diaz's unit. Team Awilda—I smile to myself because I got my way in changing the "standard" name. Small steps.

The company has been training for close to three weeks, and I have flown with each unit several times and will accompany each on a mission, though Miles is still not happy about this choice. But I am not going to be a general sitting behind a desk. I want to be there when things happen.

Colonel Tony Diaz, the pilot, is sturdy and broad through the shoulders. He has a shock of black, straight hair and an easy smile. His pilot's tattoo stretches up his neck and tickles his ear. He and I worked together close to fifteen years earlier, and we have been spending time in training getting reacquainted and sharing stories about our families. He is an excellent pilot who leads quietly and calmly. He has three kids about the same age as mine, and we have committed to getting them together soon.

His navigator is Kajetan Rivers, a lieutenant and incredibly talented. They are on the young side, but it is clear that they plan to push ahead, and they certainly have the skills and leadership to go places. His gunners are Isaac Cowan and Stefanie Ratliff, both majors, and Stef recently got married. She has had lots of questions for me about my election to the Generals' Table, and I have laughed and told her I will watch for her to show up soon. Isaac is far more laid back and balances Stefanie's unbridled enthusiasm well. He is the only child of an ill, widowed father. He seems to be a dedicated son. The engineer is Captain Elina Taylor. She is recently divorced and has one son about to graduate from university. She and I have connected through a shared love of music from the twenty-first century. I admire how she can do an astounding job as an engineer and then, when the workday is done, leave and focus on what makes her happy. Lessons to be learned for sure.

All four of the newly trained units, including Diaz's unit, with me on board, are flying to the sparsely settled small islands of the British-Irish archipelago, the officially agreed-upon name that apparently gets re-argued over every half-century or so. We Bosch simply call the group of islands the Orkneys, mostly because our pirate heart is large enough to incorporate the ancient Vikings. BI has good intel that these islands are havens for traffickers. Traffickers—or traders; the terms are interchangeable—have taken over old, abandoned buildings and refurbished them to hold, transport, and sell their human goods. Most are either found in equally deserted villages or far enough away from sparsely populated ones to not arouse suspicion.

Each unit is going to raid one suspected waystation, each on a different island. The plan is to rough up the traders, free the thralls, loot enough to make the journey marginally profitable (this hint came directly from Quartermaster Etienne Winters: "You need to keep my books happy if you are going to stay off the council's radar."), and hightail it home. We plan to transport the freed to Bosch for any medical treatment necessary, and from there, to wherever they choose to go, even if they choose to stay in Bosch.

The training I implemented calls for there to always be one member of the unit left with the vessel who can fly and one who can operate the rail guns. Of the other two or three members that make the raid, one must be a woman. I received some mild pushback on this initially, but while I agreed that many men and middles are more than capable of compassion and gentleness, I recalled aloud to the group the comfort I took from seeing Eliza and Rayna on the vessel when I escaped, and so the plan to include a woman in the raiding party was established.

The engineers have been working on the maneuverability of the vessels, adding additional axes to existing shrouded engines, and in one case, adding two additional gimballed engines. I am duly impressed and plan to see about making similar adjustments on a smaller scale on the Coupe for my own use.

Diaz's unit, with me in tow, is headed for Ipswich Island. We were told there are typically four to six thralls being confined there on any particular day, held by three guards: one stationed at the front door, one at the back, and one in direct contact with the thralls. On market day, the guard numbers more than double, and buyers and their armed teams flow through, exchanging markers for humanity. We are scheduled to drop in on a quiet day before the market.

Tony handily brings the ship to rest offshore, cutting the engines early and opening the newly attached glider wings to land us silently on the water's surface and we motor ultra-quietly into a narrow bay on the far side of the small island. Rivers and Ratliff will stay aboard the vessel, so the raiding party of Diaz, Cowan, and Taylor proceed to pull the muted green and tan camouflage covers over their uniforms. Tony grins at me and tosses me a cover, and I give a "Hot damn!" and grin back. I am here officially only to observe, but I am as keen as any of them to really partake in a full rescue. I am armed and ready to participate in whatever way the pilot orders. I have made it clear to the entire company that my rank only applies on Bosch and regarding the broad strokes of the project. Each unit is trusted to independently decide the details of how best a mission should be carried out, and I have guaranteed I will not question any orders during implementation.

There is not much foliage cover on the perimeter of the island as much of its topography is rocky beach and seagrass. Initially, we are protected from view by the high, sandy cliff that shoots up above us, but once we reach a place where we can scale the cliff, there is only beach grass interrupted by a smattering of gorse and the occasional deeply bent juniper. We make our way first at a crawl through the mounds of the Marram grass, each of us receiving several sharp stabs, then to the low gorse bushes and the occasional sparse copse of twisted birch, moving slowly and intently toward the coordinates the BI provided us. There is no decent cover until we are well inland, where a small forest of gray-trunked, wind-bent hawthorns and black poplars lean deeply away from the constant sea breeze, their branches bent at such improbable angles that they remind me of large versions of Kenichi's bonsai garden. This is where the building we seek will be found.

We finally come in sight of the property. It is just as the BI report described, little more than a two-room, tar-papered shack. The black paper is tattered and flapping in the constant wind that blows across this island. From our vantage point behind some low trees and undergrowth, we can use the bi-spy glasses to see one trafficker sitting on a stool by the front door, head leaning back on the wall, his weapon casually on his lap. Tony directs Elina Taylor and me to circle to the back and subdue the guard stationed there while he and Isaac will restrain and muzzle the fellow we can see. Then Diaz will use some Bosch encouragements to get his new captive to draw out the trader stationed inside, allowing the two of us to safely enter the back way. I nod approvingly; it's a sound plan.

Elina and I quietly move in a large, sweeping curve around the house, stopping now and then to be sure we are not off course. Soon enough, we are on the far side and able to get a visual of the back door. We see the expected guard. This one has given up all pretense of guarding and laid his weapon on the ground while he has stretched his feet onto a block of wood and pulled his hat down over his eyes.

I whisper to Elina, "Guess I can't blame him. It must get pretty dull sitting there all day."

"Well, we are here to spice up his day then, General." She gives me a wicked grin and starts to move forward.

There is no trick to taking this guy. We are on him in a moment, and Elina quickly deals him a good thump to the head before dragging him away from the door. "That was an impressive strike, Taylor," I say with sincere admiration.

"Thanks. I just think of my ex-husband during the worst times, and it makes my blows land strong and accurate." Her eyes dance as she says this, and I have to work to suppress my laughter as I roughly gag and tie the unconscious trafficker.

Within moments, we hear the two-note whistle from Isaac Cowan telling us we are clear to enter the building. I unlock the door, and Elina compliments my speed and skill with my precious lockpick set. We swing the door open, and both of our smiles fade. Elina gasps, "Sweet New Earth."

There are four "women" in the far corner of the room who

can't be more than girls barely into their teens. I cringe as I realize that one is likely only two or three years older than Grey. They are naked and bound to each other with heavy neck shackles while their hands are tied tightly behind their backs. Their eyes are empty, void of even fright at this point. And they are silent. I remember that empty feeling. They all are pale like the peoples of the North Country or of nearby Scania. They might all be blonde, but their hair is so filthy, I can't tell. From their wounds and the dried blood on their legs, it is obvious they have been the subject of their captors' entertainment. I feel my anger percolate.

I move to the girls and speak quietly first in standard FA, then in the blend of North Country speech and Scanian that I learned from a peddler years ago when I was a kid. This patois seems to spark understanding, so I use it to explain our intentions and give the reassurance that they are now safe from further harm. I see Elina watch me closely, and I realize I have probably overstepped. "Sorry, Elina, I jumped in."

She smiles and says in a quiet voice, "No, no. I appreciate it. It will help when I do this alone on the next missions, and anyway, I don't know the language you are using."

I smile ruefully. "It's from deep in the vaults." My picks and I now work on the locks holding the neck shackles, and she carefully cuts the ties from the girls' wrists.

A bell later, the girls, washed with a bar of unused soap Elina found on a shelf and clothed in the four camo coveralls the raiding party stripped off for them to wear, are ready for the return to the vessel. The three bound traders are awake and eyeing us, and I make sure to give them each a good kick as we depart. They are very fortunate our policy does not include lethal measures.

~

The mood in the hangar after the twenty, yes, twenty freed thralls are settled in with the newly developed re-integration office is one of elation and exuberance. The intelligence was spot-on, and all four raids went off without a hitch. We have decided to refer to the rescued as "souls" instead of victims or thralls, partly as a nod to our lineage both on ship and in flight, and partly to maintain a sense of humanity toward those we free. Not cargo, souls. And the fact that we brought twenty souls to freedom is exhilarating. After a short debrief, a few words of heartfelt gratitude from me, and a gift of the day off tomorrow from Miles, the units are dismissed to celebrate in whatever way they desire.

Matty and Bailey come up to me, and their smiles are radiant.

"Special Project: End Trafficking is off to a successful start!" Bailey says jubilantly.

Matty leans toward me and says, "Aren't you glad you listened to me?" And I thwack him on the arm as he laughs. "I don't know when I have ever been so proud of a mission, Gen. Seriously. Thanks for making this happen."

I, too, am delighted, though my joy is somewhat blunted by the haunted eyes of the girls in that sad little shack.

NINE

Repercussions

TOFT, SCANIA, NOVEMBER 5, 2365

"Mr. Hartvig, I do not like flying, and I do not like having to deal with situations like this." Rob Abernathy's face was relaxed, but his fingers drummed the tabletop next to where he sat in a deep-purple upholstered chair. "We agreed long ago that there would be no need for my personal involvement once I took over the Scanian trafficking cartel. However, clearly, my guidance is necessary as you seem to have utterly lost control of all situations." Rob motioned about the room.

"I am certainly looking into the archipelago situation, Mr. Abern—" Abernathy's eyes flashed dangerously. "Excuse me.... Sir...." Erik Hartvig tried to speak with his normal assuredness, but the task was difficult as he stood in the center of the room completely naked. He shifted, in turns covering himself and then simply standing as he normally would, uncertain which posture would send the right message to this dangerous man in front of him. His eyes flicked to his wife, Freya, and their three blonde teenaged children where they sat, bound and gagged on the gray, velvet-tufted couch in his mistress's living room in the most expensive neighborhood in downtown Toft. All four wore clear expressions of fear, and his older daughter's blue eyes reflected repulsion when she looked at him. He would need to speak to her at length after this situation was resolved. Sunniva, his statuesque and stunning lover, sat naked at Abernathy's feet. Her usually elegantly braided, long blonde hair was now tangled and disheveled, and her head sagged heavily as she softly sobbed. One of Abernathy's guards had slapped her hard when she ordered them out of her home as they pulled her and Erik from the bed they had been making love in not fifteen minutes earlier.

Abernathy reached out and began to fondle Sunniva's hair, and Erik could see her tense and pull slightly back. But Abernathy simply wrapped the length of hair around his hand and jerked it toward him, eliciting a small scream of pain from her. Abernathy's face did not show any indication of reaction as he calmly said, "I was dismayed by your rather cavalier response to my inquiries into last week's loss of product. A loss that occurred in your territory, on your watch."

Erik quickly responded. "I did not intend to be cavalier, sir. I was only saying..."

"That the occasional hijacking of product is simply the cost of doing business? I believe that was the gist of it. Well, let me explain, sir: I bear the upfront costs, so your dismissal of my concerns is indeed cavalier. And I don't appreciate people being cavalier with things that are mine. Perhaps the loss of one of your children will help you to understand my point.... Randall..." Abernathy motioned with his index finger to a large man who pulled a hunting knife from a sheath under his jacket and began to walk to the couch.

Freya gave a small, muffled scream, and the children also began to make begging noises through their gags. Erik had to think fast. He knew a little about this vice president of the FA and had a small piece of information that might save his child.

"Sir, I do have a line on who made the raids." Randall was almost to the couch. Erik quickly said, "They were Bosch."

Randall grabbed his youngest by the hair and pulled his head backward. Abernathy's eyebrows went up. "Hold, Randall. But don't go too far." Abernathy's voice was cool. Randall stopped, releasing the boy's head and re-sheathing his knife. He resumed his bodyguard stance. Animal-like sounds of fear and misery mixed with abject relief came from the four people on the couch. Abernathy considered Erik Hartvig.

"Bosch? And what evidence do you have of that?"

"Well, sir, one group of traders recognized their uniforms. Apparently, they removed their camo gear to clothe the thralls they stole, and the traders described their uniforms down to the vests. One man even made out the flying ship tattoo on one of the raider's arms."

Abernathy stared into Hartvig's eyes, and Erik realized there was no sense of humanity in them. It was as if he was staring into an abyss. Then Abernathy began to laugh, and the laugh made the hairs on the back of Hartvig's neck rise. "Of course. This wasn't a competitor or some upstart. It was my little Mary on a do-good mission. I'll have to pay her back."

While this statement made no sense to him, it did not include any additional blame on him, so Erik began to relax. In his mind, he patted himself on the back for his quick thinking. He might even become a confidant of this powerful man. His brain began to spin on the ways this could end up paying off, and he, too, began to chuckle.

Abernathy paused. "Well done, Mr. Hartvig, well done. That is important information. And you have purchased the lives of your family with it." Erik could hear the relieved sobs from the couch. Abernathy seemed not to notice any of the emotions in the room, but continued. "However, the cost of the collection, housing, and processing of twenty head represents a rather significant investment of my markers, and I do expect to see the anticipated return on that investment."

Erik smiled broadly. "But of course. I will liquidate some investments and see you receive recompense."

Abernathy nodded. "Excellent." Erik was about to request he be allowed to get dressed when Abernathy continued. "But I will need some immediate redress. Your second-in-command, a Mr. Skau, will be promoted to your position." His voice carried a deadly tone that warned Erik to keep quiet. "You, sir, owe me twenty fresh thralls." Now Rob stood and pulled Sunniva to her feet, holding her upper arm firmly, his fingers pressing hard into her flesh. He ran a hand along her body, though Erik detected no sensuality in the move. Instead, it brought to mind attending livestock auctions with his father when he was a boy. Abernathy half-dragged, half-walked her to the couch, where he pushed her down to sit between Freya and the children. His fingers trailed along her frightened face, then he reached out and lifted each child's chin as if evaluating their Nordic features. Their choked sobs went dry as he looked at them. Finally, he squatted down and looked into Freya's face, saying in a quiet voice, "Everything that is about to befall your family is your husband's fault. Remember that." Then he turned to Erik. "But I am a generous man. Look here, five prime products at our fingertips. Your wife and children and this...creature..." Here, Rob gestured to Sunniva. "...will be taken from here tonight. Each will be sent to the appropriate market on the planet where they will garner the best price. Of course, they won't be the same markets." A small smile curved Abernathy's lips. Both Freya and Sunniva began to vigorously protest. Rob sighed and dealt a practiced blow to each, quieting their protests into sobs. "You, Mr. Hartvig, have one week to find fifteen more that will satisfy my standards. If you fail, which is very likely, you will lose either your hand or your tongue, your choice. And any protests, to anyone, about any of this, will result in the loss of both and perhaps more." Here, the Federal Alliance VP gestured to Erik's limp penis. Erik felt his intestines turn to water.

"Good day, Mr. Hartvig." The man in charge of all seven human trafficking cartels on New Earth began to stroll to the door, his business concluded. Outside stood four other bodyguards, waiting. He paused, then turned. "Randall, see to my instructions."

Alejandro DeLeon did not want to answer his comm as he sleepily roused, but it was his work comm, and with one look at the number associated, he was wide awake. He pushed the on button. "Yes, sir?" He could tell by the slightly hollow sound that the comm was coming from inside a vehicle.

Rob Abernathy's voice was strong and clear. "I have managed the Northern European situation, but I will want the waystations targeted next to have their security tripled and additional weaponry acquired and dispersed to them."

DeLeon shook his head slightly, uncertain if he had heard correctly. He knew better than to ask for clarification or to argue with the man on the other side of the comm. "Sir, we have no way of knowing where, or even if, this type of raid will happen again. I do have all markets on the lookout for small, unknown vendors bringing in product…"

"There's no need for that. They won't appear at any market." Abernathy's voice was clipped. "And there *will* be additional raids. And you are in charge of discovering where the raids will occur."

Alejandro frowned, "Sir, I am not sure—"

Again, Rob Abernathy cut him off. "The raiders are Bosch,

Alejandro: those damnable pirates. And if I don't miss my guess, they are being directed by my own thrall who recently was elected to some type of office there. You will use the contacts in Bosch I have provided for you that you have been nurturing for the past few years to discover where the next raids will occur. I want them annihilated. It is time to break the Bosch."

The comm went dead, and Alejandro slowly dropped his hand. He hoped his employer knew what he was doing. Though it really didn't matter; DeLeon knew he had to do as he was instructed anyway.

TEN

Dinner Out

BOSCH, NOVEMBER 5, 2365

I sit back in the red leather chair at Barton's and toss the linen napkin on the table near my empty plate. I look over at my husband and stretch, running my tongue over my teeth to check for food. "That was a really good meal. My fish was perfect. How about yours, Takai?"

"Quite good. Though the sauce was a bit excessive."

I laugh, feeling relaxed and a bit on top of the world. My trafficking project has started out as an amazing success. I spent the day receiving congratulations and compliments from not only the other generals and the commanders but also even the regular troopers, who gave me a round of applause when I walked into the mess for lunch. In fact, the mess staff made me an extra-special salad with real bacon pieces—quite a coup for me.

Miles was effusive as well, but he did caution me that it was just the beginning of the project, which, naturally, I understand. Tonight, though, I'm not letting anything get me down. I smile indulgently at my husband, who has been home for almost a week and we haven't argued yet. I say warmly, "You're so Edoan. I could cook you plain veggies and a plain piece of fish and rice day in and day out, and you'd be satisfied."

Takai lifts one eyebrow and nods, a small smile on his handsome face. "Edoans like to let the food speak for itself. And you seem to enjoy that type of preparation as much as I."

"Well, yes," I concede amicably, "but I like others as well. And Bosch does do well with spice and sauce."

Takai pauses and seems to consider this. Then he pronounces his verdict. "Bosch spice is overdone, and then the sauce tries to mitigate it. Which, frankly, is a metaphor for all things Bosch: over the top and then attempt to camouflage the extreme."

This unforeseen attack on my home is like a splash of cold water on my previously convivial mood. I narrow my eyes and fold my arms across my chest as I tip my head and ask, "You ever going to get over the fact that we moved back here for my work?"

Takai looks away and sighs heavily. "I have a diplomatic trip to Edo next week."

I suppose that's an answer. I look away from Takai, contemplating what direction to take this conversation, and then a commotion at the door catches my attention. "Hey, it's my favorite unit." I watch as the four men and one middle come in laughing, brushing off the rain that has just begun and talking, perhaps a bit loudly, as they move toward a table on the far side of the room. "C'mon." I tug at Takai's shirt sleeve as I stand. "I'll introduce you."

Takai's face has taken on that blank expression it does when he really doesn't want to do something. "Is that really necessary?"

I smile saucily, hoping to breathe a bit of life into the night. "Yes, it is. They are really nice. You'll like them."

Takai looks skeptically over at the group, boisterously

talking and gesturing as they place their drink orders with the lovely, dark-haired server. "They seem very…Bosch."

His tone, and all that it connotes, grates on me, and I respond, "There was a time you thought that was a good thing." Then before he can respond, I snap, "You know your children are half-Bosch." I stand to walk away from our now joyless table, toward where the unit sits exuding merriment.

Before I turn, I see Takai's face darken slightly, and I know my comment has struck home. *Ha. Good.* I am close to halfway across the room when I feel him touch my shoulder. I pause and turn, pleased he has decided to join me, and feel a stab of guilt at my remark. I look into his face, ready to apologize, when I hear him say, "But they were born in Edo. That makes them more Edoan than Bosch." My expression shifts to one of annoyance, and I see him smile, obviously pleased to have achieved this response. Then he says with a disingenuous smile, "Let's go meet your friends."

I stand for a moment as he smoothly moves past me, walking toward the five-top table that is just receiving their drinks. *What an unbelievable tool.*

Takai arrives a split second before me at the tableside where Matty and his unit sit merrily talking and sipping on drinks. I arrive, and there is a clear pause in conversation. Bailey glances at Takai, who is wearing his diplomatic "Let's chat" face, and then at me, their face carrying a worried expression. I do a body check as Ruth has taught me and feel the tightness in my lips, chin, neck, and shoulders as anger is still steeping in me. I give a small shake of my head to relax those areas and smile broadly, not looking at my husband but instead focusing on the unit. Matty is gazing at me, and I feel like he knows I need a boost as he says, "Well, look here, folks, it's our favorite general. You must be out celebrating the amazing start to your new project, Gen." He turns his head toward Takai and says in a friendly manner, "And you are?"

My entire body now relaxes, and I want to laugh aloud as I know this tiny comment, said with what seems to be honest innocence, has undoubtedly cut Takai to the quick. I see him bristle, so I play the part of the kindly wife. "Oh, this is my husband, Takai Shima. Takai, this is Matty, I mean *Matt* Warner. I'm sure I've told you about how he helped me in the election. And this is the unit he flies: Rashan, or Rash, Holloway; Aaron Morton; and you know Demery and Bailey, of course."

Takai nods and smooths his dark hair. He lifts his head and gives a smile; his eyes are relaxed, but I can tell by the tightness in the angle of his jaw that he is still angry. Though that seems to be customary these days. He dutifully extends his still summer-bronzed arm to greet each person and pleasantly repeats the new names and asks a polite question of each of them. Such a diplomat.

Matty is the final member of the group he greets, and I hear him ask, "You are Warner, like the wine?"

"One and the same. My parents and two older brothers run the Warner vineyard. It's been in the family for generations," Matty answers.

This is a subject Takai can embrace, and I think, hopefully, that perhaps interesting conversation will allow us both to let go of our pettiness tonight. "It's a delectable vintage. District Seven, correct? It's quite beautiful out there. There are parts that remind me of my home in Edo."

I watch as Matty smiles at the praise. "It is beautiful. The vineyard itself is magnificent. And I'm made up of the soil and vines and the rain there as much as I am made of blood and bones."

I grin and add, "Matty had an idyllic childhood. That's why I occasionally call him 'Summer Child.'"

"You know, you're not wrong, Gen," he says amiably.

I laugh. "I never am." I see more than one set of eyes roll at this comment and make a mental note to cut that comment from the routine for a while.

"Idyllic in what way?" Takai is looking at Matty with interest.

Rash leans in toward the conversation, his dark eyes twinkling in his umber face, and says in a teasing tone, "Idyllic landscapes and it's an idyllic place to meet beautiful women. Matt, tell him about the string of broken hearts you left in Seven."

Without even looking or shifting his pleasant expression, Major Warner of District Seven gives his engineer a friendly shove that unseats a laughing Rash from his chair, eliciting a round of laughter from the rest of the unit. Matty acts as if nothing has happened as he responds to my husband's question amicably. "I got to frolic in the vineyards as a small boy, go to one of the most charming village schools in Bosch, play a variety of sports, get elected president of my class. All the ridiculous things that seemed regular to me until Gen pointed out that not everyone grew up like that."

At this, Takai looks at me, and I see his eyebrows raise almost imperceptibly and a small twitch in the muscles of his jaw. "Yes, well, Kat does like to remind all of us at length that her past was far more difficult than anyone else's."

I feel the words like a stab, and I know everyone at the table heard the comment by the silence that follows it, but then my husband smoothly continues, "And speaking of children, we should really return to ours and relieve your mother, Kat." He pauses for effect before adding, "Don't you agree, my love?" The smile on his lips does not reach his eyes.

As I focus on my breathing, I am also considering, and then discarding, myriad ways of killing this man I have made a life with when Bailey says, "Actually, Kat, I know you are off-duty, but if it isn't too much trouble, we did have a question about a problem we had during yesterday's mission that we wanted to clear up." They look at Takai. "I hate to pull her away from you on your date night, Takai, but maybe you could relieve Miriam now. We'll send Kat along in half a bell, max." It does not sound like a request, and I want to plant a big, wet kiss right on Bailey's lips for this rescue move.

Takai's eyes shift from Bailey to me to the table, which now has five very earnest-looking troopers sitting at it. I shrug. "Well...I suppose I could answer a couple questions...."

"I see. Then I suppose I will head home and send Miriam along." Takai's voice is even, but I know he is furious.

"All right then. I'll see you at home in a bit." I, too, am keeping my voice even, but I am no longer dealing with anger; instead, I am giddy with anticipation of a pleasant drink with friends.

He turns to go, then looks back and purses his lips. "Good night. A pleasure to meet you all." The five murmur their goodbyes in return.

Matty pushes a chair near me out with his foot, and I slide into the seat and square up, my face controlled and serious. Blond-haired Aaron stands from his seat, unfolding his tall form and stretches, leaning clearly to the right and peering over at Takai and narrating, "He's got his coat. Taking a house umbrella. Okay. He is out the door."

My forehead hits the table as I give a loud exhale. "I really need a drink."

I hear glass sliding damply across the shiny wood, and I lift my head to see a crystal tumbler with some amber liquid in it.

"Share mine for now. I'll order another." Matty lifts his hand to signal the server.

I pick up the glass without a word and take a long drink.

Rash starts, "So, what the hell…?"

I am mid-drink when I hear Bailey and Demery both murmur, "Don't do it."

I set the glass down firmly on the table and say before anyone can inquire further, "Nope. Don't want to talk about it." I look at the serious faces and then settle on Matty. "Thanks for sharing your drink. Now, let's hear about the string of broken hearts in Seven."

Suddenly, the table is abuzz with laughter, tall tales, and protests, and none of it is about me. And I am thrilled.

ELEVEN

Butler Unit: Second Mission

BOSCH AND FAR NORTH, NOVEMBER 11, 2365

"Look," I call to Team Butler as I face the southwest and look upward, pointing. "It's Orion! Good morning, Teddy!" I wave. I am feeling chipper even though it's absurdly early. The moon is just rising, and its sliver of a crescent gives little light, making the stars stand out that much more. I crane my neck some more, and I can just make out the feet and legs of the twins, one of my favorite constellations for obvious reasons.

I walk backward to get a better view and collide with Matty, who laughs. "You know I have a nice telescope. We could go stargazing sometime. Though maybe not at three bells."

I grin and readily accept the invitation. "Oh, yes, please! See his belt?" I point into the clear sky at the three stars that mark the belt. "Teddy and I decided that the middle star was his before he died. So, I always say hello to him when I see it."

Matty nods. "I like that." He looks up at the constellation and raises a hand in greeting, then leans toward me, whispering, "Should I salute?" I shake my head *no*. He continues, "Good morning, sir. I hope you know just how difficult your daughter is still being." He grins at me, and I slap his shoulder.

"Don't listen to him, Papa. No one else does."

The rest of Team Butler laugh, and then we walk on to the mess. It's mission morning and we are getting ready early. I have spent quite a bit of time the past week with the unit as we prepared and have gotten to know them well.

Of course, I know Bailey and Demery from before, and Matty and I have grown to be close friends since the election. Captain Aaron Morton is the navigator. He is a tall, blond, dashing man who is quick with a smile and a laugh. He flirts with anything that moves, and that even includes me, which I was initially uncomfortable with until I saw that he also flirted with every other man, woman, and middle over twenty. Now, I simply flirt right back, honing a skill I've never had. There's been a few missteps, but Aaron assures me I'm improving. Unsurprisingly, Captain Morton is decidedly single, playing the field like a competitive athlete.

Lieutenant Rashan Holloway, flight engineer, is equally as handsome, lithe, and lean, with a deep, dark face and eyes that twinkle like black diamonds. He has a quick wit and can throw out some biting observations. He is currently dating a university history professor named Liberty.

"Plans for the weekend, folks?" Demery asks, rubbing his bare hands together for warmth.

I weigh in with my plans. "Takai comes home this afternoon, so I plan to try to play nice and not antagonize him." My group all chuckles at this. "We might go to District Four. I love the beach in winter."

"I have to go to the 'pasta thing' in Seven." Matty sounds unimpressed with his plans as he opens the mess door, and we step into its light and warmth. I see the Awilda and Drake teams already seated and eating and raise my hand in greeting.

Rash jumps in, "You get to see Rita and all her kids!"

The rest of the unit laughs somewhat derisively, but I am mystified. "Who's Rita?"

Matty shakes his head. "We don't need to go into it."

Bailey laughs. "Sure, we do, Warner." And they grin at their CO. "Rita Altera. Matt's big relationship. What was it? Five years." We are moving with our trays down the line, picking up breakfast items. I settle on a piece of fresh bread that I toast and District Six cheese.

Rash and Aaron are grinning from ear to ear, and Demery is chuckling as Matty responds with a sigh. "Yep, five years. From university, through enlistment, until I made captain." He dolefully plops a serving of oatmeal into his bowl.

"So, what happened?" I ask, filling coffee cups for all of us, enjoying the smell of the brew as I distribute them.

Aaron spreads his hands out as he says, "The usual. She told him it was time to fish or cut bait. And he cut the line and set her loose. Thanks for the coffee, beautiful."

"You are so welcome, kind sir." I nod with a smile, then turn my attention to Matty. "I see. Not the marrying type, then?"

Now Matty shakes his head and says, "Definitely not. Marriage and kids are not for me. My parents, sure. My brothers, well, I love their wives and my nieces and nephews. And you...." He looks at me and pauses.

I laugh as we take our seats, and there is a bitter tone to it. "Oh, yeah, me. I make marriage look like a walk in the park. If you happen to be walking on needle-sharp rocks. Near shark-infested waters. Glad I can be a shining example. But I do have amazing kids."

"Rita's got, like, four kids now, doesn't she?" Rash asks.

"Five. Married Vinnie Moretti." Matty returns to sounding melancholy.

I am still confused. "But what does Rita have to do with the 'pasta thing'? And what is a 'pasta thing'?"

Matty sighs. "Vinnie owns a restaurant in Seven— Moretti's. It's good food. They bill it as 'Old Days Italian,' and they buy quite a bit of wine from the vineyard. And every November, they have a pasta dinner for the community, and my mother insists that I attend. Every fucking year."

"But that doesn't sound awful." I nibble at my cheese, trying to make the sorry serving of it last.

Rash is using his toast to wipe up the egg yolk on his plate. "I think our fearless leader's problem is that every little old lady there came up to Matt and said sorrowfully, 'Oh, dear, Matt. When will you get married and settle down? You never bring anyone home. You know you are breaking your mother's heart.' Or some version of that."

Matty is vigorously nodding his agreement with Rash. "And to be clear, my mother is fine with me not ever getting married."

"There's an obvious solution," I say as we all rise and head for the door. "You just need to take a date. Aren't you seeing someone now? Laura… Lisa…"

"Lydia. And no, I just started seeing her a few weeks ago. Those old women would have us married and moved into the place I'm renovating before the night was out." Matty shakes his head.

"So, take someone who knows the score, who can pose and deflect." I smile broadly at him. "I'd go, but I'm busy this weekend, negotiating shark-infested waters."

~

"FA vaccine shipments are due in today. All troopers are to present themselves at the mess at their previously assigned time over the next four days to receive theirs. Anyone with any prior significant reactions should report to the medical building for evaluation and consultation." The yearly announcement blares through the PA system as Team Butler and I walk toward the airfield to prep ourselves and our vessel. There are still several hours to daybreak, and the only light streams from the buildings we pass along the pathway.

Rash makes a face. "I hate needles."

"As much as dying?" Matty asks.

"You know, I'm okay with death. But I want to go big, not be taken down by something I can't even see," Rash responds with a laugh, his breath making steamy clouds in the chill early morning.

"I never got any vaccines until I was over twenty," I say, knowing the guys will be appalled.

Matty, naturally, starts in on me confrontationally. "You know that's crazy, right? Pandemics came in waves after the great fires and floods in the twenty-second century and essentially halved the human population that was left!"

I shrug and roll my eyes. "Well, you'd have to know my dad. I can still hear him when the FA medics came to town to distribute vaccines when I was in primary. 'Nobody is touching my kids with that shit. Not even the girls.'" I make my voice gruff and growly like my dad's, with a serious sprinkling of bluster. "He pulled me out of school in a flash. Then he rallied some of the other men, and they took their weapons and chased the medics off. Nobody got vaccines that year or any other year that I recall."

"Your dad really pulled you from school?" Matty has apparently settled on this issue being the most incredulous.

I hoot a laugh. "Dad was mean as a snake and had no love for 'book learning.' I got pulled out of primary a bunch of times, all for ridiculous reasons or because they needed me to work. Mom always sent me back eventually, I think mostly so I wouldn't be underfoot. The final time was just after I started secondary. I had a crush on a girl named Rebecca, and my next younger brother found out and told the family. The next thing I knew, I was on the Buckley farm breaking sod for their back ten acres, cultivating and planting and taking care of the house. That was the end of school for me."

Aaron looks at me and grins his most suggestive grin. "Rebecca, huh? Interesting. I'd like to hear more."

I laugh at his predictable antics. "In your dreams, Morton."

"Oh, I surely hope so." He gives a naughty look and sighs deeply.

Matty, however, looks horrified. "You never finished? But you talk like… And all those books… Hell, you've read more than I did in uni."

I link my arm in his and say in my best North Country accent, "That's why we make a good team, Matty-boy. You're the brains and the beauty, and me—I'm just the talent."

At this, he can't help but laugh as we arrive at the hangar, ready for adventure.

"Do people really hike in the woods for fun?" whispers Rash. "'Cause it seems to be just a frozen, giant pile of dead leaves for ticks to live in." He is picking his steps very carefully as we move through the forested land, crouched. The sky is slate-gray with clouds, but the horizon is just taking on a hint of dawn. Under the trees, it is still very dark, so we have our night vision glasses on, making the whole world take on an odd green tone. But they keep us from running into shit; so, green it is.

After the resounding success of the first mission for all four units, there is a lightness to this morning's foray. We will strike fast and hard and will once again prevail with more souls freed.

Matty, Rash, and I are moving stealthily forward through the old forest, with its large trees with bare branches. We are farther north, so snow has started to accumulate in the crooks of the branches and in the more shaded areas. Bits of what seems to be a cross between snow and sleet are swirling through the air, and each time the breeze picks up, the bits strike the parts of my face that are exposed like icy needles. Even though I don't thrive in the heat, I find myself wishing it was June. Yes, partly so it wouldn't be so damn cold but also because the leaves would add an extra layer of camouflage to pair with the morning twilight. I figure there has to be a fairly decent deer population here since the underbrush has definitely been cleared, giving the woods a park-like quality. Good news for us—likely no big predators. Bad news—not nearly enough cover.

"It's better in the spring," I whisper back to Rash. "'Cause then there are pretty flowers that make you go off the trail and into the dry, tick-filled leaf piles."

Matty snorts at this retort but says in a hushed but firm tone, "We are almost to the edge. Let's keep it down, troops."

Rash and I look at each other and shake our heads as we grin.

"Yes. Sir," I mutter as I give a small salute with an extra gesture.

Matty looks over his shoulder and points at me. He smirks

and mouths, *Fuck off*, which garners a silent laugh from me. We continue our movement toward the cleared space at the edge of the woods that will lead us to the old inn now being used as a waystation.

The vessel is stashed some distance back, with Aaron at the helm, ready for a quick getaway. Dem and Bailey are stationed, ever at the ready, in their gunner sections, in the unlikely event that heavier weaponry becomes necessary.

The plan is the same as the first mission: Get to the waystation; neutralize any guards using non-lethal means, preferably; and nab the souls that are being held—intel says four this time. They are due to be moved to the slave market the next day; so, our timing is perfect. Shift change for the traffickers happened a bell earlier, so there should be just three guards on duty outside. Easy enough.

We crouch down at the margin of the woods and pull off our night vision glasses and stow them. The clouds are taking on a purple hue and starting to break up on the eastern horizon as we crawl to a stone fence made with some pretty impressive boulders as a base and filled in over the years with rocks of various sizes. A wall like this has likely stood here for hundreds of years, probably since the Old Days. Approximately a hundred meters away is a wooden bridge, old but not as old as the wall. It stretches across a wide, rugged ravine. A shallow stream moves along beneath it, framed on either side by rough, steep banks with more rocks jutting out and a few pioneer trees trying to gain a foothold. There is snow piled in the shaded curves and a bit of ice along the banks of the stream.

We are crouched in a line facing the wall: Matty in the middle, with me on his left and Rash on his right. We all peek just over the edge of the wall. My brain starts to work out the details. "The bridge is pretty exposed." My voice is just above a whisper. I am simply narrating what I see.

Matty's voice takes up the train of thought smoothly. "But we can cross, staying close on the sides, covering one another, especially before full light."

I continue, "Yep, that'll get us across the bridge, and then we scarper to that far wall on the other side, and then..."

We both finish, "...we will be close enough to neutralize the guards."

Matty and I look at each other and grin.

Rash looks at the two of us and rolls his eyes. "Like we needed another one like you, Warner?"

"Seems like a solid plan." Matty deadpans, then gives the order. "Ready? Let's move."

We rise and start to scramble across the wall when suddenly we are met with a shout—thank the universe for amateurs—and hear the pop of a weapon and then another being fired. We throw ourselves back to our side of the stone fence and lean with our backs to the wall, heads protected by the stone as we all hear a series of feet hit the twelve-meter-long bridge and then the pings of more ammo hitting the far side of the stone.

"Fuck." This we all whisper in concert.

I return to my narration. "We've been made." I am pissed and I know my voice reflects it.

"Ya think?" Matty asks, definitely irked.

"Now, kids...it's a bit early for mutiny," Rash cajoles.

"BI said there were never more than a total of four guards in the station at a time. How many on the bridge?" I ask as I start to turn to make my own count.

Rash is quicker and peers between two stones. "I count eight, maybe more."

"Well, shit." I am becoming more annoyed by the moment. "Fucking details."

We hear distant gunfire, and Matty hits the button on his earpiece. "What's going on, Aaron?"

There is a pause and then, "Shit. Do what you have to do to stay safe. We are in a bit of a situation here as well." Pause. "Roger that." Pause. "Stay safe and stay alive."

Rash and I regard Matty. "A-okay with the vessel?" Rash asks.

"They are taking fire as well." Matty's voice comes out in a growl. "We have to get that bridge clear."

As I sit with my back against the cold and uneven stones, I glance to my right and see where the wooded area runs fully to the side of the ravine. Time to improvise. "Keep their focus as I cross the ravine. I'll get to the other side and pick some off from behind. We need to fly the *Jolly Roger* today." I roll to my knees and start to rapid-crawl toward the tree line before either of the men can present me with the downsides to the plan. Though I am pretty sure I hear a "Goddammit, Gen" from Matty.

As I make the trees, I hear Matty and Rash methodically firing to the far side of the bridge to keep the focus away from my position. I scramble through the woods, then pause, pulling two dry sacs from my sling bag and sealing my pistols in them, safeties on. I then replace them in their holsters, assuring that all my weapons are well fastened down, tight to my body. I tighten up my sling bag and fasten my helmet securely with the neck guard snug around my throat, whispering in my head a *Thanks for the reminder* to Will, and scoot to the edge of the bank. I cross my ankles and cover my face with my hands, keeping my elbows tight against my body. Then I launch myself over the edge and roll down the ravine, bumping on rocks with a few involuntary "umphs" before landing just before the water in a pile of snow. I resist the urge to jump up and shake myself off. Instead, I push up on my elbows and peer around, the hard bits of snow in the air still peppering me and making me squint. I have ended up about twenty-five meters down from the bridge. Not so bad.

I glance to the upper bank to see Matty and Rash still focused on the enemy and keeping them busy. Excellent. I move quickly to the stream and hesitate only a moment before plunging in. It's not deep but still comes up to my hips in the center. *Sweet New Earth, this is cold.* What starts out feeling like a burn fades to a deep chill in my bones. I finally wade out on the far side and crouch behind a rocky bend, where a couple of the brave pioneer saplings grow. They provide a bit of cover as I try to control the chatter of my teeth.

I look up the steep bank and sigh. Clambering up the bank will take far more time than rolling down it, especially since I am weighted down with the icy water that soaked into my clothes. I focus on the task and test a couple of the bigger rocks for stability. I start my diagonal scramble, keeping three of my limbs in constant contact with the bank. I make decent time as I move upward. The top edge of the bank is steep, and I lug myself up and over the edge, landing into a large pile of dry leaves dusted with snow. All I can think as I hear the crunch and smell the musty earthy fragrance is, *There fucking well better not be ticks.* I pop my feet under me so that I am in a crouch and shake off slightly to release the water and dirt as silently as possible. I am actually pretty exposed as there are no trees on this side, and the morning twilight is quickly giving way to actual dawn, with clouds clearing and the sun rolling up over the waystation. I grin, knowing that if I wait just another couple of minutes, the sun will be behind me as I walk the bridge, and anyone turning to shoot will be blinded, at least momentarily. I stand and pull Papa's pistols from my back holsters, stripping off the waterproofing and clicking off the safeties. I prep them for automatic fire and then set my sights for the far end of the bridge.

The *Jolly Roger* call—that lethal force will be used unless an opponent surrenders without a fight—doesn't bother me too much. It is the way of the Bosch to not kill unless directly threatened, although there have been some missions Teddy sent me on… I shake my head. I can't dwell in the past right now. We have been ambushed, and that calls for different rules of engagement. These are traders. Traffickers. Lowest of the lowlifes. And they are shooting to kill those I call friends.

I wait until I see the sunlight come rushing up toward the eight—no, I think it's actually ten men—firing on my compatriots near the rock wall. Shots are coming in from the wall, and I think I see two or three hits. I pull a breath in and begin to hum an old dance song to myself as I start to walk, obscured by the blazing sunrise path, toward the bridge with my eyes focused on the shooters concentrated at the end nearest the stone wall. *"Come dance, don't stop, we'll spin 'til we drop."* Both of Papa's pistols are raised.

Up the middle of the bridge I walk, almost casually, surrounded by sunlight. I am intent on the group of guards. I will not allow any of my friends to take a bullet. I feel my brain shift into slow time. I realize I am in easy range, but I hold my hand until I am practically on top of them. Two loud booms from the direction of the vessel pull all the shooters' focus but mine for a moment, then they turn, and hold their hands up to shade their eyes, raising their weapons. This is my opportunity. I quickly take my shots, dropping six in rapid succession.

One guard remains and fires, causing me to leap right. Blinded by the sun, the shot goes wide. Lucky Guard then shades his eyes, with his weapon trained directly on me now, and I prepare to dive left when suddenly I hear a voice close by snap, "Hey, asshole," which causes the guard to pause and turn slightly. I hear the crack of a weapon and watch the no-longer-lucky guard fall. Matty stands on the bridge just behind where the last shooter had been standing, dark glasses shading his eyes. He drops them down so they hang by a string around his neck. We look at each other. His eyes are wild, and he is breathing heavily. I suspect I look the same. "You missed one," Matty says with a wry grin.

My heart is pounding. I see Rash coming onto the bridge. My unit is intact as far as I can tell. I smile broadly. "I figured I'd leave you something to do."

Matty and I join in an adrenaline-fueled laugh as Rash comes up and looks at us with a sideways grin. "You both are truly fucking nuts."

"Thanks," I say and hear Matty say the same. We look at each other and roll our eyes. No time to discuss anything. There is still work to be done. The three of us look at our handiwork: The old, wooden bridge, with its gray, weathered planks that make up its deck, and the sturdy post and cable railings that run along each side, are now pock-marked on the posts and on the planks from the ammo that had flown moments before. Blood spatters the deck and sides and is pooling around several of the guards whose injured bodies lay askew at the end of the bridge.

"Let's get this done." I gesture to the guards.

"Yep," Matty agrees. "We'll need a clear path to move the freed souls back across."

It takes the three of us several minutes to shove the injured to the side and the dead into the ravine. Matty takes a comm from Aaron who assures him they are safe, having taken out a party of five that descended on them. That's—what—fifteen attackers? And we haven't even made the inn. This was no accident. It was a planned ambush. But how? I realize I can't focus on that yet, not when we have souls to free.

The three of us move toward the house now. The sun is fully up, so we dodge behind trees, boulders, and small outbuildings along the way. The back door is in sight and unguarded. Likely, the guards were ordered to be part of the ambush force. Unfortunately for them.

We still move cautiously, however, since we have definitely lost the element of surprise after the bridge situation. We approach the building and peer into the windows. No one is in the kitchen, so we jimmy the lock and move into the room.

"There's the basement door." Rash gestures to the right.

We stand on either side, weapons at the ready, and push the door open. A voice comes up from the bottom of the stairs. "Luke, that you? How'd it go? Hope you killed all those Bosch, 'cause that was a hell of a lot of noise."

We stand silent, looking at each other. Any thought that this was just bad luck evaporates. They knew who we were and why we were there. Quietly, I put my pistols away and reach down to my thigh, opening the slit I had sewn into my camo pants. I unsheathe the bone-handled knife Papa gave me so long ago. I still love how it feels in my hand, perfectly balanced. Matty and Rash look at me. Their expressions are quizzical at first and then brighten with understanding. I step opposite them and shift to hide myself in the shadow just beyond the open door. We hear footsteps creak on the wooden stairs, and a large man appears and turns toward my friends, his back to me. Before he can register that he is not seeing "Luke," I push the blade up to the hilt between his shoulders and to the left, feeling his muscles tighten only slightly too late. He slumps forward, and Matty and Rash catch his body and lay it carefully face-first as I pull my knife out. I wipe it, business-like, on the big man's shirt and re-sheathe it.

Matty stands after settling Luke's friend on the ground to finish the job of dying. He gives my blade and me a side-long look. "Handy little item."

"I like it." I give a brief smile. "Let's see what is being guarded downstairs." I give a gesture to the basement, and we move carefully down the stairs in the formation that has been drilled into us.

As expected, we find a locked room and hear the movement of people inside. Matty and Rash pry through the old hinges and break the newer lock. As Matty moves the door aside, Rash and I peek into the room and establish that its only occupants are four young women, three of whom stand toward the back, looking at us with fearful eyes. We are intruders. One very young woman, barely out of her teens, with a head full of curly hair, stands with a large rock raised, ready to smash whoever comes at her or at those she protects. I find I like her immediately.

I sit down on the floor crossed-legged a distance in front of the women, Rash and Matty behind me, at attention. They carefully do not look at the women as we had drilled. I roll my sleeves up, making sure my brand is apparent, and check for language understanding. Then I speak in standard FA and explain that we are from Bosch, a country where slavery and trafficking do not exist, and we are there to bring them to freedom, wherever they choose to go. I pause and see the three women in the back look at the curly-haired woman and speak a few words in languages I only barely know. Curly Hair answers, nods to them, and then looks at me. "What about them?" She gestures to Matty and Rash.

"They are under my orders. They will not look at nor touch you without your permission." I raise my arm and point at the brand. "I've been in your place," I say. "I understand."

Curly Hair nods and motions for the other three to follow

her. She pauses and looks uncertainly at the rock in her hand. She glances at me.

"Keep it," I say with a smile. "Until you know who you can trust, it's always good to be prepared. I'm Kat. Kat Wallace. What's your name?"

"Isa."

"It's good to know you, Isa."

TWELVE

Pirate's Revenge

BOSCH AND OUTSIDE MYNIA, NOVEMBER 11–12, 2365

We land on the BPF airfield and hand the vessel off to the ground crew. The newly created re-entry team is waiting to take the liberated souls. I nod encouragingly to Isa as she steps out of the vessel into freedom, but none of us are riding as high as we were after the first mission. This was clearly an ambush, and I want to get to the hangar for the debrief and to assure myself all is well with the other three units. We had held our tongues during the flight home so as not to upset the newly freed women. Now, adrenaline is running high for us as the realization that we just barely escaped settles in. As we walk double-time toward the hangar, the tension for all of us is palpable. Four of us are talking nervously about the events. Demery, though, is a few steps behind us and silent. His face is as stony as I've ever seen it.

"Hey, Dem." I fall back and gently punch his shoulder. "You did what you had to." We had passed the bodies of the ambush party that had tried to take the vessel when we returned to it with the freed. Both Bailey and Demery had looked grim when we told them. I know the idea of outright killing doesn't sit well with either of them. Yes, they're gunners, but generally, gunners just want to blow shit up, not kill people.

Demery doesn't look at me; he just shakes his head and says in a growl, "I can't even believe that happened. Were they looking to take us as thralls, or would they have...?" He trails off.

"I don't know, buddy. But I sure as hell am going to get to the bottom of it," I say, feeling fiercely committed.

He breathes out, "Oh, shit."

"I know what you mean, Dem." We arrive at the hangar just as the clock on the green chimes ten bells and head inside.

I see Rylee Bank's Cavendish Unit milling about. I do a quick head count to five and breathe a sigh of relief. Rylee turns and sees me, and I can tell by her face that they ran into trouble as well. She comes up, meets us, and gives me a salute. I return the gesture.

"General Wallace, I'm sorry. We couldn't complete the mission. We landed and there were dozens of armed opponents. They seemed to know we were coming and where we would be. We couldn't even get out of our vessel. Suarez and Collins, my gunners, cleared a few, but they just kept coming. We were lucky to get to take off."

"It's all right, Major. I'm glad you got your people out. We ran into a spot of trouble as well. Let's have you go back to your unit, and we will discuss this further in debrief." She nods and turns to rejoin her team. I look at Matty, and I know we are thinking the same thing: two of four units ambushed—that is no coincidence.

Bailey gives my hand a squeeze as they move with Butler Unit to its assigned section of the hangar. I watch worriedly as Demery walks away from the rest and stops at the door, looking out, his broad back toward the rest of us. He is taking this hard.

Olivia, my assistant, comes up to me; her young face is worried. "You are late. The other two units are as well, although Colonel Booker has reported in a few minutes ago. They are on their way. But they have a couple injuries, General." This last part she says in a hushed tone.

"Severe?" My mind is racing.

"They didn't say so and said they were coming here." She shakes her full, dark curls and points to the hangar.

I nod. "Get some medics over here. And something for the units to eat and drink." She nods in response and starts to hurry away, but I stop her. "Liv, do it quietly. We don't need to get the whole base into an uproar until we know what we are dealing with."

"Yes, ma'am." Her brown eyes are big as she nods and then turns to implement my orders.

I am standing, silently, watching the large clock on the hangar wall as the red numbers tick off the seconds, then the minutes, and finally, the bells. Booker's Drake Unit landed over a bell earlier. Their navigator and engineer both sustained flesh wounds as the rescue squad ran the six liberated souls from the waystation to the vessel. Drake had found themselves ambushed as well, though the trap was not as well implemented as the ones tripped by the Cavendish and Butler units.

There has been no word from Diaz's Awilda Unit. They should have been back over a bell ago based on the location of their target. We continue to try and raise them on their vessel comms as well as their personal ones, and I have asked Bosch Intelligence to send in any drones they have in the area to survey for them. The anxiety in the hangar lies thick, and there have been some flare-ups, like with Lily Sanchez of the alternate Easton Unit.

"Why the hell aren't we flying in *now* to find them?" she had loudly demanded to know only moments after Booker's Drake Unit arrived. I completely understand her vehemence, and if I were in her place, I'd probably already be loaded up and in the air. But I'm responsible for these people, and I am not throwing them knowingly into harm's way. I watched as Matty calmly listened to her, said a few things, and then walked over and pulled the other three pilots— Banks, Booker, and Cardenas— to the far corner of the hangar for what looked like a fairly spirited discussion. After they all returned to their units, the flare-ups ended.

"What was that all about?" I ask Matty quietly a bit later when we are both at the coffee table.

Matty looks a little annoyed as he says, "I told them to get a fucking handle on their people and deal with whatever emotion was coming, and that questioning superior officers wasn't going to get Awilda back any sooner."

I sigh, nod, and look at my coffee.

He drops his voice as he says, "Also, Sanchez and Cowan had been seeing each other. That's why..."

"Oh, fuck. This just gets better by the minute," I growl. Then I look at Matty and try to give a smile. "Thanks for handling that. And thanks for letting me know about Lily and Isaac. I'll talk with her."

I look back at the clock and at the people waiting in the hangar. There is a weight in my gut that gets heavier by the moment.

I commed Miles after I arrived back and informed him of the situation. He listened carefully, asked a few questions, then simply said, "I understand. You can handle this, General. I'll wait for a report each bell, or when you deem it appropriate.

I'm here if you need to talk it through." Part of me wishes he would have swooped in and taken over, and another part is grateful that he trusts me at a time like this.

Another half-bell passes, and the noon bells ring as I walk through the section of the hangar, talking to each trooper. We have cordoned off the area with some portable room dividers to allow for the units' privacy. I am attempting to be as honest as I can be while still holding onto hope. But we are all ready for the worst. As I turn from talking to Salim Carr and checking his dressing, I see someone enter the hangar. It's a tall man with a shock of red hair that can only belong to Major Cal Greene of Bosch Intelligence. Information.

I walk briskly to meet him, and his face is grim. He holds a large envelope in his hands. His light blue eyes lock with mine. "We should go somewhere private." I nod and walk with him to one of the small offices, Olivia in tow. I can feel the twenty sets of eyes of my company on us as we go.

I have Olivia wait outside as Cal and I go into the office. I shut the door, flipping on the harsh overhead light and pulling the shade on the window in the door. "Okay, Cal. What do you have for me?"

Cal pauses for the briefest moment, and I realize it is bad. "This image was pulled from Astrid, a part of the interwebs out of China that cater to less-than-legal activities." He holds up the envelope, and I reach for it. "Kat—I mean, General. It's brutal."

I look at this man who I have known since he was an awkward teen working for Teddy and keeping my whiskey glass full. "Cal, it will always be Kat to you. Hand it here." I open my hand expectantly. He hands me the packet, and I open it and draw out the image. The heavy weight in my gut rolls over and over, and I have to swallow several times.

I can't bear to look at it, but at the same time, I can't look away. It is an image of a pile of bodies haphazardly tossed one atop the other. I can see Tony Diaz's pilot's tattoo, but his face is gone. Elina Taylor's signature blue hair is now dark with blood. Kajetan Rivers' young body lies face-up, staring unseeing, with Isaac Cowan tossed face-down over them. Stefanie Ratliff lies half-naked on the top of the pile. Across the bottom is the caption: *Fuck the Bosch. Too mean to sell as thralls and too stupid to live.* I feel the weight inside me start to swell with anger, and I feel angry tears prick at my eyes.

I slide the image back into the envelope and fold it and tuck it in my sling bag, then turn to Cal and say briskly to cover my rising fury, "Do we know this is real?"

Cal nods. "As far as our tech folks can tell, it is not doctored, only captioned."

I sigh and nod. "I appreciate you being the one to bring this over, Cal."

Cal clears his throat and begins, "Kat, I…"

I look straight at him. "I'll take it from here, Cal. Please see to it that no copies of this are in existence." He nods his agreement. "Also, I'm going to want an internal investigation into leaks. Four different waystations were expecting us, and I want to know where they got that information."

Cal nods and his face is grim. "Agreed. I've already started to trace who had access to the information. I'll put my best team on it. I'll get you what you need."

"I know you will, Cal." We walk to the door, and I open it. "Olivia, lock the hangar down. No one is to come in or out with the exception of Major Greene here, the Master Commander, and me. Everyone is 'working late.'" My voice is brisk and business-like. Olivia's usually lively face looks pale, and her eyes reflect concern, but she nods. I soften my tone. "Liv, you'll have to miss your date tonight. We have work to do before we deal with this situation publicly. Also, double-check that I have the accurate coordinates Awilda was headed to. And pull the unit's personnel files for me. I'll talk to the other units in a quarter-bell." I need to call Miles and then think of how to tell my company this.

The afternoon is chilly and gray, appropriate for my spirit, as I walk up to the service entrance near the trash collectors of the university library. I look left and right and, seeing no one, try the door and am rewarded with a click as it opens. Carisa has been enrolled in the university for the past three years, and I see her for lunch regularly and at Mama's almost every Sunday. She is loving her world history classes and hopes to teach at the university someday. She also has been working at the library, and she let me in on the secret of this door. I love everything about the library, including its vaguely dusty smell, and I find it gives me comfort even now. I start to move along my well-trodden path toward the ancient fiction section but then stop and remember why I am here.

I reorient, turn, and silently make my way to a very long, very broad hallway with full-length windows on one side behind shades that filter the dim afternoon light. It is the Hall of Heroes, and it is my good fortune that it is currently cordoned off for some kind of installment maintenance. The far wall is painted with an elaborate mural, displaying a choppy sea filled with the history of pirate ships. Posed nearer the window are mannequins costumed and armed like the pirates from each historical time. I duck under the rope barrier and trail my fingers past the Egyptian and Greek galleys, to the Phoenician biremes and the Illyrian lembos, where I glance appreciatively at the mannequin of Queen Teuta. I continue past the Viking drakkar and the Chinese junk. I take a moment to admire Zheng Sao's robes. When I pass the atakebune of the ancient Wokou, I give a slight chuckle at how their inclusion offends Takai. He does like to tidy up Edoan history. I pass the Turkish tartanes and the Barbary galiots until I come to the sleek sloops, schooners, and brigantines from over six hundred years ago. If I kept walking, I'd pass the frigates and the motored skiffs that came after the Golden Age.

But this is the era I have come for. I move through the dim light to the mannequins representing the Golden Age of Pirates. There's Ed Teach, Sam Bellamy, Ben Hornigold, and the Barbarossa Brothers. Stede Bonnet used to be here but got relocated over to the theater when it was renamed. I know who I am looking for as I make my way along the privateers. And there she is: Mary Read, in between Calico Jack and Anne Bonny. I remember the day I met Carisa at the library, and we walked through the display. We had a good laugh and suggested some actions "Anne" and "Mary" could take on a certain FA senator, now ridiculously their vice president. My old vengeance desire flames up as I think of Abernathy, but I put it to the side for now. I have a more pressing duty today. I make a final glance over my shoulder and approach the mannequin, Mary.

In my gold-lettered office, I strip off my uniform and stand in my underclothes, looking at the costume I have liberated: a white shirt with billowing sleeves, a black jacket with two rows of shiny brass buttons, a pair of knee britches that also has large buttons at the fly, and a red waist sash. I took the stockings but left the shoes as they looked highly impractical. I finished the outfit with my own leather boots and my own dagger with the thigh holster adjusted to fit at my waist. I carefully dress in the garb and then eye myself in the small mirror on the wall. Mary, indeed—I still won't answer to the name. But I certainly don't look like a Bosch general. Good.

When I spoke to the project's company before my raid on the library, I told them that Awilda Unit had dropped off. I didn't say the unit members were dead because I wanted full confirmation.

I stood in front of them, saying close to the worst thing I could imagine. "There will be a special envoy deployed to determine Awilda's fate. Until that report is back, all of you need to stay put on base, even Easton Unit. We can't have twenty troopers leave and fifteen come back home, leaving five families in limbo. You each can comm your immediate family briefly—no details, just 'I'm home.' I don't even want any talk of injuries." I nodded over to Booker's Drake Unit. "The Awilda Unit's families will be notified that they are missing, but until we know their fate for certain, everyone needs to sit tight." All twenty accepted the plan with grace.

My conversation over the secure comm with Miles was pointed and painful. "Miles, they are dead. BI brought me the evidence."

I heard a deep sigh. "I'm so sorry, Kat." His tone was sober but even.

I continued, "This was a planned ambush, Miles. All four units were attacked. It was clear they were waiting for us, which means someone on the inside tipped them. Cal Greene is starting the investigation into where the leak occurred. I've also drawn up the necessary papers for each unit member to be sent to the quartermaster. The families will receive full ongoing equity as well as the death gratuity. And I've had Olivia arrange for the families to be brought to base and put up in the VIP quarters. I have medics and chaplains standing by."

"It sounds like you've managed all the essentials. What can I do for you?" I knew this loss had to cut Miles deeply, and I was touched that his concern was for me.

I took a deep breath. "Miles, I'm going in to get them."

I heard him breathe out in a whoosh, and then there was a long pause. "You know, I want to tell you no, but honestly, I expected as much. What's the plan?"

"The plan? I'm going to get a transport to the old airfield and fly myself to Awilda Unit's last-known location and see for myself if they all are really dead. If so, I'll bring them home. If not, I'll bring them home." My voice was steady as I laid it out.

There was another pause on the far end of the secure comm. "You know it's not a one-person job. We don't need to lose you as well. Don't let old fears keep you from accepting help if it is offered."

I gave a smile and blinked quickly. "I understand. Thanks, Miles."

"Stay safe and stay alive, Kat Wallace. Bosch needs you. And I personally would miss the hell out of you." I heard a small tremor in his voice.

Now my voice had some emotion in it. "Yes, sir. Same to you." I turned off the comm.

I adjust the straps of the twin pistols of Teddy's on my back under my billowing shirt. I hear the door squeak open slightly. "Hey, Gen?" Matty's voice cuts through the fog of fury I am floating on.

I look over. "What's up?"

He looks tired and drawn but manages a small grin as he looks at me. "Nice get-up. You setting sail soon?"

I nod and my face remains sober. "I don't want this to be a known Bosch rescue—or retrieval—mission, so, costume."

He and Bailey stand slightly in front of Aaron and Rash with Demery still in the hall. Bailey says, "You need backup. Especially if you plan to get anyone out—whatever condition they are in."

I frown. Bailey and Demery have been through a shitshow mission with me before—when Will was killed. "Bailey, I can't risk..."

"You aren't asking us. This is an individual decision. I'm guessing you are flying out from the old airfield. You gonna take the help?" They look expectantly at me.

I sigh, look at each of them, and know that Miles is right. I need help. "Yes. I plan to leave from there in one bell. No hard feelings if you decide to stay behind, but I could use the backup." I adjust my sash.

Aaron flashes a ghost of his usual flirting grin and looks me up and down. "You are looking quite fetching in that outfit, your General-pirate-shipness. It makes your cheeks look ever so rosy."

"Yeah?" A wry smile crosses my face. "Then that's who I am: Rosie. No 'General.' Just Rosie." I find I like this new name. General Wallace needs to follow protocols and traditions. Rosie can do whatever she wants."

Matty's brows knit together, and he gives Aaron a withering look that just bounces off. He says to his unit, "Okay, those of you that want to come, be at the old airfield in a bell dressed.... Now, how in the hell are we going to match that?" He points at me.

I give a wink. "First floor of the library. Hall of Heroes." I see the understanding on their faces. "Service door by the trash collectors currently doesn't latch."

Matty nods. "Good to know." He turns toward me. "Besides weapons, should we secure anything additional?"

"If there are souls to free, we'll need blankets and provisions." I pause, not wanting to go on. I take a deep breath and look at them all. They need to know the reality. Each vessel has a special sealed compartment with two white sails and a ball of red cord, along with cloths and oils to be used to cleanse and prepare a body or even two in case there is some tragedy. The only time I ever opened the compartment was after Will was killed. This feels so similar that I want to vomit. I pull air in through my nose. "We will need additional sails and more cord and more oils." There is silence as they take in my meaning.

Rash says steadily, "I'll take care of it."

I look at him gratefully. "One bell."

I make a muted landing on the lake in the dark near where the waystation is reported to be, maneuver it through the marshy edge onto the shore, and park it. We hop out of one of Teddy's larger pet vessels that he had stored—and now, I store—at the old airstrip near the cave. We are a merry band of not-Bosch pirates: me in my Mary Read garb, now answering to the name of Rosie; Matty dressed as Calico Jack; Aaron, who apparently went even more rogue and broke into the theater for the fancy Bonnet outfit; Rash as a Barbossa brother ("Had to honor my ancestors," he had said with a wicked grin); and Bailey, who went full-on Edward Teach and applied a wild beard. Demery, though, decided to stay back, and, given how hard he is taking all this, I understand. It stings a bit, but I understand.

Aaron pulls his night vision on and takes off down the

water's edge in big strides, then stops and peers at the ground, waving us over as we put our own glasses on. We all join him, shifting the rule to never leave a vessel unattended. We will need all hands tonight. We see the vessel tracks he is pointing to. "They pulled up here. Let's follow the path." We turn and move into the brush in formation, tracking the broken branches in the green glow of our NVs. In seconds, we come upon Diaz's Whydah-64 Banshee.

I hold up a fist, signaling for all to stop. "We need to assess if traffickers found it." There could be another ambush set up, or the vessel could be set with explosives, or there could be dead troopers inside, though I remind myself that is unlikely, given the photo evidence.

Nevertheless, I will not be taking any chances here. We spread out and slowly approach from all sides. There is no movement. We creep closer and hear no sound. Rash checks for any indication of tripwires, physical or electronic, and finds none. I motion the unit far back and move to the panel, putting in the master code and beating a quick retreat. I whisper to Rash, "We need master remotes," and he nods his agreement. The door descends without incident. Silence. After some discussion, Matty stays at the door as rear guard while the rest of us board the eerily empty vessel.

As we step into the main compartment, its automatic lights come on, and we quickly pull our NVs down. It is clear that no one is here. The Whydah sits as if it is on the BPF airfield, patiently waiting for its flight unit to arrive. *Sorry,* Banshee, *loyal vessel, they aren't coming back,* I think bitterly.

"I don't get it," Bailey says, their tone slightly low. "Somebody always stays with the vessel."

"Unless they got a distress call," Aaron reasons grimly. Seeing the usual happy-go-lucky man so burdened adds to the grave nature of this mission. Even his frilly Bonnet get-up doesn't lighten the weight of what we have to do.

"The on-board crew could have been ambushed," Rash says with concern. He goes to the flight engineer panel and pushes a few buttons. "Fuel is secure, and no self-destruct was initiated." FEs are always checking the security of the vessel's fuel.

"Whatever happened, there is no one here. And it doesn't look like there was any struggle around or inside of it." I am stating the obvious, but it helps me think. "Intel said there were half a dozen thralls they were going after. So, let's head to the waystation and see what's up."

We move down the hatch door and tell Matty what we found or didn't find. He nods and gives a small sigh. "I was hoping…" The rest of us nod somberly. On the flight here, I had told them about the image Cal had brought me, and while none of them looked surprised, all were appalled. Now covering each other carefully, our weapons raised and cocked, we walk single-file along the path that Aaron discovered, the only sounds our breathing and the crunch of fallen leaves beneath our feet. After a good quarter-bell of a quick march, we reach the tree line. Beyond it, there is a clearing, its grasses tired and dry, rolling toward a building. Electric light glows in a couple of the windows, and a thin wisp of smoke drifts from the chimney.

"I can do recon," Bailey says as the five of us crouch near a rocky outcropping.

I eye them and can't help but give a dismal grin. "In that get-up? I'm pretty sure you will be spotted, even in the dark."

They pull off their beard and tuck their braids inside their jacket, tossing me the red sash they had been sporting. "Better?" Their face is resolute.

"Go." I nod. We watch as they stealthily make their way

forward toward the building. I use the bi-spy glass to track them as they get farther away, though it's awkward over the NVs. Matty nudges me several times, and I pass the bi-spies to him each time. I see them start at the far end of the building, peeking into one window after another. After the fourth window, I see them drop down and cover their face briefly. After a moment, though, they stand back up and take another look for several seconds, fiddling with their hands, and then make a beeline back to where the four of us wait.

There is enough desolation in Bailey's eyes that we all know this is a retrieval, not a rescue. They turn their hand to us, showing a sketch with hatch marks in two places and an "X" near one set of the hatch marks. "The three backrooms are a storage room and two sleeping quarters, all unoccupied. There are likely rooms across the hall in a similar configuration.

"This one large room is the only one that is occupied. Two doors—the one we can see." They nod across the clearing toward what appears to be the main entrance. "And one at the far side. The six thralls are there." They point to the set of hatch marks near the "X." "Four adult women and two young boys, maybe eleven or twelve. They are tied together with rope and appear to be fastened to the floor next to the bodies." They don't need to elaborate on who "the bodies" are. Bailey goes on, pointing to the second set of hatch marks. "I counted seven traders in the room. I could see seven Chinese QBZ-60s—looks like old, double-based style. There are three empties and one half-full bottle of some kind of booze. Did the job: They did seem pretty drunk. That's it. I can't be sure there aren't others on the far side." They take a breath in. "I can't believe…"

I put my hand on Bailey's shoulder and squeeze, and they tip their cheek toward my hand. I turn it up and caress their cheek as I watch one tear run down their face from agonized eyes. We give each other a tiny nod. "Okay, let's get the living souls out and to safety, and then we will get the unit," I say.

We all check our weapons, which are definitely not from the Golden Age of Pirates. "Bailey, you and Aaron go around to the far side and work your way toward the back door off the main room. Matty, Rash, and I will approach from this side. If we can secure the scene before you arrive, we will. Let's use the earphones to stay in touch." We each pull out the small boxes that hold our tiny comm devices, place them in our ears, and run a test.

Satisfied we are connected, my pirate crew nods in unison, and we all move out.

As Matty, Rash, and I approach the house, there is none of the lightheartedness of our mission earlier in the day. Instead, we are fixed on our task and consumed with our own thoughts. We get to the window, and each take a look. Matty pulls back and says, "Rage."

I nod. "Old Homer had it right."

The traders are indeed drunk, and a couple are sleeping or even passed out near the fireplace. One of them has his arm bandaged, one has bruises near his eye, and another has scratches on his cheek. Awilda Unit must have put up a fight. The enslaved look pretty battered as well, but their bruising looks older. Two of the women have their arms protectively around the boys, both of whom are pale and thin. Four QBZs are leaning on the wall near the chimney, with one carelessly laid on the hearth in front of the fire. Only two traders are wearing their weapons. That plus the two asleep leaves the odds pretty fucking good for us. We develop a plan, whispering it through the earphone mic to Bailey and Aaron.

Aaron's voice comes into our ears with the first piece of good news we have had all day. "Negative on any other mortals—souls or traffickers."

Rash, Matty, and I look at each other and nod. "Good," I respond to the report. "We are going in." I step up to the door, take a deep breath, and pound my fist on it. Matty and Rash stand a step behind me, weapons shown. I only have my dagger visible. The door is jerked open, and a rifle is pointed at my face.

I reach up and shove the barrel aside. "Ahh, get that fucking thing outta my face." I stride inside and my men follow me, holding their weapons at the ready. "Keep your paws away from those cubes if you know what's good for ye." I point at the two traders who are armed, using the slang for the QBZs. "And you lot, don't even try to get your guns. You are surrounded." At this word, a re-bearded Bailey Blackbeard and Aaron in his Bonnet finery appear with weapons drawn and ready. The traders going for their guns wisely stop in their tracks, and the two armed men move their hands away from the rifles slung on their chests.

"Who the fuck are you, and what do ya want?" one of the armed traders, a big man with a full, dark beard, asks with just the hint of a slur in his voice. I register he is wearing Diaz's vest, loose and unfastened. I take a small breath and tamp down the rage that seeing this lights in me. *All in good time.* The sleeping two slowly come to awareness, rising cautiously up on their elbows.

I grin widely and let my eyes go wild. "Name's Rosie, and this here's me crew. You idiots put out that brag on the dark-nets, showing how you offed those asshole Bosch that fancy themselves pirates." I jerk my thumb briefly at what remains of my fallen comrades. It is a sight that sickens me, and yet, it also hardens my resolve to even the score. I draw my dagger out and, pointing it upward, move it sensuously about, showing it off. "Well, idiots, you showed your location with that move, and you left yourselves open to being pillaged. We are the real pirates. And we've come for the booty you hold." I gesture with my dagger to the thralls.

"They aren't for sale to you," the big trader says, his voice a low growl as his fingers move back toward his rifle.

I don't hesitate, but I slow my inner clock, dropping the hand holding the dagger behind my right shoulder and pushing my right elbow straight up. Then I send the blade spinning end over end. I can hear the slight whoosh it makes as it sails through the air. I wonder if my target can too. Probably not. My inner clock returns to real time as with a moist *thunk,* the dagger finds its resting place deep in the big man's throat, who, with shocked eyes, chokes, blood spraying from his mouth, his hands uselessly grasping at his chest and neck before he collapses on the floor in shock, trying to breathe through a marginally severed windpipe. "I don't remember saying we was shopping," I say without blinking.

One of the other men goes for his weapon, and I hear the report of a rifle behind me and see him drop, howling in pain as Matty has blown his kneecap off. I continue as if nothing has happened. "So, sit down, you bunch of drunken fools. We will be taking the booty. Teach, Stede, take the thralls back to the ship, back to *The Kingston,* and take anything else of value you find—those cubes to start."

I see Aaron and Bailey pause for a millisecond to translate "ship," and then they force five of the traders into a seated position with hands on their heads in front of the fire. The knee-capped man is writhing on the floor already, and the bearded sheath for my blade is sprawled against a chair. They remove his weapon and roughly relieve the second armed man of his. Then they gather the cache of QBZs near the fire. Finally, with the slightest bit of roughness for show, they hustle the four women and two boys out the door and toward safety.

I turn to Rash. "Barbossa, take that one outside." Rash looks at me curiously but leans to grab a trader by the arm. I cuff "Barbossa" and yell, "Idiot, not that one. The one that just lost a knee."

Now Rash is in full character. "Oh, yes, Cap'n Rosie. Sorry, ma'am." And he hustles the wounded man outside. The door clicks shut, leaving Matty and me alone with the traders and our dead friends. I quickly glance toward where the bodies lay unceremoniously piled, and then I look at Matty and tilt my head in the direction of the remains. He turns his head for a brief moment and then returns his gaze to the traders. Finally, his eyes shift to capture mine. This was not a mission gone bad for Awilda Unit. It was an ambush. It was a fucking act of war. We murmur together, "Red flag," and we nod in agreement. Then we both turn our focus to our task.

We stare momentarily at the drunken traders, and I think about how many have suffered at their hands. Well, no more. No quarter will be given. I walk over to where the bearded man is sprawled. He is curiously still alive and semi-conscious. "I want that vest." He burbles slightly but unsurprisingly, makes no move, so I muscle him out of it and slip it on over my jacket as the other traffickers watch. Matty is now standing amongst them, watching me. I place my foot on the wounded man's chest, then I lean over and grasp the bone handle of my dagger and pull it sharply back, hearing a second moist sound as it exits. I wipe the blood off the blade onto the man's shirt as I grin in his dying face. Then I re-sheathe it as he bubbles a protest before collapsing back to begin the job of bleeding out. I sneer. "You all are nothing but scum. I doubt even hell will take you."

I reach into my pocket and methodically pull out my earplugs, and Matty does the same. Fear sparks in some of the faces of the seated men as Matty raises his rifle, and I draw my pistols. The five on the floor begin to shift and try to stand. Matty uses the butt of his rifle to disable one trafficker who begins to make for the door. The other four sit back down, groveling for their lives.

I walk to one and shoot once. "That's for Diaz."

I hear the snap of Matty's rifle as it shoots and hear him say, "For Cowan."

"Rivers," I call as I aim for a shoulder. "Ratliff," I hear Matty say with a growl and then hear the rifle shot. I look at the man with scratches on his face, and I somehow am sure how he got them. My eyes narrow as I gut-shoot him, calling out, "Taylor." We methodically walk through our little section of the room, firing up-close as we take our pirate's revenge. We make it last so that each trooper has their justice time and again. "Diaz. Cowan. Rivers. Ratliff. Taylor." We recite their names over and over like a sacrament as we empty our weapons. Then we stop and look at each other, faces, hands, and chests spattered with blood, breathing heavily from emotion and exertion. Then we reload and walk again among the trash, firing into the still forms and calling the names.

We swing the door open, and a block of light falls onto the dark ground outside. Silently, still breathing hard from the emotion of the task we completed, Matty and I step out, pausing to let our eyes adjust to the dark.

A few meters away, we can make out Rash standing with Aaron, a small flashlight on, pointing at the ground, making a pool of light. We make our way to them. They are both staring at Matty and me, but their eyes hold no shock, only grim appreciation. Bailey must be at the vessel with the liberated. The wounded man, his face terrified, sits bound and gagged on the stump that has been used to split wood, a kerchief tied around his knee in a sloppy bandage. I shift back to being Rosie and step over to him. I lift his chin up so he can see me well. I know my face and front are spattered with the blood of his fellow traders. I lean over and whisper in his ear, though it is loud enough for my crew to hear, "Tell your bosses, this is what happens when you cross real pirates." Then I signal Aaron who deals him a blow to the head. He crumples, and I check to assure he is still alive.

"Well done. Now let's get the sails."

The four of us prepare for the work in front of us. Bailey has connected with a couple of the women we have freed and has opted to stay with them on my vessel. They have been fed and given blankets and the assurance of freedom and seem okay, given the circumstances. Aaron and Rash will return when our work is complete and pilot that vessel and the newly freed souls to Bosch while Matty and I will fly Diaz's vessel and its crew home.

The task of un-piling and readying the bodies of Diaz, Cowan, Rivers, Ratliff, and Taylor is heart-wrenching. Aaron estimates, based on their bodies' condition, they have been dead for about ten bells. He looks at me, and his eyes are serious but gentle. "General, they were dead when we touched down in Bosch after our mission. We couldn't have rescued them. No one could've."

I close my eyes and take a deep breath. "Thanks for letting me know. Let's take care of them now."

We have to gently massage their rapidly stiffening joints to straighten them for preparation. Once laid out, we search their bodies for personal belongings, finding rings, bracelets, necklaces, and photos of family. We carefully package each trooper's things together to be returned to their home. Then we remove their vests and painstakingly wipe the medals and the decorations. I remove Diaz's vest and wipe it down. Each one is folded and placed with personal belongings. Then we cut their remaining clothes off and bathe them with water warmed over the fire.

When every spot of blood and grime and death fluids are removed, we then rub each body with the fragrant oils that are stored with the sails. The scent has both a heavy musky part and a finish of lavender and mint— I guess to give us hope. I'm not sure it is working now, though.

As I pour the oil on my hands and begin to anoint Elina Taylor's broken body, I remember the last time I performed this ritual after Will was killed, and I find I have to breathe through several waves of emotions that break on my heart. I keep my focus by quietly singing one of the Old Days songs Elina and I shared a love for as I gently move my hands over her cold arms and legs. When my fingers reach her belly and feel the scar that she received birthing her son, new pain stabs into me as I know the grief and anguish that he and even her ex-husband will have to endure. I glance up from my toiling and see the three men each bent over a body, gently preparing it for the final journey. I can see each of them quietly talking or singing to their charge as they work, and I find myself loving these people that much more.

Once Elina's oiling is complete, I move to the final body: Antonio Diaz, pilot and friend. We have wrapped his head in swaths of gauze from the first aid kit, so the damage is not immediately visible and the part of his cheek still intact is exposed, so his family can touch it. I look at his strong arms that now will never lift his little ones again. I take a deep breath, open the bottle of oil, pour a measure into my hands and stare at it, tears flowing freely. I hear Matty's voice: "He had the best laugh." Then his big, brown hand appears palm-open as if in supplication, and then two more appear, and the four of us kneel around Colonel Diaz and share the oil as Matty spins the tale of Tony and him running a New Lisbon turnaround mission. We all are laughing and crying as we tenderly stroke and prepare the body of this man whom we knew we could always depend on.

Next, we lift the cleaned and perfumed body onto a white, opened sail, and then, to the rhythm of Old Days sea shanties, we carefully roll our friend up, tucking in the top and bottom and wrapping it with the traditional red cord, fastening the sail securely. We take the bundle of personal belongings and carefully attach it to the front for his family. This task, we repeat four more times.

Finally, we finish. Five carefully wrapped bundles in white sails with red cord lie at our feet, and we are reverential in our silence. We begin the process of carrying them to Diaz's vessel, two of us lifting and carrying each lost friend. We only move one body at a time so as to never leave the dead alone in a strange place. Rivers is the last to be returned to the vessel, just before one bell: so young, with so much ahead of them, now lost. We all return for the next step as the newly freed are now deeply asleep on my vessel, and we know the *Banshee* will safeguard the spirits of Awilda. The five of us walk up to the building where so much horror occurred, and Aaron goes to the chopping block and drags the still unconscious One-Knee a distance from the structure before returning to stand with us and stare.

Bailey says, "We can never go back to how it was before."

"No, we can only go forward," I answer.

"I remember a story from the time of sailing ships, when a ship arrived to a new land, and the captain brought his crew ashore and ordered the ship they had arrived in to be burned so that they would all be committed to moving forward," Matty says, his rich baritone filling the night after the quiet of our earlier tasks.

I consider this story, then nod and gesture to the building. "Burn it to the ground."

I hear a chorus of "Aye-Aye, Cap'n Rosie."

The fires Aaron and Rash light start small but quickly grow and climb, joining together and consuming the atrocious site. We stand watching, our faces glowing red and orange in the reflected light, until the heat of the flames drives us back, and then we turn, the night alight behind us, to take our comrades and our freed souls home.

"Dammit, Teddy! Did you ever have to do this?" I throw my empty glass at the pedestal, and it explodes with a satisfying crash in the dim light of the very early morning. The statue of Teddy just keeps looking off to the horizon, hands on his hips, but I can see it is bedecked with a black, three-cornered hat on its head and a red sash around its stone waist. Apparently, my spontaneous gift to Teddy of my hat and sash after my second graduation has now become something of a tradition. Each graduation since, twice a year, one new trooper has climbed the pedestal to do the same. In fact, there now is a special hat and sash set aside just for this so troopers don't have to lose their graduation mementos. I come here often when I need to talk. Or just feel close to Papa.

I heard the clock chime five bells before I left the VIP quarters and arrived at the statue in the deep dark and started drinking from the bottle of Teddy's stash I had brought with me. Now, I lean against the corner of the pedestal, screw my eyes shut, and sob, my cheek on cold stone, wishing I had his grizzled voice in my ear and his hand to guide me through this. Even though it's a Friday, I know it will be at least another half-bell before the base comes properly alive. Except this morning, there will be five souls that don't. I lean into my grief and let out a small wail.

I feel a hand on my shoulder, and a deep, familiar voice says, "There you are. I've been looking everywhere for you. You shouldn't be alone after everything."

I reach up and put my chilly hand on top of Matty's big warm one, squeeze, and receive a reassuring squeeze onto my shoulder.

"It was awful, Matty. All their faces, so broken when I told them." I choke on another sob. He turns me toward him like I am a child, and I let him. I am just so exhausted and heartsick. I feel his strong arms wrap me in an embrace as he whispers into my hair.

"General Kat Wallace, this was not your fault. The project, your project—our project—is the right thing. You didn't kill Awilda. Someone else took their lives. And by all the gods and goddesses of New Earth and Old, we avenged their deaths. And then we brought them home." Now he pushes me a little away and bends down to look in my face. "I went to find you, and the MC told me you took them to their families in the VIP quarters and broke the news yourself. And then sat with each family for hours. When I heard that…" Now Matty breathes in a ragged sob, and I see tears well in his eyes.

I swipe at my puffy eyes and runny nose. "It was my duty. I sent them there. I had to…" More tears and a small gasp. "… see them home, if not safely then at least into their loved ones' keep. Their families deserved to hear it from someone who knew them—who cared about them." I close my eyes and remember each father, mother, husband, and wife's eyes as I broke the news they had already steeled themselves for. "I'll never forget their pain, Matty."

His arms go around me again and pull me close. "No, you won't. But you did the brave thing—the right thing." I hear him give a sad little laugh. "You know, you have what my mother would describe as 'valor.' You gave them the greatest final gift: dignity and respect and compassion for those they had to leave behind. You make me proud to be Bosch, Kat Wallace." He steps back. "Now, let's get you home. You need your family."

I try to manage a small smile at the thought of my children, and then a wave of guilt starts to wash in, and my head drops slightly.

I feel Matty's hand lift my chin so he can look at me. "Hey. No guilt." I am constantly amazed at how he knows exactly what I am feeling. He goes on, holding me with his gaze. "We will live for them. Every laugh. Every mission. Every joy. Every hug. Every kindness will be in their memory. We won't sully it with guilt."

I close my eyes and take a deep breath in as I slowly nod my agreement and look at my friend. "Okay. No guilt. Only joy."

Matty leans over and picks up the bottle of Old Fire Hill from where I had left it, uncorks it, and raises it to the pre-dawn sky. "To Diaz, Cowan, Rivers, Ratliff, and Taylor. We will do their memory proud." He takes a drink, wipes his mouth with his sleeve, and hands me the bottle.

I don't hesitate. I take the bottle and lift it high. "To Diaz, Cowan, Rivers, Ratliff, and Taylor." I take my drink. "So, do you think there is a place we all meet after death?" I ask after wiping my mouth.

"Like Heaven? I don't know. My mom believes that. Her

people were from the Christian section of Old Zimbabwe." Matty's voice is soft and calm.

"Yeah, maybe. In the North Country, there was some of that. Though I preferred the stories of Hel and Valhalla. I'd like to think…" I trail off.

And then Matty takes the bottle back from me and tips it, splashing a measure on Teddy's stone feet. "He's been a part of this from the start. If there's a place, he'll be there, and he'll take care of them." This finally brings me a sad smile, and I feel my burden lighten a tiny bit.

Then the two of us turn to the east, standing shoulder to shoulder in comfortable silence, and watch the new day break on the horizon.

Part II

THIRTEEN

What's Next?

BOSCH AND TRUVALE, NOVEMBER 12–13, 2365

I sit in my usual chair in front of Miles' desk, holding the cup of piping-hot coffee Betsy has just brought in. I'm glad for it because the midmorning sunlight that comes through the windows feels cold. As I hold my hands near the steamy mug to warm them after my chilly walk from home, I can see through the windows of his office the flat, gray clouds that rolled in to cover the sky from horizon to horizon just after dawn as if even the very atmosphere is in mourning along with Bosch. I feel beaten and washed out, but there is a flame in my chest that burns steadily, and I know it is my unwavering commitment to my anti-trafficking project.

Matty had walked me home just after dawn, and I went directly to the twins' room and lifted each of their gangly, seven-year-old, sleepy bodies one at a time from their beds, carrying them carefully, then settling them in Grey's bigger but not too big bed. I tucked them on the side farthest from her, and then I peed and drank a big glass of water and snaked myself into the middle, pulling all three children to me. They gave small, sleepy sounds as they gravitated to my body, conforming to the curves they themselves had created. I reveled in their warmth, their breath, their squirms and wiggles, their actual living selves as tears flowed from me until I joined them in sleep like a pile of puppies.

Takai woke us all up a couple hours later with before-school pancakes for the children and coffee for me. I told him about my previous day as he stood at the stove making more pancakes while the children ate their first round of breakfast and giggled at the table in the next room. He was stricken and sympathetic when he heard what happened to Diaz's unit, but his compassion evaporated when I told him what took place at the retrieval.

"You executed those men, Kat?" His voice was a whisper pushed through his teeth, making his repugnance apparent.

I dropped my brows low and looked at him. "We avenged the murders of our friends and compatriots, Takai." My voice was low as well.

"But that makes you no better than them. There are other ways..." He stood at the stove, his face stricken, shaking his head slowly back and forth.

My temper flared and I stepped toward him and watched him take a step back, practically hugging the wall next to the stove. My voice, while still low, was forceful. "Listen, I will not have you or anyone sully my troopers' actions, nor the memory of those who fell." I took another step closer and heard a dangerous edge to my voice as I leaned in. "And what would you have done, dear diplomatic husband? Discussed reparations over a glass of champagne? Held a roundtable over a light breakfast? Perhaps you would want to set an agenda, with one of the traders taking the minutes." I snort out a scoff. "Your head would have been on a spike quicker than you could say 'negotiate.' We did what needed to be done. We are Bosch, we are pirates, and we are at war for freedom. And this is only the beginning." I moved toward the shower with my cooling coffee.

He pivoted from the stove and just stared at me, his upper lip curling in disgust. "Who are you anymore?"

"I am Kat Wallace." I smelled a hint of burnt flour and butter and gestured with my chin. "And *you* are burning the pancakes." He quickly turned and flipped them, but I was gone before he could turn back.

Now Miles looks at me as I recall the morning's events and says, "You must be exhausted."

I shrug. "A little. Does it matter?"

He sighs. "Kat, for what it's worth, I admire the way you handled the entire situation. You kept the troops informed, but you did not alarm them. You nurtured the families of the lost. You collected the information. You took the necessary steps to retrieve our people, freeing some enslaved at the same time." He paused and then looked at me. "Now, a more seasoned general might have given the order and sent in a unit, not gone in herself...."

I put my hand up. "I'm not sending people into situations I won't face myself. You know that about me."

Miles nods, and I see there is more gray on his head than I remembered. I think, *Probably mostly due to me*. He says, "I know. I don't like it, but I trust you and your judgment."

This buoys me and I give a weak smile. "So, you aren't shutting the project down?"

"Kat, that's not for me to do. It's your project. Yours and the company you have created." He looks seriously at me. "It is up to you and them." He takes a breath. "But Kat, a project like this moves Bosch forward to a new place, and while we value our Bosch devotion to our nation's independence as well as our own individual autonomy, the people of Bosch, not just the BPF, have to support the direction of progress."

I hear the echo of Matty's story in Miles' phrase "move Bosch forward." I wrinkle my forehead. "What are you saying, Miles? Do I have to go door-to-door, asking for the approval of everyone in the city and the districts?"

"No, Kat. But you need to be able to read the room, something you are very capable of doing if you take a breath and take your time."

"But Miles, there are people who are enslaved. They may not have time."

Miles smiles at me across the desk. "Let the people of Bosch see your passion, Kat Wallace, the way I have. You have been working toward this for, what, fifteen years? We sat right here and talked of strength and power and allies. You have two now. It's time to align the third."

Betsy placed a gentle hand on Kat's arm before she left. "Take care of yourself, Kat. Get some rest and know that the families truly appreciated the time you spent with them. I heard it straight from Lena Rivers, and you know she doesn't say anything she doesn't mean." She patted the young general's cheek and smiled.

"Thanks, Betsy. That means so much. I'll get some rest after I see to a few things today." Kat gave a tired smile back.

Betsy nodded and watched the woman she had come to cherish walk out the door, her shoulders slightly hunched as if she carried the weight of the world. *Which she does,* Betsy thought and frowned a bit, looking at the MC's office. She headed over to the cart where she kept her coffee and tea supplies.

"So, you aren't going to be the one to speak to the table and the company, sir?" Betsy asked in a pleasant voice as she set a cup of deep-brown tea in front of the Master Commander. "You normally would be out in front. Are you leaving General Wallace to hang in the wind?" Her tone was still light, but she was looking directly at Miles Baldwin-Bosch.

Miles looked up from his desk and raised his eyebrows. "Do you really think I would do that, Bets? You know she has to learn how to manage in a crisis."

Betsy nodded at her boss's words. "So, you are still set on your plan?"

"Not just my plan. It's been *the* plan for almost fifteen years. I've always been set on it, of course. Teddy made sure I was on board before he retired." Miles blew on the proffered tea and took a tiny slurp to test the temperature.

"Well, I'm glad to hear it." Betty straightened a small stack of papers on the master commander's desk. "This is as tragic a circumstance as I have ever known, except for perhaps the Khumi City situation, but that was over a quarter-century ago. But I believe Kat is more than capable of managing this one." Miles nodded his agreement. "Do you have a timeline?" Betsy asked.

Miles surveyed his long-time assistant. "I need to see how this all plays out before I talk with her. But I expect the wheels will be in motion next year."

Betsy smiled again. "That's lovely. I consider myself most fortunate to serve such gifted master commanders: first, Teddy; then you; and one day soon, Kat." She picked up the stack of papers in Miles's outbox and moved efficiently back to her desk.

Alejandro DeLeon picked at the skin around his thumbnail as the auto he rode in drew closer to the location where he had been told to meet with the vice president. He hadn't chewed his nails since he was in university, but this command meeting and the information he had to convey made him as tense as he had been since those long-ago days. How had he ended up having to cater to this man's whims? *Because otherwise, he would have had me killed and my body left to rot,* he reminded himself.

He had landed in the dark of night at the luxurious Truvale airship field, with its busy apron segmented by gates where passengers could board and disembark, never going outside. He had been escorted to the auto, and then they had driven for several hours, though DeLeon had no idea where they were, given the time of day and the deeply tinted windows around him. *As long as I live to see the sunrise,* he thought. He was sticking to short-term goals. He shut his eyes and allowed himself to drift into welcome sleep.

"Sir, we are here." The driver's voice nudged DeLeon awake, and he opened his eyes to see the door open, though it was still quite dark. He stepped out of the auto and saw what seemed to be a small house on wheels parked under a tree near an expanse of water. There was almost no moonlight, though Alejandro knew it must be early morning as the tiny sliver of the moon hung just above the eastern horizon.

Suddenly, the door to the wheeled house opened, and light streamed out, silhouetting the vice president of the Federal Alliance, Rob Abernathy. "DeLeon. Come in. I don't have all day."

"So, let's hear the report. Did we crush them? Or did you fail?" Vice President Abernathy leaned back in the attached seat that looked crafted of leather. Alejandro DeLeon sat on a small bench in front of him. He was choosing his words carefully as neither option was strictly true.

"Archer's information was accurate regarding the four sites the Bosch intended to raid. The traders, with the help of the sentries we sent and the additional weaponry, were able to fend off one Bosch team that then took off in their airship without even disembarking. Two other heavily fortified trader groups were unable to keep the Bosch teams from stealing the commodity, though one did state they believed they had injured some of the raiders." DeLeon paused and his eyes flicked to Abernathy's face, which was dark and dangerous. "The fourth group of traders...well, they did indeed annihilate the Bosch team as directed." Now DeLeon saw the lines on Abernathy's face relax, and while he wasn't smiling, he also did not look quite so murderous.

The VP paused and then said, "I see. We should make an example of that group. A one-time sizable payment, perhaps some other small luxuries, whatever those types of men desire. The other groups should be penalized for fumbling the effort. And we must be sure these outcomes are known across the cartels."

DeLeon took a deep breath in. "I think this story is already spreading. You see, I was informed late last night by the head of the North American cartel..."

"*I* am the head of all the cartels." Abernathy's voice was sharp.

"Oh, yes, sir. The *manager* of the North American cartel..." Again his eyes flicked to his employer who nodded approvingly at the title. "...reported that the group of traders that had killed the Bosch were then set upon by...by... Well, it seems highly unlikely, and the man that brought the tale to the... manager...did say they had been drinking..."

"What. Happened?" The words were clipped and the tone menacing.

Alejandro DeLeon sighed. "They were set upon by actual pirates, not Bosch pirates. The report was, they wore clothing of the Old Days and were led by a bloodthirsty woman named Rosie. She and her band stole the thralls, killed all but one man, whom they knee-capped, and then burned the entire waystation to the ground. The injured man reportedly was told to tell his bosses, 'This is what happens when you cross real pirates.'"

Abernathy stood quickly, causing DeLeon to jump in his seat, fearing a weapon coming at him. Instead, his employer turned his back, pulled back the cream-colored curtains, and peered out at the dark through the side window. "So, with the funds I released to you for intelligence and security, I have now lost three-quarters of the commodity they were to protect, a band of trained and vetted traders, and an entire waystation." He turned and stared at DeLeon until DeLeon felt he was forced to nod his agreement.

"Perhaps I need a different second-in-command of this business?'

DeLeon stood. "No, sir. I will track down this Rosie and her mercenary band and put an end to them. I will also continue to have Archer surveil the Bosch and be ready to crush them when they attempt any more raids. The other groups will have learned from this." DeLeon did not share the rumor he had heard that was spreading through the traders in his cartel—that killing the Bosch would lead to their own deaths. "I have already put these mitigation strategies in motion." He hoped he didn't look as green as he felt as he made these statements.

Abernathy's eyes narrowed. "What about the new Bosch general? I need information about her, so I can break her."

"Sir, I can arrange for an assassin…," DeLeon began.

"No!" Abernathy leaned in, his gaze intense. "No one is to kill her. That is to be my personal treat." He straightened and smiled. "But I will pay a significant bonus to the person, or the person's employer…" Here, he looked significantly at DeLeon. "…who brings her to me. She has a family and children. Those things could be enticements to snare her. And if perhaps her home is destroyed along the way, all the better." A beam of morning sunlight shot through the little wheeled luxury house, and the Vice President looked back through the window. "I must return to the city and my work. I expect regular updates and that progress will be made. Quickly." He tapped on the window, and a moment later, the door opened, and the driver who had delivered DeLeon opened the door, motioning the second-in-command of the New Earth trafficking cartel outside to be delivered back to his chartered airship.

FOURTEEN

Burn the Ship

BOSCH, NOVEMBER 19, 2365

"It's filling up out there," Olivia says to me as I stand in a small anteroom, running through my speech.

I look at her. "Oh, boy. Couldn't I have kept my mouth shut about this being an open meeting?"

"You could have, but that doesn't seem like you. Do you want the podium?" Liv asks.

"No, as nervous as I am, I'll likely pace."

She smiles. "No podium then."

The final funeral for the Awilda team occurred three days ago as Major Antonio Diaz was memorialized. I stood with Marie and their children and listened to the priest of their church give them assurance of Tony's rebirth in the afterlife. I had thought to Tony, *I sure as hell hope so, buddy. But Bosch and I will make sure your family is cared for here in this life and that no one ever forgets you or any of your crew.* Then I watched as his oldest son, TJ, just a year younger than Grey, stood at attention with his fist on his heart, trying to keep a trooper's stance but with a young son's tears on his face. Heartbreak stood right with me.

Storms have picked up offshore, so the five bodies are stored in the coldest section of the Glitter mines, surrounded by some of last winter's harvested ice until the weather moderates in the spring, and they can go to their rest in the sea.

Now it is time for me to posit the question to my company and the generals and to Bosch: Do we continue with the project, or do we put it aside?

The little room I have claimed off the main chamber sparks the memory of being held here briefly after being brought up from the basement cells while I was awaiting trial after Teddy's death. *Does that fact make this time auspicious or bleak?* I can't answer that, so I return to surveilling the data on trafficking that I have pulled from the interwebs. I then go to my carefully written speech and whisper it to myself again, though I have it memorized. I asked Mama to come and sit in the back because, honestly, I am fucking scared to death how this will go, and I figure seeing her face will help me stay on track.

I head to the toilet for the third time and pause after washing my hands to splash water on my face. I stare at my reflection. "Don't fuck this up, Kat Wallace. Lives are depending on you." I see Pressure standing behind my back, peering at me in the mirror. *Do you really count as an emotion?* I ask. Pressure shrugs. *If you say I do.*

I return to the anteroom and crack the door to peer into the chamber. I see dozens of troopers from all areas, Cal Greene included, but I also see townies—Ray is here, as is Badru Azizi, and Dawn, whose last name escapes me, from the drugstore. I see bankers, bakers, teachers, and tailors. Many are standing. I continue to scan the room and can feel my tension grow. There in the back is Marie Diaz and Elina's mostly grown son, Wilder. Next to him is Samuel Cowan, Isaac's father; supported by Ross Ratliff, Stephanie's husband; and the Rivers: Lena and Marek. I see Naya Clark, head of the civilian council, and Jace Richmond, who was recently elected to the council. I think I may even see Howard Archer standing near the far door, looking sour and disagreeable as usual. I shut the door and back up to the far wall: something solid. I breathe a *thank you.* I close my eyes. *Sweet New Earth, what if I go down? What will become of the enslaved?* I have to make them understand. I hear Olivia say my name, and I open my eyes and step to the door she holds open.

The moment my feet pass the door, every word I had prepared and memorized evaporates. I stand for a moment, looking at the serious faces. Miles said to take a breath and take my time. I breathe in and out. I look for the faces I can depend on. There are Matty, Rash, Aaron, Bailey, Dem, and Gia. I look around a bit more and see Mama and Carisa with Miles' partner, Stuart. I breathe and step forward.

"Hello." I glance at Miles where he sits with my fellow generals. Again, I remember his advice: "Let the people of Bosch see your passion." *Okay, Miles, I will try.* "I am struck and pleased to see all these faces from all parts of Bosch. We in the Force can sometimes forget there is an actual city and districts outside of our fence, so I am grateful you have come to remind me and the rest of the BPF what we are here for." I give a nod to the Awilda families.

"I had a speech all prepared to tell you about trafficking and the important work of this special project. But, it appears, I've forgotten all of it." A roll of laughter runs across the group. "Well, not all of it. But I don't need to give you the history lesson that I had rehearsed. Sorry, Professor Warner." I smile at Matty, who smiles back, nodding. "What I do remember is that I am here, to paraphrase our MC, 'to take the temperature of the room.'

"I have desired to work against human trafficking since I arrived in Bosch some sixteen years ago, having escaped my own enslavement. No one who knows me will be surprised at this. Then I was elected general, thanks to your support, troopers, and with it came the first real opportunity to fight this evil.

"We began this anti-trafficking project to save lives, and we have done just that. But trafficking is an industry with millions upon millions of markers involved, and the cartels take the markers and ruin lives. They took our incursion seriously. And they struck back. The cartels took the lives of our friends. Friends that we cared for. Friends who died trying to save others. And when we as a nation and as individuals suffer such a loss, it requires that we pause and consider our next steps as we honor our fallen. So, today, we stand at a crossroads: Do we close the project and back quietly away, returning to our Glitter runs and extractions and the way life was, or do we move forward?"

I smile and glance at Matty. "A wise man told me the story of a captain from the Old Days who brought his crew to an unfamiliar shore, and in order to commit them to the task of exploring the land, ordered their ships be burned to commit them all to the future."

I look at the people of Bosch gathered here and smile. "But that was a captain of old, and he was not a pirate. We are. We believe in listening to each voice. Yes, this project is a passion for me. But it is a passion I want to share, not impose. I have been banished, marooned unwillingly if you will, and I will not ask that of my company or my people. I will not burn our ship without consensus." I look around and sigh. "I do not have the power to see the future, and I cannot promise that the project's company will not encounter opposition and danger.

But I can promise that we will learn lessons from Awilda and honor them by working to keep our units secure.

"We Bosch began our journey breaking free of thralldom on the seas over two hundred years ago. We have grown strong as we have embraced opportunities, and we have become secure, perhaps even a bit comfortable. Now here we stand, together, on the shore of new land: a land that will allow us to pass the gift of freedom to others who are in bondage." I look at the faces. "So, what say you all? Do we stay safe and comfortable on our ship and sail on to our harbor, leaving the enslaved of the planet to find their own way, or do we burn the ship, releasing the reticence of the past, and look to a future where we commit ourselves to freeing those kept in subjugation?"

My chin is up, and I am breathing fast. I look around the audience.

The room is silent, first, for a few seconds, then for three breaths, then a full minute and beyond. My heart drops, and I focus on keeping my face friendly, not crushed or angry.

Then I hear a single voice from someone in the Awilda families. "I say, burn the ship." And I hear people in the council chamber shifting to look around.

Then another voice from the other side of the chamber: "Burn the ship." And on its heels, another. "Burn the ship." Then silence, like a storm mustering its power. Then, "Burn the ship." And then the storm breaks. "Burn the ship." "Burn the ship." "Burn the ship." Now it comes so fast that it overlaps: "Burn the Burn the ship the ship."

As I stand in the vortex of the storm, my eyes fill with tears, both of pain for my fallen troopers and with gratitude for the people who adopted me into their nation.

I turn to where the twenty members of the company sit, and as I do, I see Howard Archer slip out the door. All the better. I look at these brave people. "Company?" I speak loudly to be heard over the storm.

They all stand, and the room quiets immediately. Then my company members look to one another and then to me and in unison clap their fists to their chests as they chorus, "Burn the ship."

FIFTEEN

Lydia

BOSCH, EARLY DECEMBER 2365

"You ready to go, Lyd?" Matt Warner called from the foyer of his third-floor apartment that sat just off-base in a neighborhood graced with dozens of hardwood trees. The neighborhood abutted a park that stretched to the small creek that wandered through and around the neighborhoods at the Bosch's central city.

"I'll be right there! Just finishing my makeup," Lydia's soft voice called.

Matt didn't know why she bothered with makeup. Her lovely face was rosy-cheeked, with a smooth complexion of deep sepia that was still tanned deeply from the hot summer months. He knew and deeply appreciated the lighter tones on her body that did not get the same sun exposure as her face, shoulders, arms, and legs. In fact, as he started to consider those varied hues and their locations, a smile spread over his face. "If you don't hurry, I'm going to think of something to do that will make us very, very late!" he hollered down the hall and was rewarded with her pleasant laugh. It sounded like ice tinkling in a crystal glass, like the ones she provided him when he had first met her at Barton's. If he remembered correctly, it was on one of his nights playing with his band.

She appeared from the bathroom, and his smile broadened. She had done up her long, deep-brown hair into two soft braids and fastened them together behind her head, leaving a few soft tendrils near her ears and forehead that framed her lovely, large, dark eyes; high cheekbones; and full lips. He had to admit while looking at her face that her makeup was done exquisitely, accentuating all her best features. Well, not all of them. His eyes traveled down her and lingered on the curves that her close-fitting, deep-orange shirt accentuated, and he knew she had left the top several buttons undone for effect. Her denim pants fit snugly around her tiny waist and then swept over her hips to cling to her long legs. She had finished the outfit with a pair of shoes with impossibly thin heels that always amazed Matt that a woman could walk in. But Lydia did more than walk; she practically glided in such a sensuous way yet was seemingly unaware of the effect her movements had on other people.

"I'm ready to go and meet your friend, the general." She flashed a smile at him as she picked up her red coat from the chair near the door. "Then we can come back here, and you can tell me about your delay ideas." She ran her hand along the back of his neck and across his cheek as she reached up slightly to kiss him and then leaned back and winked. *Damn.* Matt grinned. He knew he was a lucky guy. But then, he had always been pretty fortunate and didn't take that for granted.

He was, however, a bit surprised by how nervous he was to take Lydia over to the general's house. Of course, he had been over there a few other times, both with his unit and on his own. His relationship with General Kat Wallace had started as a purely political one, but over a short period had moved quickly toward friendship. Their temperaments and personalities were similar, sometimes leading to heated arguments, but they also shared the same values. It was entertaining to find they liked the same foods and some of the same Old Days music and movies, but when they had gone in for the retrieval of Diaz's unit and responded to the situation in perfect concert, he had known that this was a person like him. That day, tragic as it was, had cemented their friendship into something deep and permanent.

So, Matt was taking Lydia over to meet Kat. Of course, Lydia knew Rash, Aaron, and Demery from their Friday nights at Barton's, and everyone knew Bailey, and Bailey knew everyone. But Kat was home on most Friday nights with her kids. He had only seen her at Barton's once, with her husband, and that had been a bit awkward at first.

The truth was, Matt valued Kat's opinion, and he really wanted her to like … hell, even approve of this woman he had been dating for a few months, and he wanted Lydia to meet Kat and like her too. He slipped into his fur-trimmed aviator jacket.

"Let's get going, Lyd. Sooner we get there, the sooner we can get home." He leaned over and kissed her gently while reaching inside her coat and giving her bottom a playful squeeze that elicited a giggle as they headed out the door for the older, established neighborhood where Kat's little white house with the blue door was located.

"So, what do you think of Lydia?" Matty looks at me, his eyes hopeful and eager. I can't believe he puts this much stock in what I think. But I kinda like it.

"I think you two would make beautiful babies." I grin

naughtily at him because he has made it clear there are no babies in his future.

His balled-up napkin hits me on the side of my head, and I cackle, delighted that I got the reaction I expected. I scoop up the errant piece of fabric and lob it back at him, and he carelessly bats it away with a short laugh.

"No, seriously, Gen." He is in earnest.

Lydia is upstairs reading to Mac and Kik. Mac knows a beautiful woman when he sees one, and Kik, well, Kik goes along with Mac in wanting someone other than me to read stories, but I don't think she holds the same charms for him as she does for Mac. I turn to my friend. "Why do you like her?"

Matty snorts. "I would think that was fairly clear."

"Okay, okay. She is most definitely beautiful. Young as shit. Can she even drink the stuff she serves?"

"Ha-ha. You are so not funny, Gen."

Matty has been calling me "Gen" more than "Kat" since the election. "Seriously, Matty. Do you just date the girls you do because of their looks? What about connection and partnership and conversation? You know, intellectual stimulation?" I gesture to my head.

"That's not the stimulation I am looking for in a date." He gives me a suggestive smile and raises his eyebrow up and down devilishly.

I roll my eyes. "Oh, Sweet New Earth, do you really just think with your dick on dates?"

He gesticulates with his hands. "Kat, if I want to have a connection and intellectual conversation and partnership, I can come here." He points with both index fingers to where he currently sits in the easy chair in my front room. "If I want to have a gorgeous woman on my arm and in my bed, then I have Lydia."

I growl at this man I have come to admire in all aspects but this. "You understand you just insulted both Lydia and me, right?"

Matty looks genuinely perplexed as he tips his head quizzically like the farm dog I liked back in the North Country. "Huh?"

I sigh and shake my head, laughing. "Did you hear your subtext? Lydia gets no credit for having any brains or substance, and I am apparently a wrinkled, old hag but a great conversationalist. Kudos on the double insult."

"Shit. I didn't mean that. I mean Lydia and I talk about stuff. And you are… Well, shit, Kat, you are one of my commanding officers, and you are married with three kids." As he says this, somewhere in my brain, I hear, *No, four,* and want to say it but don't. I make a mental note to tell Ruth about it on Tuesday. I hear Matty go on, stammering, "I didn't mean you aren't, umm, well..."

I laugh. "Stop before you get your whole leg in your mouth, Major. I like Lydia. But it's more important to me that you actually like Lydia, not just her great boobs, which are magnificent, if I may say so."

Matty grins. "They are, aren't they? Okay, I promise to have a substantive conversation with her tonight."

"Not enough…." I make the *c'mon* move with both of my hands.

He hangs his head like a recalcitrant child. "Okay, the conversation will happen before I even touch her 'magnificent' breasts." One of his hands reaches slightly up, fingers cupping an imaginary breast, but then he jerks them back for effect.

"Good man." I nod, pleased. We hear Lydia coming down the stairs and transition our conversation topic smoothly.

Matty puts his feet onto the ottoman. "The new recruitment class has some interesting talent." He pulled officer-in-charge duty for the first two weeks.

I nod. "Oh, yeah? That's good. Hey, how are you here if you are OIC?"

"Booker is covering for me—the whole damn weekend. I'm sure payback will hurt, but I'm enjoying myself now." He gives me a huge grin as he stretches out and settles into his chair.

We laugh together, and then Lydia appears, and I see her glance from me to Matty and back. Her eyes linger on me for just a second longer than typical, and she gives me a small smile that I return as warmly as possible. She then goes directly to the chair Matty is in and slips into his lap, her long legs dangling over the side of the chair as she snuggles under his arm. His face shows delighted surprise. Weirdly, a desire to hit her flows over me. I shake that old feeling off and put it on the list of things to talk with RTT about. I ask, "Do you two want some more wine? We could drink the crap Matty brought, or I could break out the good stuff."

I hear Matty's laugh as I stand. "Them's fightin' words."

I laugh as well and go open another bottle of Warner Wine.

Matty looked over at Lydia as they walked slowly home hand-in-hand from General Wallace's. He thought about what Kat had said about conversation and partnership and figured he might as well try it out. "You're being awfully quiet. Do you want to talk?"

Lydia looked up at him in the moonlight; her brows were knit, and she wore a frown.

"It looks like you have something important on your mind," he prompted. "Tell me what you are thinking."

There was a pause before Lydia said, "I thought she would be lots older and like a mom."

Matty was perplexed. "Who? Kat? She is a mom." He shook his head and grinned. "So much so."

"Yeah, but not like your mom or mine." Lydia tossed her head, causing those lovely braids to bounce attractively. "You never told me she was so pretty. And she calls you Matty." Lydia's voice was taking on a bit of a whine.

Matt paused for a moment before he answered, "Uh, is she? I guess I never noticed." *Bullshit, Matt Warner. You noticed over three years ago when you first met her and again on empanada day. Lock that shit down, though. She is married. She's your friend. Nothing will ever happen between the two of you.* Matt shrugged, turned to the lovely young woman next to him, and activated his most charming voice. "I guess I can't see anyone else when you are part of my life." He watched as Lydia's frown faded and was replaced with a shy smile. He gave her the gaze he knew women liked and closed the conversation with, "And, hell, my mother calls me Matty too." *But no one else.* He felt Lydia's body melt into his as he gathered her up, kissed her, and was a bit appalled when he heard his brain think, *Oh, Kat.*

SIXTEEN

New Plans

BOSCH, EARLY JANUARY 2366

"So, any changes suggested for Project Burn the Ship this week?" I look at the faces in front of me. There's General Philip Patel, the general in charge of tactical planning and defense; Cal Greene has been assigned to the project as intelligence officer; Matty is here, representing the Pilot's Coalition; Kaitlin Pruitt of Drake Unit is here to provide her expertise in flight and weapons engineering; and as a guest today, Etienne Winters, Quartermaster. I am on strategy and, apparently, leadership.

Etienne speaks up in his quiet but firm voice, "Well, you could quit spending so many markers."

The rest of the table chuckles, and I respond, "We could. But Etienne, you and I and the group knew there'd be a sizable upfront investment. But it is just that: an investment. There will be an equally sizable return as you saw in my proposal."

Etienne flips through pages on his device, murmuring, "Hmmm. Uh-huh. Okay. But wait, what is this bill for cleaning and repair of library property? The BPF does not underwrite the university."

I clear my throat and glance at Matty, who covers the smile

on his face with his hand. "Yes, well, some library materials were borrowed for an early mission, and it was important they were returned in good form. After all, we do want to keep our relationship with the library and the university amicable." *Amicable to the tune of a personal donation of fifteen thousand markers from my pocket,* I think with just the slightest bit of reproach. Those were damned expensive costumes.

Matty says casually, "I remember those materials. They were invaluable."

"I see…." The quartermaster flips through some more documents, then nods and stands. "I have no additional concerns, assuming the return will occur on schedule. Now, I have another meeting. Good day." Etienne Winters is a slight man in his middle years, with silver hair and a ruddiness to his brown complexion. He wears silver, wire-framed glasses and has the most organized mind I have ever encountered. There's a reason the BPF's books always balance. The table murmurs "Good day" back as he leaves. Then he pauses at the door, turns, and says briskly, "General Wallace, please be aware that on a personal level, I am 100 percent behind this project. I also anticipate it will be a professional success." Without waiting for a response, he turns and leaves, pulling the door gently shut behind him.

The table sits in silence for a moment.

"Well, well, well." Phil Patel breaks the quiet, a jovial tone to his voice. "I don't think I've ever heard Etienne get so emotional. You have yourself a fan, General Wallace."

I grin. "Apparently. And since that fan happens to control the purse strings, all the better."

We all laugh quietly before continuing with our meeting.

Project Burn the Ship has been running well. We paused for a couple of weeks after the ambush to reassess strategy, and that led to the group that sits in front of me. We now meet twice a week to continue to answer the questions: "What have we learned from this?" and, "What's the best way to take the next step?"

We have doubled our company now, adding in a partner unit for each of the four established liberator units. The partner units, who we have dubbed "cleaners," have a dual mission: protect the unit on the ground, and, once they and the freed souls are out of harm's way, burn the waystations to the ground, ensuring there is but one survivor. Our Red Flag policy has met with almost no resistance among those in the company. Though the photo evidence of Awilda's murders that Cal provided me did not become public, it was only right that my people were informed of what happened to Awilda. They are ready to do what it takes to prevent a recurrence.

We have made some significant changes that we will keep implemented until we know where the ambush leak occurred.

We no longer go in looking like the Bosch to protect the nation. Instead, our project vessels' exteriors have been altered to look battered and dilapidated, with no indication of their origin. Inside, the weaponry is being refashioned to give more firepower and offer more distance. Cleaners' vessels have also been armed with incendiary artillery using magnesium casings. It makes a proper fire of the stations. Uniforms are left behind, with two small clothing businesses in District Two creating modified Golden Age wear and then distressing it, though they believe they are creating theater costumes. This allows our ground units to look like mercenaries, and they are indistinguishable from one unit to the next. We believe it is to our advantage to keep the impression of our numbers low in case we are seen by others near the waystations.

We have gone as far as having Miles put out a statement condemning the "mercenaries calling themselves pirates who are attempting to take over control of the trafficking of humans on New Earth." In fact, as far as anyone not directly involved is concerned, Project Burn the Ship is likely on permanent hold.

Our fliers go out on a staggered basis which allows our company units to also make their Glitter runs, which keeps the QM office happy. It also helps to stagger the influx of freed thralls since we have essentially disbanded the re-entry team to mask the project. We still provide medical care, support, and transport but can only manage a few at a time.

I continue to rotate my observational presence with each unit, liberators and cleaners alike. To be honest, I could step back as they don't need me. But I really love the sense of exhilaration and purpose running the missions gives me, and I love showing up as Rosie and watching the fear the name is beginning to produce in the traders due to the tales spread by the single survivors.

Cal stayed after a recent meeting, and I told Matty I'd catch up with him at the food trucks.

"What have you found out about the leak?" I assume this is what he wants to discuss as I close my office door.

He tips his head non-committedly. "That process is slow. Interviewing everyone with access and then interviewing all the people they could have accidentally…"

"Or intentionally," I add.

Cal nods. "...or intentionally told."

I press, because I want my people safe, and I also want to burn whoever went to the enemy and made it possible for the ambushes to occur. "But is there progress?"

"Yes. I have a lead I'm investigating." Cal pauses. "I'd like to get your permission to open my investigation up a bit."

I give a small chuckle. "You need my permission to investigate?"

Again, he tips his head side to side, this time a bit more

markedly. "Not to investigate a BPF member, but I do need official backing to investigate a civilian." He scratches his red beard nervously.

I stare at Cal. "A civilian? This sounds juicy. Who?"

"Howard Archer." The name drops from his lips, and I stare at him.

I then raise my eyebrows in question. "Does he even have the brains to be that clandestine?"

Cal shrugs. "Well, there's been some interesting talk about his finances that I'd like to look into. And he is wearing an awful lot of blue these days."

I nod. "I've noticed. Did you see him at that meeting in the chamber…?"

"You mean, when you first started the Burn the Ship movement, and he slipped out when it became clear you weren't going to be roasted?" Cal smiles knowingly.

Now I actually laugh. "Well, you don't miss much, do you? Maybe you should think about a career in intelligence."

Cal grins. "I'll consider it. Do I have your permission, General?"

"Absolutely, Major. Let's squash that little bug."

SEVENTEEN

Dominoes

BOSCH AND EDO, LATE JANUARY 2366

"How about hot-buttered rums?" Bailey asks as we sit on the back porch bundled up with the firepit blazing and the stars twinkling above us on a Saturday night. I glance at them.

"That's a great idea! I'll do it: I know how to make them. Beril taught me last week," Lydia says as she eases out from under the shared blanket that she and Matty have wrapped around themselves and gives him a kiss.

I feel a muscle in my neck twitch as I watch. I like Lydia. I really do. But there's just something that grates on me when they kiss and moon in public. I must be getting old. I shake my head and smile. "I'll come in with you and check on the kids and pull out enough cups." I leave my solo blanket and feel the chill hit me as I stand. I act as if I am counting heads, but I know it will be an odd number. Gia and Red are here; Bailey and Gino, who are having their second date in front of all of us; Rash with his regular date, Liberty; Matty and Lydia, of course; and Aaron and...Chloe, I think. I'm always afraid to say a name for his dates because he is always dating multiple people. Astonishingly, they all know he is and are okay with it.

My past history with Takai would never allow for that if I

ever had to date again. I grimace inwardly. I was never much for dating. Things may be a bit distant between my oft-absent husband and me, but it must be better than the alternative. And even though he is once again in Edo, he has promised me that he is keeping to his vow to be faithful to his commitment. "I'm a family man, Kat. I am settled" was his response the last time I voiced my worry that he had ample opportunity to seek new romance during his many travels. And I believe him. I know he wasn't thrilled about the generalcy, but he no longer even suggests that we return to Edo. I take that as a sign of his support.

I mull all this as I peek into the boys' room, readjust their blankets, slip the book from Grey's sleep-limp hands, and turn her reading light off. I come back downstairs, pull out the five regular cups, open the company cupboard, retrieve six more, and line them up on the counter just as Lydia finishes her concoction of butter, sugar, and spices. It speaks to how often she has been here that she knows my kitchen this well. It's been almost two months since Matty was here without her. That's good. *Is it?*

My reverie is interrupted by a knock on the front door, and then I hear the unlocked door start to open. "Knock-knock, Kat. Are you up?" Mama's whispered words greet me before I round the door and see her, all bundled up against the cold.

"Mama, what's wrong? What are you doing here at this time of night?" It's only around twenty-two bells, but she is usually long asleep by now. I go to her, give her a kiss, and help her unwind her long, blue, knitted scarf. "Your face is freezing. Come into the kitchen. Lydia is making hot-buttered rums."

As I walk with Mama into the kitchen, I see Matty has come in to help with the drinks.

"Miriam! What are you doing out in this cold? Let's get

some pink back into those lovely cheeks of yours." Matty's face blossoms into his warm smile as he comes over and kisses my mama on her forehead.

She actually gives a little school-girl giggle. "Oh, Matthieu, having a handsome fellow like you passing out kisses is enough to warm an old woman's heart." I look at Mama with a touch of surprise. She's flirting.

Matty's deep laugh joins with Mama's, and he gives her a hug. "You are definitely my best girl!"

Huh, the things you can get away with when you pass sixty, I contemplate. "So, why are you here, Mama?"

She leans against the counter and gratefully takes a sip from the cup of sweet and spicy rum. "I got the oddest comm just a bit ago. It was from Yumiko."

I feel my insides tense up, and anxiety flows through me. "Yumiko? Did something happen to Takai?"

"No, no, dear. Nothing with Takai. It's Shigeo. Yumiko says he is..." She reaches out and touches my arm. "...well, he is dying."

"What?! No! That can't be..." I practically yell this and then remember that my babies are sleeping; I modulate the volume. "But I didn't know... Takai never said..." My hand goes up and covers my mouth, and I knit my brows. I am feeling significant remorse as I had doubted the existence of any illness in all the times Takai returned to Edo. I thought he just wanted to spend his time there instead of Bosch. I even at times wondered... *I'm so sorry, Takai.*

Mama continues, "Yumiko wants me to bring the children to see him before he passes. I wanted to ask why she wasn't calling you but thought perhaps she was just upset, and then after I got off the comm, I got concerned that maybe she couldn't raise you. I tried to comm, but you didn't answer."

I quickly go and grab my comm from where I put it at

dinner. There are three missed comms from Mama, nothing from Takai, nor anyone else in Edo.

As I walk back into the kitchen, I hear, "Mama? Is Jiji going to die?" The small voice comes from the hall, and I turn and see Grey with tousled hair holding both her seven-year-old brothers by their hands.

"Oh, babies, did I wake you with my loud voice? I'm so sorry." I go to them, kneel on the floor in front of them, and wrap them in my arms, giving them a snuggle. "Grandmother called and wants us to go to Edo because Grandfather is not well at all."

Mac gives a snuffle. "I don't want Jiji to die, Mama."

"Neither do I, but we aren't in control of life and death. We just need to be sure he has the people he loves with him before he journeys," I gently say.

"Hayami will be very sad. She loves him lots," Kik says in a mournful tone.

Time screeches to a halt, allowing the universe to throw a strong punch to my midsection. My brain slowly processes what I've heard. *Hayami? In Edo? With Shigeo and Yumiko. With Takai. With my children. Oh, Sweet New Earth, Kat Wallace. Have you been played for a fool yet again?*

I am vaguely aware of Mac and Grey starting to scold Kik. I hear, "Shhh, you aren't supposed to talk about Hayami in Bosch," and, "Mama will get mad." Kik is starting to cry from all the admonishments his siblings are giving. The reality of what they are saying ignites an outrage I have never felt before. *He taught the children to deceive me.* I quickly turn my focus to my innocent babes. I am going to have to do something I swore I never would: I'm going to lie to my children. I move back to real time. "No, no. It's all right," I murmur to them all, but most especially Kik. I make my voice light and try to infuse it with the right amount of happiness. "I know all about Hayami. A long time ago, we didn't get along. But everything is fine now. I am glad she is there with Papa and Grandfather and Grandmother."

Kik smears at his eyes and nose with his fist. "Truly?" His voice is so tiny. "You are glad Hayami is there?"

"Oh, my sweet boy, of course, I am." I am shocked by how convincing I sound.

Kik gazes at me with eyes that are so much like his papa's. But he will never deceive someone the way Takai has me—I will teach him that. I look over at Mac and Grey and give them all a reassuring smile, opening my arms and sitting back to make room for them. Mac and Kik happily crawl into my lap for cuddles. They are smiling contentedly, their burden released. Grey has come to sit next to me, snuggled under my arm, but I saw it as her ten-year-old eyes searched my face before she sat. She knows I am play-acting.

Mac runs his finger over my neck scar, the way all the children did when they were nurslings. "Are you glad about the baby too?" *Baby? Baby too?* Jealousy and Suspicion come out of the box I have kept them in, and even they look stunned. They call Humiliation over to take charge. I feel as if I've been sucker-punched. And that phrase takes on a whole new level of meaning for me.

Now Mama bustles over. "You three need to get to bed. We all will be leaving early in the morning." She starts to hustle them upstairs away from where I am frozen on the floor.

"Mama?" Mac's fingers trail along my cheek as their Mama M helps them to stand. "Are you?"

I swallow. "Of course." My voice is unnaturally high, and I feel my face curve in what is intended to be a reassuring smile, but on the inside, it feels like someone has pressed pins into my cheeks. "A baby is all joy…. And you and Kik…will be big brothers…. Isn't that exciting?" I feel three kisses on my cheeks before Mama walks them upstairs, murmuring answers to their questions. *What would I do without Mama?*

I am glued to the floor, sitting with my knees to the side, my eyes staring at the wooden planks but not seeing them. I know if I move, I will likely start to break things, so I am trying to stay as still as possible. I just keep hearing Takai say, "I'm a family man." The man needs to work on his plurals.

I see movement out of the corner of my eye, and Matty folds his big frame as he sits down on the floor in front of me. He picks up my hand and wraps it around a glass, holding it with me. "Drink," his deep voice directs me. I look at his strong forearm with the tattoos of grapevines heavy with fruit intertwined around a wine press and a wine barrel. It's one of my favorites of his. I start to put the glass to my lips, but my arm sags. He helps me lift it to my lips, and I feel the sweet taste of bourbon with its butterscotch aftertaste flow onto my tongue and just the right amount of burn as it slips down my throat. I look up at his face, and his eyes shift from hard and angry to soft and caring as he looks at me.

"A baby," I whisper. "I suppose there are probably quite a few of those out there. All waiting for the same papa to come home." My voice takes on some venom as I say this, and I watch as he closes his eyes and shakes his head ever so slightly.

"Bastard," we whisper as one.

"Kat, wake up. We will be coming in for final approach in a few minutes, and I'd like you to negotiate that." Mama's voice cuts into my pleasant dream about sailing on the ships in the library mural, jumping from one to the other as I laugh with pirates through time. As I come to full consciousness, I am yet again surprised to see Mama at the helm of the *Coupe*, comfortably flying us to Edo. It still does not look right.

After Matty got the glass of bourbon in me last night, I had finally stood, shaking out my legs that had fallen asleep as I sat practically paralyzed on the floor, and turned around. My guests were there in my not-very-large kitchen trying not to stare but all throwing sympathetic glances at me and being exceptionally quiet as they sipped their now-cooling hot-buttered rums.

It was Lydia who broke the silence as she opened the bottle of Teddy's best bourbon and poured another measure expertly into my glass. "Who the fuck does he think he is, doing that to you?" She said it with such quiet intensity that I couldn't help but laugh, which broke the tension and sent everyone, including me, into peals of disgusted laughter. I waved them all back outside so we could talk without disturbing the kids, and for over a bell, we discussed various means of disfigurement and maiming for my soon-to-be late husband. Even the non-troopers among us jumped enthusiastically on the torture train, as apparently, his transgressions evoked the same visceral response in us all. It surprised me that I wanted them there, though as the clocks chimed midnight, each couple in turn began to stand, say goodbye, fiercely hug me, and make their exit. Matty and Lydia were the last to go. We walked inside together and saw Mama with her hands in a sink full of soapy water, washing dishes.

"Oh, Mama, you don't need to do that. I can take care of it," I reproved her gently.

She looked at me, and I was taken aback as I had never seen her eyes so angry. Her voice was the same gentle tone, though. "I needed something rote to soothe my soul, dear one."

Matty automatically began drying and putting cups and

glassware away while Lydia put the drink fixings away and wiped the counters.

"We'll help you finish up, Miriam, and then walk you home," Matty said.

Mama nodded. "Thank you, Matthieu, Lydia. That would be lovely. I'll need to pack for tomorrow. Kat, I went ahead and laid out clothes I thought you would want the children to take. You can look them over and then decide. I did pull their travel bags out and their toothbrushes and such."

I looked at this woman who is always there for me and thought about protesting that she need not come, but I knew it would be a futile effort. I went to her, kissed her on the cheek, and said quietly, "Thank you, Mama." And she turned and wrapped her arms with soapy hands around me as I started to cry for the first time that night, and I knew both of us were recalling the first time I cried in her arms, soap suds surrounding us, so many years ago. And just like then, she asked nothing of me and just held me while Matty and Lydia moved quietly out toward the door to wait for Mama.

Now I slide into my place at the helm after settling the children with various video stories on the small Obis I keep stashed on the *Coupe* and look at my pilot and navigator, Mama. "Did Papa teach you to fly?"

"Mmm, hmm. When we were on our honeymoon outside of Paris. We had all sorts of adventures planned, and he said I needed to be ready to take over the helm if he wasn't able." She smiles at the memory.

I grin. "I did not know that, nor about Paris."

She gives a small laugh and says with an air of mystery, "I am a complex woman of many talents. At least, that's what your papa used to say."

I consider her and ask in a small voice so the children don't hear, "Is it hard…being alone?"

She looks kindly at me. "Your papa has never truly left me. Oh, of course, we had our ups and downs, but I have always been secure in his love while he was alive and even after death. So, I am not actually alone." She pauses and I see her carefully choosing her next words with a quick glance back at the children. "But honestly, I do long for the companionship and the touch of another person, Kat. I may even decide to go on a date or two."

I almost jerk the yoke back from where I am pushing it as I glide toward landing, chatting in Edonese to the tower as I draw close to the runway. "Sorry, what?"

"Keep an eye on your altitude," she says smoothly and continues, "Kat, I am not dead yet, and neither are you. And you, my sweet girl, are far younger than I. There will be love for you to find and, who knows, maybe even for me. It won't be what Papa and I shared, but it could be…comfortable, perhaps even fun. And for you, I believe you will find a partner who sees you and celebrates you and loves you and only you for all your traits, not in spite of any of them. Don't let this horrible event close your heart, sweet Kat."

The tires bump on the ground a bit harder than I usually land as I snuffle up the tears that began. As we glide to a slow ground speed and move toward our parking area, I finally respond. "I think that ship has sailed over the horizon, Mama. In flames."

"Mama, there's a place where we can make a snow pirate!" Grey says excitedly.

I called in the wee hours last night and reserved rooms at the old Kiharu inn for Mama, the children, and me. I made it under the name of Keaton, Papa and Mama's last name from years earlier, before he became Master Commander, in order to keep some semblance of privacy in the tiny village prone to gossip. There is a large back garden that is currently covered with the season's first snow. "You three should go and play and stretch for a few minutes while Mama M and I get us settled in. Then we will go over to your grandparents' home and see them and Papa." I want to choke on this last word, or perhaps choke the subject. But I keep my voice even as I know Grey is watching me carefully.

I never went to bed last night after Matty and Lydia saw Mama home. I sat for half a bell on the sofa not knowing what to do, and then I prowled the house looking on shelves and in cupboards in the living room and the bedroom for something I couldn't quite define. Until I stopped at Takai's study door. Then I knew. I wanted evidence. A man who had gaslighted me for the entirety of our relationship, who used his own children to play into the deception, would try and smooth-talk his way out of this accusation even as his now pregnant—What, mistress? Additional wife?—stood next to him. I wanted what Othello wanted, "the ocular proof." I never went into the study before because I respected his privacy. *Fuck that,* I thought and swung the door open.

After about a bell and a half of me pulling books off shelves and shaking them, emptying desk drawers, and feeling around for secret compartments, I found what I was looking for in a lovely, solid walnut box that I had assumed Takai kept diplomatic papers in. It sat in plain sight on the shelf behind his desk. Hell, it wasn't even locked. Inside was a stack of letters tied ceremoniously with a green ribbon. A green ribbon. The irony of that little touch was not lost on me as the hair tie I had left behind at Abernathy's during my escape from Bellcoast had been close to the same shade of green. *And I am escaping again.*

I sat down in the comfortable chair at Takai's desk and stared at the pile of dozens of letters. I pulled one from near the base—it was addressed to *The Venturer.* I opened it and glanced at the salutation: *Most Beloved* and the closing, *Yours forever, Hayami.* I really didn't need to see more, but just out of curiosity, I pulled one closer to the top and glanced at the address. *Central Mail Service, City of Bosch. Pick-up only.* Huh. I'd be paying a visit to Dewey in CMS. I didn't need to open it but planned just to glance on the off chance the letters were from a variety of lovers. I saw the same opening, but as I scanned down to the closing, my name in the delicate Edonese script caught my eye, and I read the paragraph.

I do so hope that dear Kat will soon be recovered from her mental imbalance… Here, I paused, reread the line, and then took three deep breaths to keep my rage from exploding and my hands from tearing the letter to shreds. Once I felt I had regained my foothold, I continued:

…and you will be free to tell her that we are all but married. I am sorry to say that at times, I wish that if she cannot recover that you would place her in a facility where she could receive care. I do worry that the children, dear as they are to my heart, are not safe in her unstable hands, though I trust that you know best, my love, and that The Way will help you to keep them safe, heal Kat, and bring us together finally as husband and wife.

I dropped my hands and sat stunned. Then I carefully untied the ribbon and started from the first letter and read my way through the romance of Takai and Hayami, realizing I was not the only one who had been deceived with pretty words and tales spun of gossamer.

Now, from my suitcase, I carefully unpack the letters that are all back in their envelopes and tied neatly with their green ribbon. I have artfully added my wedding ring to the bow on top, tied securely. I tuck the packet into my sling bag and set it aside as I dress in my nicest, most conservative outfit, though this one fits my curves well and my weapons make clearly visible bumps beneath the fabric.

Years earlier, as part of our marital negotiations, when Takai vowed he would be faithful to me, I had promised him I would lock my weapons outside of the house each night when I came home, and I did so dutifully, even when he was not home. Last night, I dismantled the weapon storage box and returned my blade and my papa's twin pistols to their rightful place: within my arm's reach at all times. I was done trying to be someone else. I am a Bosch pirate, and I will rain down quiet hell today.

Mama, the children, and I walk slowly up to the Shima residence. It is very traditional, with its curved and tiled roof and the outer, glassed-in walls that enclose the engawa now that the cold has arrived. In the summer, the walls are gone, and the inner walls are slid open to allow for fresh air and light. The meticulously curated plantings in the front of the house are covered with snow, and I see some of the plants I placed there years earlier thriving, though currently dormant. It is apparent by the trampled snow on the path that many visitors have come, and likely there will be quite a few people inside to provide support for the family.

The children are both eager to see their papa and their grandparents and anxious about what to expect of Shigeo's condition. We pause at the genkan to remove our snow-covered shoes and slide our feet into the slippers that are at the ready. The children have a special cubby with their own while Mama simply uses the generic guest ones. From my sling bag, I pull out some black slip-ons that are traditional enough to be marginally acceptable but are not the style provided by the hostess: a small but significant insult. We step inside and I hold my head up high as I scan the room for the man I had called husband for so many years.

I see him standing over in a corner with a teacup in one hand as he chats with a village elder. Yumiko is settled in the farthest corner next to a raised futon where Shigeo lies. He is pale, thin, and drawn, his dark hair sprayed with far more white than I ever recalled. His eyes are partway closed, and his mouth hangs gently open. Hayami Miyamoto, her belly softly burgeoning, sits on the bedside, one hand holding each of Takai's parents' hands. First things first. I lean down to the children and remind them of how to greet their Ojiisan.

We walk to the far corner. Yumiko looks up, and her drawn, sad face turns shocked and angry as she sees me. I do not drop my gaze from hers until she looks away, focusing on the children. I hear Hayami give a small gasp, and I look over to her. She regains her composure as the children greet her. She gives the boys gentle hugs that are returned warmly. I feel an icy knife twist in my heart at their expressions of affection. Grey, however, hangs back and bows to her formally, which causes an expression of dismay to cross Hayami's delicate features. This creates a small, warm flame in me. I am not particularly proud of either of my felt—but unnamed—emotions, but I'll sort that out later.

Each child, in turn, sits near Shigeo, greeting him, saying their name, and touching his hands. He stirs and his eyes flutter, and I see a small smile creep onto his face. He is pleased. He always loved his grandchildren if not their mother. I stand far back. While I don't care if Yumiko is upset by my presence, I have no desire to create ripples in Shigeo's final days. Hayami rises and begins to walk slowly across the room toward Takai, who is still engrossed in his conversation with the elder.

I gently touch Mama's arm and whisper to her to keep the children on this side of the large, visitor-filled room. She nods her understanding and, keeping her eyes on my three young pirates, begins to chat compassionately with Yumiko. She is a way better person than I am. I turn and walk purposefully to the other corner of the room, not wanting to lose the advantage of surprise. Predictably, Hayami is not able to get a word in while Takai pontificates about some issue deeply important to him. It is not until I step up and say to the elder in Edonese, "Excuse me, but I have important issues to discuss with my husband and his mistress," that Takai even registers that I am in the room.

The elder beats a hasty retreat and buzzes off to discuss this delightful piece of gossip. This day's stories will provide many hours of story and speculation for the villagers through the coming winter.

Takai stammers, "Kat, I… Where…? The children…"

I keep my voice even and low. "Save your breath, Shima. Your mother called Miriam for the children to come last night, so I have brought them. But I shall not leave them alone with you to once again ask them to deceive and lie to protect their father's duplicity." I watch as his face goes pale, and I see him close his eyes and put his hand to his forehead. My jaw twitches. The remorse is far too late.

I continue, "I have also brought you these." I slowly and ceremoniously unzip my sling bag and carefully pull out the stack of love letters, plus a cast-aside wedding ring, holding them out but not handing them over yet. "This was a remarkable read. So many highs and lows, heartbreaks and reunions, a love complicated by a loveless marriage to a woman gone mad, and you, torn in your love, committed to standing by to support her, ever faithful." There is venom in my tone as I pause meaningfully at this word. "Truly, a marvelous tale. Unfortunately for Hayami, she doesn't realize which parts are fiction and which are not. I wonder if you even know. Who now is the one who is…how did you put it…? 'Disturbed and disabled?' It sure as fuck isn't me. I see the past decade very clearly, and it is a pack of lies. Your lies."

I turn to Hayami, who keeps her hand protectively on her round belly as her eyes dart between Takai and me. She looks thunderstruck. I can't say I don't still harbor some measure of ill will toward her; after all, she knew her captain was married, but she has been drawn into this deception as well.

I soften my voice as I speak to her. "Congratulations on your coming child. The children are excited for a sibling. You have always been more than kind to them, and they have love for you. You and your child will be welcome to visit them in Bosch at any time. But Hayami, as you can see, I am well and strong, and any 'mental breakdown' that occurred happened years ago and was brief and dealt with. Let me provide you with a small history lesson: You are not the first in the parade of lovers, and there is no indication you will be the last. Take steps to protect your heart and your family. I wish I had."

I drop the bundle of letters, my ring glinting off the top, onto the small tea table to Takai's left, turn on my heel, and stride out into the chill of the Kiharu November. Notably, no tears are on my flushed cheeks.

"Aiko? What's all this?" I am smiling for the first time today.

Mama agreed to look after the children for the day, keeping a careful eye and ear on them as they visit with their papa and grandparents. She and I had talked, and she knew I would need time to center myself after I had my say, and we agreed that the children should not have to feel the tension that would be present if I had stayed.

So, after leaving Takai with his web of lies and a mistress with questions, I made a quick stop at the inn to gather a few items in a basket. Then I headed to see Aiko, my Edoan friend and a priestess of The Way, the state-sanctioned system of culture, beliefs, and practices. The Way emphasizes learning, patience, emotional control, diplomacy, and rejection of violence in any form. As I walked through the village toward the address Aiko had given me, I thought briefly that perhaps The Way should add honesty and loyalty to the list, but hell, that's not my issue any longer. Let Hayami deal with that.

Aiko had told me when I commed her to arrange a visit that she had moved into the village group home for elderly priests and priestesses. She assured me she was fine. "I just don't want to climb that damn mountain anymore." She had given her signature laugh as she made this statement.

I approached the "home" that was actually a beautifully appointed traditional building surrounded by gardens that still retained some late-fall color under the light snow, offset with meditative sand and rockscapes. A fountain constructed of bamboo sat outside to the right of the door with tiny icicles artfully extending from the spout through which ran the barest trickle of what was surely icy-cold water. I knocked and the door was answered by a tiny Edoan woman, at least a head shorter than me, practically Grey's height, all dressed in black and covered with a blue flowered apron.

"Good day. I am Kiyo. Welcome." She addressed me in formal Edonese and motioned me inside.

I gave the appropriate formal bow and greeting. "Good day, Kiyo. I am Kat Wallace." I stepped inside and saw another fountain trickling next to the far wall at the end of the genkan, the water falling quietly in soft sheets. "I am seeking Madame Aiko, please." I glanced around the place as I slipped off my shoes and slid into the slippers provided.

One older gentleman occupied one of the four chairs in the common space. The chairs were comfortable-looking, but none looked so squashy as to be difficult for the elderly residents to rise from. The man held his meditation beads in his hands and was softly murmuring to himself, eyes half-closed. There was a decent-sized Obi in the room, and it was currently tuned to a picture of a forest with the sounds of breezes blowing, birds singing, and the occasional temple bell chime. To the left of the common space was a large table with several unoccupied chairs. Kiyo conferred with a young man who was preparing lunch, then motioned me to the back porch with a smile.

"Thank you." I gave another small bow and slid the porch door open, stepped out, and carefully closed it behind me. The porch was covered in and enclosed with sliding glass, essentially making it a wide engawa. It is expansive, with several rocking chairs, straight-back wooden chairs, and chairs woven of bamboo. Standing in the corner, facing away from me, slightly bent, near a bird feeder, is Madam Aiko. And next to her sits my other great friend, Kenichi Tsukasa, head of the most powerful yakuza family in Edo. What is all this, indeed?

I say her name, and Aiko turns her head sharply in my direction. "Kat Wallace! It has taken you long enough to visit an old woman!" Aiko, and Kenichi, for that matter, have definitely aged, but then again, so have I. It has been almost four years since I left Edo to return to Bosch. And during those years, my visits back to Edo were very sparse. Certainly, sparse enough for my husband to start a new family. I shake my head a bit. That is not where I want to dwell. I am here to see a friend—correction, friends.

Aiko still has jet-black hair, but there are a few more strands of gray in it. She is a tiny bit shorter, if that is possible, with a face full of wrinkles, though that part is not new. It is clear from her bright eyes that it is only her body that has aged.

Kenichi stands, his hair more silver, though his body looks strong for a man who must be looking at his seventh decade. He gives me a broad smile. "You look well, Kat-san." His voice is also strong.

I laugh with delight and move quickly over to embrace them both, setting my basket on the table nearest Aiko.

My heart feels full, and I am so glad to see these friends as they remind me of the best of Edo. Aiko leans over to the basket and lifts the cloth on top, whispering conspiratorially, "I hope you have brought me some good Bosch wine. District 7, correct?"

I smile. "Actually, I have done one better. I now know someone who keeps me supplied with the best reserve bottles from the best vintner." I reach in and retrieve a bottle of Warner Reserve. Aiko's eyes go wide, and her smile glows.

Even Kenichi gives a low whistle as he lifts the bottle and reads the label, settling a pair of spectacles on his nose as he does so. "This is an excellent year, and hard to come by."

I nod. "Yeah, I'm like *you* now, Kenichi. I know a guy." I say this last part in my best gangster-speak from the Old Days films Kenichi and I both enjoy. He laughs.

"Let us go to my room to indulge in this," Aiko says. "They don't approve of spirits here or at the temple," she muses, "but I believe that is a result of mistranslation." She gives me a wink. As we approach the door inside, she says under her breath, "You distract the cook. I'll snag three glasses."

I chuckle at the intrigue and make a point of chatting about lunch preparations with Itami-san, the young man in the kitchen, until I see Aiko boost herself up on the counter and hand three pottery teacups of varied sizes to Kenichi, who sequesters them quickly under his jacket. I make a note of the small smile I see on Kiyo's face as she studiously wipes at a spot on the immaculate table. My guess is, nothing happens here that she doesn't know about.

In Aiko's comfortable and remarkably ample room, I open the wine and pour it into the cups. We sit and speak of the mountain Aiko loves but no longer wants to climb, Kenichi's home on the big island and on the city-ship that slowly sails in a circle offshore, and of my children. I show them photos on my Obi and promise to bring them by tomorrow or the next day.

I see a glance pass between Aiko and Kenichi, and Aiko reaches for my hand. "I am so grieved that your marriage to Takai has unraveled." They both look at me, anticipating tears.

I, too, sit for a moment, waiting for them to come, but they don't. I furrow my brow and then give a sad smile. "'Unraveled' actually sounds like a good thing. It appears I have shed my final tears over Takai Shima. Perhaps one day, I will reflect and find where I contributed to the end of this marriage, but that day is not today. Today, it's all on him." I see Kenichi pull in his lips and give a small nod. I look at him. "Did you know? About Hayami? The baby?"

Kenichi draws in a deep breath. "There is little that occurs in Edo I do not know or have access to. Family situations rarely concern me, though, unless it involves my family." Here, he looks at me with his deep, dark eyes. "I promised Teddy that I would care for you, Kat. So, yes, I was informed." His eyebrows come together in what looks like consternation. "I chose to keep the information to myself, though I had resolved to speak with you once I heard a child was on the way. I hope you can understand my choice."

I search around in my head and heart for any feeling of betrayal from this man. There is none. "I understand. I expect that deep down, I knew something was happening as well, but I, too, kept it set aside." A sly smile curls my lips. "However, if you wish to take action to assuage any guilt, you could expedite the dissolution of my marriage. The wheels of the Edoan government move so slowly otherwise." I give him a small, spoiled child pout.

Kenichi reaches out and cups my cheek. "Done." We both chuckle at the deal.

Another look passes between the two old friends. Aiko leans forward. "Kat, now that you are not part of the Shima clan…" She bites her lip and looks at Kenichi.

He picks up the thread. "Yumiko is currently distracted with Shigeo's illness and his approaching end. But once he is gone, you must be very careful of her. She does not hold your best interests at heart."

I give a small hoot of somber laughter. "That I know. She would like me to disappear from her life."

"More to the point, she would like you to disappear from life altogether." Kenichi looks at me, and his eyes seem to bore into me; his look is so intense.

I frown. "Are you saying…?"

"Winter Festival, the attack on the path home," Aiko says quietly.

I turn my head and stare at her for several seconds and then look at Kenichi, who gives the barest nod, affirming this. I quickly stand and go to the large window.

"That can't be true. She…" And then I pause and scroll through my memory. I consider her attitude toward me… Well, not everyone can be like Miriam, so I can't hold her dislike for me against her. Shigeo never approved of me either. Then I think back to the Winterfest incident when traders had tried to kidnap me, along with Kenichi's daughters, and how strangely Yumiko acted, practically pulling Grey from my arms. But it was so many years ago.

The ambush on the path: I was coming home from the physicians' office I had worked at when the children were small when I was jumped by a man intent on killing me. After I dispatched him, Riki appeared, telling me the assailant was from Kenichi's yakuza family and had taken a rogue assignment. I had assumed it was Abernathy who had hired the assassin, but I remember Kenichi had said that it had "looked like a domestic hire," and then he refused to comment any further. I had just figured it was some conflict between families. Shit. I guess it was—just not the families I figured.

I let my breath out in a low whoosh. "You are quite sure of this?"

"The men from the Winterfest gave some information before they, unfortunately, passed on. It was incriminating but a bit vague. I did not know all the circumstances leading up to the event, so I held my tongue." Kenichi's voice is level and clear, and I detect no hint of pretense. "The Jiro situation, however, left no doubt. We confiscated his comm and found Yumiko's number in it from several occasions leading up to the event and one message after requesting her markers be returned."

"Then why didn't you…?" I begin.

Kenichi sighs deeply and interrupts me. "I am unsure, Kat. You would likely call it male egotism and arrogance, and perhaps you would be correct, but I liked to think of it as an acting father's protective nature. But it did make me realize that keeping you in Edo would not keep you safe. However, I did play to Yumiko's fear of me exposing her to Shigeo who knew nothing of either event. That has seemed to work until now."

"Until now…." My body is taut as I assess the risk. "Are the children safe with her?" My voice is urgent and low.

"There has never been any indication that she has anything but an obaachan's deep affection for the children," Kenichi says quickly. I feel my body relax a tiny bit.

"Well, then. I can take care of myself…. But…" I am still coming to terms with the news and what that will mean for my babies, whose world is about to be turned upside down already.

"May I make a suggestion?" Kenichi asks casually.

I turn back to look at my friends and try to keep my voice normal, but I am shaken. "Of course."

"Riki adores your children and has been dismayed by their absence. If I were to send him with the children when they visit Kiharu…," Kenichi begins, but I jump in.

"Oh, Kenichi. Could you? Would you? Would he? That could solve so much." Riki is one of the biggest, strongest Japanese men I have ever met. He works as a bodyguard for Kenichi, and he and the children have a warm friendship, especially him and Grey. "It's not just this Yumiko situation, which I'm still trying to come to terms with, though his presence will certainly be invaluable for that. It's also…" I stammer a bit as there is no way for what I am about to say to sound good. "It's just, I don't want them alone with Takai right now. I can't trust what he tells them, but I know they will want to see their papa, and I can't refuse that, and if Riki were there… Well, it would be another set of ears and an impressive aura."

Kenichi chuckles a bit and nods. "I had hoped you would feel that way. Let me comm him and arrange for him to wait for Miriam and the children at the Shima home this afternoon.

The three of us can discuss details of the assignment tomorrow."

I feel more tension flow off me, and I smile. "Yes. Perfect. Thank you, Kenichi."

"It is my pleasure to see you and your children safe and well. Now, let us pour more wine and get the Shogi board out. I believe it is you and I playing, Kat-san."

I pull my chair over as Aiko opens the elegant wooden box holding her board and pieces, and the three of us sit down for a game and conversation.

"It's mine!" Kik's voice is angry and insistent.

"Papa said we should share them," Mac replies in his superior tone that he knows annoys his brother. I don't need to turn around from where I sit piloting the *Coupe*. They must be arguing about one of the games Takai gave the children in his over-the-top attempt to curry favor with them.

I glance over at Mama, who sits in the navigator's seat, elbows on the helm, two fingers on either temple, not paying any heed to this newest round of bickering. She looks exhausted. I imagine she is. I know I am.

Grey's voice intervenes, "Here, Kik, you can play with the one he got me. I don't want it."

I cringe inwardly and a little outwardly. Her tone, especially the way she says "he," is so disdainful. She has spent little time with either Takai or Hayami over the past five days we have been in Edo, preferring either Yumiko's company, mine, or Mama's—and now Riki's. I can tell she is feeling anger, responsibility, and some guilt over following her papa's instructions to keep Hayami's presence from me. I have held her and reassured her as best I can, but I am afraid there is now a deep chasm in her connection with her beloved papa whom she had previously thought was infallible. I will speak to RTT about her. I am sure she will have wisdom that I cannot find at this point.

Shigeo passed fairly peacefully the second afternoon, with the children, Takai, Hayami, and Yumiko present at his side. I actually shed a real tear for this man who was an excellent diplomat and, frankly, a fucking saint to stay married to Yumiko all those years. He never thought Takai and I were, as he once said to my soon-to-be ex-husband when he thought I couldn't hear, "a good fit." Turns out he was spot-on.

I spoke to the children the night after Shigeo died as we were snuggled on futons together before we all fell asleep, talking about serious things like life and death. "So, Papa will be staying in Edo from now on with Grandmother and Hayami and the baby. You three can visit him here." I tried to keep my voice light. I hated to pile on after their Ojiisan's death, but they needed to know.

There was silence from all three for several moments, and then Grey asked the question they likely all had in their minds. "Are you and Papa going to stay married?"

I took a deep breath in. "No."

"Can Papa come visit in Bosch like he used to?" Kik asked. I hadn't considered this. I also thought it was interesting that he saw his papa's time in Bosch as simply visits.

"We'll work something out," I hedged slightly.

Mac took the next question. "Is it because of Hayami and the baby?"

I did know the answer to this one. "No, Mac. It's because Papa and I have decided that it doesn't work for us to be married to each other anymore. We feel like we'd be happier apart." I realized I was making it sound like Takai was part of the discussion, which he wasn't. But he sure as hell contributed to the decision. I gave three kisses to three little heads. "But we both still love you three with all our hearts, and that will never change." *Please don't let it change, Takai,* I plead in my head.

Grey reached up and touched my face. "I want you to be happy."

"Me too, sweet girl. Me too." I sighed. "Time to sleep now."

We stayed for two days after the funeral and cremation, and then came home with Riki now following us in a vessel authorized by Kenichi and piloted by an Edonese FA pilot. Sweet New Earth, that man's reach is long. Riki came to the inn after the funeral with a startling proposal: "Kat-san, I know we agreed I would accompany the children to Kiharu when they visit, but I believe I could be of help to you and to them in Bosch." He had turned to Mama and said carefully, "Miriam-san, I mean no disrespect, but you should have time to do the work you love and enjoy your golden years and simply be an Obaachan, not a caregiver to the children." Mama had started to protest, but Riki pushed on, "I also believe it would help the children accept my presence in Kiharu if I was present with them on a daily basis." Then he gestured to Miriam and me. "And I would like to see the land that has produced two such women as yourselves."

Here I had laughed and said, "It sounds like you are looking to be fixed up with a date from Bosch, Riki." At this, he grinned and shrugged, causing the atmosphere of the conversation to lighten. I looked at Mama, and she gave a smile and nod.

So, I said to my large friend, "What you are offering is more than generous, though I don't know that being a nanny is really going to fit your skill set." I considered the scraps the boys were having lately for a moment. "But then again, it may actually be right up your alley." Here, he had frowned a little at the idiom, not quite understanding it, so I reached out and touched his arm. "If this is something you honestly want, Riki, then I want it too. Let us try it for, say, three months? And then you can decide if you wish to remain longer." So, now, we are six returning home.

EIGHTEEN

X Marks the Spot

BOSCH, LATE JANUARY 2366

The house seems strangely empty as I open the door. We have dropped Mama off at her place and Riki at the apartment I rented for him. They were both quite tired, not being used to flying long distances as the children and I are. Takai has been away from Bosch so often that it should not feel different now. But it does. I know I am doing the right thing because I cannot tolerate the deception—either his or my own—that our marriage is salvageable but knowing he will never walk in the door again feels…alien. I shake my head and look at the door to the study as the emotions threaten to wash over me.

Seeing that room renews my resolve, and I take in a breath and say to the children, "Let's get cleaned up and into pajamas. Then we can have some eggs for dinner and then cuddle on the big bed and read stories to each other." This idea is met with three small cheers. "Then early sleep as you need to get up and head to school in the morning." This statement evokes some disgruntled remarks. "No arguing. It will be Friday, and you have already missed far too many days." I try to keep my tone light but firm, and it seems to work as there is the barest of protests, and they head to take their bags to their rooms. I imagine they are tired as well.

On Friday, after I see the children off to school, I skip work and instead pack up Takai's things into boxes and stuff them, fairly unceremoniously, in the study. I pull out the old ship's captain's desk and chair and move them up to Grey's room and then take the two small tables Takai has had with him since the *Kingfisher* and put them in the boys' room. I select three small, framed pictures of Takai with each of the children and place them on the furniture for the children, grumbling that "I bet there are no pictures of me in the love nest in Edo." I am unused to taking the moral high road and think that RTT will be pleased with this story on Tuesday, peevishness aside. Then I shut the door to the study and pull the large ottoman in front of it. After he removes his shit, I will gut the room, rub salt in the cavity to cleanse it like Hallward claimed the Romans did to Carthage, and build some kind of space for myself, but that won't happen for some time. So, the ottoman will currently serve as a "no trespassing" sign.

Riki retrieves the children from school, much to their delight and, I am sure, the astonishment of all the other children and most of the staff. Riki tends to stand out even in Edo, so here, he is definitely a phenomenon. I invite him for dinner and pull together a rough meal as my single-minded task today has kept me from the store. My comm buzzes and I see Matty is calling. I smile and a little weight eases off my shoulders. I was feeling a bit forgotten today because none of my friends had commed, even though I really hadn't told anyone but Matty I was home yet.

"Hey, Gen. How are you doing?" His voice holds just the right balance of lightness and concern.

"I am hanging in there. Did a furious job of housekeeping today. What about you?" I don't want to spend my time always talking about my woes.

"Well, good, but…" He hesitates.

I frown. "Uh-oh. What's up?"

"I'm fine. But there's a couple loose ends here that really need to get cleaned up, and you are the one in charge of them, so…" He definitely sounds regretful that he needs to ask this of me, but he is right. I am the general.

I puff out a breath. "No problem. I'll come over tomorrow. Riki can watch the kids."

"Who?" As he asks, I realize I hadn't told anyone that I was bringing home a 120-kilo Edoan nanny.

"Um, he's one of Kenichi's bodyguards that is going to take care of the kids for a while." I figure the straight story is best.

There is a pause over the comm. "Sure, Kat. Why wouldn't you have a yakuza foot soldier as a nursemaid? Makes perfect sense. And I mean that sincerely, given how well I know you."

There is a tease in his voice that pulls a smile to my face, and I simply say, "Fuck you." I hear laughter from the other side of the comm.

He continues, "Well, I know things are likely to be tricky with the kids for a bit, and I didn't know you had an Edoan Sumo au pair, so I arranged some things for the kids to do while we hashed out some business. You can bring this…Riki, did you say?"

"Yes, Riki. But wait, you did stuff for the kids?" I am genuinely touched. "That's really nice, Matty."

"Yeah, I can occasionally do nice things. Don't spread it around. It'll ruin my reputation as an asshole," he says congenially.

I laugh. "Oh, I don't think there's any danger of that rep being damaged in the near future."

"Great. See you all at, say, eight bells at the hangar?" It's not really a question.

I nod, though he can't see it. "We'll be there. See you tomorrow."

"See ya, Gen."

We arrive at the hangar on Saturday morning just before eight bells. All three children are jet-lagged and cranky, and I am ready to cash in some tightly held investments and ship all three of them to one of the fancy Swiss boarding schools that, for the past several centuries, have marketed themselves as "impervious to changes that plague the masses."

Matty seems all-business, with a stack of papers for me to go through in the hangar office. He says casually to the children, "Oh, there's some stuff in those bags over there if you're interested." He points to three old sacks, like the kind we stuff into storage holds for extra carrying capacity. They are lumpy and sad looking, tossed haphazardly on the ground. I wasn't expecting too much, and I figured at that point I was rewarded by being correct. Riki can always walk them home. It is not too cold today. Good thing Matty never plans to have kids.

I stand at my desk, having sat way too long for the past few days, and start to work through the papers. I ask Matty a question about an expense for the quartermaster but get no answer. I look up, and he is peering through the open door at the kids. "What's going on?" I walk over and see all three kids dressed in Golden Era pirate hats and sashes with little wooden swords at their belts. That could end badly. But they aren't beating each other over the heads with them; instead, each one has a piece of paper they are staring at. "What on New Earth?" I ask and glance at Matty.

His face is alight, and his eyes are twinkling as he watches them. "Treasure hunt! Figured they could use a treat."

I am astonished. I look to see each child run to different places in the hangar as they follow their clues. I watch long enough to see Kik uncertain of one clue and Mac come and help him figure it out. Then Kik helps Mac with one of his, and they both yell victoriously and run to tell Grey about it. She is giggling and as relaxed as I have seen her since the night of the party and the revelation. "You are too much, Matty Warner. If you think I'm not going to tell on you about this, you're crazy." I nudge my friend with my shoulder. "Thanks. They needed something like this."

He grins. "Okay. Back to work with you." And he turns back to watch the kids.

I scowl and head back to my desk. I find the receipt to go with the expense voucher, file it in the proper box, and then go back to the next paper in the pile. I frown. The paper looks yellowed with age, but the paper feels new. There is an old-style ship in one corner and what looks like a palm tree in another, but the map is not one of an island but of the hangar. "Matty, what the hell is this?" I look up, confused.

He is no longer watching the kids, but his dark eyes are twinkling at me. "I imagine it's not only the children of the house who need a bit of fun." He grins as he says this.

I look suspiciously at him, but I can feel a smile starting on my face. I turn the map over, and there is a note:

To start your adventure

You need not leave the shore

Just look to your left

In the smallest desk drawer.

Now I am fully grinning as I move to my desk drawer and

open it, finding another small slip of paper. "You didn't…?" I look up at him. "Do I get a hat too?"

"Hell, no. You have one— no, two, counting the one you gave Teddy. No, three—you have your Rosie one." He shakes his head but is still grinning.

I pout just a bit and hear him laugh.

The next clue leads me to behind the door, where I find my Rosie hat and a clue inside of it. I whoop, put it on, and run out to the oldest vessel to check on the front tire. I am having a ball!

I run from clue to clue. One time, I have to stop and really think about where the clue is sending me. Grey comes over on her way to her clue, wraps her arms around me, and reads over my arm.

"Maybe the coffee bar?" she suggests.

"Absolutely!" I hug her and we head off to our respective locations for our next clues. I stop, look around, and see Matty and Riki sitting on chairs off to the far side of the hangar, chatting amiably, but then Matty turns his head to survey his handiwork and sees me slacking. "Back to work, General. None of you have found the treasures yet."

I hear Grey squeal, "There's treasure?!"

"It would be a sorry treasure hunt without some booty!" Matty laughs.

The four of us redouble our efforts.

After about three-quarters of a bell, Kik is the first to find his, followed quickly by Mac and Grey. They are exclaiming and I really want to see their treasures, but I also want mine. This is the first game I have played since I was in primary that was purely for my own enjoyment, and I am giddy about it.

Finally, I find the wrench that the penultimate clue leads me to and am then directed to use it to open the third smuggling panel to the left of the helm on the newest Whydah.

After some convoluted shifting and contriving, as well as some time spent wondering how Matty ever fit into this space, I get into the ideal position and loosen the bolts, then carefully lift off the panel. And there, inside, is my booty, stuffed in a bag like the kids had at the start.

I run to the cargo door, hold it up, and holler, and the kids start to applaud. Matty is standing with a fist in the air and using the fingers of his other hand to whistle. Riki looks at the children, then at Matty for a long moment, and then gives a slow clap as well, a smile crossing his enormous face. I run and slide to the ground, asking the boys and Grey about their treasures. All three of them each have a can of lemonade from Azizi's; an actual chocolate bar (*Wonder where he liberated those from?);* a bag of hard candy; and a small, flyable model plane. Kik has a gift certificate for four writing sessions with Charles Warner, Bosch's most noted poet and author. He has published a number of books and was one of Papa's favorite modern poets. And because Bosch is not that big, he is apparently Matty's grandfather on his dad's side.

"I'll get to work on stories, and Matt says he'll fly me out to District 7 for two of the meetings, and for two, Mr. Warner will come to our house!" Kik is breathless and I'm not sure which he sounds more excited for. Kik has loved playing with words since he has been able to make them.

"It's incredible, Kik." I am smiling first at him and then up at Matty.

"Thank you so much, Matt!" My dark-haired boy is positively glowing.

Mac is gazing earnestly at his piece of paper and says quietly, "Mama, it's guitar lessons. How did he know?"

I beam over at Matty. Because I had mentioned Mac's burning desire to be a musician and play guitar just in passing weeks earlier.

He grins back. "A little pirate told me, matey!" And he winks a pirate wink at Mac, who laughs, jumps up, and throws his arms around Matty's waist in a little-boy hug, saying, "Thanks!" I watch as both surprise and then delight cross Matty's face.

The boys look at me. Kik asks, "Can we eat the candy, Mama?"

"And drink the lemonade?" Mac adds.

My usual impulse would be to tell them to ration it and wait until after lunch. But today feels different. "You can decide."

Excited by this option, the boys shift into twins mode and begin to discuss and compare their treasures and when to consume the treats.

Grey stands and comes right to Matty. "Oh, Mr. Matthieu, thank you. You'll really do voice lessons for me?"

Matty smiles warmly at my girl. "Absolutely, Grey. You have a good voice, and your range and projection can be even better with a bit of training."

Riki speaks up and is smiling at Grey. "I would be most pleased and honored to hear you sing, Grey-chan."

"Well, then, if it's okay with Grey, you should come with her, Riki. You can be her audience. And afterward, he and I can show you some fighting tips." Matty winks at Riki, who surprisingly winks back. He continues, "Your mama told me how strong your moves were."

I am waiting for the groan of mortification from my daughter, but instead she says, "Did you really say that, Mama?" And I am rewarded with a smile. "Now what's in your bag, Mama?"

The boys cease their chatter in the corner and come closer.

I had almost forgotten my booty, held tightly in my hand, as I shared in the children's excitement. All three children are now sitting near me, and Matty is sitting back in his chair, elbows on his knees, leaning forward. "Well, I don't know. Let's see. Better hope it's not voice lessons. That attempt would break poor Matty's spirit." I open the sack and peer inside.

A smattering of laughter comes, but the boys are asking urgently, "What's inside?!"

I have similar items, though some are decidedly more adult. Instead of lemonade, I pull out a lovely bottle of Warner Wine. I have a small box with what looks like four chocolate truffles, which makes me look at Matty in amazement.

"I ran a solo mission near Carhuac a few weeks ago. And I know the chocolatier in 7." He shrugs. Cacao is so rare, and the mountainous area of Carhuac is one of the few places it can be grown. This is a special treat. But there is more: an Old Days book entitled *The House of Spirits* by Isabelle Allende that looks amazing. I hold it out, questioning its origin. "Yeah." He looks proud. "I liberated that when I got the cacao."

The last item is a small envelope. From inside, I pull out four light cardboard rectangles. I read them. "The smoker?"

"I can't believe you've never been." His voice is incredulous.

The smoker is an elimination fighting exhibition that happens twice a year, the night before each graduation where the almost-graduated troopers get a chance to take on more seasoned fighters. It consists of three short rounds and apparently is wild. I missed both of mine for a variety of reasons, avoidance of court martial being one of them, and never got around to going, especially since no one wanted to fight me after my first year; hence, the bar brawls I had to instigate.

Matty grins. "Figured Aaron, Rash, you, and I could go next week. Maybe you can get in there and mix it up."

I grin back. "That would be a sight, but I'm pretty sure

there's a rule that says I am not supposed to beat up any junior officers or noncoms."

"Do you think that's a rule for all the generals or specifically you?" He points at me.

I consider the question. "I don't know. But Schneider could be a sight in the ring." General Jamal Schneider is well past fifty but still in pretty good shape. Matty nods his agreement.

I hop to my feet. "Hey, kids, wrap your booty up, and we'll take Riki and Matty over to Donna May's for some lost bread and stewed apples." Cheers go up from everyone but Riki, who looks unsure. As the six of us leave the hangar, four of us with bags full of treasured booty, Grey takes his hand as we walk, explaining to her friend the delights of the eggy, grilled bread topped with sweet, cinnamon-y apples and is rewarded by Riki's enthusiastic sounds of appreciation.

NINETEEN

Rats on the Ship

SOBAYTON BAY; JORGE MONTT, PATAGONIA; AND BOSCH, JANUARY 2366

Major Cal Greene looked at himself in the mirror. He rubbed his newly shaved face and sighed. What was the saying? "In for a marker, in for a mission." He shrugged. He knew Maia, his three-year-old daughter, would be dismayed by the change. But he had been tracking this lead for weeks, and his new look was part of the persona he needed to get close. His hair was now a deep, dark brown, and he hoped the facial scar he had applied would distract from all the freckles that populated his face. He looked at his clothes and nodded approvingly. The costumers in BI had done well outfitting him, even to the point of adding enough padding to make him look markedly thicker than the old Cal Greene. He looked like just another port worker, local to Sobayton Bay, just planning to get a few drinks. He set his cap on his head and slipped into his costume coat.

He left the ramshackle room he had rented, taking a deep breath of the cold, salty air that also had overtones of old beer and waste, both garbage and human. He made his way along the gray, cobbled road that was populated with workers like him, a few sailors either going to or coming from the bars that were abundant along this section of town, some mothers pushing their bundled-up infants in carts, a few gentlemen in very clean coats with shiny buttons, and loads of children running about and shouting. He even saw a few sex workers out, but it wasn't really their prime business hours.

He made his way to the Tilted Sip. He had been here earlier as red-haired Cal Greene chatting up the bartender. Now he walked in as Mark Brady, workman, ordered a beer, kept his coat collar high and his hat low, and looked the opposite way until he was served. Then he made his way to a rough table and positioned his chair where he could see the door. He hoped he wouldn't have long to wait. He had paid the bartender well to hear that a Paddy Owens was running a grift on the Bosch and had a regular Bosch contact who seemed to provide plenty of both loot and information for Paddy's scam. A modicum of digging revealed that Paddy had been a regular on the Bosch Glitter drops, including ones made by Kat herself. Those drops ceased about three years earlier, and there was reliable information that tied Paddy to meetings with Senator—strike that—Vice President Rob Abernathy right around that time.

Cal leaned back and listened to the music and slowly sipped his beer.

About two bells and one more slowly warming beer later, his patience was rewarded as a man fitting Paddy's description came into the bar laughing with another man on his heels. Cal was not a man easily shocked after years in Intelligence, and though he could find out almost anything about almost anyone on Bosch, he certainly did not know everyone on sight. However, he did know all the members of the Burn the Ship company. And he knew that Demery Ludlow was a friend of Kat's. This would hit her hard. From his pocket, he pulled out the small camera that looked like a large man's ring, slipped it on, and began to collect the evidence he would need to plug the leak.

Paddy Owens grinned as he excused himself from the table to use the toilet. Then, he made his way past the wooden doors that concealed the privies and continued on through the kitchen door, nodding to the cooks that he made sure he kept supplied with "complimentary" Glitter until he came to the manager's office, which was currently not occupied as the reprobates who worked here had a habit of chasing off anyone who tried to manage them. He slipped in and considered what the information he had was worth.

Paddy had been growing tired of playing Owen Patricks, friend to the Bosch pirate Demery Ludlow, for the past four months. While the regular weekly hauls and the Glitter he provided made Paddy a reasonable profit, Ludlow's information had generally been unproductive. Yes, he had given Paddy detailed and colorful descriptions of Bosch and the people in his unit and even of Kat Wallace, who apparently had not only survived the mission that Paddy had sent her way in hopes of dispatching her but also sounded as if she had fully rebounded from the encounter with Abernathy when her special friend was killed. But there were precious little saleable scoops that came from him.

Ludlow had let it slip in October that now that Kat Wallace was a general in the Bosch Pirate Force, there was to be some kind of a "save the thralls" project, but that information had not been profitable as Paddy discovered it had become public.

And their "friendship" almost came to an end in mid-November when Demery cornered him, angry and ready to deliver blows, asking if Paddy was pumping him for information. Apparently, several Bosch units had been ambushed, one successfully. Paddy's first thought as Ludlow was threatening him with mayhem was that he wished he had been the one to collect and deliver that information. Now Paddy wanted to know who else was working as a snitch in Bosch. It took several rums and hours of cajoling for Paddy to reassure Ludlow, who had devolved into drunken tears, that he would never carry a tale (unless he was well paid, though he didn't share this) and, in fact, Demery had not told him the location of the mission site where the Bosch unit had bought it.

The only saleable piece of information he had provided had been that the project was halted after that. And Ludlow had been far more careful about his rum consumption over the past couple of months. But tonight, the grog flowed, and Demery Ludlow was back to spinning tales. And now, finally, there was a tale that would make Paddy a nice little sum.

He pushed the door shut in the office and punched in the numbers to Howard Archer that would garner him fifty thousand markers.

"So, what could possibly be so important to bring you all the way to my door?" DeLeon sat in his office in the mountainous village of Jorge Montt and looked at the slight figure dressed in a blue suit in front of him. Howard Archer was not an imposing figure by any means. Strands of thinning hair were swooped over the top of his head in a poor attempt to create the illusion of some type of growth on his crown, and he wore a thin mustache that traced his upper lip.

Perhaps on another man, it may have looked fashionable, but DeLeon always had the urge to simply hand Archer a napkin.

"It's about Wallace's project." Archer patted his brow, where beads of sweat were dripping. Deleon sneered in his head. *Northerners—can't deal with the heat.*

"Burn the Ship? You already reported that and got paid. Also, you and our other sources have told us it's dead in the water." The dark, handsome man shrugged and brushed a stray crumb off his desk.

An unpleasant smile curled on his snitch's lips. "That is what we all have been told in Bosch. But I have learned something about the project that could be very useful for you."

DeLeon's patience with Archer was fraying. "And what is it?"

"I want double the payment from now on."

DeLeon laughed. "I'm not even sure you've given me enough to merit what we do pay you."

Archer stood, leaned over DeLeon's desk, and hissed, "I gave you the correct locations of the intended mission sites back in November. And I've kept you informed on Wallace's movements."

DeLeon leaned back as a wave of noxious breath came at him. He didn't like any traitors, even ones that were turncoats to his advantage, and a person who would inform on his countrymen, knowing that it would lead to their deaths, was a special kind of despicable. He would have dispatched this man by now if Abernathy wasn't so damned obsessed with that Wallace woman.

"But there has been precious little else. You told us of Wallace's Burn the Ship movement, but there have been no Bosch raiders since November. So, unless there is something else, I have actual business to conduct...."

The smile returned. "I know plenty. I know you aren't at the top of this food chain."

DeLeon paused and looked hard at Archer.

Howard gave a laugh, and a little spittle flew from his mouth. "Ha, your face tells me I'm right. You tell your boss I have information about pirates killing your people, and if he wants it, it'll cost him. Triple now." Archer turned to walk to the door.

DeLeon looked stunned. He had not shared the trouble they had been having with mercenaries slaughtering traders and stealing commodity with Archer or anyone, not even with Abernathy. He had moved markers around to mask the losses, but they were continuing to accumulate. He spoke loudly as Archer's hand touched the doorknob. "What do you know?"

"Payment?" the little man asked firmly.

DeLeon locked eyes with Archer, picked up his comm, and pushed in a number. He instructed the person on the other end to transfer a ridiculous amount of markers to Archer's account.

Archer lifted his device and pushed a few buttons. "Well, that wasn't so hard, was it, Alejandro?"

Alejandro DeLeon took three breaths to avoid killing the rude little rat. "What do you know?" he repeated.

Howard Archer smiled. "The renegade pirates and the Bosch raiders are one and the same. Project Burn the Ship is in full swing."

I sit in my chair, anger boiling up in me, as I look across my desk at this man whom I thought was a friend. He is slumped in the chair, and his face is crumpled in misery as it should be. I hear Ruth in my head and conflate it with my own voice when the boys were three-year-olds and violent with each other. *Use your words.*

I take a deep breath and glance to my door to see the shadow of the guards I asked to be stationed there after I called Demery to my office. I decide to start small. "You know I have no problem with side jobs and making extra markers, Dem. But why the hell didn't you do a little digging into your contact? Fuck, I could have told you to watch out for Paddy. He is only interested in what he can get from anyone."

Demery's face shifts from miserable to annoyed. "Not everybody needs Kat Wallace to swoop in and play best friend and hero."

I stare at him, perplexed. "What the fuck are you talking about?" I pause on my interrogation to follow this.

He looks at me, and his eyes aren't warm. "You gave Tom Pikari all those markers, and now you sit on his board. And you and Gia became fast friends after you made your way into our unit. Then you just had to pull Bailey in as your confidante. And now you go off drinking with The Three Handsomes. Yep, everybody is raking in markers, and if you're close to Kat Wallace, you'll rake in the most. And where does that leave me? Waiting for a boon from her highness?"

I continue to stare at him and try to make sense of his words. Apparently, our friendship was one-sided. I narrow my eyes and hold my hands out, palms up. "So, you are telling me, you betrayed your friends, your unit, your company, and your nation because you were butt-hurt I didn't pay for your drinks?" Now I point at him. "You know, you are going to prison for the rest of your life."

He says sharply, "I didn't betray anyone. Not intentionally."

I stand up and hit my desk with both hands, causing Demery to jump and one of the guards to open the door and peer in. I wave him off, and he closes the door as I growl fiercely, "Do you think Awilda gives a shit if it was intentional or not?"

Demery is on his feet as well, shouting, "I never gave up that information. I swear on my life."

"Bullshit! It's why you didn't fly the retrieval with us, isn't it? You figured we'd end up like Awilda. Two-for-one." My volume is climbing.

"No! Never!"

"You skimmed Glitter and sold information to Paddy Owens!" I snap.

"No. I didn't." His voice drops. "I mean…yes, I skimmed a bit of Glitter. But I never sold information." His tone is insistent.

"Well, then you gave it away. I had you pegged as a better negotiator." I am not even trying to disguise the contempt I am feeling.

Demery Ludlow's face falls. "I… I…didn't mean… I never meant… You have to believe me."

We stay standing for several breaths. "Sit down, Ludlow, or I guarantee, you won't leave here under your own steam." My voice carries an unyielding tone. He pauses for just an instant, then sits obediently.

I slowly sit back down, not taking my eyes off this man I have laughed with, cried with, fought next to, and yes, even bought drinks for. Cal Greene is still tracing the leak; Ludlow is only one possibility. He may be telling the truth. But if it turns out he is lying and did give away our position, nothing will stop me from killing him. But for now, I modulate my voice. "Do you want to finish your days in prison, Dem?"

His jaw works as the anger recedes from his face, and he sighs and shakes his head. "No."

"Okay. Then here's what's going to happen: You will resign

from the Force, effective immediately. You will tell the unit you are wanting to pursue other projects. You will not be specific."

I watch as Ludlow's face shifts from shocked at the demand to resigned. Now to add more. "You will not have any contact with any base members after that, either professionally or socially. You are banned from base and all base activities."

Again, I pause for his face to show me he accepts this punishment I am meting out. I see him sigh and rub his brow.

"You now work for me and only me." I reach into my desk and pull out a comm. "This is the comm you will use to report to me, and I will call you on it. When it rings, Dem, you fucking pick it up, whatever the time or place. Savvy?" He nods as I hand it to him, and he pockets it. "You will continue to nurture your relationship with Paddy—I'm sorry... Owen Patricks. And you will now feed him information as I direct. Any, and let me repeat that, *any* deviation from my instructions will land you back in my personal custody." I put on my Rosie death stare. "And I promise, it won't end fast, and you'll wish it had."

I lean back in my chair. "Are we clear?"

He nods. "Yes, we are, Kat."

"The title is General, Mr. Ludlow. I expect you to use it." I stand, walk to the door, and open it for him to leave, hoping the bad taste in my mouth will recede with time.

TWENTY

The Smoker

BOSCH, JANUARY 28, 2366

"Anybody heard from Demery lately?" Rash asks. There's a murmur to the negative, and he continues, "Kat, do you know why he really resigned?"

I keep my face neutral. "Only what he told everyone. He has other projects he wants to pursue."

Matty frowns. "I never got the sense he was the kind of guy to quit in the middle of a mission, though."

I shrug noncommittally. "I think the ambush hit him hard. He likely just needs space."

"Maybe so. What's the deal with you, Kat? That's the slowest I've ever seen you consume a drink." Rash points to my still half-full bourbon cocktail.

The four of us—Rash, Matty, Aaron, and me—are at Barton's for some pre-smoker drinks, and I am being cautious about my consumption and am glad for a shift in the topic. "Well, tomorrow is the first time I have to sit up on stage and be all general-ly and speak in front of everyone, and I don't want to be hungover for it."

Aaron laughs. "The entire graduating class will be

hungover. You'll stand out if you aren't." The other two men laughingly agree with Aaron's summation.

"Still. I'm going to pace myself." I shrug.

"Suit yourself, Gen. I'm ordering another from the lovely Lydia—if she'll look this way." Matty's hand goes up as he tries to catch Lydia's eye, but she seems intent on her other tables.

Rash hoots a laugh. "What happened, Warner? Is she peeved because you're seeing your girlfriend tonight?" Aaron joins the laughter, but Matty looks annoyed.

"Yeah, she wouldn't have known about it if you two jerks hadn't started spinning tales last night." Matty takes a drink from his almost empty glass and scowls.

I go quiet as I process this information. When I finally speak, it is in a small voice. "You...have another girlfriend, Matty? And Lydia doesn't know?" I feel a stab at my heart. Disappointment whispers to me, *That's just how men are. Did you think he was special? Honestly?*

He glances at me and then does a double take, reading my face the way he always does. "Oh, Kat..." And his voice is soft and sincere. "No. It's nothing like that. I don't..." Then he turns to our tablemates. "Look what you assholes did— you made Gen sad."

I shake my head and try to cover. "What you do is your business...."

Aaron looks a little sheepish, and Rash jumps in. "Oh, she's not a real girlfriend. She's a video one."

I frown at this odd statement. Disappointment looks a bit pissed as Relief shoves him to the back to let Friendship settle in. "Okay, now I'm confused." *A video one?* I look at Matty's honest face that now flushes with what seems to be embarrassment, and I chuckle. "So what video is this? Or should I say, what kind of video? Is it the kind that doesn't require much conversation?"

This evokes ribald laughter that starts with Aaron and flows to Rash, who coughs as he hurries to say, over Matty's developing protest, "There's this old video they've been showing before the championship round of the smoker for the past few years of this woman." Rash looks at Matty and grins. "And I'll grant you, she's impressive. But one night, Warner was three sheets to the wind and loudly proclaimed—"

"Enough. No one needs to know what Drunk-Matt said." Matty is definitely looking embarrassed now.

"Oh, sure they do," Rash says quickly, avoiding the swipe of Matty's long arm as he leans to keep eye contact with me.

I admit, "I want to know!"

Rash laughs. "See?"

With a disgusted breath, Matty sits back, defeated and abashed, allowing Rash to continue gleefully, "So, Matt announced to the entire gym during the video that she was the only woman he would ever marry, and all other women were a distant second. It went over really well with Diamond, who he had brought as a date."

I look at Matty. "Diamond Miata? You dated her? Wow. That's impressive, even for you." Diamond is a noncom who is drop-dead gorgeous, with a series of diamond studs and hoops in her ears, her nose, and, well, likely other spots as well. She is tall and fit and has a reputation for being a dead-eye shot. She works in tactical and security.

Matty nods his agreement. "Yeah, I had asked her out weekly for about two years, and she had just started saying 'yes' a few weeks earlier, but that was our last date, given my mouth and her right hook." He gingerly rubs the left side of his face as if remembering a wound. "Hence, the reason I don't drink much when going out anymore." He gestures at his now empty glass.

I look at him. "You asked her out weekly for two years? Weren't you dating anyone then?"

"Oh, well, sure. But, Kat, everybody understands that there's a Diamond Miata waitlist, and if you aren't on it, it'll never happen."

I grin. "You know what's amazing is, I have heard exactly that." I nod my approval. "I'll allow it." I snort at Matty's eye roll. "But all that doesn't explain why Lydia is clearly ignoring you tonight."

Aaron chuckles. "Because Matt Warner doubled down on his claim last night when he was stone-cold sober."

I laugh and tilt my head. "Aww, Matty. Is it time to move on already? I was just really getting to like Lydia." I give an exaggerated sigh. "But that is how it goes for those of us who are not the marrying kind." I like being able to hop into that group, even though my divorce is still several weeks from being final.

Matty shrugs. "Hell, I'll make up with Lydia for you, Gen. But it's always the same. I am upfront on the first couple of dates that, for me, marriage is ridiculous, and they either agree or we go our separate ways, no harm done. But so far, all the ones that stay end up hurt and offended a few months in when they haven't changed my mind."

"Do you explain that you were first in your class in Not-Getting-Married? Maybe that would help." I propose this in an innocent tone, and I am rewarded with a rousing round of laughter from all three men. Matty gives me a punch in the shoulder, and I rub it, play-acting pain. "Assaulting a superior officer, sir. That could get you into trouble." I grin.

"Superior in rank only," he starts and then continues as he

sees me start to get ready to retort. "And equal, in all others." He puts his hand up as if to calm me.

I smile. "I like that. Okay, I'll go up and order one more round from Beril, and then we go. I have to see this video dream girl of Matty Warner's." I stand and leave the table for the bar, hearing the continued banter and laughter behind me. I am surprised to find Envy walking with me, and I wonder what she must be like to pull his attention so fully.

We step through the door of the officers' gym, and I am hit by that which defines a smoker. Clouds of tobacco smoke float about my head and blend with the smell of sweat and leather, creating a delicious amalgamation. Tobacco is hard to come by and expensive; so, generally speaking, most Bosch don't smoke, but troopers have a tendency to liberate it when they can and hoard it for special occasions, apparently, like this one.

We have to talk loudly for each other to be heard above the loud rumble of voices from the impressive crowd, and moving through the gym requires serpentining through scores of troopers and a fair number of townies. Two of the gym trainers thrust bracket papers and stubby pencils into our hands that we shove into our pockets. Most of the equipment is moved aside, and the area around the center ring is clear to make room for the throng of spectators. A couple of officers from security are moving through the crowd as well, just to demonstrate a presence, but are only here to police if hell really breaks out. I find myself hoping it might. It's been a while. I do some torso twists to loosen up just in case.

There are four smaller rings set up on the sides, and Aaron leans toward me, practically yelling in my ear, to explain the system: Anyone can sign up, but recruits fight first, starting in the smaller rings on their own bracket until the top four recruits move on to fights in the center ring. The recruit victor is then briefly celebrated. It is an impressive accomplishment on its own, and I damn well know it could have been me in both of my classes. The recruit victor (RV) goes into the full bracket to fight more experienced troopers as the night progresses. I look around and see a fair number of women in fighting gear stretching, bouncing, and shadow boxing but far more young, well-built men, all shirtless and going through the same maneuvers.

I lean in to my group. "It's like a candy store for this almost-divorced woman. I'm not buying, but window shopping is fun!" I grin suggestively.

I hear Rash and Aaron laugh, then Rash teases, "You could always ask for a sample or two."

"There's an idea!" I give a laugh and look up, seeing Matty looking offended. "Aww, what's your problem?"

"I don't think you should be acting that way. I mean, you're a mom, Gen." He states this as if informing me of something I have completely forgotten and gives me a disapproving look, which causes me to react.

"Yeah. And guess how I got to be one?" I bite my lower lip and blink, then flatten my expression as I let my annoyance grow and show. "Newsflash, Major. Some wretched creature, bereft of decent vision, and left alone for decades somewhere, may actually crawl out from under a rock and find me attractive, surprising though that may be. Not to worry— it won't bother you and yours as it would be fully blinded from the radiance of those in your rarified circle of beauty." I turn away and then say over my shoulder as I point to the far ring, "If anyone cares, I'll be over there, staring at some sweaty, half-naked men and likely thinking very naughty thoughts. Shocking! Call the mom police!" I stomp off and hear Rash say, "Nice move, Warner."

A quarter-bell later, I am ringside, rooting for Trooper Kumar to take down Trooper Bauer when I feel a presence at my shoulder, and Matty hands me a cold beer in a paper cup. "I'm an idiot and an asshole."

I grin as I take the beer. "You coming over here to give me yesterday's news?" I hear him chuckle. I sip my beer and say, "I'll add to it. I have a tendency to overreact."

"You?" I hear the smile on Matty's face. "I never noticed." Now I get to chuckle.

We laugh softly together, and I say a bit soulfully, "The two of us make quite the case for not being the marrying kind, don't we?"

"Maybe you do, but don't forget, you get to meet my intended tonight on screen." He elbows me gently.

I turn and we tip our cups together. "I can't wait. Here's to your true love!" We both laugh and then delightedly, I see Bauer go down, and so I grab my pencil stub from behind my ear to mark my bracket.

After about two bells, the brackets are close to completed, and the ring is being prepped for the championship match between Lieutenant Devin Kidd and Major Bishop Goodman. It promises to be impressive, and I watch as loads of markers get shifted to the people taking wagers. Not me today, but if I had bet my bracket, I would be heading home heavy.

There is a thrum of excitement as the referee and one of the trainers bring out two large screens and place them back-to-back in the center of the ring. I have discarded the idea that this is a sex video because those tend to play to personal preferences, and everybody seems excited for this screening: men, women, and middles. The four of us have claimed a spot at ringside right in front, and I am surprised by how amped-up Matty looks. I start to ask if she's typical for him—young and top-heavy—but decide to hold my tongue until after I see what I figure is some old fight video between a couple of women fighters.

The lights go down, and the crowd quiets as the announcer takes to the ring. "And now, what is quickly becoming the most popular part of the Bosch smoker." He gestures to the screens in a flourish as he says, "Motorcycle Woman!" A cheer goes up. The projectors start on either side of the ring, and I feel my stomach drop to my feet. It can't be.

But it is. The video made of the motorcycle rescue I embarked on three years ago when I was living on the edge after Will's death. The video of me cutting loose a young couple who were to be executed while taking ample fire and then riding them out on my bike. The video that prompted Takai to threaten to take my children from me. The video that made Miles angrier than I had ever seen him. The video that he swore would never be seen again.

My emotions are careering from shocked to mortified to furious as I see and hear the episode play in a loop over and over. My first impulse is to go and kick the projectors down, and I turn to do so. Then I start to listen to the crowd, and I turn and look at the screen as I hear the troops cheer when I ride in. A few yell, "Look out" as incoming ammo hits the ground. And then someone calls "Use your knife!" and then another cheer as Philip and Arruda scramble onto the bike. I look around: These are not angry, disgusted faces; these faces are cheering me—or rather, Motorcycle Woman—onward, excited by the action. I watch as they lean to the left in unison with my bike.

I look back to the screen to see the bike leaving the arena, and now Matty pounds my shoulder, completely entranced by what he is watching, and yells to me, "Here it comes—best part!" and the entire room shouts "Teep!" as "video me" kicks my leg out from the bike, toppling the guards at the gate. And finally, the screens go dark and plunge the room into blackness as a loud round of cheering and applause goes up, and I stand, considering.

"You've been pretty quiet since the championship round. Did you lose a bunch of markers?" Matty asks as we walk in the chill January night, bundled up, hands in our pockets. We walked with Rash and Aaron to their street, and Matty has developed a habit of walking me home, even though he lives in the opposite direction.

"No. I didn't bet tonight. Maybe next time," I say quietly.

He looks over at me, and I look back. "Then what's wrong? You haven't even ribbed me about my future bride." He grins.

"I thought you weren't the marrying kind?" I ask smoothly as we turn up my street.

He scoffs. "I'm not. Motorcycle Woman is make-believe. That was all staged. Nobody could do all that and not get killed."

"Oh? You think?" I murmur noncommittally.

Matty nods. "Absolutely. It was probably some FA movie outtake." He sounds a little wistful.

We reach my gate, where Matty typically veers back to head home. I look at him. "I can one hundred percent guarantee you that video is not staged, and she is a real person doing real things."

Matty gives a small, derisive snort and looks at me with that superior look he gets when he has had a few and is certain he has already won an argument. "Kat..." He leans toward me, and I can smell the bourbon and cigar smoke on his breath. His tone sounds pretty close to condescending as he pats my shoulder. "You are just taken in because it's the first time you've seen it. After you watch it a bunch, it becomes obvious that it is staged. But I get it. Rash thought it was real for a long time. I think he still sort of does." He gives a chuckle and says in a growl more to himself than me, "Gotta admit, though, she is sexy as hell."

I take in all this information without response, my brain happily filing the comments for use later. I smile at his distant look. "Fascinating." Then I open my gate and start to walk to the door. Close to the front stoop, I turn and say in a voice just loud enough to carry back to the gate where Matty is turning to leave, "I mean, I get that the helmet hides my face, but I would have thought you'd recognize my knife." The night is so still, you can almost hear my words echo as I wait a moment. I see his back go up, and he starts to pivot. I smile. "Night, Matty."

I scoot inside, opening and shutting the door in a flash behind me. From where I stand, I see Riki's enormous form, one arm thrown over his head, snoring softly on my sofa with a blanket tucked around his legs. I grin and lean back on my door in my dark living room. *I will have some fun with this tomorrow and beyond.* My comm starts to vibrate in my pocket, and my grin expands. Gotcha, Major.

I peek outside through the small window in my beautiful, blue door and see at my front gate a tall, handsome, copper-skinned man all bundled up against the cold, standing, his comm at his ear and his mouth hanging open. I send his comm to my voicemail, and watch as my message begins in his ear. He jerks his hand down, and I think I can read his lips and make out the word "fuuuuuck" in the moonlight. *So. Much. Fun.*

TWENTY-ONE

Graduation Day

BOSCH, JANUARY 29, 2366

I am up early and at Miles' office even before he gets in. Betsy just waves me through the door, so I am comfortably seated in my chair with my feet up when my Master Commander walks in.

"Well, General Wallace. Up with the dawn, are we? Are you ready for your first graduation speech?" Miles' voice is rich and chipper.

I look over at him, attempting to keep my face neutral. "I have a small talk prepared."

He narrows his eyes slightly and tilts his head as he looks at me. "What's going on? I can feel the tension from here."

I give a droll laugh. "Am I that transparent? You know me well, Miles."

I see him nod. "You are making me nervous, Kat. Out with it."

"When was the last time you went to the pre-graduation smoker?" I ask, making sure my voice sounds pleasant and even.

"The smoker?" Miles brings his coffee and sits down in his chair. "It's been…maybe ten years? Why?"

I smile predatorily. "I went for the first time ever last night. It was quite…illuminating. Guess what tradition I got to see?"

"Kat, just tell me. I can't take this game of…" Miles starts to chuckle.

"It will go worse for you if you say 'cat and mouse,' Miles." I am working to keep myself from laughing.

He gives a sigh. "So, let's hear the issue with the smoker. Not enough women? What?" Miles is starting to sound desperate, and that is just where I want him.

"There was a video shown…just before the championship round. And, apparently, it's a sort of tradition." I choose my words carefully as I lay my trap.

"Oh, boy. A bunch of troopers with recruits that have been essentially confined to base for eight weeks—I can imagine what the video was." Miles rubs his brow.

I put a hand up. "No, not a sex video. Well, not exactly… though it certainly evoked emotion and reaction." I draw out my sentence.

Miles glances at me, then scoots his chair back and carefully pulls open his center desk drawer, drawing out his favorite pistol—a replica of a Colt from the Old Days. It is a beautiful piece with a wood grip and a sleek, flared barrel. He checks it for ammo, flicks his wrist to close the cylinder, and clicks off the safety, then leans across his mahogany desk with its map of New Earth and compass rose and BPF symbol inlaid on it in beautiful shades of natural wood and sets it on the edge nearest me. "Fuck it, Kat. Just shoot me and get it over with."

Now I do start to laugh as I gaze at the loaded pistol lying on the beautiful desk. "Oh, no." I pick up the pistol and click the safety back on. "That would be far too easy on you." I run my hands along the pistol as I admire its lines. I sit with it in my hand, quietly turning it to see all the parts before I sigh, setting it back on the desk, and figure I'd better get on with it. I have others to torment today. "It was a video of a certain motorcycle-based rescue in Parida that I was told would never again be seen. But it has been, over and over in a loop on two large screens at every smoker since…well, just after it was made as far as I can figure."

Miles has gone practically as pale as I am in deep winter. He begins to sputter, his words falling over one another. "Kat, I swear. I ordered that video destroyed, and I even had BI scramble the feed from Parida so it wouldn't be visible here. I never heard…" His voice is shocked, and I can hear a plea in it.

I put my hand up. "Miles, I was pissed as hell initially when it came on. Considered some significant brawl-at-Ray's kind of behavior. But then I took a moment and looked around, and no one else was bothered. They were actually cheering for their 'Motorcycle Woman.' After about the third loop, I looked at it and thought: Well, shit, it may have been foolhardy, but it was a pretty piece of rescue." I laugh quietly. "So, don't beat yourself up. Though you may want to reflect on whether your reach is as far as you think."

He smiles a tiny bit and shrugs. "I probably should've had Betsy take care of it."

Now I laugh a bit louder and point to him. "Now that would have guaranteed it would be gone forever. Not to worry, though: I have it from a reliable source that the video was likely all staged, just for effect." I hear Miles snort, and I stand. "I guess I better go get pulled together for graduation." I smile at my Master Commander and friend who is shaking his head and starting to grin, probably in relief that I didn't shoot him. "Good to know where you keep that piece." I nod at the Colt. "I may have to go for it someday." I wink and watch him relax back in his chair and laugh. "See you on the green, MC."

~

I am the last general to speak as I am the newest. The crowd is restless, and the graduates look like hell.

> "Congratulations, new troopers. You have come from all over Bosch and some from beyond our borders to become something special: a trooper of the Bosch Pirate Force. You all bring your own unique gifts to the BPF, and that is important to remember. Let me give you a metaphor because I do love words. Almost, and I mean, almost, as much as I love Bosch weapons."

I draw my thigh blade and hold it up.

> "This is the knife that my papa gave me years ago. It was crafted in the artisan community in District Five by Kyran Watson, who has been crafting blades for close to half a century. It almost never leaves my side and has been with me on many a riveting adventure. It is unique and valuable.
>
> "In other lands, like many of those that make up the FA, most blades and knives are made in a factory—they are mass-produced so that each one is the same. Of high quality to be sure, but one blade made in these factories cannot be distinguished from the others. And counterfeits are difficult to discern.
>
> "But here in Bosch, we have artisans who lovingly craft our blades one at a time. Each one is unique, and a careful eye can spot the distinctive qualities and even know which artist created it. Each blade brings to those who wield it its own

strengths that the user will discover as they employ it. You are like those blades, lovingly crafted and about to embark on finding your own strengths. And know that as part of a unit or a company, you will all learn to forge your strengths together. One blade is strong. Many together are unstoppable.

"So, go forth, troopers, and make your mark. And be sure everyone knows you by your blade."

I nod to the applause and look pointedly at Matty, who sits in the officer's section with a hand on his forehead looking extremely tired and very mortified. I really want to stick my tongue out at him but figure that might not go over well, so instead, I give him a broad smile before sitting down and giving the floor to Miles to close the ceremony.

I walk into Barton's after all the festivities for lunch with Bailey. They have taken Demery's departure hard. I've tried to assure them he just needs space, and it is not a personal snub, but I can only reveal so much. It makes my heart hurt to see them sad, and I want to spend time with them.

I see them at a booth, but they aren't alone. Matty, Aaron, and Rash are with them. I start to chuckle as I make my way through the place, crowded with parents, grandparents, and siblings of our newest BPF members. I'll be able to accomplish a couple of things this way.

I slide into the booth, sandwiching Matty between Rash and me. He sits staring at the tabletop, hands on either side of his head, elbows on the table. "You look like shit, Warner. What's your problem?" I look around and the rest of the table is staring at me. I nod with nonchalance. "Aha, I see Matty told you about our little conversation last night."

Bailey turns their head and gives me a side-eye. "How come I never knew about this?"

I shrug. "It was right after...you know.... And I was in that Bad Place." I see a dawning realization on Bailey's face, and we lock eyes, remembering.

Then Rash says, "I fucking told you that was real." And he smacks Matty in the arm. Aaron is just gazing at me dreamily, and I flutter my lashes, evoking a laugh.

Finally, Major Matty Warner speaks, droning, still staring at the spot in front of him on the table. "After I left you, I went back to the gym and tracked down the troopers who were cleaning up and made them give me a copy. Then I took it home and watched it over and over, eventually slowing it down to watch it frame by frame. It was about four bells when I finally really saw it."

I look at Bailey, then Aaron, then Rash and smile my most evil smile and cut my eyes toward Matty before giving a schoolgirl titter, linking my arm through Matty's and beginning a rapid-fire monologue. "Oh, sweetheart, I really think spring is the best time for a wedding. Much better than summer. Of course, it does depend on when my divorce is final. I am hoping for a great, big, public proposal. Maybe skywriting, or you could write me a song and perform it, even though you have certainly made your intentions known to everyone, but that's not really the same as a good, old-fashioned proposal, is it? No, no, not at all. I, of course, will want to meet your folks in that charming little vineyard you speak of and let them know just how adorable our little love story is. Maybe we could even leave the church—we go to church, don't we?— on my bike. That would lend a roundness to it all, but I do wonder if it would muss my dress. I will want a big creampuff of a dress. And a long, flowing veil, and about six attendants all in shades of pink. And you, you handsome devil, you: We will get you all gussied up in a bright pink suit with nice, tight neckwear. And then we'll have to discuss children. Of course, there are my three, but what's three or four more...?"

"You have got to stop...," moans Matty. And the entire table erupts in laughter. He finally looks at me. "I still can't even fucking believe it."

I give him a sideways grin, waggle my eyebrows, and say, "Believe it, buddy. I was on my way to crazy town then. And here, I didn't know you went in for the crazy, Matty. Best be careful." I pat his cheek, and he rests his face in my palm, his eyes studying me. I look at him and smile. "Maybe not a pink suit...." I wink and give his cheek a gentle slap, turning to look at our other friends, who have gone quiet during this exchange. "So, how'd y'all like my speech? You know, the knife being unique and all, since I was using it in the video...."

Bailey raises their eyebrows and glances between Matty and me. "It was a bit obtuse."

I wrinkle my nose and finally get to stick my tongue out. "You're obtuse. What are we drinking?" I look up to signal an order and see Lydia looking at our table, and she looks pissed. "Uh-oh. I may have just made things more difficult for you, Matty."

"How?" He glances over and then drops his head back on the table, blowing out a puff of air defeatedly. "You are the absolute worst, Kat Wallace."

"Thank you," I say brightly. "And by the way, this is far from over, fly-boy. I plan to get lots of mileage from this. Now, who wants a beer?"

I hear Matty say, "And a bump."

TWENTY-TWO

This Thursday

BOSCH, FEBRUARY 3, 2365

Quiet is not the norm at my house. But it is so very quiet. Usually, I am met at the door by two boys talking over each other and asking about snacks, dinner, and such, and then a pre-teen girl typically appears at my elbow with some complaint about the boys getting into something of hers. And there's typically an adult. I see no sign of Riki—hard to miss—nor is Mama anywhere to be seen. Where is everyone?

The first indication something was amiss really came when I got to the gate and saw no toys strewn across the yard and the drive, though I wouldn't realize that clue until later. I made my way to the stoop and opened the blue door I like more every time I see it. I dropped my coat and bag in the living room chair, sighed because I had a lousy week and there was still another day to go, and looked around, perplexed. So quiet. That's when I began to get nervous. Now, I check my weapons and start to move intently through the house.

When I get to the bottom of the stairs, I hear muffled voices. I breathe a sigh of relief; they are here, but I'm still cautious and feel a bit on edge. Then I hear another sound.

Something I haven't heard before in the house. It's a guitar being strummed a bit laboriously.

I tiptoe upstairs and follow the voices to the boys' room, where I push the unlatched door open slightly and see Kik and Grey each safely curled on the top bunk, absorbed in watching something. I follow their eyes, and what I see astonishes and delights me: Sitting cross-legged on the large pillows the boys often use to build vessels and bases is Mac, holding a guitar that looks as big as he is, peering at his fingers intently as he strums a chord. Next to him, Major Matty Warner is hunched over, long legs also folded beneath him, scrutinizing my son's small fingers and adjusting them with his own large ones and murmuring suggestions. If that wasn't remarkable enough, I see a gleam on Matty's head and realize he is wearing the tiara that Grey typically keeps securely on her desk in a place of honor, having been given it during a dance recital some five years earlier.

I give the door a push to fully open it, and Kik says brightly, "Hi, Mama!" Grey smiles down from her perch as well. I wiggle my fingers and blow them both a kiss.

Mac glances toward me and calls excitedly, "Mama! Look what I know so far." And he strums. "This is a C chord." Strum. "This is a D one." Strum. "And this..." His fingers fumble a bit, and Matty helps place them properly. "...is an F chord." Strum. "My hands are small, but Matt says he'll bring a three-quarter-sized guitar next week for me to use, and I'll be able to get to the chords better!" His face is glowing. I can't help but mirror it.

"That's so amazing, Mac!" I am delighted for him. He has wanted for this a long time.

"We should probably wrap it up for today." I hear Matty's deep voice, and I realize it's the first time I've heard it in days.

I frown and think back. Graduation was last Saturday. He

was pretty tired then and ended up in what looked like an intense conversation with Lydia after we ordered a round of beers. I had to leave before he returned from that as I had promised the kids a long-delayed winter beach trip. Yes, he was at the BtS meetings, which is what the project is now being called, but he showed up with Kaitlin Pruitt, didn't really say much, and then left quickly once the meeting was concluded, not staying to just talk and maybe get an empanada. But then, I've been pretty busy this week as well.

I look at Matty. His eyes glance back and forth between me and the floor, and he smiles, but it is tight-lipped. I mouth "thank you" and smile warmly when I catch him on an up-glance. He nods. I'm now beginning to think I may have gone a bit overboard with my "Motorcycle Woman" teasing. I have been known to push things a bit far. I'll talk to him later and probably apologize.

"Well. I should probably get dinner started…," I say.

Grey pipes up from the top bunk. "Can Matthieu stay?" *Hmm. Matthieu, huh? Not Mr. Matthieu. Interesting.*

"Of course. It's the least we can do for this generous gift of a lesson," I say.

"No, Mama. Two lessons. He and I worked on breathing… No, breathe…" She looks to him for help.

"Breath management," he says with a smile.

She smiles as big a smile as I have seen since Edo. "Right. Breath management. Breathe in for three, hold for three, breathe out for three." She breathes along with her words. "And…" She takes a belly-breath in and blows it out in a hiss.

Matty stands up, shaking his legs slightly, then nods approvingly and ruffles her hair. "You are a quick study, Grey."

I look at Mac and Grey. "Well, we should definitely feed

him. Two lessons? He must be tired." I look at Matty. "Can you stay for dinner?"

He glances at me, and I say, "Teasing will be kept at a minimum."

He grins and nods. "I told Kik I would talk with you about him going to Seven this weekend for his first Gramps lesson."

"Well, that's exciting as well. I'm sure he will have a great time." I start back toward the stairs.

"Hey," Matty calls, and his voice sounds friendly and regular. "I'll help.

I had planned a simple meal of fish and some broccoli I got at Azizi's on Monday and start to the icebox to pull things out, but Matty stops me, saying, "Wait." He fiddles with his device, and I show him how to link to our speakers, and before I know it, there is music reverberating through the kitchen.

"Okay, then. Let's see what our options are." He opens the icebox and begins to pull things out, tossing items to me and each kid with directions for preparations.

Matty looks at me as he hands me the broccoli and smiles a full Matty smile. "You chop. I understand you are good with a knife."

I roll my eyes and laugh, taking the vegetable from him. Then the kids and I watch as he shuffle-twists over to the stove in time with the music, and that is enough for my three miscreants. They are all in, peeling, stirring, and toasting as directed, as well as spinning and dancing, which causes a few collisions.

"That's why I had your mama use the knife," Matty says merrily as he helps Kik up from where he fell after bumping into Grey during a spin and dropping carrots on the floor.

I laugh, hold the blade above my head, and offer a few dance moves, which causes the children to whoop and Matty to laugh.

Grey starts to say something to Matty about his crown, but I wave her off and wink, and that makes her giggle furiously.

A raucous half-bell later, we sit down to five plates of orange-glazed salmon with roasted broccoli and carrots sprinkled with toasted almonds. The children are delighted by the meal they helped create and eat every bite.

After we clean up and the children head to their rooms to take care of any lingering schoolwork that needs to be finished before the morning. I offer Matty a glass of wine, and we sit down in the living room.

"Hey. Sorry if…," I begin.

"Stop. Don't even think of apologizing." His hand comes up like a traffic cop from an Old Days movie.

I laugh. "Well, it seemed like you were avoiding me this week, so I thought…"

"You thought I was mad? Let me tell you, it's been a shit week, and I really wanted you to be to blame for it."

I laugh. "Maybe I was. Or maybe Motorcycle Woman was." I wink.

He waggles a finger at me. "One and the same. Which I'm still wrapping my head around." He grins.

"I get that. But still, thanks for making good on your presents to the kids. People don't always keep their promises. You did. It means a lot. Grey and Mac were obviously thrilled. And Kik seems excited for this weekend."

There is a pause, and I see Matty take a drink of wine, then look off to the side and actually bite his lower lip. "Um, about Kik's trip to Seven..."

"Yeah…?" *Oh, please, don't back out, Matty—he'll be so sad,* I beg in my brain.

He looks at me. "I was thinking maybe you all could come. Riki too." He leans his head back. "Shit, Kat. That damn pasta thing got postponed because of the ambush, and now it's happening this weekend, and I thought…" He gesticulates so vigorously that wine slops out of his glass and lands on his lap and the sofa. "Oh, shit, I'm sorry." He stands up and heads to the kitchen for something. I am currently in the midst of a laughing jag.

I am just winding down when he returns with some cleaner and a cloth and begins blotting the stain. "So, wait. You want Motorcycle Woman to go as your fake date, huh? Won't that piss Lydia off?"

Matty turns, cleaner in one hand and rag in the other, and gives me a dejected look. "I don't think so. Remember the shit week I mentioned? It started with Lydia telling me she had someone else she wanted to see and that we had 'run our course.'"

I pull air in through my teeth. "Ouch. But, hey—at least she wasn't champing to get married."

He nods as he gives the spot another spritz and a scrub. "Yeah, but I'm usually the one to break things off, and this felt...unpleasant. It really has made me rethink dating."

I puff a short laugh. "I hear you there. That shit is ugly from where I sit. But sorry about Lyd. She is sweet. With great…"

"Stop it—don't remind me." He sighs. "Anyway…pasta thing?"

I shrug. "Why the hell not? I no longer have to negotiate the shark-infested waters of my marriage. Can I be all 'take no prisoners,' or do I have to play nice?"

Matty shrugs back. "Mmmm, we can ask Mae, my mom. She knows those old birds best."

I stand up and grab the wine bottle to refill Matty's now mostly empty glass. "Sounds good." I look at him, and I feel my face soften. "Hey, I didn't like spending the week without talking to my friend."

He grins and looks at me, his dark eyes friendly and warm. "Me neither. I think that's what really made it a shit week. Let's not repeat it." He lifts his glass.

"Agreed." I clink it with the bottle in my hand, and we each take a healthy swig to seal our deal. "By the way, nice crown."

I watch his hand go to his head, and he begins to laugh.

TWENTY-THREE

Pasta Thing

SEVEN, FEBRUARY 5, 2366

"Kat, dear?" Mae's voice comes up the stairs. "Are you ready? We need to be at the restaurant a bit early."

I am eyeing myself in the mirror, with Grey sitting on the bed behind me in our guest room. The boys have a room that shares a bath and toilet with us, and Riki has a spot across the hall. Matty, I imagine, is getting dressed in his boyhood room that likely is lined with ribbons, trophies, school projects, and cards from a long line of sweethearts tucked neatly in the frame of his mirror.

"I'll be down in a flash, Mae," I call. "So, what do you think, Grey? Over the top?" I tug at the sides of my snug, leather-like skirt that stops just a hair below my mid-thigh and press in my still vaguely round, twins-did-me-in belly. I am wearing the skirt and a short-sleeved gray knit top that fits closely and ends just at the very top of my skirt, with a square neckline that dips slightly to the tops of my breasts. Mimi let me borrow a silver necklace of hers I love, and gold and silver earrings that Bailey lent me dangle from my ears. I feel attractive and fit, and maybe just a little bit sexy, though I can barely remember that part of my life.

"Oh, no, Mama," Grey says breathlessly. "You look beautiful."

I grin at her. "Thanks!"

"I wish I could go to the pasta dinner," she says wistfully.

I run my fingers through her wavy brown hair, combing it and twirling it with my first finger. "It's just for adults, sweetie. Don't rush it. You'll be there all too soon." I kiss the top of her head as she gives a deep groan.

I feel a bit sweaty, even though it is chilly both inside the big, rambling house and outside. I imagine that's the nerves. I promised Matty to make enough of an impression that the old ladies would leave him alone, which seems important to him. After all, that's the whole reason I'm here, right?

The Warners have been so gracious and welcoming. We arrived last night, and Mae and Matty's dad, Stephen, had laid out bread, cheese, and fruit, along with grape juice for the kids and wine for us. Matty's unit had said coming here was a treat, and they are right. After I got the kids tucked in, Mae even asked if she could come and read a story to the boys and then to Grey, which all three were quick to agree to.

Mae is lovely both inside and out. She is not tall, maybe half a head shorter than me, with her dark, tightly curled hair cut short and a bit of silver shot through it. One look at her, and it is apparent where Matty got his gorgeous skin from—hers is the same lovely copper color. His height, though, came from Stephen, who is tall and broad-shouldered like his son. His skin has a mahogany tone to it, though I imagine lots of his color has been enriched by years working outdoors in the vineyards.

We stayed up a bit late and drank, perhaps, a bit more wine than usual, but we had a wonderful time getting to know one another. Riki told stories of his childhood in Edo and dodged other questions artfully, and Mae was on a roll, telling stories about Matty that had him blushing and laughing into the wee hours. Stephen also shared some delightful tales about serving with Papa "back in the day," and those I couldn't get enough of.

Both of them were beside themselves with excitement and laughter when they heard of Matty's and my plan to ward off the older women who were committed to finding him a wife. Mae had several good suggestions, and as I look at myself in the mirror one last time, I believe I have implemented them.

Grey skips downstairs ahead of me, where Riki waits with Mac. Kik is with Grandpa Charles Warner today, working on stories and poems, and Mac is a bit adrift without his twin and has been hanging on Riki. I slip on my low-heeled black dress shoes and come down the broad, wooden staircase. When I am on the landing, four steps up, I hear Mae give a little gasp. "Well, General Wallace. You certainly don't look regulation today! And I mean that in the very best way."

I beam and see both she and Stephen smiling at me and nodding in an approving way. Mae looks quite lovely as well in a cream colored sheath dress with a coral wrap and a strand of black pearls. She had shown the pearls to me earlier in the day.

"Matt brought these back years ago from some adventure in the Southern Sea." She had said when I commented on them.

"They are so lovely and so rare," I had said as I admired them. "I remember my friend, Dale, bought two from an island peddler, back when I was on the *Kingfisher*. Matty must have had to use all his negotiating savvy to come away with enough for a full necklace." I made a note to ask him about that adventure later.

I give a little turn on the landing, and Mac gifts me with a little round of applause, and Grey is glowing. Matty, on the other hand, went from his eyes wide and his mouth hanging a bit loose to tightly drawn eyebrows with his lips pressed together. He is dressed very nicely as well, with dark-brown pants and a jade-green sweater with the collar of a white shirt peeking out.

"Yeah, yeah," I say, vaguely annoyed at his expression, "I know. I'm a mom and moms don't dress like this. But you want those old birds off your back—or don't you?" I trot swiftly down the stairs and go to kiss Grey and then Mac, who is ensconced in Riki's lap. Riki glances over at Matty and whispers to me, "I think Warner-san is quite pleased by what he sees." Then he gives me a nod and a small smile.

I tilt my head, consider that, and lean in toward his ear so my children don't hear. "Then he fucking better figure out how not to look like he is offended by the sight of me." I lean back and grin. "I'm going to have some fun today." Riki gives a slow, low chuckle. "You'll come over to the restaurant in a bit? The Warner brothers have arranged for a sitter, and I've left directions." He nods his assent. I smile back. "Wonderful."

I wave to the kids as I head to the door. "Have fun meeting Grumpy Matt's nieces and nephews!" We all head to the vehicle, Mae and Stephen chatting and Matty scowling.

"Wait, my bag..." I run back to the house and grab my small black bag from the front hallway table.

I slide into the back seat next to Matty. It is silent until Mae gives a little cough, and I see in the rearview mirror her glance toward her son.

Matty clears his throat. 'Um, Thanks for doing this, Kat. You... You look nice."

I glance up to the mirror again, catch Mae's eyes, and give a little smile. "Listen, Major, I don't look nice. I look fucking amazing, and those old women won't know what hit 'em."

We all start to laugh, washing away any lingering tension, and head for "the pasta thing."

The "pasta thing" is really quite fun. Upon arrival, Mae and I go straight to the kitchen to help out with the setup. The smells are amazing and send my mouth watering as I watch chefs chop herbs and stir a variety of sauces. The entire kitchen staff is lovely, and we are laughing and preparing platters, already taking a few nips of wine.

Then from the swing door of the kitchen, I hear, "Mae Warner, whatever are you doing? You should put your feet up and let my staff wait on you." I look over and see a very pretty woman in a shimmery, rose-colored dress and very high heels with a golden complexion and her blonde-streaked hair up in a bun. I put two and two together and realize this is Rita Altera, née Moretti: *the* Rita. Her green eyes move to me and flick over my face and body, her eyebrows creasing slightly. *Judge much?* I decide while she is not in the group I came here to wow, I can include her.

I grin and don't wait for Mae to introduce us. I extend my hand and arm, turning it so my pilot's tattoo is apparent. "Hi, I'm General Kat Wallace. You said 'your staff.' You must be one of the Morettis. It's my first time at this 'pasta thing' of yours."

Rita frowns a bit, lifting her hand, and I see her eyes cut to my tattoo. *That's right, I fly with the big boys.* She lightly lays her hand on my arm, barely touching it. I grasp her elbow firmly and give it a gentle but clear shake, which causes her to inhale slightly. "I'm Rita Moretti. It's actually called the annual Moretti Community Foundation Charity Event," she corrects as I release her arm.

I shrug and feel my sweater come up, exposing my belly slightly and showing a bit of the birds in flight I have tattooed there. "Oh, Matty just calls it the 'pasta thing.'" I turn to a young server struggling with a heavy tray. "Here, Kian, let me help." I take it easily onto my shoulder and head toward the door that Rita leans on, saying, "'Scuse me. Nice to meet you, uh…Rita, right?" as I push by, leaving her holding the door for me. As I glance back, I see Mae biting back a grin.

I am now in the main part of the restaurant, and I see what can only be my target audience come in as a group moving as one, plump little women all shoulder to shoulder and peering about at the people already here with nervous but interested eyes. They make me think of a covey of partridges, and I intend to bag them all. I have been chatting with Jeanette, who is finishing secondary and is unsure whether to enlist or go to a university first. I point out the old women and smile at her. "Gotta go. Showtime." She looks curiously at me, and I grab my first real glass of wine of the day from a tray and then grab another, scanning the room for Matty.

He is standing and talking with his father and what must be his two brothers; they look so similar to Stephen and to Matty. I make a beeline for him, remove the beer from his hand, and hand him the wine. "Ready?"

He looks over his shoulder, sees the covey, and lets out a groan. I glance at the probably-brothers and give a small wave. "Hi. Kat Wallace: savior to your brother. We'll catch up later." Then I look at Matty and pick a speck of lint off his sweater. "Now, sweetheart, you don't have to do anything. Just look pretty." I flash a mischievous smile that makes him laugh, and he stands up straight and offers me his arm.

We slowly promenade about the room, greeting people who know Matty and not me. It occurs to me that this is just one of seven districts, and each seems so removed from the base and even the city. That should change.... I smile and nod as I am introduced, but I make sure we don't get caught before we are close to the nesting grounds of my marks. Upon approach, I release Matty and push him toward them. I lean up to his ear and whisper, "Flush 'em out and I'll take them down."

One sees Matty and flutters over, placing a hand on his arm. "Oh, Matthieu. Here alone again...?" This apparently is a call to the rest of the covey who all begin their approach. Time to use Dad's old shotgun. I slip next to him and take his arm with both my hands, leaning in closely and possessively and looking at the lead partridge. "Oh, no. I've heard all about you ladies from my Matty." I release his arm with one hand and shake a finger merrily at the birds, saying, "He may have been coming to this 'pasta thing' alone up until now, but I won't be letting him out of my sight around you naughty women." I look rapturously at him and give a sigh. "He's all mine now, and you will just have to look elsewhere."

After a brief moment of stunned silence, as much from Matty as the covey, they begin their *chuk, chuk, chuks* with me, asking me questions and giggling. Matty stands still for a moment, then slowly peels his arm from my hand and backs away toward his brothers and father, who have been watching the spectacle unfold. When I glance over, I see them raise their beers to me in a toast as they start to rib the youngest member of their group.

~

It is to my advantage to have a colossal Edoan friend. At just about the point I was getting tired of being the center of attention and acting the new girlfriend, Riki arrived, and I became delightfully inconsequential except as a vehicle to get near this vast, exotic man. I have now handed him off to Rita, who looks incredibly tiny next to him and is escorting him about the room, making introductions.

I return to what apparently is the Warner stronghold of the place. Matty and his brothers sit on tall stools, leaning on the wall while Stephen stands and leans on the high-top talking with a rather handsome, lighter-skinned man with thick, dark hair. I grab a beer from the ice barrel and hold it up.

Matty holds his out. "To a job well done, General." Our bottles meet and we drink.

One of the brothers, who is a little shorter than Matty and a bit thicker through the middle, grins. "Until next year, when they'll want a wedding invite or a baby."

"Or both, preferably," says other brother, who is lean and colored like his father.

I scoff. "Well, that shit ain't happening. Unless maybe Riki finds the girl of his dreams."

Thicker brother leans in. "I'm Franklin. I'm this kid's oldest brother." He points the neck of his beer at Matty. "Call me Frank. What the hell is that guy?"

I smile and tilt my head as I watch Riki, the social butterfly. "Oh, him? He's my kids' nanny. And a yakuza foot soldier."

The man standing with Stephen looks at me and then at Riki with a bit of concern. "Is he dangerous?"

Matty doesn't move from his perch. "Take it easy, Vinnie. Riki is a great guy. Unless you threaten Kat or the kids. Then he'll snap you in two like a dry twig."

Lean brother is also languidly leaning on the wall. "Seems like a helpful sort." He raises his beer to me. "Paul. I live in the middle between these two clowns." He gestures between Frank and Matty. I nod to him and smile as he continues, "I met Riki when I dropped the kids at the house. When I left, they were climbing him like a mountain, and he was throwing each one to the floor with just the right amount of *umph*. A tiny bit for the littles and a bit more for the big kids. They were having a ball."

"I completely adore him. He has more patience than I do. And is so very kind. I've never seen him angry...even when..." I trail off, figuring that I don't need to tell the tale of the fumbled assassination attempt in Edo, but my hand goes automatically to my neck. Matty grins at me because he knows the story.

Vinnie, who must be Vinnie Moretti, Rita's husband, stands. "Okay. We need to get our seats. Pasta is coming out." He motions to the door, and I see Jeanette and other servers begin to carry large bowls to the bench tables.

I have now eaten all the pasta I possibly can, in all its permutations. But it was delicious. I am leaning back from my seat against the brick wall behind me, contemplating my newly gestating pasta baby and rubbing it lovingly when I look up and see Aaron walking in. "Hey, Matty, look." I smack my pretend boyfriend's shoulder. "It's Aaron with a new woma ..." I trail off as the "new woman" turns, and I see Carisa's tiny form laughing and holding onto Aaron's hand. I push away from the table, standing up quickly, my fork falling to the floor with a clatter. "Oh, hell, no." And I start to move behind all the seated bodies to get to a space to put a stop to that. Matty is on my tail.

"Kat, wait...." He reaches for me and misses. "C'mon, don't go off half-cocked."

I freeze. "What did you say?" I turn to him.

"I said, 'Don't go off half-cocked.'" He is looking at me intently with a plea in his eyes.

I see Aaron spy us and raise a hand to wave. "You channeling Teddy now?" I ask.

A look of confusion crosses his face, and then he shrugs and nods. "If that's what it takes. Kat, Carisa is a grown woman. She can date whomever she wants. And it's just the 'pasta thing.'"

I wrinkle my nose and give a little growl. "Fine. Scene avoided. But I don't have to like it. And I will speak to her later."

"You do you, Kat. Like anyone could stop you." He breathes a small sigh. The two people in question come up. "Hey, Aaron, glad you made it...and it's Carisa, right?" Matty's voice is hearty, and I see him clasp Aaron's arm in a warm greeting.

"That's right. You're Matt?" Carisa's voice is small and light and needs to not be so close to Aaron, the Don Juan of Bosch. "Kat!" She comes and gives me a hug. Her head barely reaches my chin; she is so petite. I put my arms protectively around her. I can feel happiness exude from her, and I look at Aaron.

"How you doing, Kat?" Aaron's voice is friendly and sincere.

I keep my arm on Carisa. My eyes narrow slightly, and my tone is flat. "Aaron," I say shortly and see Aaron's eyes widen. He glances at Matty, who shakes his head and waves his hands vaguely.

"Come say hi to my brothers, and I'll get you two some pasta and wine," Matty says and then punches my shoulder. "Right, Kat?"

I give a disgusted exhale. "I suppose." And we walk with the two people, who are most definitely not a couple, back to where we had been sitting.

I'm spending the latter part of the evening visiting with some of the District Seven folks. Partly because I don't want to be around Aaron and Carisa because I will likely come unglued, and partly because I want to know who these people are and what they want. I haven't spent much time in the districts other than brief visits, and listening to the people talk makes me realize how different their views are from the city and especially the base. These are the people of Bosch, but the things important to them are a far cry from the priorities of Glitter runners and troopers. I wonder how different the other districts are.

A man's voice pulls me from my musings. "General Wallace, huh?"

I smile and, while not in uniform, nod and see an older man, taller than me and broad through the shoulders with silver hair and a round face. The face isn't particularly friendly, though. "Yes, sir. And you are?"

"Name's Gilbert Denton. I own the heavy equipment shop in the central village."

I smile pleasantly. "Good to meet you, sir."

He looks at me. His eyes are cool, and his tone carries doubt. "Is it? You know, I went to school with Naomi Dawes. She was Isaac Cowan's mother."

I lower my head and take a breath. "No, sir, I didn't know that. What was she like?"

He seems a bit thrown by the question but answers, "She was a damn good woman. Caring, great mother. She loved Isaac. And you got him killed."

I hear another man say, "Gilbert, this isn't the place."

He turns to the man. "Why the hell isn't it? It's the first

time I've seen any type of Force brass out here. I got a right to say my piece."

"But it's a charity event, Gilbert," a woman in the group says.

I put up my hand. "Gilbert's right. He should get to say his piece, whatever the place. Go ahead, Gilbert."

So, Gilbert does. "You and that Generals' Table and Miles Bosch and hell, even Teddy Bosch before him, sit in the center of the island making rules and sending our kids off to foreign lands, teaching them to loot and sell Glitter. But out here, we respect others' property, and we don't use Glitter and don't need to sell it. Now you come in with all that talk about saving thralls. And, yeah, I read enough to know you used to be one..." He points to my arm as I stand quietly. "...and I'm sorry that happened to you, and I don't hold with thralldom like some of those blue folk, but that doesn't mean I want my markers spent on sending kids off to get themselves shot and killed..." Gilbert takes a breath here. "...trying to rescue thralls and breaking their father's hearts." The whole side of the room has gone quiet, even though Gilbert isn't yelling, just speaking his piece.

"The trouble with you generals is you think you know what's best for everyone. But, hell, you never even ask what we want. The damn Council doesn't even ask anyone beyond the city. We in the districts...we might as well be living in another land until you want some wine or fruit, or cheese, bread, or bricks, or your precious Glitter. All the City does is take. Never gives. Never once. And I was okay with that, mostly. Until you started taking our young people and sending them back in sails." He stops and stares at me.

I have no idea what to say. But I know I have to say something. "I'm so sorry about Isaac's death, Gilbert. And Tony's,

Stef's, Kajetan's, and Elina's. And I never, ever want to have another trooper return from a mission in a sail.

"Now, I am new to being a general, so I can't speak for those more seasoned. But you are right, I am ignorant of the districts—a fact I am just starting to realize and, though in Teddy and Miles, you would not find two more compassionate hearts or two hearts more dedicated to Bosch, it may be that they also neglected to get to know all the people of Bosch. And you are right: We of the table and the Force and the city need to not close our eyes and turn our backs to the needs of the districts just because we have done so for so long while still profiting from the riches that are produced from the peoples in One, Two, Three, Four, Five, Six, and Seven."

I pause and think for a moment. "But in the same way, those in the Force and the city *and* the districts must not close their eyes and turn their backs to the plight of those kept enslaved across our planet whose blood and sweat and tears produce so much of what even we import. Even *you* import. We began as a nation of thralls. They are us. We are them.

"The truth is, Gilbert, we are both right. And we are both wrong. And the only way for us to find the right path is by listening to each other's piece. Thank you for sharing yours."

I look at Gilbert Denton, whose face is now not quite so hard. He nods. Then he gestures over to the bar. "Can I buy you a glass of wine, General? I believe we both have more to say."

I nod, and we walk to the bar as the room around us begins to buzz with life.

By the time we leave the "pasta thing," the stars are out, and I have had more than my share of wine. Riki tucks, if a man his size can actually tuck, into the back seat. With many grunts and Edonese "hmphs," "ughs," and, "pardon mes," he slowly fits himself into the space, knees almost under his chin, effectively crushing me between Matty and him. I am exhausted. I lean my head back on the seat, and Matty grins at me. "Has my little general had a busy day?"

I laugh and give my voice its North Country spin. "You district folk, you sure get a whole lot of living done in one day. I'm not sure I can keep up the pace."

"Gotta get it in while we can. Tomorrow will be quieter. I'll take you by my great-grandparents' abandoned place that I'm restoring before we head home." And he begins to describe a rambling house with a wide front porch and a view of a vineyard, and I smile at the image of what he wants it to be, but then my head dips, my eyes close, and I fall asleep on his shoulder.

TWENTY-FOUR

Okay, So Therapy Is an Ongoing Process

BOSCH, MID-FEBRUARY 2366

"You can't go out with Aaron anymore, Carisa." I am in Carisa's small apartment near the university, laying down the law on this. "He just plays with the people he dates. You'll end up hurt, and I don't want that for you."

Her eyebrows go up, and she looks at me with a shadow of a smile. I see her reach up and finger the large scar on her right shoulder. After a somewhat uncomfortable pause, she asks, "Why did you come for me at Abernathy's that day, Kat?"

"What? That's not what we are talking about."

"Answer the question."

I toss my hands in the air. "To get you away from him. You know that. We had tried to run together from Bellcoast, and I hated leaving you behind. I wanted you to have..." I trail off.

"What did you want me to have, Kat?" Her voice is steady and as strong as I've ever heard it.

I swallow and look off to the side and mumble, "Freedom."

"I'm sorry, I didn't hear you. What was it you wanted for me?" There is almost an amused tone to her voice.

I sigh and speak louder. "Freedom. But I still am responsible for you, Ris."

"No. You still *feel* responsible for me. There's a difference." She looks at me reasonably.

I growl slightly. "You've really embraced the therapy talk, haven't you? Nanette must be thrilled," I say with a begrudging tone.

Her laugh is like little bells tinkling. "Actually, yes. She is proud of me, and I'm proud of me, and, I dare say, so are you." I look at her happy face and know she is telling the truth.

My voice is now pleading. "But Ris, Aaron is...well, he's not right for you. You need someone who will cherish you. Someone who won't cheat and break your heart."

Carisa tilts her head to the side and asks with a half-grin, "Are we still talking about me, Kat, or you?"

I stare at her and have no idea how to respond.

Then I see her face become serious. "I'm a grown woman, Kat, like you. And just like you, I've survived Abernathy's horrors. But unlike you, I'm not going to lock my heart and soul away just to avoid possible pain. I like Aaron and he likes me. It may end well, or it may end hard, or maybe, it might not end. But I get to discover that." Her voice has increased in volume just a hair, and she points to her chest fiercely. Then she takes a breath and shakes her blonde head, and when she speaks, her voice is once again soft and gentle. "You didn't rescue me from being a thrall to keep me safe in a box on the shelf here in Bosch. That would still be captivity. I'm going to make my own choices and my own mistakes, and I am going to love every minute of it."

I study her face and remember when all she wanted to do was hide under a shelf, and I feel a wave of love for her. "Oh, Ris...when did you get so much smarter than me?"

She smiles. "Smarter? Or braver?"

~

I sit in my big gray chair in Ruth's office and pick at a spot on the brick wall.

"Which part was the hardest to hear? That she no longer needs you to protect her, or that she sees that you avoid intimacy?"

I study the bubbles in one of the bricks and trace my finger from one to the other. "I have kids. I don't avoid intimacy. I just don't have anyone to be intimate with anymore."

"Intimacy is different than sex, Kat, and you know it."

"Yeah, well. I don't have either, and I'm just fine." I shrug.

"Fine? Intimacy is closeness to another person that makes you feel validated and safe. Are you intimate with your friends?" She glances at her notes. She must have a whole room for the notes she takes on me. "Besides Carisa, there's Gia, Matty, Bailey... Do you still talk with Dale?"

"Yeah. A few times a month. He's halfway around New Earth, though, and has a partner now, so intimacy has…shifted." I look at the brick dust under my fingernail.

"And the ones here in Bosch?"

"Bailey, Gia, Carisa, and I are close. I can talk to them about most everything."

"Most? Deeply or superficially?"

"Some deep, some not. They don't need to hear all the gory details of my fucked-up soul."

Her pen scratches.

She looks up. "And…Matty?" Ruth's voice is level. "What can you talk to him about?"

"Everything."

"Everything?" Her voice carries some surprise.

I nod. "Yep, everything. Even things we talk about in here…. So, everything. Well, everything but…"

"What don't you talk about?" she prompts.

I start to rub hard at the brick with my thumbnail now. "You know, I just don't want her to get hurt."

"Carisa? You see that as your responsibility? Why?"

I glance over and frown at RTT. "Because I... I need to... She needs to be safe."

"And it's your job to keep her safe? To keep everyone safe? You know that is outside of the locus of your control. We've talked about it."

I nod and return to my brick-picking.

"You changed the subject when we started talking about what you and Matty don't talk about."

"Yes, I did." I use the tone that says *don't ask again*.

Ruth pauses, and I hear her pen scratch again.

"Okay then, let's go back and talk about your sense of safety and how that ties into your need to protect."

I am not looking at her. "What's wrong with staying safe? What's wrong with helping others stay safe?"

"Nothing, Kat. But you have made a career of rescuing people. And why?"

I give a shrug. "The people I rescued seem okay with it," I say with a deliberately flippant tone.

Ruth waits for a moment and then says gently, "I am sure they all are, Kat, and that they appreciate your efforts, but I think you need to explore where so many of your feelings about safety and protection stem from to help you understand your desire to rescue. And from what we've spoken of lately, you think some of it comes from when you were taken from the North Country."

My picking gets more furious, small red particles falling to the floor. I shake my head. "No. I don't think so." Thanks, Denial, you can be so helpful at times.

Ruth presses on. "Let go of the denial, Kat."

I hold my breath. *Dammit, look out, Denial, she's coming for you.* I guess three years of Kat renovation has made her wise to my go-tos.

"Last week, you said we should talk about this sometime. I think now is sometime." Her voice is soft but clear in its focus.

I can feel my pulse increase and my breathing accelerate as Ruth shuffles through her notes and continues. "You had described running into the woods when the traders came for you. You told me that you thought you had your baby with you. The baby that you think was lost in the North Country."

I punch the brick I have been clawing at, scraping my knuckle and drawing blood. I quickly put it in my mouth and taste the coppery flavor. I close my eyes; I can see myself running, but it's like I am watching myself from far away and above. The young woman-me has long hair in a braid and a long skirt, and there's a bundle in her arms...and she's scared, so scared. I can hear heavy footsteps behind her and underbrush cracking. Then…I gasp, wrap my arms around myself, and draw my legs up, so I am in a ball. "I think the traders hurt him. I couldn't…" I am breathing hard.

Ruth's voice is kind. "Take your time, Kat. What couldn't you do?"

"I couldn't...keep him safe." My brain shuts off the image, and I drop my head down to my knees and start to cry. Who needs tissues when you have leggings?

TWENTY-FIVE

Another Thursday

BOSCH, MARCH 3, 2366

I am sitting on the sofa watching and listening to Matty play Spanish guitar while he sits on the edge of the gray living room chair. I smile to myself. My three perfectly safe children are sitting on the floor at his feet, watching his hands and fingers move rapidly and listening intently. When Mac first asked if Matty would play a song or two before they went to bed during their now-routine Thursday night lesson, I was expecting some cleaned-up version of the rock and roll songs he'd often play at Barton's or for base festivals. So, when he launched into a five-minute, Latin guitar piece, I was astonished. In a good way. The music is so evocative and intriguing. It is even a bit sexy, which is nice and a little weird at the same time.

He plays two or three songs and then wraps up the recital, and I walk the kids in to brush their teeth before they get into their pajamas to be tucked in. I consider offering Matty a glass of wine as I have done the past four weeks but suddenly think that he may have better offers than sitting and shooting the shit with the general in my living room while three kids sleep.

So, while the children are busy brushing and washing, I walk to the dining room to release him from any obligation. I find him at the bar cart surveying the options.

"You want a glass of wine now or after the kids get to bed?" His back is to me, and I smile. I am thankful for a friend like him.

"Does it have to be either/or?" I ask warmly.

He lifts a bottle and turns with a glass in hand and extends it to me, his face relaxed and apparently happy. "Nope." Then he pours his own, walks to the sofa, and sits down with a sigh. "I like this spot." He moves his butt back and forth on the cushion. "I think it's beginning to form to my ass just right."

I laugh. "Well, I'm glad, but that certainly is not something they teach about in hostess school, or whatever the hell they call that." I sit down on the edge of the gray chair, where not long before some amazing music was created.

He leans his head back and closes his eyes. "They only teach about taking care of guests in hostess school or whatever. I'm not a guest. I'm a…fixture."

"Like a faucet?"

"Mmm-hmm, but I don't leak."

"That wine spot on the couch begs to differ."

"Was that Mac calling you?"

I stand up quickly and then realize the house is silent. "Fuck you."

Matty just laughs, and I go to check on the kids since I am already standing up.

A quarter-bell later, I return and sit back down, happily seeing my wine glass is refilled. I look over at the sofa, where Matty has turned and has stretched his sock feet out, flipping through a book of poetry Teddy got me from Old Days by the poet May Sarton. I sit back in my chair. "So, I'm flying out tomorrow early. Abernathy is due to be traveling to New Detroit by vehicle, and I think I'll have a pretty good shot at him."

Matty looks over to me, and there is the slightest pause. "Why?"

"Why what?" I am perplexed. "Do you mean why do I think I'll think I have a good shot?"

"No," He looks across at me. "Why are you even going?"

I consider the question. "Because it is on my yearly to-do list. Because I have backed off it being a monthly list item because RTT thinks it borders on Obsession, who I might add is big and kinda pushy but also immaculately groomed, unsurprisingly." I see Matty chuckle. He has asked me to describe what my personified emotions look like, and it's pretty fun. I go on. "Because it's my job to prove RTT wrong. And because Abernathy is a sadistic son of a bitch who needs to die."

He looks over at me and says placidly, "I've never actually been in therapy, but I'm still pretty sure that's not how it works."

I scowl at him. "What do you know?" He knows a lot. I have shared most all of what Ruth and I talk about with him.

"I guess I just wonder. What do you hope to gain from it? Assuming you are successful, which I think is a legitimate assumption."

"Are you saying revenge has no gain? Because I felt gain when we took out those traders." I rotate in my chair to let my legs swing over the arm, and my head rests on the wall.

"Well, yes and no. And I've really thought about this these past months." He gestures with his hands, and now he turns and plants his feet on the floor in front of the sofa. "There was the immediate gratification, sure. But, shit, Kat, it didn't bring Awilda back. Not that I expected it to. And you killing Abernathy won't bring McCloud back, and it won't give you back the years he enslaved you or remove the pain he dealt you. He is vice president of the FA. Kat, he is well protected. What if you get arrested by his security? What if it sparks an international incident? Can you imagine the headlines? *Bosch General Attempts Assassination of VP.* The FA would declare war on Bosch. They wouldn't have any other choice. And the absolute worst thing that could happen is, what if he gets his revenge first? Without you, where will that leave the rest of us? Hell, to be completely selfish, where would it leave me?"

My thumbnail has been working between my teeth during this monologue as I consider the questions. "I don't know...." That's all I can think of to say. Then I go quiet and realize that was the first time Matty has said any part of Will's name around me.

My thoughts are rushing in my brain. I maintain a lengthy silence trying to sort through them. There it is. The one thing we have never spoken of together: Will McCloud. I finally break the quiet because I have to know. "Bailey said a long time ago that you don't carry a grudge."

I glance over and he is looking at me, his face open and friendly with just a slight squint as he waits for me to say more. The book of poetry is still half-open in his hands. I take a deep draught of my wine and gaze over into the dying embers of a late-winter fire in the fireplace. "Do you blame me for getting Will killed?" I don't want to see the friendly look ebb, so as I say this, I look directly into the fireplace, watching the greens and blues of the cooler flames spurt up occasionally.

There is a long pause. Long enough that I am forced to tear

my eyes from the fire and look at my best friend's face. His brows are drawn, and there are a couple of folds on his forehead like copper-colored clay has been compressed. He is staring, seemingly toward the rug that is worn thin in places. There are lines on his face that I've never seen there before. He blinks rapidly.

"I'm a coward." His deep voice carries the hint of a shake as he says this surprising reply.

I am confused. I kick my feet back and turn them to meet the ground as I sit in the chair looking at Matty. "What are you talking about? You are not a..."

His eyes come up as if heavily pulled from the ground to meet mine. His look is stricken. He gestures between us. "Gen... Kat... What we have..." He tips his head back and inhales and exhales shakily. "You are the best friend I have ever had. You know me. You accept me. Both the good and the ugly. And there's plenty of ugly." He glances back at me for a tiny second and then drops his eyes as if he doesn't want to meet my gaze. "But I have kept something from you. Because...I..." He lets out an exhale, and I can hear the suppressed tears in it. "Because—shit—I don't want you to hate me. And I don't want to lose what we have."

"Matty, there is nothing—" I start, but he interrupts.

"No, don't say that until you hear me through." Now he does look at me with those dark eyes penetrating me with their intensity.

Say what you will about politics, but it has taught me to know when to keep my mouth shut and just listen. It also helps if someone simply tells you that too.

His full voice starts in. "People have always listened to me. 'Let's ask Matt.' 'See what Matt thinks.' 'What should I do, Matt?' I don't know why. It's been that way since secondary and into uni and even after. And I would simply tell people what I thought: Take the job. Leave the girl. Go back to school. Hell, enlist, enlist, enlist. And after I directed their path, I never even gave it another fucking thought." He shakes his head and rubs his scrubby beard with one hand. "Until Will McCloud came to me one spring day and told me about a woman he had fallen in love with."

I can barely breathe as I feel my tears well and obscure my vision as I silently listen.

Matty continues, "He told me the whole story, even the parts he had left out when the MC had reassigned him. He told me that this woman was married with a family, and he had to move on." He glances at me, and I quickly try and wipe any tears away, but they return. "And I agreed. He was doing the right thing. We talked, and he wanted to leave the BPF, and from what he said, I thought it was a good plan. And then…" I hear Matty take a ragged breath. "…then he told me that there was a mission he had started with your unit. He didn't give details, and honestly, I would have blown past them. I simply said, 'McCloud, you started a mission. You are honor-bound to finish it. It's your…last mission with that unit. Make it happen.'"

I sit frozen at these words, thinking a million things all at once, and a wave of nausea engulfs me.

Then I hear my friend let out a small sigh that ends almost in a sob. "You didn't get him killed, Gen. I did. Because I had to tell him what was 'the right thing to do.' Because I am Matt Warner, keeper of all knowledge and right." He shakes his head slowly. "I'm such an asshole." His right hand comes to his eyes.

I stand and move quickly over to the sofa where he sits. I gather his big left hand between my two smaller, paler ones, and give it a good squeeze. "No, Matty. No. I get it. I really do.

I still plague myself with 'what ifs.' But it's like RTT says, I didn't—we didn't—pull the trigger. Abernathy did. And he did it because he wanted to teach me a lesson. He wanted me to feel responsible. But dammit, I'm not. And neither are you. He is." My tears are flowing freely now, and I look at Matty and see his are as well.

Matty slowly withdraws his hand from mine after a few moments and pulls the neck of his shirt up to dry his eyes and nose. Then he reaches out and wipes my face of tears with his hand as I snuffle and drops both hands back to mine. I hear him take a deep breath in and out, and then the cycle repeats before he says, "Belay those tears, Kat Wallace. You are right." His voice takes on a harder tone. "It wasn't you and…" He gives a short scornful laugh. "…apparently, it wasn't me either. It was that dog, Abernathy." Here, I grin a little through the pain as I remember Teddy referring to Abernathy that way.

I stay quiet, though, and Matty breathes audibly out and continues, "Kat, I get wanting revenge and wanting to feel… maybe forgiven…maybe triumphant…maybe peaceful. But after Awilda, I'm not sure the retribution we meted out gave me any of that." He gives a rueful chuckle and shakes his head. "My nightmares would indicate it didn't. And by all the gods and goddesses of New Earth and Old, I don't want you to chase the unattainable." He turns to look at me, and his dark eyes bore into mine. "Let the past go, Kat. Burn the fucking ship."

We sit looking at each other in silence, and then we both look down at our intertwined hands and then at each other. We both smile and then glance away. Something has happened here. And I need to give it some space to see where it goes. So, I nod and say quietly, so as not to disturb what might be growing, "I'll take tomorrow off my agenda, Matty. But I can't burn that ship. Not quite yet." I feel his hands squeeze mine, and his deep voice says two amazing words, "I understand." And then he releases one of my hands and wraps a strong arm around my shoulders, pulling me toward his chest, and we lean back on the couch and enjoy the peace and pleasure of just being together.

TWENTY-SIX

The Proposal

BOSCH, MARCH 7, 2366

"You've given us a lot to think about, Wallace. Especially me," General Jamal Schneider says as he and the other three generals stand to leave our weekly table meeting. Jamal is responsible for district relations and, after I told my Seven story, which I have spent several weeks following up on and fleshing out with travel to Three, Five, and Six, the districts most neglected, we all had an animated discussion regarding what to do about it. Miles was unusually quiet throughout, nodding at our statements, watching the interactions, but saying almost nothing. So, I asked Helen Wolcott, who is in charge of internal base communication and communication within the city, if she and Jamal could meet with me the following day to come up with a preliminary plan.

"I see no reason to sit on this and let it die in discussion," I had said and received resounding agreement from all the generals.

We are now wrapping up and gathering our material to go back to our offices and attend to our agendas. Phil Patel, the tactical general, and I are the last to leave and are still discussing my weapons wish list when I hear Miles say, "General Wallace, a moment please."

I glance back and see him standing near the French doors to the small balcony, looking out through the glass to the green that is alive with troopers. "Sure, Miles." I turn to Phil. "We can finish this later." And he nods and continues out the door, letting it close behind him.

I walk over to the opposite side of the doors where Miles stands and move the curtain aside. "It's a great view." I see Teddy's statue from here, though it looks tiny, and a little distance away, I see the hangar and airfield. I watch a vessel take off into the clear blue sky and smile. To the left, I see the top of the two-story, brick barracks building and the mess close by. The gyms are on my right, and there are various half-buildings set up outside that get used for drills. In the very distance, I can see the taller buildings downtown that bleed into District One. The trees that are scattered on base have a mist of green on their branches, and I can see places off base with actual wooded areas that have a mix of evergreen and hardwood.

"Have you figured out what you are doing with Ludlow in the long run?" Miles' voice is casual. This is a topic we have discussed a few times.

I watch some tiny troopers chatting on their way to somewhere on the green. "No, not entirely. I told him I wouldn't imprison him, and I can't banish him, and I guess killing him is off the table, so I'm just moving him around like a chess piece."

"Well, be careful. Eventually, he'll want something, and if you can't provide it, he'll go shopping."

"You are right." I nod and we return to watching the day progress from our vantage point.

After a few minutes, Miles steps back from the door, letting his side of the sheer curtain slip back into its place. "Have a seat, General." His voice is pleasant, but there is a tone to it I can't quite make out.

"What's with all the title use, Miles?" I look at him curiously and smile as I move toward his desk and my chair in front of it.

He sits down and runs his hands along the edge of his desk, smiling, and then looks at me as I flop into my familiar seat. "That's sort of your spot, isn't it, Kat?"

I look at the chair and the area around it and give a little laugh. "I guess so. I've been sitting or standing in this general area since I was a brand-new recruit."

He nods. "First time I really saw you was when you came barreling in here, demanding we put an end to the thrall trafficking on New Earth." He grins.

"Not much has changed." I grin back.

Another nod. "Well, your entrances have become less dramatic."

"I'll work on that."

We both sit and smile. I am looking at the edge of the desk, becoming lost in memories of times with Teddy at the helm and with Miles.

"What do you think about changing where you sit, Kat?"

I pull back to the present and look up to see what the hell Miles is talking about. He is pointing with both of his index fingers to the chair where he sits.

"You want to switch chairs?"

Miles tips his head to the right and gives me his reproachful stare.

"You are redecorating?"

I watch as his head slowly tips to the left, eyes on me, expression unchanged.

He can't be suggesting what I think he is. I furrow my brow

and look at his face. He has now put on a congenial smile and is nodding.

I lift a forefinger. "Wait. Are you proposing...? No..." I scoff. "You must be kidding."

Now I see his head move side to side in what I used to believe was a universal gesture for "no," but now I'm thinking it must mean something else.

"Miles, I've been a general for..." I hold my hands up, lifting one finger at a time as I silently count the months. "... six months. I barely have figured out this job. And there is no way I'm qualified for..." I can't even bring myself to name it. Suddenly, a horrible thought occurs to me. "You're not sick, are you, Miles? This isn't...?"

Finally, he speaks. "No, no, no. I am fine. And I'm not talking about you taking over tomorrow. But this chair is meant to be yours when I leave it."

I breathe a sigh of relief. "Well, thank the universe you are healthy." I grin. "That's quite an offer, Miles. I guess it is something I could consider in the future. I mean, you have another good twenty years I could use to learn from you."

Now he starts to laugh. "Just because Teddy put in thirty-five years doesn't mean I will. Stuart and I have agreed that I'll stay until the house in Four is finished. Then I'm done."

I look at him with wide eyes. "Shit. Please tell me that you are taking it down to the studs, redoing the foundation, all that stuff."

Now he returns to shaking his head. "We did all that years ago. I'd say, it's got six, maybe seven months, tops."

My brain is ready to explode with the information it's been given. I lean over, my elbows on my knees and my fingers at my temples. "Sweet New Earth..." My mouth hangs slightly open, and I can hear and feel my breath coming fast. "Sweet

New Earth…if I can't make it through the suggestion, what makes you think I can do the job?"

Now I see his grin. "And what, General Kat Wallace, makes you think you can't? There has yet to be a job, a mission, an assignment, a project that you have not embraced and made a success of. Even if there are some missteps along the way."

Now I hoot a nervous laugh. "Missteps along the way? I think most people call those failures."

"No, Kat. Failure only occurs when you decide to never try again, when you don't learn from a mistake. Neither have ever been true for you. This chair has been waiting for you since the day you crawled onto Teddy's vessel. Now it's almost time to take your seat. I want you to be the next Master Commander of Bosch, General Kat Wallace."

TWENTY-SEVEN

Commitment

BOSCH, MARCH 10-11, 2366

There's a knock on my cobalt-blue door, and I move from where I am laughing in the kitchen to open it, anticipating feeling the warm March breeze blow in. Instead, I freeze. "What the fuck are you doing here?" Takai stands on my doorstep, clothes satchel in hand, late on a Thursday evening. I haven't seen him since my farewell scene in Edo, though we have talked, stiltedly, on our comms, about the children a few times.

Takai seems nonplussed by my greeting. "We agreed I would take the children to Edo for their week off school."

I frown. "The week off starts on Monday. And we have weekend plans. And you said nothing about coming to get them in Bosch. And certainly nothing about you appearing here at *my* home."

Takai has his "I'm so reasonable" diplomat voice on. "I think it's important they know I am still part of their lives wherever they are, Edo or Bosch."

I am unimpressed. "Mmm. How noble." I eye him with distaste. "But why are you here now?"

"I want to be here when they wake up. I can stay in the study." He glances toward the ottoman-barricaded door.

Nope. You are sure as hell not staying here. "The study is currently being restored," I lied. "I hear that Dawn has a nice spot to rent by the night just off base."

He glances over my shoulder to Matty, who stands with two glasses of wine in his hands, watching this pageant unfold, and then back to me. "You have someone else staying here now?"

I keep my face neutral, but in my head, there is knifing occurring. "It's none of your goddamn business if I have the entire base staying over and sharing my bed. Go away, Takai. Come back in the morning early to see the children and then find something to do. We are headed to Four and will be back Saturday morning for the exchange as agreed upon."

He throws his hands up. "Fine."

"Great." I swing the door shut in his face, which is what I wanted to do from the start.

Matty, the kids, Riki, and I are indeed headed to Four this holiday weekend. Tomorrow is Remembrance Day, and the sea commitments for all five Awilda team members are happening. There is always a compulsory, base-wide general ceremony at Friday dawn to honor all the troopers through the years who gave their lives for Bosch, and afterward, the majority of the base is dismissed for the three-day leave. This year, the ceremony will be more poignant with the recent loss.

The families have asked if the people who retrieved and returned their troopers would attend the sea commitments. We have not made the identities of the special unit public because the mission wasn't about us. But Miles said the families' request should be honored, and Aaron, Rash, Bailey, Matty, and I agreed. Matty has a small sloop and a slip in Saltend and has offered to take Rosie and her pirates out to say goodbye. Riki will stay with the kids on the beach until the ceremony is done; afterward, we will have a lovely day exploring Four and eating fresh-off-the-boat seafood. Then we will return on Saturday for the children and Riki to travel to Edo. Given my unpleasant and unexpected caller, I guess that they will also be traveling with Takai.

It's been a week. Miles' MC bombshell has had my mind in a whirl. I haven't had a chance to share it with anyone, not even Matty. The BtS project is still finding and freeing souls and removing waystations across the planet with no further attacks on our people. I have been carefully planting information via Demery. Grey had a small cold at the beginning of the week, and I stayed home with her, taking comms, writing reports, and making tea.

Then it was Mama's birthday yesterday, and we all gathered at the family home to celebrate. Jace Richmond was there, and it became apparent, because he kissed her in front of everyone, that the two of them had been seeing each other socially. (Is kissing in public and in front of family social or something else? I'm not really sure.) It caused a bit of a stir, particularly with Peter and Paul, but Mimi, Ryann, and I calmed them. I caught Mama in the kitchen later, and I gave her my own kiss, whispering, "Go for happiness, Mama" into her wavy silver and black locks.

She giggled, sounding about twenty, and said, "We'll see."

Carisa was there, too, alone, and I had smiled and asked after Aaron, to which she responded, looking at me with grateful eyes, "He's good. Thanks for asking." Hey, almost a month of dating—that's some kind of an Aaron record. I still worry but am trying to let go.

Matty took Kik back to Seven for a Gramps session the weekend after the handholding. Charles and Kik have formed a delightful attachment, and the four-lesson gift has, at Charles' request, been extended indefinitely. Kik is spending much of his time after school writing, and he and Mac are collaborating on a song.

Grey is definitely enjoying her voice lessons but has commented more about the fighting tips that seem to have shifted into fighting lessons from Matty and Riki. She was beside herself when she told me about the last lesson. "Matthieu jumped onto Riki's back, and Riki just looked like he didn't notice and leaned forward and just kinda did something to Matt's leg and then Matthieu ended up on the ground on his back. He kept saying, 'I can't breathe. Am I dead, Grey? I think I'm dead,' and Riki was laughing and then helped him up and brushed him off like he was Kik or Mac. It was so funny, Mama!"

I laughed along with her as she acted out both parts, first as Riki throwing Matty and then as Matty struggling on his back. "I wish I had been home to see that! Maybe they can re-enact it for us."

That made Grey laugh harder. "Oh, no, Mama. Matthieu kept saying, 'Never again. Never again.' Over and over!" She is practically falling over; she is laughing so hard.

I am so fortunate that Riki is here. He has made the transition to single parenthood so easy. He is becoming family, and I never worry about the children when they are with him. He is both teddy bear and razor-wire fence. And he helps us see Bosch with new eyes.

As far as Matty and me, we have spent much of the week

shyly smiling at one another during work hours. He left soon after our Will and Abernathy conversation. We held hands as I walked him to the door, and we both just looked at each other and grinned as he stepped out to walk home. Neither of us was ready for anything more.

Bailey has asked me why I am so distracted this week, and I have been vague, but I have spent almost every night since last Thursday spinning out scenarios in my head, a few that ended quite pleasantly. But neither Matty nor I have spoken about whatever started that night…yet. And tonight, Takai's appearance has put me in a foul mood, and I told Matty to head home. Riki, the children, and I will pick him up in the morning and head to Saltend.

The March breeze is blowing in my face, and I feel the cool salt spray of the sea as we cut through the water. I never learned how to sail, something all Bosch children learn practically in primary, but I do love the freedom and exhilaration I feel when the sail is full and the boat is running. I also like watching Matty as he maneuvers the sheets and the sails of the *Rune of Bosch,* the name of the boat. I have been told to manage the tiller, and I have to work to focus on my task when tacking and gybing are necessary. Aaron comes and sits next to me.

"You seem to have that figured out, General." His voice is kind, which is generous, given that the last time I saw him, I raged at him regarding Carisa. Of course, that was before she set me straight.

I look at him and give an abashed smile. "Well, you know how much I like to be in charge of the direction everything goes."

He laughs. "I've heard."

I take a deep breath of the delicious air and look at the marvel of the deep blue-green sea meeting the light blue of the sky at the horizon. "Sorry for being a jerk, Aaron. I'm glad you and Ris are both having a nice time together."

I feel his big arm go around my shoulder. "Now, was that so hard, beautiful?"

Now I laugh and shake my head. But then Aaron leans in. "Here's a little secret: I really like her."

I look at him, and there is a seriousness to his face, even though his eyes are twinkling. I grin. "Well, that makes two of us."

We approach the sacred site and see the five funeral ships just tying up to the mooring buoys. Miles' twelve-meter sloop, *The Escape*, is already there.

"That is a proud ship you have there, MC," Matty radios Miles as he brings his sloop around to moor it. He is close enough that he could talk loudly and Miles would hear him, but we want to be respectful of why we are here.

"Thanks, Warner. Yours is a graceful ship as well" comes the response.

"It used to belong to Gramps. Hence, all the brightwork," Matty says with a smile.

"What's brightwork?" I ask quietly.

Matty points at the shining wood around us. "All of that." Then he adds, "It's a whole lot of work, but it is real pretty."

The ceremony begins and we all stand at attention on the *Rune* as Miles does on the *Escape*. Stuart simply stands next to Miles with his hands clasped in front of him. We watch as each family says their final goodbyes to their loved ones, and then we salute as Diaz, Rivers, Cowan, Ratliff, and Taylor are gently released into the sea to their ultimate rest. I've never been to a commitment, so I am not sure what to expect next. I watch as each family tosses a few flowers off the side of their ships to float on the surface and everyone begins to sing "The Farewell Shanty," and I join in. When we finish, I hear Maria Diaz's voice on a loudspeaker.

"I speak for all the family members of Awilda when I say 'Thank you' to the troopers who risked their lives to bring Tony, Kajetan, Isaac, Stef, and Elina home. Thank you for honoring them and honoring our request to come to their last farewell. We will honor your desire to remain anonymous but will always carry your names in our hearts along with our fallen." Then on each ship, each family member, even the Diaz children, return with small, paper boats to the sides where they had cast their flowers. They pause for a moment, holding them to the sky, and then light each one on fire, with Maria and Tony's mother, Beatrice, helping the children. There is another tiny pause, and they drop them to the sea. The little ships float and spin and look like flaming flowers among the other blossoms. Then they are consumed, and the blackened bits sink to join those they are meant to honor. The families step back, and the funeral ships unmoor and turn for shore.

There is total silence on both the *Rune* and the *Escape*. When the funeral ships are quite a distance away, Miles calls from his place near the railing. "That was amazing. I've never seen anything like that."

"Roger that," I hear Rash say quietly.

I look around to see what he means, and I see stunned looks on my friends' faces. "What was different? This is the first one I've attended."

Bailey is looking into the sea. "The paper ships, Kat. Don't you see? They burned the ships to move forward."

The *Rune* is quiet as we sail back to shore, all of us consumed by our private thoughts about what happened. When we get near the slip, I see Matty chat quietly with Aaron who nods and then steps onto the dock and holds but doesn't fasten the mooring line. As I move to disembark, I hear Matty say, "Hold on, Kat." So, I hold on.

He comes near me and says, "We need to go back out. You and I." His face is serious, and I decide not to ask any questions at that moment. So, I simply nod in agreement.

The rest of the unit stands on the dock. Aaron says as we push off, "I'll find Riki and let him and the kids know you'll be back in a bit."

I nod and wave as Matty puts the motor on to maneuver the *Rune of Bosch* back out of the harbor.

Once we are in open water, I sit down at my spot near the tiller. "So, what's going on?" I ask quietly.

"The boats they dropped in gave me an idea. Can you manage for a moment while I go below?"

I nod and Matty disappears into the tiny cabin that is outfitted with a small sink and counter and a wraparound seating area, as well as a cramped head. He returns in a moment with some paper and pencils and sits down next to me, after surveying our position.

"Homework?" I ask with a smile.

He smiles, though his eyes are still serious. "Sort of. I never knew you hadn't been to a sea burial."

"Well, Teddy circumvented that, and Will…well, his family wouldn't have wanted me there and…"

"I didn't go to Will's either. Because I felt like shit." He rolls the pencils in his hands. "Kat, I want to write Will a letter and, I don't know, maybe apologize, or maybe just say goodbye.

And I brought extra paper and pencil in case you might want to as well."

I take a deep breath in and feel the tears threaten. "You know, for a couple months after…I would talk with him, like, a lot, and it was like he was right there, and he'd… It sounds crazy, which I kinda was…but he'd talk back. But then, when I decided to rejoin the living, he stopped showing up, and I realize now I…" I am crying now. "…never said goodbye." I pull in another shaky breath. "Let me have one of those pencils, Warner." I manage a sad smile.

We arrive at the Sacred Site and tie up to a mooring. And then Matty sits on the foredeck writing furiously, and I sit by the tiller and stare at the empty page. About half a bell later, I have finally said what I need to, and I fold my paper in half. I look up and see Matty standing next to me. "Ready?" he asks.

I nod. I stand up with my single page and look in Matty's hand, where he holds what looks like three pages covered with his half-print, half-script writing front and back. He shrugs and folds them together. I hold up mine and shrug back with a little smile.

We go to the side and look at the water. The flowers from before have already dispersed from the tight circle they had been dropped in. We look at each other, and Matty pulls the flint sparker from his pocket and compresses it in his hand, holding his letter close to catch the spark. It takes a couple of tries, but then the paper catches. Matty holds it for a few moments, letting the flames grow until the letter is almost consumed. Then he drops it to the sea. "Fair Winds, my friend." Then he steps back and wipes his face.

He turns toward me and hands me the flint. I click it a couple of times and set my page on fire, wait briefly, and drop the sheet of paper that contains four lines.

Thank you for loving me so completely.

I did love you and will always remember you.

Now, I'm ready to let you go.

Goodbye, My Will. Safe Travels.

I watch as the sea swallows the page, and the flame is no more.

TWENTY-EIGHT

It Pays to Listen

SALTEND, BOSCH MARCH 11–14, 2366

Riki sat back and leaned against the big rock, shifting the sand under his backside to make himself comfortable. He could hear the seagulls laughing and squawking as they glided above him, and the early afternoon sun warmed his face. He scanned the beach, did a headcount, and saw Kik and Mac digging multiple holes and laughing as the tide filled them. Grey was a bit farther up on shore, building a sandcastle and embellishing it with drips of wet sand from her fists. Riki remembered doing the same thing when he was a child when his mother and aunts would take him to the beach.

He continued to run his eyes up and down the beach; there was a family with two children playing some distance away, and a couple walking hand in hand away from him back the short distance to Saltend. He took a swig of the beer that Warner-san's friend, the smiling Aaron Morton, had brought him, along with lunches for him and the children. Kat-san and Warner-san had gone back out in the boat, apparently. Riki grinned to himself. He liked Warner-san. He and his friends treated Riki as a friend and an equal. He liked Bosch: the food, the people, the women. The Bosch were much less formal with their hierarchy than he was used to in the Koshijiya-rengo family. He knew his duty to Kenichi Tsukasa, the head of his work family, and to Kat-san. He worked diligently and was constantly vigilant. But he found that here, in Bosch, he was also happy. He hoped Kat-san would find happiness with his friend who always said, "Just call me Matt, Riki."

He suddenly remembered it was Friday and pulled out his comm and sent an update on Kat and the children to Tsukasa-san. He typically sent the updates when he woke to allow for the time change, but this morning had been a rush of preparation as Kat-san had her general's work to do on base before they traveled to this district, and they had to be ready to return to Edo the following afternoon. Riki frowned as he thought of traveling with Takai Shima. He did not like the man or his mother.

Suddenly, he heard a small squeal, and he immediately looked up. He assessed the scene in a flash. There were three men near the children; two held the boys, who were struggling, and the third was running to catch his Grey-chan, who was scampering quickly down the beach but away from him. Without a thought other than to protect that which was precious to him, and with the speed and agility that belied a man of Riki's size, he was on his feet running full-steam, his eyes on the children. He made no sound except the pounding of his feet on the sand.

As he came close to Kik and Mac, he yelled, "Lie down." The men dragging them toward a small boat anchored offshore turned, and both went for their weapons, momentarily releasing both twins. Each boy immediately threw themselves to the sand and went flat. Before either man could fully draw his weapon, Riki began a guttural yell and raised his arms to either side of him, stiffening his shoulders and tightening his core. He struck both men at the neck almost simultaneously and heard the satisfying crack of the spine from the man on his right. The man on the left made a choking sound, and both fell to the ground.

Riki looked up. The running man had almost caught up to Grey, and the family down the beach was retreating fast, though it looked like the man was preparing to return. He hoped he would not. "Boys. Run to town. Find Aaron. Now." The boys scrambled up and began to run.

Riki began to run again toward Grey-chan. He saw the family man yell something and begin to run toward the pursuer and the pursued. Almost immediately, he saw the man chasing Grey pull a gun and shoot. The shots landed in front of the family man, and he turned and ran, calling to his partner, who was out of sight with the children.

Riki could feel his lungs burn, and even though he was closing the distance, he knew he would be too late. They were too far ahead of him. Suddenly he saw Grey slow, then stop. She must have been exhausted. He saw the man catch up and reach around, grabbing Grey under her arms to lift and take her. Riki put on more steam, and his eyes began to water with the effort. He could barely see anything, just the shape of the man taking his Grey-chan from him. But suddenly, the man-shape was on the sand, and Grey was running toward him, yelling, "Riiikiiii, help!" She reached him and threw herself into his immense arms, and he lifted her to him. He saw the man get to his feet and draw his gun again. Riki turned his back, shielding Grey. He had taken several bullets in his time and would certainly take one now for this little girl.

As he turned, he glanced toward the town and saw, running toward him through the sand, Kat-san's friends: Aaron; the one with the braids, Bailey; and the one who always was laughing…Rush? Each had a weapon in hand, and their faces were set for battle. He began to run toward them with Grey safely in his arms.

He heard Bailey shout, "He's headed for the boat." Riki glanced over and paused in his run, setting Grey-chan down. "Wait for me here." She nodded, eyes big. Riki turned and ran splashing into the surf, shifting the angle of his pursuit to intercept the third man. The seabed dropped away suddenly, and Riki threw himself into the water and swam. He was no longer concerned for the children, but he was intent on finishing his job. He caught up to him as the man was climbing into the small boat with two motors on the back. Treading water, Riki grabbed his shirt and pulled him backward into the water, knocking his gun from his hands to land harmlessly in the depths. He used the boat to buoy him for a moment and then turned on this man who dared to try to harm the family he cared for.

The man surfaced, sputtering and gasping for breath. Riki struck him in the face and then struck him again, landing hard punches, and then grabbed him by his neck and dove, dragging him down, squeezing. He held him, watching him struggle and flail helplessly until bubbles came from his mouth and nose and trailed toward the surface, leaving a lifeless body behind.

Riki kicked hard and broke the surface with his own gasp. He swam until his feet touched sand and then trudged, dripping and breathing heavily, to the beach. Aaron was on the part of the beach where the two other men lay broken in the sand, and Bailey stood a distance back with Grey and now both Kik and Mac. Rash came up to him. "You saved the children. Thank you, Riki." He reached out two hands to Riki's arm as if to escort him. After hesitating, unsure how to configure the grasp, Rash dropped his hands, looking at the large man. "Sweet New Earth, Riki. You obviously don't need any help, and, quite honestly, me trying to help you is like the flea carrying the dog."

Riki thought carefully about the expression for a moment. The Bosch had many odd idioms. "No, Rush-san. Fleas annoy. You are a good man." And he put his arm gently over the wiry man's shoulder and leaned slightly. "Thank you. You can help me."

Rash staggered slightly, put his arm partway around the larger man's waist, and walked with Riki to shore.

We arrive at the dock, and I am surprised to see the unit and Riki sitting on chairs with Kik on Bailey's lap, Mac on Aaron's, and Grey sitting between Rash and Riki. As we near the dock, Riki and Aaron stand. Aaron gives his chair to Mac, who immediately invites Kik over.

"Something's wrong," I say to Matty, and I don't wait for the mooring lines to be tied, instead jumping to the dock. "What's happened?" I say to Riki as I step up toward him.

"Mama, you should have seen it!" Grey pops in between me and Riki before he can speak. We both look down at her. There's a small scrape on her cheek, and her eyes are lit up like it's her birthday. Her expression does not match the adults. "Come here!" Grey grabs my hand and starts to pull me to another deck chair that Aaron has brought around. The boys are cuddled together in their chair, no visible marks, though their eyes are a bit wider than usual. I see Bailey reach out and gently tousle each boy's hair, which evokes two small smiles. Grey runs back and pulls Riki in a similar fashion to sit next to me, and Matty comes and stands behind me.

Grey begins, "So we were playing on the beach...." And she speaks for about five minutes, describing in detail the sandcastle she was making and who she envisioned was living in it. I try to hurry her to get to the meat of the story, but as is typical for Grey, she just puts her hands on her hips and asks, "Mama, who is telling this story?" I see Bailey look away and cough, and Aaron covers his mouth.

I force a smile and nod. "Okay. Go on then."

And she does. I am beginning to relax a bit as the story circles around the number of holes Mac dug compared to Kik and the sweet, ordinary quality it has, when she says, "And then we saw a boat pull up, and me and Kik and Mac were watching it, and then three men waded to shore fast and said…" And here she puts her chin down and bends her elbows and talks in a deeper voice. "'Nice castle, kid. You one of them Wallace kids?' and I said, "'Nope. We're Shima kids, but our mama is General Kat Wallace.'"

My hand goes to my neck, fingering the scar, and I feel Matty's hand on my shoulder, steadying me.

"And then they grabbed Kik and Mac, and I ran and yelled."

"*What?!*" I jump from my seat. My heart is beating fast, and my mind is racing but making no sense. There are murmurs of reassurance from my friends, but I can't hear them properly. "What do you mean, grabbed your brothers?" I glance over at them and see them jump up.

"Like this…" And Mac proceeds to body-check Kik and wrestle him to the ground. For his part, Kik flails for a moment and then starts to roll and laugh.

Finally, Riki speaks, but it is brief. "Kat-san…"

"No, Riki, you aren't in the story quite yet. Sit down, Mama." Grey shushes him with a dimpled smile that guarantees he will comply, and, indeed, he nods equably and sits back, albeit with a very deep sigh. I take my seat as well.

And she continues, "So then I am running and running

down the beach, but I'm not yelling anymore, because you always say to focus on your breathing when you run, so I did a two-one pattern for fast running." I am silent, my hand at my mouth and my eyes wide.

Kik jumps in. "And the two men were trying to carry us to the boat, and Riki came running down the beach like he got shot out of one of those old cannons in the Pirate Park on base…"

"…and he told us to lie down and then he ran into the guys," Mac says grinning at Riki, who nods his agreement with the way the tale is being told.

Kik adds, "He...what does Mama M call that?" He looks at his sister.

"Clotheslined them."

My eyebrows go up, and I look at Riki, who frowns. "I do not know this expression."

Grey, still fully in control of the dramatic presentation, answers, "It means, like, they ran into a rope that you hang laundry on, right at their necks." And she pretends to hit herself in the neck with the blade of her hand, making a little choking sound and sticking out her tongue.

Riki pauses and has the look he gets when he learns something new, a look we have seen often during the past six weeks. He nods. "Yes, then. I *clotheslined* them."

Grey smiles approvingly. "Then he started running for me, and I was getting tired, so I stopped running."

"What?!" Apparently, that is my only approved line in this Grey Shima production because Grey smiles and repeats herself.

"I stopped running, and I let him grab me."

I am about to explode into a million pieces.

"And then I did that leg thing to him that Riki did to

Matthieu, and it worked! He fell over and I turned around and ran back to Riki."

I am simply staring at my daughter. Riki has the good grace to look away, eyes to the side. I can feel Matty's body and hand vibrating with suppressed laughter. I flash a look back to him, and it immediately subsides. There is not one scenario I have ever heard of or considered to prepare me for this parental moment. I run through all the possible responses in my head. And I breathe, and breathe, and breathe some more. *Watch this fucking emotional-control moment, RTT.* "Well…" My voice comes out high, and I clear my throat. "Well…it certainly sounds like…" I smile and catch my breath. "…it was exciting…and a bit dangerous."

Grey says emphatically, "Oh, no, Mama. It wasn't dangerous. We had Riki there."

And all I can think is, *And thank the fucking stars of the universe for that.* I am stunned at how they can be so unflustered by their attempted kidnapping. I will need to hear about this situation from the adults, though not with the children present. I glance over to the ice pop shop and reach into my bag for a few markers. "Seems like some ice pops might be needed. Can you three go get some for all of us?"

Kik, the truth-teller, says, "We already had some. Rash bought them for us."

Rash shrugs.

"Well, a day like today is a two-ice pop day. Go on," I urge them, pressing the markers into Grey's hand.

They have never before had something that merited two ice pops in a single day, which I am currently equating as the child's version of a shot of really good bourbon. They whoop and run off.

"Quick. What really happened?"

"Grey-chan told the story correctly. I am sorry, Kat-san...," Riki begins.

"Nope, Riki. Please don't do the traditional apology. I am not disappointed in you. I am more thankful for you than you can imagine. Was it Abernathy?"

Aaron answers, "I don't think so. The guy who was still alive on the beach wrote the name Deleen or maybe Dereen in the sand after I encouraged him to tell me who his boss was."

I look at Aaron. "Encouraged, huh?"

"Gently motivated. First name might have started with an 'A,' but he got tired." Aaron grins.

"I bet he did." I reach an arm out to Aaron, and we bump our fists and elbows together. "I'll get Cal to run the name."

Matty says, "It sounds vaguely familiar."

I nod my agreement, then turn to Riki again. "Did she really upend the guy?"

"Yes, Kat-san. Quite well. Clearly, she has practiced. And the twins were very good. They did as I asked right away. They are all good children."

Rash jumps in. "We saw it too from farther down the beach. Kat. It was a solid move."

Bailey puts their hand on my arm. "She's her mother's daughter, Kat."

It's late Monday afternoon after the holiday, and Ludlow stands in the backroom of Ray's, where I have arranged this meeting to keep my chess piece off-base and safely anonymous. It looks like he's lost some weight. I would like to assist with that by cutting out his fucking tongue.

I've known since the kids and Riki told me about the kidnapping attempt that I'd have to confront Demery because while I hadn't told him my personal plans, I also hadn't made them a secret.

I stand and walk over so I am close to Demery Ludlow. He has been standing at attention, but now looks at me. "General?"

"Who's Dereen?" I ask quietly, intentionally swallowing the *R* sound to make it go to either possible name.

Ludlow frowns. "I don't know that name."

"Don't lie to me, Ludlow." I hear my fury creeping into my voice.

He moves out of attention and looks me in the eye. "I'm not lying. I don't know anybody named that. Do you want me to ask Paddy?"

"You know they failed." I watch his face.

He narrows his eyes, and I can't see deception in them. "Who failed?"

"The kids are fine. The kidnapping failed." I still struggle to keep my voice steady saying this, though this is the fifth time I have said it, first to Miles, then to Cal, then Mama, then Takai.

Demery's face comes alive, and I see anger in it. "Your kids? Grey and Mac and Kik?" Who did it?"

"I thought maybe you'd know."

There is a long pause, and Demery is looking at me open-mouthed and with questioning eyes. "Dammit, do not tell me you think I had anything to do with this. I like those kids. I've played with them at *your* house. Remember? Back when I had friends? I'd never do anything… Do you really think…?"

"Then who?" I am leaning toward believing him.

He turns from me, walks over to a window, and looks out for a long moment. "New Earth, I miss the base." He stands silent for a minute, and I let him. Then he turns and there are tears in his eyes, but his face is angry. "Give me more detailed, more seemingly classified information." He walks closer to me.

"Instead of letting it slip like a boozy clown…like the clown I was, I can play a traitor. I'll start selling the information." He shrugs a little. "Paddy already trusts me more since I had a few choice words about you." He glances up to try to read my face, which I am working to keep blank. He leans in. "General, they are just kids. They shouldn't… No one should… Let me find out who's behind this. Who this Dereen is."

Miles leans back, puts his feet on his desk, closes his eyes, rolls his neck, and moans quietly as he does. "Before you tell me your news, let me tell you mine." He says this without opening his eyes.

I commed Miles after I returned to base in the early evening to tell him about my meeting with Ludlow, and he said, "I just got back from the Council meeting. Come talk to me in my office." So, I headed up to the third floor, and I am now seated in my chair.

"Okay…shoot." I am in no hurry as I have nowhere to go. The kids are in Edo and Mama and Jace are visiting District Five for the Five Alive Arts Festival.

"First, old news: Howard Archer hates your very existence."

I nod. "That tracks. The feeling is mutual. Has he painted himself fully blue yet?"

"Pretty close. But he was talking all kinds of shit about you, first, in general in the open session, and then, you and the BtS project in the closed session."

"What the fuck does he know about the project?" I lean forward.

"Well, that's the thing. He should just know what I report…"

"Why do you have to give him a report about BtS?" I realize that this is something I have overlooked.

Miles opens one eye. "Well, he's on the Council. And I report to the Council."

"You report on everything?" I am getting nervous.

Now he opens both eyes. "Yes, Kat. It's part of the charter: The MC reports the goings-on at the base to the Council."

"Wait. So, do you have to report details about the Burn the Ship project?"

"No. I can maintain classified information to keep troopers safe and I do. And this was what was interesting: Archer started ranting that you were trying to get more troopers killed by sending them out dressed like marauders, and he was surprised there hadn't been more ambushes. But I never said in my report the project was operational; I just said it was moving forward." He looks at me.

I let out the breath I have held as he says this. "So, this might be a good time to tell you that I approved of Cal Greene's investigation into Howard Archer?" I smile and try to look innocent and charming.

Miles now sits up and stares at me through narrowed eyes. He is not smiling. "Excuse me? General Wallace, I think you overlooked a step in the approved process."

"So, can I approve…?" I begin unnecessarily.

"Sweet New Earth, Kat. He's a senior council member. What are you thinking?"

"Cal and I are both thinking he could be a leak."

He inhales deeply. "That could blow up in your face."

"Or it could plug the leak." I decide to push on so he can't get too wound up about my supposed oversight. "Speaking of which…" I give him a quick overview of my conversation with Demery Ludlow.

"Do you trust him?" Miles looks at me.

I pause and consider. "Mmm. He seemed in earnest. And I think there is no harm feeding Paddy false-ish information. And having two people investigate the Dereen name—Cal and Dem—doubles our chances of figuring this out."

"Agreed." Miles nods then tips his head. "You know, that's the first time you haven't called him Ludlow."

I give a quiet snort. "You sound like my therapist. There's no hidden agenda or feelings, though. He is a tool to be used, and he may be able to get us the information we need."

"You want to tell me you won't feel responsible if something happens to him?" Miles asks.

I look steadily at him. "You know, that is a theme in my Tuesday sessions, but if you are offering me this office one day, which I have not yet said I want, won't I be ultimately responsible for everything that happens? Aren't you?"

Miles looks at me and slowly nods. "Yes, if I have all the information." And he raises his eyebrows to me meaningfully.

TWENTY-NINE

It's for the Best

BOSCH MARCH 14, 2366–LATER THAT MONDAY EVENING

I stomp into the hangar and see a stray wrench on the ground. Leaving tools out always annoys me, but right now, it really pisses me off. I pick it up and wing it against the large metal doors, where it gives a loud *clang* and then a satisfying *clatter* as it falls to the floor, causing the rest of the late-evening crew to hush momentarily and look to see who is making a point.

"It's just me. I'll take care of it," I say to the open air around me, loud enough to reassure the troops. The hum of work resumes as I walk over to retrieve the offending tool and put it away.

As I am returning it to its place on the workbench, I hear a familiar voice. "What'd that poor wrench do to you? Or the wall, for that matter?"

I look up at Matty as he stands in work pants and a plain, tan, short-sleeved shirt. "Wrong place at the wrong time. What are you doing here so late?"

He shrugs. "Just running some flight checks before mission tomorrow evening." Then he tilts his head. "What made you so mad?"

"Not what, who. Three guesses," I say and can feel my jaw tighten.

"Hmm, let's see. How about Takai, Takai, Takai?"

"I can't stand sharing a planet with him, much less the best kids on that planet. He wants them to stay for some fucking festival through next weekend, and they, of course, want to. I swear, Matty, except for those three exceptional people, those thirteen years were a fucking waste of my time." I stomp and growl.

Matty looks at me and leans back onto a Whydah tire. He frowns and tips his head. "Shit."

I know he sympathizes with me, but this particular expletive does not seem related to my current rant. "Shit what?"

"Did you know that Lydia has requested that I not be seated in her section at Barton's anymore?"

"Ouch."

There's a long pause. "You know that little deli over on Third?"

"Skyman's?"

"That's the one."

"Yeah. I go there a lot. It's the only place to get bagels that the kids like."

"Right. Get me one sometime. I can't go there anymore. I used to date Eliana, the owner's daughter. And afterward, her mom threatened to poison me if I came in."

"Seriously?"

Matty nods. We glance at each other. I think I see where this conversation is going. It's something I've thought about as well, and I suspect it is what has kept us both from moving beyond the handholding, shoulder-leaning, and moony looks of the past week.

"I just don't seem to be able to do the amicable partings

that Aaron manages. I'm actually persona non grata all over town."

"How about on base?"

"Diamond Miata sneers every time she sees me."

"Careful. She's a good shot. Did she really hit you when you broke up?"

"So hard." He rubs the left side of his face.

"Now I know why you go for the young ones. You've alienated all the ones your own age."

"That sounds…frighteningly accurate." He releases an audible breath.

"Well, I can't criticize you. While I don't have the breadth, I make up for it in depth. I mean, I have to fight the urge to attempt to flay Takai every time I hear his voice. And when he showed up the other day..."

"You looked pretty murderous that night."

"Yep. I'd be delighted to never have to see his stupid, lying, diplomatic face again. Unless it was pressed into the dirt as I pounded the back of his head with a hammer."

"Nice image."

"Thanks."

Our eyes connect and we both know where this is going. But we have to give it a voice.

"You and Gia ever fight?"

"Sure. But then we talk, and it's all good."

"Bailey?"

"Oh, yeah. But you know Bailey. Can't stay mad at them."

"Rash and I don't actually fight because he is so easygoing. But he's been pretty annoyed with me before."

"Who hasn't?"

Matty laughs but there's a sad tone underneath it. "Aaron and I have actually come to blows a couple times over the years. But the next day, we are out having a beer."

I lean back onto the tool table I had set the wrench on and sigh. I can feel the tears that want to come, but I cram them into a box for Remorse and his little brother, Regret, to hold for me until the walk home. I wonder why my bad feelings all identify as male. There's a Tuesday topic. "Well...shit."

"Yep. Shit."

We look at each other for several long moments.

"I can't lose my best friend."

"I can't lose mine."

I see all the scenarios I had spun waver, fade, and disappear.

We both give a deep sigh, almost in concert. As usual. "Well, then, I'm glad we didn't let things get out of hand."

"Me too."

"Still on for Thursdays?"

"Oh, definitely. Well, once the kids are home."

"Right. Good."

"I guess I'll see you next Thursday then."

"No. Tomorrow. We have a BtS logistics meeting."

"Right."

"Let's not let this be weird. Empanadas as usual tomorrow?"

There's a pause and a breath.

"Absolutely. Empanadas as usual."

"Okay. See you then."

"See you then."

Then my best friend, Matty Warner, and I look at each other, nod, turn, and take separate paths.

Part III

THIRTY

Information

BOSCH, APRIL 2366

Commander Eliot Conrad ran his fingers over the spines of the books in the military history of Bosch section as he glanced up and down the aisle. The early afternoon sun shot rays through the window, and there were dust motes dancing and floating in the beams. He spoke in a low tone, but his words were clipped. "I'm sorry, Howard. I can't help you."

Howard Archer's voice was almost a whine as he said, "But you got me those coordinates before."

Conrad frowned. "Shhhh!"

Howard scoffed. "Oh, please, there's no one in this section. Probably no one on this whole floor. Anyway, you picked this meeting place."

The commander nodded slightly, accompanied by a shrug, but he still dropped his voice to a whisper. "That was before Awilda was lost. Since Awilda, the coordinates for the BtS missions are only known by the company members and Wallace." He paused and looked down at the small man with the peculiar mustache. "And I probably wouldn't tell you if I did know."

A puff of a laugh came from the blue-suited man. "Oh,

please, Eliot, why not?" Archer kept his voice in a normal range.

"Because I don't want to see innocents die." He straightened his vest, a hand checking the medals and ribbons, including the small blue one, and stood a little straighter.

"Innocents? Have you seen how they fall in line behind her?" Howard sneered. "They get what they get following that woman. And we talked about the fact that a few pawns would have to be lost to win the crown."

"Well, you didn't get me elected general, so any crown will go elsewhere." Conrad's voice was bitter.

Archer paused and carelessly picked up a book titled *Strategies and Counterstrategies of Extraction Work* and thumbed through it as he said without looking at his co-conspirator, "If Wallace is taken out, then the space opens up again. And you know she flies with her units, so…"

Eliot Conrad glanced at the Council member and looked toward the top shelf in the stacks. "If I could get the coordinates of where she was in particular, then…"

A slow smile began to develop on Howard Archer's face. "Exactly. Remember what she did to Master Commander Emeritus. She is no innocent. She is a foreigner who wants to contaminate Bosch with all those escaped thralls. You want your kids in school with theirs? Or hers?"

"No. I do not." The commander's head shake was definitive.

"Then why don't you see what you can do? It's not for me. It's not for you. It's for Bosch."

The tall man curled his smooth hands into fists and nodded his beautifully coiffed head. "For Bosch."

Council Member Archer shut the book in his hand with a small thump, dropping it onto a random shelf as he urged, "For Bosch."

The two men dipped their heads to one another, then turned and left the university library through separate exits, both different than the ones they had used to enter. On the other side of the military history stacks, where she had placed herself after following the first man, feeling his behavior was odd, Carisa stood still and silent, eyes wide. She took a breath and thought, *Kat.*

It's a warm, late April day, and Bailey and their new gunner partner, Tania, as well as Matty and I are sitting in the grass on the green, just outside my office, enjoying after-lunch conversation and sunshine when Matty looks up, and I see his face curve in delighted surprise. "Dem?"

I whip my head around and see Demery Ludlow coming at me at a trot. He seems unwaveringly focused on me as he hustles up. "I need to talk to you." His voice is urgent. Then he pauses and looks around as if just seeing there are other people present. "Uh…hey, Matt. Hi, Bailey."

"How the hell are you, Dem?" Matty's voice is hearty and friendly, and he stands and grasps Demery's arm in greeting.

"Demery." Bailey's voice is neither hearty nor friendly.

I don't have time to sort out the emotions of the people around me. Mine are complicated enough at the moment. I want to know how in the hell Demery Ludlow got on base with no ID and against my expressed instructions. I tamp down my annoyance that is steeping into anger, then stand and say with as casual a tone as I can muster, "Demery, good to see you. Why don't we go into my office, and you can tell me what brings you over to the base?"

"Yeah, okay, Gener… Uh…well…," he says, frowning slightly. Before we turn to go, he says to the group, "It was good to see you." But he is looking at Bailey, who looks away. I see Matty furrow his brow at the interaction and then look at me with a question on his face. I give a smile, but I know it is tight, and I know Matty can see through the ruse. I'm going to have to confess some of this to him later.

"Let's go, Dem," I say, and I hear the tension in my voice as we walk quickly to the Bosch Hall. He starts to speak, and I hush him through gritted teeth. "Not until we are in my office."

I take the stairs two at a time, making Ludlow hustle to keep up with me, and walk briskly past Olivia as she starts to tell me, "Demery Ludlow…" and trails off as she sees him come in on my heels.

"I know." I shut the door.

I don't even speak. I am so angry. I just sit down and stare.

Ludlow leans forward and his face is animated with excitement. "So be pissed, Kat. But listen—it isn't Deleen or Dereen or Desseen, or any of those fuckin' names we've been a chasin'. It's DeLeon, Alejandro DeLeon, of the South-Central Continent thrall cartel, and that bit only cost me rum and flattery. But I bartered something more."

"Hold. Spell it." I lift one finger to pause him as my anger evaporates.

"D-e-L-e-o-n." I write the name on a pad of paper on my desk and then look at Demery. I start to grin, and so does he. I reach for my comm and dial it, still looking at Dem. "Cal—how about: DeLeon?"

~

"So, I want to bring Paddy in. I think it's time. He knows this DeLeon. Who knows what other information he has stashed in that swindling brain of his? We can press him to flip. Cal agrees," I say earnestly to Miles.

He nods. "I am on board with that. But I don't have to tell you to watch your step with Paddy Owens: both in the grab and the interview. He seems to be something of a wizard at getting out of situations."

"More like a snake. But I've dealt with him so much, I know how to snake charm him," I say disgustedly and think of all the markers I paid him for Abernathy information over the years. I am about to comment on that when Betsy opens the door and walks over to the desk.

"Kat, Olivia just commed. She says you are needed down in your office right away."

I look at Miles and sigh. "Can we continue this in a few minutes?"

"Go. I'm not going anywhere. For a few months."

I grin and shake my head. "You just stay put for now." I head for the door and the stairs.

I start talking as I walk into the office. "Olivia, what's up?" And then I see a tiny blonde woman pacing restlessly inside the open door to my inner office. It takes me a moment to process as she is out of place. "Ris?"

She turns at her name and comes and grabs my hands. "I have to tell you something." And she pulls me into my office and shuts the door.

A moment later, I stick my head out. "Olivia, get Miles down here. Now."

THIRTY-ONE

Mission

BOSCH AND AN EQUATORIAL JUNGLE, MAY 2366

Two of Papa's favorite authors from the Old Days both wrote in their works, "The game's afoot." And indeed, it is.

The combination of Demery acquiring DeLeon's name and business, and Carisa having done amazing work tracking, overhearing, and memorizing the conversation between Eliot "The Tool" Conrad and Howard "The Fuck" Archer in the stacks pretty much have made these past few weeks better than any birthday.

Paddy is still in play per Demery's recommendation a few days earlier. "General, you know Paddy: He has his fingers in everything. I am sure he knows more, and I can get it before you pull him. What I get won't be nearly as colored with the wheedling and truth-bending you are liable to get from him when he feels cornered."

He is right and I will tell him that, but first I have something I need to say at today's meet-up. "So, Dem…we found the leak that led to Awilda's deaths. You're off the hook for that."

He sits, unspeaking, and stares at me.

"You still broke the code, what with the Glitter-skimming and some of your loose talk, but..."

When he finally speaks, his voice is quiet. "I told you, I never gave the locations. And I was sure I hadn't, but that day, when we got back...I was sick with worry wondering if I had said something, anything, when I was drunk. That's why I couldn't go on the retrieval. I was afraid to see what I might have contributed to...."

I nod. "Dem, I did what I had to do as general to protect the company, the force, and Bosch." I blow out a sigh. "But as a friend, because that's what I thought I was, I owe you an apology, not just for thinking you could have given Awilda and the rest of us up, but I'm sorry if, before that, I came across as some asshole fairy godmother, barreling in and taking over. That's not how I wanted to do things. I'm sorry if I've excluded you."

Demery stands and again walks to the window and gazes out.

I take a breath. "You still have to answer for what you did do, but I see no reason you can't reconnect with your friends. Our friends."

"Bailey wouldn't even look at me," he says, and I hear sorrow in his voice.

"Everything with us has been in confidence." I want to provide some hope. "They don't think you set anybody up. They just don't get that you left so abruptly."

"That wasn't my choice, was it? They just seemed so angry with me."

"Oh, I think their anger may get redirected after you talk to them." I really hope Matty is right, and friendship can weather most anything. I decide to return to business. "Also, you are right about Paddy. If you are willing, you can keep up the pretense."

He turns and looks at me. "Yes, General. I'd like that."

I look at Demery Ludlow. "Good. And when, and if, you want, call me Kat."

He nods and leaves me to sit and consider the choices I may have to make if I take the job Miles is suggesting.

The second piece of information Demery gleaned from Paddy, he had to barter. Demery sold the tidbit that my ex-husband (officially now!) had angrily taken the children from me after the kidnapping attempt and sequestered them on some ship in the Southern Ocean. He would sell the name of the ship in a subsequent deal. I, of course, was heartbroken and devastated and was taking cavalier chances with my company and my own life. There was enough backstory legitimacy to the well-constructed lie that Paddy had bought it all. And he had paid well. Along with a pretty tall stack of markers, which Demery dutifully turned in, he sweetened the deal with the information that DeLeon was going to consolidate a large thrall transport, and Demery could earn some markers as a trader. Demery jumped at the chance to earn some "heavy markers" and so was told when and where to show up. Just so happens, he has invited a few friends along.

The Conrad/Archer situation has been passed to Cal. Neither of them can be taken into custody based solely on what Carisa overheard, but Archer is no longer being simply investigated. Cal and his hand-picked team are now compiling the necessary evidence to guarantee full convictions for both Conrad and him. Conrad's accesses have been shut down, and the tech people that are "working on the problem" are actually working for Cal. I don't like that either of them is still at large, but Cal says that they can both be useful in tracking if there are other leaks. His BI team plans to slip false data to them to lead to my supposed ambush and death. I won't be there, but it's still kinda creepy to know it's being planned.

"And then Shari just threw the whole thing away!" Tania laughed, describing a failed dinner experiment she and her wife had had over the weekend.

Bailey joined in the laughter wholeheartedly. They really did like Tania, or rather, Second Lieutenant Tatiana Santiago. She was young and vivacious with a roundness and balance in both her body and personality. She wore her vivid orange hair to her shoulder on her left and shorn close to her scalp on her right. And she was a damn good gunner, already picking up the rhythms and flows of partnership in the two months she had been assigned to the unit. Kat had encouraged Bailey back in January to hand-select their partner, which helped soothe the professional sting when Demery simply up and left after more than eight years of gunning together. It did nothing for the personal pain they had felt when he seemingly cut off all contact with Bailey and the rest of the unit.

Tania looked over to the far side of the hangar, where her pilot, Major Matt Warner, and General Wallace stood talking. She looked at Bailey. "So…what's the deal with those two?"

They looked over as Wallace touched the back of her hair and leaned in to say something to Warner, and then they both started laughing, their heads and bodies moving gently in what looked like a choreographed dance. Bailey shook their head and failed to suppress a smile.

They weren't quite ready to forgive Kat, who had spoken up in support of Demery when he reappeared, saying, "There was a situation that required me to dismiss him from base for a time." But she wouldn't say anything else, and Bailey knew there had to be more. They also were still hesitant to fully embrace Demery again, much for the same reason. But they knew they would soften to both of them likely sooner rather than later. So now, Bailey couldn't help but grin at their young friend's observation. "Those two? What do you think?"

Tania giggled and leaned over to whisper, "I think they are shooting twixt wind and water."

Bailey looked over at Kat and Matt and shook their head. "Nope. They are just good friends." They saw Tania look at the not-a-couple, and then back at Bailey with an expression of disbelief, which evoked a laugh from Bailey. "Or so they think. Honestly, it's just a matter of time."

"It's about what we figured," Rash says, pulling off his night vision glasses as he reports to us in the steamy equatorial night. We are about 450 kilometers south of Parida. "Big, old, dilapidated two-story school with a basement that has outside egress on the far side. We counted evidence of between twenty-five to thirty traders and guards, which is in the range Demery gave us."

Since Awilda, one person has been going in as a point-trooper to do recon before the unit rushes. With Butler unit, Rash and Bailey have taken turns. Tonight, Bailey is staying with Aaron on the vessel, and I am taking Tania through her first extraction. Demery told us that the estimate was between forty to fifty thralls being moved. So, all four liberator units were on the ground for this, and I am jumpy as hell about that. "Are those trader and guard numbers confirmed?" I asked.

"Just estimates, but that's confirmed times three," Rash answers.

"I hate estimates. I like hard details. Did you see Demery?"

"Negative. But he had said he was going to try to be part of the basement thrall team." Demery has been embedded for several days and has been able to give very few updates, though what he has is valuable. The unit now knows that Demery is working for me as an asset.

I nod. "Right. So, we will have each team take one hostage, preferably a DeLeon guard, not a trader. We'll take Demery as ours to keep his cover. One of them has got to know something about where to find DeLeon's place." That was information that Demery had tried to pry out of Paddy, but he is convinced Paddy simply doesn't know, saying, "Somewhere in the godforsaken mountains of Patagonia is all I know." That doesn't narrow it down.

Rash adds, "Dem said that lights out is at twenty-two bells, and booze has been rationed, though that comes from DeLeon's soldier-guards. The traders don't like being told when to sleep, and they really don't like their drink limited, but they are going along with it. The skeleton crew is only about ten guards and traders."

"I like those numbers." I press my earpiece and check with the four pilots. "Are we ready to roll at twenty-three bells?"

"Butler, good to go."

"Cavendish, good to go."

"Drake, good to go."

"Easton, good to go."

The game is most definitely afoot.

Twelve company members, plus me, make our way through the wilds. The moonlight trickles down in drops in the thickest part of these woods only to pour out in puddles in the clearings. We have a numerical advantage—except for the fifteen to twenty others ostensibly asleep. *Let's be real quiet, company.*

As we move through the jungle, I feel strangely unnerved. There's just something niggling in the back of my mind. I keep thinking I hear the echo of feet, different from the quiet steps of my company. I fall back to check several times, but there's no one. I chalk it up to nerves, something I didn't have to deal with while running solo. Being responsible for others comes at a price.

We come to a wire-link fence, and Pruitt cuts through it. We can see the school across a wide-open expanse. It is run-down; there're even a couple of sets of rusted swings and other play equipment not far from it. Leaving Tania with Rash, I move forward with Matty, Booker, and Carr to silence any outside guards.

There are only two, and they are quickly and quietly dispatched. Probably traders—they didn't put up the fight a trained soldier would. Cavendish and Easton report the same. That's four of ten. We call in Rash, Tania, and Pruitt. Booker slowly opens the door, and a guard stands from his post in front of another door. I reach for my knife and then halt. "Dem," I whisper.

His eyes shift and he says low, "Affirmative. This is the basement door. Two DeLeon guards are in the basement, one by each thrall hold. One guard upstairs. Two on patrol."

We start to head down to the basement, leaving him to guard, and he stops me. "When you take me, make it look real."

I look at him and wrinkle my brow. I see the old Demery twinkle as he says, "You know you want to." I shrug and give a small nod.

The basement stairs are solid, so no squeaks. The plan is to bring two of us down as if we are extra thralls. Tania and I stow our small arms out of sight in the concealed pockets and holsters under our pirate garb. Matty and Booker have thrown on the jackets and hats of the traders we took out and have armed themselves with the weapons we liberated. They take each of us by an arm and march us down the stairs. Matty calls out, "Got two more."

A lantern flares and we hear a voice from the dim. "What do you mean? No one told me…" As soon as the voice shows a face, Matty deals him a hard elbow, and he goes down. Booker jumps to restrain and gag him. At the same time, a big woman comes up to Tania and me, and before I can do anything, Tania has dealt her a double-kick, one to the middle and one sweeping her legs out from under her. *Damn, am I getting slow or is she wild-fast?* I put that on the list of things to find out. Later. For now, I take the tying and gagging job. We look around. There are four doors; one leads to the outdoor bulkhead doors, and we unlock that, letting in the rest of the Cavendish and Easton teams. We have left one member posted at each of the two doors and two inside with Demery.

Another door looks unlocked, and Tania starts to quietly open it, but an awful smell comes out. She falls back toward me, gagging. I pull the door shut, and the smell still lingers but less of it. "There's at least one dead body in there." I shake my head. "And it's been a while."

Tania looks at me. "Why?'

I shrug, though it's a cover for my disgust. "Not all thralls live to go to market, and no one in the trade gives two shits about a dead thrall."

"That's horrible." Her face is aghast.

"Yep," I say. "That's why we are here."

Sanchez, Kidd, Matty, and Banks are working on both of the other doors. These doors are newly installed and solid steel, each with a keyed lock and a small pass-through window for food. The company members are cutting through the hinges, and while I could probably manage to pick the locks, we don't have time for that; so, drills it is. Booker and I, with Tania next to me, each open one of the small windows. We can hear murmurs inside, and the smell of urine, sweat, and feces blows through it.

"Better than the other room," I murmur before calling in through the slot as loud as I dare, "Get back from the door. We are taking it down and getting you all out of here."

The room beyond the steel door goes silent briefly, followed by urgent whispers going through the room.

The hinges are now cut, and the locks have been destroyed. A couple of troopers move the door aside while two members of the company do a peek and then a push as they scan the room for any hostiles. I look first in one room and then the other as Sanchez with Tania, watching and learning, and Banks on her own, each goes in to speak to the about-to-be-liberated. I count eighteen fairly young women and six children between about nine and thirteen years old in one room and twenty women and three children of the same general ages in the second room. Forty-seven. Sweet New Earth.

The pilots and I quickly confer. Butler will take eleven since they are flying heavy with me and Dem, and the other three will take twelve. Banks and Tania, on her own, divide up the rooms. I grin at Sanchez, who gives me a thumbs-up. They ask for volunteers to pair with each child. Within five minutes, we are ready to move out.

Sanchez and Booker each take a bound guard, and I put a hand up where the soldiers can't see. I call Rash on my earpiece, and the door at the top of the stairs opens. He hustles Demery downstairs, hands bound in front of him. The Cavendish, Drake, and Easton units, along with Tania, move the freed out through the cellar bulkhead.

I glance at Dem, who gives a small nod.

"Fuck you, you traitor," I say to him with my best venom, and then I lay a good cross on him. I didn't use all I had, but I have to admit, it felt good. Suddenly, though, Demery turns back from where he had staggered and swings his bound arms like a club into my chin, knocking me sideways off my feet. Matty and Rash go to grab at him, partly in a big show and partly because they aren't sure what's happening. I'm not exactly positive either.

Demery shakes them and comes close to me with a menacing look. He glances at DeLeon's men, turns his head a little, and winks, whispering, "Now, I'll call you Kat." I want to laugh, but it would give the ruse away, and damn, my jaw hurts. Matty and Rash hustle him outside, and Booker and Sanchez march their prisoners out as well. I follow, shaking my head a little and moving my jaw side to side.

We move across what used to be a playground toward the fence that tries to keep the jungle at bay. Before we are halfway, a tall woman with a fresh, oblong-shaped welt on her face and blonde hair pulled back asks, "Who is going to get the new ones?"

We all freeze. "What do you mean, the new ones?" I ask.

The blonde gestures with her head to the house. "Ten new youngsters were brought in tonight." Her voice sounds like she is from one of those northern countries of the Eastern Continent.

I look at Demery for more info, and he shrugs. "I don't know anything about new ones. But they had me on patrol earlier. They could've come in then. And I'm not the guy they share a whole lot with."

"Where would they stash them?"

Dem shrugs again.

Blonde says, "I watched through the food slot. I even

talked to one of them. That's how I got this." She points to the welt. "They put them in the room in the basement. Where the bodies are."

Tania makes a horrified sound. I check my timepiece. And I look at Matty. The cleaners are going to be flying in to burn the place down in less than half a bell. I decide. "I can get them."

Matty speaks up. "I'll go with you."

I shake my head as I check my weapons. "No. I'll take her…" I throw a thumb toward Blonde. "…if she's willing." She nods. "One of the kids knows her, and that will make it easier. The rest of you get to the vessel." I turn to her. "What's your name?"

"Sunniva. Do I get a weapon? I can shoot."

I like her nerve. "I'm Kat, Sunniva. Somebody give her a spare," I say briskly. Rash hands her one of the confiscated rifles, and his hand goes through the essentials of it with her.

Matty steps closer to me and says quietly, "I'd rather be the one covering you."

"Nope." I shake my head. "They'll need you to fly if this goes sideways."

"Is it going to go sideways?" He looks into my eyes.

"I sure as hell hope not."

"Kat?" He raises one hand as if reaching to touch me and then drops it before he does.

I take a breath. There won't be any more Bosch blood on my hands if I can help it. "Go, Major. That's an order. Make sure the other units are clear." Then I smile at my friend. "I'll be fine, Matty. I always am."

He growls and furrows his eyebrows. "You better be. Stay safe, stay alive. Seriously."

Rash gives me a little Bosch salute, followed by a raised fist and nod. I see Dem and Tania both raise their hands in farewell.

Matty signals the group to move, and Sunniva and I watch them go until they clear the fence before turning back to the schoolhouse.

We move rapidly back toward the building, but as we turn the corner to get to the door, we find the patrol guys checking out my past handiwork with the two traders who had been posted there. I glance at Sunniva. "We need to make this quiet." She nods and I grab her arm. Maybe they don't know everyone. "The thralls have escaped. I nabbed this one." I am walking her forward, and she is doing an excellent job of sniveling.

The soldiers look up as we approach. "Who are you?" the bigger one demands.

I shove Sunniva toward the smaller one, and I push toward Big Man, drawing my pistol that I have equipped with a silencer and keeping it close to my body. He instinctively tries to push me away, but I use the advantage of being shorter and smaller. I burrow toward his chest and then turn my weapon to his midsection and fire in and up twice. I look up and his face moves quickly from surprise to slack, and I use my body to quiet his fall.

I glance to my right and see Sunniva with one hand on the other guard's crotch, making sultry moans while her other hand releases his large knife. In a flash, she takes a tiny step back and slashes his throat, blood spattering across her, me, and the wall, smiling into his eyes the whole time. I help her catch the body and then look at her with questioning eyes.

"I've been trafficked on and off since November, and I have learned things. Owners don't keep me long because..." She gestured at the body. "...I don't like being fucked with, and that's all they are interested in. One of the caveats of my sale is that I can't be allowed anywhere near weapons. But many things can be weapons."

"O-kay." I smile at Sunniva. "You may want to consider a career as a pirate."

She grins and spits on the body she has just created. "Let's go."

We slowly open the door and are relieved it is empty. We must have come across the guards before they could raise the alarm. We slip into the basement and head for the room Tania and I had passed earlier. Now I push the door open, and the smell is heavy and foul. The room itself is pitch-black. I pull a small hand light out and shine it around the room. The beam hits what looks like three adult-sized bodies shoved next to the wall. There's where the smell is.

I continue to sweep the small room with my light, and in the far corner, the light illuminates a pile of young and filthy children, a couple of whom look like they can't be more than three years old. They all stare at us, terrified into abject silence. I am sickened.

As Sunniva and I move toward them, they draw back, almost moving as one entity. I let Sunniva take the lead, and she speaks to an older girl. Older. She is perhaps eight. But she remembers Sunniva, and they share names. Sunniva turns to me. "This is Adella."

I squat down to eye level and whisper, "Hi Adella, I'm Kat. We are getting you all out of here and getting you safe." She nods wordlessly, looking at me with big, brown eyes that probably don't believe a word I am saying. I turn to Sunniva, who is touching each child's head and murmuring.

"Let's pair the littles with a bigger child. We can carry the tiniest. Let's move."

"There's only nine." Sunniva sounds unsure. "I swear there were ten."

I quickly count. Nine. "Adella?"

"A guard took a little one upstairs when they moved us to

this room." Her voice is childlike but resigned and matter-of-fact.

I feel all my systems move to the edge as my body prepares for battle. I look at Sunniva and hand her my rifle. I won't need it. "Move this group through the fence and into the cover of the jungle. I will send someone to guide you to the vessel. Just be sure you and the children are well away from the building because it's going to get hot." *The cleaners will be here soon.*

She nods and we move the children through the bulkhead doors, and I watch in the moonlight until they have all moved safely through the cut in the fence. I look at my timepiece. I will not call the cleaners off. This place needs to be shut down. I put my earpiece comm receiver on mute so I don't have to listen to the inevitable argument. "There's a kid still in the house. I'm going back in. Send two people to pick up Sunniva and the other children. They are on the outskirts of the playground, just beyond the fence. Do not come to the schoolhouse. Get them back to the vessel. Give me a quarter-bell and then get the hell out of here, whether I'm on board or not. That is an order."

I slip back to the schoolhouse and this time head for the stairs leading to the second floor. I start to mount them but find they are not as solid as the basement ones. One of the treads I can see is rotted through, and they all squeak and moan. I stay to the edge and take them three at a time, pausing after each to listen for any of the possible twenty other sleeping opponents to wake, come out, and shoot me where I stand.

But I make the top of the stairs. I look down a long hall with several doors on either side and see a small light at the end, where a guard sits with earphones plugged into an Obi device trying to stay awake. Easy enough. I toy with the idea of another hostage, but I don't have time for that. I pull my bone-handle knife and move quickly and quietly down the hall. The guard looks up as my feet appear in his vision. I go full Sunniva on him, leaning in with a hint of a smile and running my hand through his hair until I reach the back of his head. I come close as if to kiss him, then I bury my knife upward into the center of his chest. He was dead before he could say a word.

I wipe my blade on his pants and sheath it. I pull the dead man's knife from where it lay sheathed on his leg, tucking it securely into my sash.

There are eight doors in the hall, four on each side; none look like they have locks. But the question is, which one? I steal through the hall, zigzagging door to door, pressing my ear against them. Silence from the first four, but from the fifth, I think I can hear…something. I concentrate. It's quiet weeping, and it's a child; my memory hears the echoes of my own babies in the crying, but this is tinged with fear and agony. Then a memory of a past cry ignites in my brain, and the red miasma of rage flows into me.

I shove the door open, and the moonlight through the window illuminates the bedroll on the floor, and I see a pair of adult arms reaching out to grasp a small being. My body shoots forward independent of reason or logic. I have no idea if there is anyone else in the room. "Fucker!" I throw a knee to this big man's right kidney, and he falls onto the child with a grunt. I grab him by either shoulder and haul him bodily backward. As I do, he gets his feet under him and shoves me sharply with his shoulders, and I lose my balance, landing on my back. That's twice tonight I've ended up on the ground. I need to practice more. He turns and, seeing a woman on the floor, leers and points to his hard cock. "Oh, you want some? I got enough for everybody." He grins lecherously and comes at me. My body cedes a bit of control to my brain, allowing it to calculate the angles. I give a gasp and a look at him with vulnerability and fear. I remember this. I scoot slightly backward on my elbows. He leans and grabs the front of my shirt, tearing it, but I am in perfect position. I kick upward, nailing his testicles solidly. He collapses forward with a gasp and moan of agony, and I roll to the side. Quickly, I force him from his fetal position onto his back, where I deal several hard blows with my elbows to the side of his face until I hear bone crack. I hope it's his and not mine, but there's enough adrenaline running through me that I won't notice for quite some time. I finish the rip he started in my shirt and pull a length of the fabric loose, stuffing it into his mouth. He is flailing, trying to throw blows toward me. One slightly connects and I taste blood. So, I knee his groin a second time, and he shudders and the flailing ceases, and I only hear his gagged sobs.

I quickly scrabble in my black sling bag and pull out some line, neatly and tightly tying his hands and feet. I sneer at him. "You are trash and you'll be incinerated," I whisper.

Now I turn my attention to the bedroll. There is a little boy, maybe four, maybe less, naked, softly crying, and curled into a ball against the wall just past the bedroll. My battle-self steps aside to let Mama me in. I grab an old buckskin blanket lying there and wrap it around him, then lift him to my shoulder, whispering, "Shhh, shhh, baby. Mama will take care of you. Just be very quiet. No one is ever going to hurt you again." He clings to me like some of the small tree monkeys I've seen in these jungles and sobs. I take a deep breath, and the scent of the buckskin is strong. Something stirs in my brain, and I am momentarily transported to the North Country in fall.

. . .

I feel a chill wind gust briskly through the trees. It rustles the orange and red leaves that are starting to turn to a late-fall brown before they pile up on the forest floor. I can smell woodsmoke in the air as well as the ever-present smudgy scent of coal burning. I even hear the faint sound of geese honking directions to each other high in the sky as they wing their way south.

I shake my head, hold the boy closer, and move to the door. I pause next to the evil creature on the floor, and the red miasma flows again. I pull the tanned hide over my sweet little one's head, and with one hand, hold him close to my shoulder. With the other, I pull the hall guard's knife from my sash and, kneeling, jam the borrowed knife down into the man's genitals, pinning them to the floorboards. He lets out a muffled howl.

"Don't bleed out before you burn," I say with scorn.

Then I rise and, holding the boy tightly on my left shoulder, I open the door and run for the stairs, murmuring words of comfort and humming a little lullaby into his ears.

As I move down the hall, I hear voices in the rooms. I was not quiet enough. I hear the soldiers and traders getting up, coming to life, grabbing comms, yelling, and pulling on clothes. I take the stairs by threes, avoiding the ones that I saw were rotted, all while still murmuring reassurances to the sweet bundle I carry. I jet through the door I left open into the overgrown schoolyard and make for the fence, hearing pounding footsteps in the house. I am almost at the fence when I am knocked forward by a searing pain in my right shoulder. I let out a cry and catch myself with my right hand, which sends stabs of agony through my shoulder and down my back. "Shh, baby, shh. Mama is here." I continue my reassurances as the boy gasps when we tumble forward. "Mama still has got you."

What the fuck was that?! I look at my shoulder and see an arrow embedded, with its carbon shaft sticking out of the back of my shoulder. Those fuckers! "Seriously? An arrow?!" I say this out loud to no one. The little boy whimpers, so I reassure him as sweetly as I can muster, "Shhh, shhh, baby. We are going through this fence, and then you and Mama are going to fly away from here." I add my own quiet plea: "Please don't have left yet, Matty, please don't have left ..." I wriggle through the fence cut, and the long arrow shaft catches and pulls at the flesh of my shoulder. "Fuck, fuck, fuck!" I shake it free and push on toward the jungle. My foot hits a tuft of grass, and a rabbit shoots out from it, and I am once again transported.

I see the rabbit dash from a clump of shrubbery where it has been flushed by my round, chuckling child, crawling full-steam after it.

"You'll never catch him, Sean. Bunnies are too fast for fat babies." I reach down and scoop up my child, tossing my braid behind me. He always likes to pull my hair. I nuzzle his neck and blow my lips on it and am rewarded with a cackle of delight. "Let's see what your dad is up to, shall we?"

I walk with the baby on my hip, skirting the edge of the woods to where Zach, young and bearded, is building a small deer blind to prepare for hunting now that fall is here. I know that last year, he had waited until freezing weather had arrived to take the first deer because I was so very pregnant and couldn't face the task of butchering. It was far more than most other North Country men would have done. I flash on my dad talking about how he had made my mom help fell the trees and haul them to build the cabin that I was born in a few weeks later.

"Didn't hurt either of them. Unless it knocked the peg off the baby inside of her, and that's why we ended up with just a girl first

time around." I hear my dad laughing loudly and raucously as he takes another swig from the ever-present bottle in his pocket. I see Zach listening to my dad and shaking his head as he looks at me apologetically.

I come back to the present and I am panting heavily as I run. I am in the jungle. I hear multiple feet in pursuit. They are gaining. I dodge among the trees, murmuring reassurances to the little one I carry. I have to outrun them. Time telescopes again.

"It looks good," I say, eyeing the small, rough building with a slot in it for viewing and shooting. "Are you going out tomorrow?"

"I figured I would. We can place this tonight and put out a carrot pile, and then I'll tuck in before dawn and have a deer to you by lunchtime." He reaches over and lifts our son from my arms, tossing him into the air, and is rewarded with screams of delighted laughter.

"Just don't take the doe with the yearling. She reminds me of Sean and me."

"You are far too sentimental, Kat Wallace. But that's something I like about you." Zach tugs on my braid and smiles at me. I smile back and shrug.

Then we both turn as movement catches our eyes farther down the tree line. Four strange men are approaching, and they all carry weapons. "Fuck," Zach swears. "Traders. Kat, take Sean and go into the woods. Now." His voice is urgent and low.

My eyes go wide as my son is pushed into my arms. I pull him close and turn, then look over my shoulder. "Be careful, Zach. I've heard they can be mean." Then I duck into the trees.

• • •

I weave through the trees and try to make out where my pursuers are. They seem to be everywhere. "Shh, baby, shh. Mama is here." I pat his back reassuringly. I glance down at the ground as my feet just keep moving and then I trip on a root, catching myself.

I can hear the voices raised as I weave through the woods, picking my way around trees and undergrowth. I pause, turn, and can just see the men bearing down on Zach. He lifts his hands in a defensive posture. I hear the crack of a weapon and see him fall back slightly and then crumple to the ground. I start to call out but stop and, pulling my son close, I begin to run helter-skelter farther into the woods.

I trip and fall to my knees and elbows, instinctively drawing my little boy closer to my heart. I start to crawl, and the baby yells in protest. "Shhh, shhh, baby. Mama will take care of you. Just be very quiet," I murmur in his ear, and he quiets as I struggle to my feet with him still in my arms. I just have to get deep enough into the woods. Maybe I can make it to the creek and the old mineshaft. I hear nothing and see nothing but my feet moving underneath me. I smell the scent of Sean's head, which has changed since he came into my arms in blood and work but is still the sweetest smell I know. I keep up an ongoing rumble to him. "Shh, baby, shh. Mama is here."

I keep my feet under me and serpentine through the trees, but still stay true to my course to the vessel. We have to make it.

I know I will make it. But suddenly, I feel my braid grasped and pulled and hands on my arms pulling me backward, and I feel Sean wrenched from me. He starts to cry. I begin to flail and kick and hit and spit and bite at the hands and arms that are pulling me away from my son. "No!" I scream, "I need my baby! He needs me!"

He is sitting next to the sumac bush crying. I hear a voice say, "Not anymore." The report of the weapon is so deafening that I flinch and blink, and I can no longer hear my baby's cries. My eyes go wild as I search for him. Where is he? I struggle wildly against the arms that hold me. I feel myself lifted and tossed onto the trader's shoulder. I look up and can see the small legs and feet lying unmoving under the scarlet bush. I scream a scream that tears my very soul and begin to hit and kick and scratch anew. "No! No! You did not do that! You didn't! You didn't! No! Let me go! I need to go to him! No!"

There are tears pouring from me. I remember it all. The trader and soldiers are gaining on me again. "Fuckers. Not this time." And those words steel my soul, and my eyes dry immediately. Time to make a stand and make them sorry. I duck behind the largest tree I see and, breathing deeply, I tuck the little boy down between the trunk and my feet, telling him, "It's going to be okay. Mama will keep you safe." My right hand is not responding well. I am yet again glad Tommy taught me to shoot with both hands. I pull my non-silenced weapon with my left hand and check my ammo, lifting the boy with my right and wincing in pain as the weight of him pulls at my shoulder still decorated with an arrow shaft. I put my face in the boy's hair and breathe in his scent—not the same, but comforting, nonetheless. Then I murmur, "Hold your ears tight, sweetie. Mama is going to make the bad guys go away."

I begin to quietly sing an old sea shanty. "Blow the man down, bullies, blow the man down, way, hey…" Then I listen as my pursuers approach. I lean out from the tree to the left, keeping the boy safe against the trunk, and I methodically aim and shoot at each head that appears, one after another, over and over, with the deadly accuracy that I learned from Teddy until there is no more movement. I take a deep breath, look left and right, and run full steam to the vessel.

The engines are on, and I start to call, "Matty! Open up!" The cargo ramp drops before I can fully get the words out. Matty, Rash, and Aaron stand there, fully armed, ready to do battle, but seeing no enemy, they grab me and pull me aboard, shutting the ramp. Matty and Aaron jump to the helm, and we are airborne in moments, Bailey and Tania sending suppressive fire over the landscape.

Moments later, Bailey comes to me where I sit on the deck, rocking and sobbing with my little bundle, who is glued to me. "Do you want me to take him so we can look at your shoulder?"

I shake my head, pulling him closer, and whisper, "No, not yet."

They nod and move back as Matty comes and wraps me and the child in his arms, carefully negotiating my shoulder wound. He talks into my hair, and I can feel his warm breath. "We heard it all, Kat. You once again forgot to turn your comm mike off. You'd be a terrible spy." I can tell his words carry amusement, but his voice shakes a little.

I give a sobbing laugh that shifts back to full weeping into his chest. "Matty, when I was running, I remembered it all. The North Country. When they took me, they killed him. The traders, they killed Zach and Sean. They killed my baby, Matty."

He gives a soft moan and pulls me even closer, and I don't care about the small shot of pain the arrow gives me. "Oh, Kat. My sweet, strong Kat."

After a minute or two, I shift back the tiniest amount and look up at him. "I couldn't let it happen again."

His rich, brown eyes look into mine, and he smiles. "You

didn't. You got him out, see?" He pulls the buckskin back so I can see the little face now peacefully asleep on my breast. Matty turns to Bailey and Rash, who have been standing near, discussing the best way to remove the arrow in my shoulder. "Can we get a better blanket here?"

I stare at him as I hear the echo of Teddy on my first flight to Bosch. "What?"

He shrugs and smiles at me. "You don't want something softer and cleaner for him?"

I shake my head in astonishment but say, "Sure, that'd be good."

As we tuck a soft blanket around the child, Aaron says, "Cleaners are in and out. It's burning."

We are less than half a bell from Bosch with a heavy crew of seven and eleven women and ten children as freed souls. The flight home took a bit longer with the increased payload, but Rash has done some engine modifications to keep us moving at a good pace. Good man.

I am moving tenuously about the vessel, checking on the souls, especially the children. Rash has cut the shaft of the arrow off after some debate with Aaron and Bailey on the best technique, rinsed the wound with sterile saline, and put a bandage over it, admonishing me to keep my arm still after I refused a sling.

The little boy is still asleep, now snuggled in with the other children, having eaten the paltry snacks we had brought. I texted Mama, asking her to let the civilian hospital know the company will have some people we are bringing in. I didn't mention that I would be one of them. There are far too many souls to burden the base medics with, and I felt like

Mama would know the right person to call instead of Miles. I wanted it to be a request, not an order from the Master Commander.

I sit on the deck for a few minutes, watching the newly freed and remembering when I was in their place and hoping they can embrace their lives after enslavement just as much as I have. Cavendish, Drake, and Easton are a quarter-bell ahead of us, so I am surprised when Booker comms me. "General, we are going to wait to disembark until you arrive. I think you need to see this."

"See what, Ocean? It's the middle of the night."

"Yes, ma'am. That it is."

"What's going on?"

"It's a visual thing," Colonel Booker says.

"Well, we'll land in…" I look over at Aaron who holds up five fingers. "…about five minutes."

"Roger that."

A few minutes later, we are rolling up toward the hangar, and I see the other three vessels lit up in the electric lights of the hangar and airfield. Just beyond them, cordoned off with a rope, I see a crowd of people, some holding signs. "What the hell?" I turn to the unit. "Let me get out first and figure this out. What are all those civilians doing here?"

I step out and walk down the ramp. I hear someone yell, "We don't want those thralls here!" and my heart sinks. Are these Archer's followers? Have I misread the people of Bosch so thoroughly? And then I see Miles walking toward me.

"Kat!" He is smiling, but then he gets close and his face drops. "What happened to you?"

I likely look a mess. I know there is blood from my shoulder covering my shirt mixed with blood from the vanquished. I am sure my face has swelling from the blow Dem gave me as well as the one the perverted, now-roasted trader dealt me. "I'm fine. What is going on here, Miles? Since when do we have civilian protesters on base?"

Miles looks over and shakes his head dismissively. "We had to let them in because we let all the others in."

"Others?"

"Kat. Look." And he points to the crowd. There's more than the protesters. Now I see Peter and Sharon, Paul and Elise, Mimi and Ryann, the Azizis, the Skymans, Ray, Max Cooke, the whole Warner clan.... There's even Alannah Campos, who teaches the boys art. In fact, I see most of the teachers from the kids' school, and there are other faces I recognize but can't necessarily name. And Mama is walking among them all, talking and directing. I have to ask again: "What's going on, Miles? What are they doing here?"

Miles laughs. "Have you ever asked Miriam for something and only gotten what you asked for? Some are here to bring food, some clothes, some toys. Some are even here to take the freed home, Kat, to give them warmth and a safe place to rest, and some are just here to show support. They are here because you asked for help."

I am stunned and I feel tears pricking my eyes, though I have little left to cry. "What about them?" I point at the folks looking sour and holding *Go Home Thralls* signs.

Miles shrugs. "There's maybe half a dozen who disagree. But don't let it worry you. You'll never have everybody support everything you do, Kat. Hell, when Teddy tapped me for the job, I had a group of folk come and try and talk me out of taking the master commander position because of Stuart."

I look at him and frown. "I did not know that." I consider and then look out at the protesters, who look smaller and more tired than the group waiting to help. "I guess some people have very strong opinions about his art."

I glance at Miles who looks down at me and grins. "I'm going to tell him you said that."

"Oh, don't," I say quickly. "He's working on a piece for Mama for me."

I hear my friend chuckle. "Don't expect unanimous support, not if you want to change things for the better. You have enough today. Look at them, Kat: both groups. Those are your people, Kat, the people of Bosch. Now, let's get the freed settled. The hospital set up a space in the hangar."

I turn and see the four units on the ramps of their vessels waiting for a signal, and I give it.

THIRTY-TWO

Best Laid Plans

BOSCH, LATE-MAY AND EARLY JUNE 2366

"Sorry, Ruth. I know I'm late. Had some loose ends to tie up at the office. And this fucking thing isn't helping me accomplish much." I gesture at my right arm and shoulder, which is held close to my chest in a sling.

Ruth smiles at me as she welcomes me to her office and closes the door. "You're almost never late, Kat. And you've had quite a time of it the past week." I stare at my seat but hesitate to sit. I'm not sure I want to delve into the feelings of the past week. I look at her, frowning, and her warm eyes are soft, and she smiles. "We need to continue our conversation from the other night. Major Warner did the right thing by calling me to come to the base to listen. You needed to talk then, but now you've had time to process your memories of your loss and I want to hear where you are."

I sigh. Ruth knows me. "I've had good support from Matty and Mama. And even from my friends. It's...just odd. The memory of Sean was so buried, *I* didn't even have it. And now so many people know what happened." I look out the window behind the chair that I am avoiding sitting in. "Losing him and Zach feels so fresh even though it was so long ago." I glance over at her where she sits calmly in her chair. "You know, I did the math—Sean should be almost the same age now as I was when I came to Bosch. But he isn't. He never even saw one." I sit down and pull a tissue from the box and our session begins.

Grey and her friend, Leia, ran back to the house from where they had been encamped in their tree fort, sailing past the adults who stood and sat on the back porch. Grey grinned at Riki, who was manning the grill, tending to the food, and talking to a young woman she hadn't yet met. Riki's eyes were almost always on her and her brothers, which she didn't mind. Now they weren't, though, and she was glad because he looked happy.

The kitchen was bustling with adults as well, so no one bothered with the two girls who slipped in and grabbed several first-of-the-season strawberries and popped them into their mouths, giggling. Leia started to head back outside, but Grey decided to share her secret fun with her friend. "No, come here." She tugged at Leia's shirt and motioned to the stairs. Leia looked at her curiously but followed. Grey showed her the small air vent in the floor at the top of the steps, just below the stair window that opened to the backyard.

"This is my spot to learn what's going on," Grey whispered. "You can hear everything that people say in the kitchen with this." She pointed at the vent. "And everything outside through the window." She grinned as she watched Leia's eyes widen and a smile spread over her face. The friends settled in for some reconnaissance, one at the window and one at the vent.

After several minutes collecting information, they were about to switch places when Leia motioned Grey to the vent.

"Listen, they're talking about your mom." Grey quickly pressed her ear to the vent next to Leia's.

"They are both too stubborn to admit what already exists." Grey recognized Aaron's voice.

"Yes, that part of it. Also, Kat is pretty self-protective. She doesn't want to get hurt again." This was Carisa, whom Grey liked quite well. But her words made the girl sad and a bit angrier than usual with her papa. Mama was always careful to not say unkind things about Papa, but Grey wasn't a little kid like her brothers. She knew what Papa had done was wrong, though she still loved him and missed him. Leia's voice broke into Grey's thoughts.

"Who else are they talking about?" her friend whispered.

"It's got to be Matthieu."

They quieted as Aaron spoke. "And Matt doesn't ever get too serious with the women he dates. He doesn't want them to expect commitment."

Carisa's laugh rang like a bell. "Well, who does that sound like?"

Aaron's laugh joined in. "True. Well, we know that can change."

"Well, I guess we just have to be patient with them." Carisa's voice was a bit muffled, and Grey whispered to Leia, "They're hugging." The two girls stifled giggles.

Leia grinned and whispered, "Let's go to your room!"

They hustled into the bedroom and Leia turned to Grey. "So how are you going to get them together?" Grey looked thoughtful for a moment and as she began to smile, the two girls began to plan in earnest.

~

I walk up to my beautiful blue door a bit later than usual on a warm Thursday afternoon in June. I immediately can tell there is something going on. The door is wide open, and someone has put two pots of colorful flowers, just like the ones at Gia's house, on the stoop. I can hear classical music flowing from the house speakers. *Is that Rachmaninov*? I do a peek and peer at the door as if I might need to clear the room. Matty is sitting with his hands between his knees on the couch looking very uncomfortable. I tilt my head at him in inquiry.

"I was told to sit here quietly until after you came home," he says. He gestures with his head to the table.

I turn and see my simple wooden dining table—which at this time of day typically holds several leftover plates, cups, and bowls from children's snacking—looking sharp and elegant. It now sports a white tablecloth and is set for two with my best dishes. At each place are wine glasses and in the center a vase of flowers exquisitely arranged. *Well, someone who has been taught that art by her grandmother created that*. On either side of the vase are a pair of taper candles, which look exactly like the ones that are usually on Mama's mantel. If Matty wasn't here, I'd go back out and see if I stepped into the wrong place.

I walk over to the couch and sit next to him. I hear bustling in the kitchen. "Well, this has Grey written all over it."

He nods in agreement. I sit back and call out, "Hi, kids, I'm home!" I am about to chuckle and make another comment when suddenly two young men who had previously been my seven-year-old sons appear with matching jackets on—*they don't even own jackets*—and with white towels on their arms. We look at them.

"Not missing the details, are they?" Matty is grinning.

"They sure aren't." I shake my head.

Mac's face is very solemn, and he says formally, "Dinner is served."

"Seriously?" I ask.

"Yes, Mama." Kik nods. "Seriously."

I shrug and whisper to Matty, "We'd better play along; they could get dangerous otherwise." And I am rewarded by his warm laugh and a nod of agreement.

We head to the table and start to sit when Kik clears his throat and says to Matty, "Perhaps you could get the lady's chair?"

I choke back a guffaw and see Matty actually flush. He pulls out my chair and motions to it with a gallant wave of his arm.

"Why thank you, kind sir," I say as I take my seat. The boys disappear and I lean over to Matty, grinning and saying in a low tone, "I think you just got schooled by a seven-year-old."

"I totally did." He grins as well and picks up a card that is in the center of his plate. "What's this?"

I have one as well and turn my attention to it, a smile spreading over my face as I read it. "Is yours a poem, too?"

"Mm-hm. Written by Kita Keaton Shima. It's good, but he put an extra *s* in kisses."

I look across the table at Matty, and we both begin to laugh as silently as we can.

We have had a really nice meal. The courses were tasty and gave a fuller picture to the lengths the kids went to for this evening. There was the vegetable soup that I know came from Carisa, and then a pasta dish that Rash is famous for in our circle. It was accompanied by Grey's green salad, and the wine glasses never were left empty of some of the best red Warner

Wines produces. We've been trying to keep track of how many people are in on this little plot, but we keep losing count, as we are both now a little tipsy.

"I'm hoping for Bailey's cream-cheese brownies for dessert," I say, leaning over to Matty and almost tipping into him.

He starts to giggle as he catches me. "Careful there, General…" Our faces are close together and we pause for a long moment and regard each other. His face starts to move toward mine…

Abruptly, all three children appear in the room, and I quickly sit back and Matty scoots his chair a little bit farther away. I see Mac has his guitar and Kik has a small drum. Grey has on the dress she wore in the fall for her first showcase. I notice how short it is and make a mom note to take her shopping. She is growing fast.

Kik announces, "Now you will have a dance before dessert."

Matty and I look at each other, and we both shrug and stand. This will be easy. Matty's unit and I have gone out to both Ray's and Barton's, and we have all danced together to the fast beats of current-day music, and some of the fun rock and roll from the Old Days. We face each other about a meter apart.

Then Kik begins to tap out a slow rhythm as Mac starts to strum his guitar, and Grey begins to sing, "Can't Help Falling in Love."

Her voice is beautiful, and the music enchanting. I stand frozen for a moment, then look at Matty. He smiles and holds out a hand; with no hesitation, I take it.

I feel him draw me close, his other hand going around my waist, and I feel my breath catch as a thrill of desire that I haven't felt for years burns through me. As we start to sway, I lean in toward him and take a deep breath. I smell the deep earthiness of the vineyard and the salt spray of the sea and Matty. It's not the first time he has held me, but somehow it feels like it. I close my eyes and see careful Caution and doleful Doubt eye me with skepticism and then, shrugging, they open a sturdy box they have been guarding, and my heart, whole and healthy, is released, but I don't reach for it as it flies free. I let it go to where it has always belonged. To Matty.

THIRTY-THREE

Politics and Scheming

TRUVALE, JUNE 2366

President Alyssa Russell looked across the room and smiled at her Attorney General Phil Reston as he spoke to the delegation from Rus. He glanced up, smiled back, and then did a double take, his eyes and smile lingering on his bride of seven months, clearly missing something the Rus Chancellor asked, requiring Phil to shake his head and ask for Chancellor Lobov to repeat himself. The older man turned and looked in the direction of Alyssa and began to laugh, slapping Phil on the back and almost knocking him forward. She wanted to laugh as well but instead quickly turned back to listen to the Berlin-born foreign dignitary from The League of States of the Eastern Continent.

"So, tell me about your desire to change the name of International Friendship Day," Minister Steinboch inquired.

President Russell seized the opportunity. "Well, Minister, you see, by next year, I'd like to make this a day we celebrate not only our international friendships but also international freedom. International Friendship and Freedom Day would speak to our shared values regarding the essential quality of human autonomy that allows us all to choose to be friends."

"The LSEC does agree with you, in principle. However, workers are scarce for the larger industries that are developing," the minister said.

Alyssa nodded. "An adequate labor force is essential, that is true. And there are steps we all can take to attract workers that will want to call our countries their home. I believe the first step in the freedom movement would be to outlaw the actual trafficking of human beings across national borders as it has been demonstrated that the cartel-controlled movement of enslaved people is inhumane."

Minister Steinboch nodded. "Very true. I will support this." She looked at the new FA president, and then looked across the room. "It must be difficult when your second-in-command does not seek the same outcomes."

Alyssa followed her gaze to where Vice President Rob Abernathy was talking intently to a member of the delegation from Edo. She forced a smile. "The vice president's contrasting views allow me to strengthen my arguments. Come, let me show you the gardens. They are blooming beautifully now."

Rob Abernathy had worked the room for over two hours to ensure that he had discussed the economic disaster that would befall any nation that fully forbade the "service for safety" exchange of the impoverished from other lands and to assure each head of state or dignitary that would listen that the FA was actually considering legalizing thralldom for humanitarian reasons. He has swayed several. Enough to stymie that woman's plans.

Now he could concentrate on his personal agenda. "Ambassador Shima-san, I was so grieved to hear of your husband's passing." He bowed slightly. "He was a brilliant diplomat. Please accept my deepest condolences."

Yumiko Shima nodded. "Thank you, Vice President. You are well-schooled in the proper and respectful way to address Edoans, a rare gift indeed. I appreciate your kind words for Shigeo. It has been hard, but I do have family to support me." She pointed proudly to the small oval pin she wore that held a picture of a mature Edoan man; his young, very lovely Edoan wife; and their infant, who looked as wrinkled and ugly as all infants did.

"What a lovely family. And a beautiful baby. Is this your first grandchild?" He smiled falsely at the Edoan woman. He knew a bit of flattery would move his plan forward. Her ambition and ego would allow her to believe he had forgotten her connection to Mary and the trial that markedly delayed his arrival as a top leader in the FA. He had not.

Predictably, the old woman laughed girlishly, a sound that grated on Rob's ears. Then she opened her small silk bag covered in a pattern of blue water and white cranes and removed three small pictures. "No, these are my grandchildren as well." She stood even straighter, demonstrating the annoying conceit Rob believed the Edoans maintained as she presented the images. Rob took them with seeming politeness, making the necessary murmurs of approval. But this was what he was wanting. He scanned them quickly but intently. The two boys were young: one looking strikingly like the man on the pin while the other had the definite facial features of Mary. They could be sold after being used to draw his Bosch pirate to him. But the girl—he gazed at the photo hungrily…while not yet a woman, she was also not far away from it. She could be both bait and prize.

He handed the images back with a mannerly smile. "What a lovely family. My children, I'm afraid, are grown, and it is quite lonely without them. I did so love the energy in the house with children."

"They are a blessing of The Way," Yumiko agreed.

Rob Abernathy paused. "I just had a crazy thought. Now I know we in Eternia tend to be more audacious than you in Edo, but I would love for my wife and I to host you and your family at our villa in Haida sometime. It is on a beautiful stretch of land, and there are ruins from Old Earth that can be easily explored." *And it is isolated by dozens upon dozens of kilometers.*

Yumiko Shima looked quite pleased with this offer. "I doubt my son and his new wife and baby could make such a trip. He is busy working on Chinese treaties, and she is occupied with little Sumiko."

"Then you and your older grandchildren should come later this summer. The breeze from the bay is quite delightful." The vice president spoke encouragingly. "But perhaps, I overstep. Please forgive me. No insult intended, Ambassador."

Yumiko quickly said, "Oh, goodness, no. We would love to accept."

Rob smiled, and this time it was real. "Marvelous. I will have my office contact your assistant to set up the details. Thank you for honoring me with your presence and allowing me to have the delight of children in my home again. My wife, Sandra, will be so happy." *Though she will not be there.*

Yumiko Shima smiled, bowed, and moved back to her Edoan contingency. Rob walked back to his table and sat down, stretching his feet in front of him. It was all working just right.

THIRTY-FOUR

Finally

BOSCH, JUNE 2366

"New Earth, General! You are soaked to the skin!" Olivia exclaims as I appear at my office door, dripping from the June rainstorm that just rolled across the island.

I sigh. "I'm fine, Olivia." I walk, dripping, past her desk and toward my door, smiling. "The rain was so warm and inviting, I just couldn't bring myself to make a run for it like everyone else." I know there is a dreamy look on my face. "It's going to be a great day, you know?"

"But your bag?" Olivia motions to the lovely black and brown bag Mama gave me when I was elected. "All your papers?"

"It's fine." I pat my case. "It's fish leather—totally waterproof." I distractedly hand the bag to her and walk to my washroom to grab a towel. I am squeezing my curls with the towel as I return and lean on the wall, feeling the chill damp of my uniform press against me. "I had forgotten how much I love the rain." I smile. "How are you? Are you having a wonderful day?"

Now Olivia stands from her desk and comes over to me,

taking the towel and using it to dry my face and arms. "Are you okay, ma'am? You're acting...well, weird." As she says this, she starts to help me out of my vest, and I start laughing.

"Liv, I'm as good as I have ever been. I had a wonderful night last night and..." I pause for dramatic effect. "I have a date tonight." I grin and hear a schoolgirl giggle come from me.

Liv stops her fussing and looks at me, her face warm and her eyes bright. "Oh, please tell me it's with Major Warner." I nod, biting my lower lip as she continues. "Thank goodness you two finally figured *that* out. Tell me how it finally happened."

I set aside being indignant about her "finally figured" comment in order to tell her all about last night's dinner and dancing. "...and dessert did turn out to be Bailey's brownies! I even saved one for you." I gesture to my bag as Liv claps her hands.

"But did he kiss you?" she asks.

I shake my head. "The kids were pretty omnipresent, but tonight..." I give a sigh. "He did say as he left that he had never kissed a general before."

"Well, there's a first time for everything." Olivia starts her efficient bustle. "Now go get changed, and I'll call someone to come pick up this wet uniform and get it cleaned. Let's get to the business of the day, so you can get to what's important."

"To beginnings." Matty raises his glass and smiles across the table. We are sitting on the porch at the Riverhouse and have just been served two of the house's signature cocktails.

I raise my glass in response and can feel the smile that is

spreading on my face. "Beginnings." Our glasses touch and we both drink.

We chose the Riverhouse since it is a bit out of town and not frequented by base folk. "That way if this whole thing goes sideways, we won't have an audience," Matty had said with a chuckle.

"Is it going to go sideways?" I had asked as I slid into his vehicle.

He grinned. "I sure as hell hope not."

We are enjoying our drinks and just chatting about our days. I am enjoying the sweet familiarity of our conversation coupled with the underlying tension I feel from both of us. And not the bad kind of tension—the good, sexy kind.

My comm buzzes.

"Shit. Sorry, Matty. I have to see who it is. It might be Riki. Hazards of dating a mom." I shrug apologetically.

"Not a problem for me." He smiles.

I look at the comm and frown. "It's Cal Greene." I press the answer button. "Hey, Cal. What's up?"

"I'm sorry to interrupt your Friday night, Kat, but I need you to come over to the base and hear something."

"Can't you just tell me over the comm?"

"No, you want to come in for this. I don't want to say more over an unsecured line." Cal's voice is serious.

I sigh and look at Matty. "Sure, Cal. I'll be right there. Your office?"

"Yes. See you soon." The comm clicks off.

Matty holds up a hand and smiles warmly at me. "This is unanticipated, but it is not a problem. I'll drive you, and we'll resume the date portion of the evening afterwards."

I stand and sigh again. "Rotten timing, but thanks."

Matty grabs two rolls from the breadbasket a server is

walking with and hands them to me. "This will tide us over. I'll go settle the bill and meet you at the vehicle."

"So, what is so damned important that you need to drag me in from my first date in close to fifteen years, Cal?"

Cal looks at me and then at Matty, eyes squinting. "What do you mean first date?"

Matty shrugs. "We were on our first date."

"No." Cal's voice is definitive. "According to intelligence, you two have been together for a while now." Then he looks again between our faces. "Haven't you?" He shrugs. "Well, at least you two finally figured it out."

"Let's get to business, Cal." I can feel the blush forming on my face as I hear Matty chuckle.

"Okay, so this came up to Bosch Intelligence from Immigration after an intake interview with a woman. And then the regular BI investigator kicked it to my office, and my guy brought it to me late this afternoon." Cal has his hand on the doorknob of his inner office.

I frown. "And you were worried about saying something over a comm. Sounds like everyone on Bosch already knows about this."

Cal grins carelessly. "Well, up until now, you two didn't." He opens the door and motions us in. I give him a smack on the arm as I pass him.

"You are still an unruly kid, you know," I say as he laughs.

A tall, very attractive, woman looks up from where she sits tensely in a chair near Cal's desk. Her hands are in tight fists, and I look at her strong face and blonde hair and know her in an instant. "Sunniva!" She looks up, and I see her shoulders relax. "Kat, you are the general Major Greene said was coming? Your arm is better now?"

"It is."

"You two know each other?" Cal looks surprised.

I decide to get back at him. "You're in intelligence. Are you telling me you didn't know?" I give him a mischievous smile.

Cal responds with a roll of his eyes and a shake of his head. "Where did you meet?"

"That last mission. The big one," I say.

Sunniva grins as she watches Cal and I banter. "The one where we killed some traffickers together." Then she pauses and looks concerned. "That will not keep me from immigrating, will it?"

"I told you that you should be a pirate. Your work in that mission should move you ahead, not keep you wrapped up in bureaucracy." I frown. "Cal, what is all this about?"

Sunniva looks over at Cal and Matty and I see recognition in her face. "And you are the pilot that flew us out: Kat's partner." There is no question in her tone.

Matty sighs and looks at me and we both smile. "I remember you too," he says with a tone of resignation. Apparently our yet-to-occur relationship was already known to everyone but us.

Cal looks at Sunniva. "Please, tell the general what you've told me." He draws up two chairs for Matty and me and pulls his around from behind his desk.

Sunniva's pale eyebrows draw close together and she takes a deep breath. "I was a well-kept woman in Toft. My lover was rich and powerful. His name was Erik Hartvig."

I look quickly at Cal. "That was one of the cartel bosses, before Skau." He nods.

Sunniva continues, "Yes. I knew his businesses were not

good. But they were very profitable, and I benefitted from them. But then something went wrong, and Erik's boss came."

"His boss? But I thought he was in charge?" I tilt my head, trying to make sense of what she is saying.

Sunniva shakes her head. "He was in control of his area. But he told me a man had come several years earlier and had taken control of the business. Now he was the top…" She pauses to consider her word. "…manager, was the word he used. He didn't care. He still made plenty of markers."

Cal asks, "Did the man just take over Hartvig's area? Like Skau?"

"No. Skau was Erik's second. Erik said this other man was in charge of all the cartels."

I look at Cal. "A kingpin?"

He nods.

"Of all the cartels?" I feel my excitement build as puzzle pieces start to fit.

Cal smiles. "It gets better."

"DeLeon?" I ask.

Cal holds up a finger to me and nods to Sunniva. "Go on, Sunniva…"

"The man came, and he was unhappy with Erik because of the loss of several groups of thralls. Erik called the man Amber or Ander. He threatened to kill one of Erik's children. That was when Erik told the man his people had identified the culprits as Bosch. That saved his child's life. He ordered his men to take Erik's family and me to be sold as thralls to repay Erik's debt, and he said something about a woman named Mary and that he would get even with her."

My stomach drops and my eyes widen; I feel Matty reach for my hand, and I take it and give it a squeeze before releasing it as I stand up and move closer to Sunniva.

I squat in front of her and take her hands in mine and say gently but eagerly, "Sunniva, what did he look like?"

"Hang on, Kat. We can do better than that." Cal lays out five headshots of blonde men across his desk. "Is it any one of these, Sunniva?"

She looks at the photos carefully. "This one. This is the man." And her finger falls to the photo of the Federal Alliance vice president, Rob Abernathy.

Acknowledgments

The more I have become enmeshed in the work of writing and publishing, the more I am grateful to those who are so generous of their time and skills to enable an idea to become a book.

I'd like to thank those who have been part of this from the start: Martha Bullen, who gets the title "book coach," but is so much more. It's her voice and focus that keep me pushing forward. Everyone should have someone like Martha in their lives.

My editors, Dave Aretha and Andrea Vanryken, who help me craft a better book, but also trust my instincts as well.

My cover guys, Alan Hebel and Ian Koviak of The Book Designers, who continue to show me what excellent work and responsive service looks like.

And there are new voices: The authors of my Women's Fiction Indie Publishing group have demonstrated on the regular how to provide support and continue to show that a rising tide does lift all boats.

I have been delighted and touched by the growing group of Kat Wallace enthusiasts from across the United States and across the world. After all, I love Kat, and I am so honored when others come to love her in all her ridiculous messiness as well.

Thank you to each and every reader who is taking this journey. Your affection for Kat and her people and your interest in Pirates of New Earth means the world to me.

And as always, my love and appreciate to all three of my children, their partners, and those amazing grandboys.

And Rick, you are the best partner ever. None of this would have happened without your love and unwavering support. Thanks for being the best beverage manager around.

About the Author

Sarah Branson started conjuring stories of pirates at seven years old when her family hopped a freighter to Australia. Since then, she has grown up, traveling the globe, teaching middle and high school students, raising a family, and working as a receptionist, retail clerk, writing tutor, and certified nurse midwife.

She has lived in the US, Australia, Japan and Brazil and traveled elsewhere extensively. Through these myriad experiences, she has developed a deep appreciation for people's strength and endurance and believes that badass women will inherit the earth.

Sarah now works full-time as a writer and an author creating stories of action, adventure, revenge and romance with characters you'll never forget. She lives with her husband in Connecticut.

For more information and updates:
www.sarahbranson.com

Coming Soon:

Pirates of New Earth, Book Four: Blow the Man Down

When the unimaginable happens:

Kat Wallace's life is finally on track. She is poised to become the next leader of Bosch. She finally has a path to break up human trafficking on New Earth and destroy the man who enslaved her. And as an extra delight, she is starting to explore love with a man who knows her worth. Suddenly, though, the most precious parts of Kat's world, her children, are stolen, and it is up to her and her allies to retrieve them before they are lost forever.

Blow the Man Down

BOOK 4 PIRATES OF NEW EARTH

Monday, June 27, 2366

The horizon is a deep pink that fades into a sky streaked with gold and a few clouds are turning purple with tiny pink edges. The trees are dark silhouettes against the magnificence of the morning show, audience members to a play that has repeated daily since the beginning of time. I have my own place in the audience, watching from the front porch as I lean on the gray door jamb staring.

I smell the coffee and sense the warmth of Matty as he places my mug in my hand. "Did you sleep at all?" His warm voice rumbles as I feel his arm go around me.

I don't answer the question, but continue to watch the colors shift and change. "All three of the kids love sunrises. I mean they should." My voice gets husky. "They are always up so damned early, and I can't count the number of times I've barked at them for waking me up." I take a sip of the steaming coffee, and it struggles to get past the lump in my throat. "I wonder if they are up early, watching it now?" I feel the emotions build. "Matty, what if I never get…."

He takes my cup and sets it with his on the stoop as he

wraps me up in his arms and pulls me against his shirtless chest. "Kat. We will find them. We will bring them home. And we'll never let them out of our sight again." I hear the emotion in his voice, and the two of us stand holding each other. I allow myself a few minutes of tears and take the comfort from this man who has been at my side almost continuously since Takai called to tell me our babies and his mother were missing. Then I feel his body give a small shake, and I know his tears have started and I reach up to kiss them away.

I look at his eyes and nod. "We will. We will find them soon." I hear a noise in the house and turn my head to see Mama, up from where she was sleeping in Grey's room, looking bereft and bedraggled, as I imagine I look. Matty opens one arm and she comes close and we stand with our arms about each other as the sky shifts to an ordinary blue in a day that is anything but ordinary.

I come awake with a sudden gasp and am disoriented. I look around, not moving my body. Then I relax and smile as I realize I am on the sofa in my living room, asleep on Matty's chest with his arms about me. Then I remember and the heaviness settles in. I sit up and Matty wakes with the same suddenness I just did. We look at each other, and I lean in to kiss him, hoping for this magic to fix the horror. And for the tiniest moment, it does. We move apart, and I smell eggs and toast.

I stand and pull my nightshirt down over my naked bottom. "Mama? Are you cooking?"

I walk into the kitchen and see Carisa and Aaron at the counter and Carisa presses her finger to her lips. "She fell asleep about half a bell ago. It was hard to convince her to move from where you were."

"What time is it? How long did we sleep?" I am still groggy. Matty comes in, lays a hand on my cheek, and grunts a greeting to our friends as he makes his way to the toilet. *That sounds like a good idea.*

Aaron shakes his head, "It's about nine bells, you two only slept for about three hours I figure." He points to the food Carisa is plating. "We are on breakfast today."

"I don't think I can eat." My voice sounds dull and blank.

Carisa comes and takes my hand. "No, first we will go upstairs, and you will shower."

"And pee." I say flatly.

I see her smile gently. "Yes. You should do that as well. Then shower, then eat. Matthieu, you as well." Matty has come back in and nods obediently. He takes my hand from Carisa, and we head upstairs.

I hear the clocks mark ten bells as Matty and I sit at the table pushing the eggs around on our plates more than actually eating any.

"What did Riki say?" He asks.

I sigh. "He and Kenichi are trying to track how they left Kiharu. They don't even know if it was by vessel, ship or vehicle. They could be twenty kilometers away or two thousand. He did say he had found the comm I gave to Grey in Yumiko's kitchen, all my missed comms and messages were on it. So they don't have any way to contact us." I hear a disgusted sigh from across the table and I am right there with it. In a sudden appearance, Anger and Hatred join forces and bubble up in me at Yumiko, and I slap the table. "Damn her to oblivion! How dare she?! How dare she take my children!?" I pick up my plate and fling it across the room at the wall and it shatters, shards of plate and bits of egg and toast flying everywhere. Then I grab Matty's plate and lob it, hitting the same spot, a mass of plate and egg and toast and butter and jam spattered on the wall and scattered on the floor. I reach for another missile and grab my coffee mug and pull my arm back to launch and feel Matty's gentle grasp on my arm and the hand that grasps the cup.

In my ear I hear his voice, deep and calm. "No, you love that mug. Grey made it for you."

I drop my arm and look at the mug. It is a bit lop-sided and glazed in purple and blue. On one side I see where she had traced a heart with her little girl finger. I collapse in Matty's arms and sob, pulling the mug to my chest like it's my child.

Carisa and Aaron appear through the kitchen door. "What happened?! Are you both okay?" They stop short as they take in the scene: food spread over the far wall and me, a mess, wrapped in Matty's arms.

Aaron looks at Carisa. "I'll get a broom." I feel Carisa gently rub my back.

"Oh my…" It's Mama's voice. I turn my head from where it is burrowed in Matty's chest and guiltily realize I pulled her from sleep with my tantrum. Her eyes move slowly around the room, and I can see dark circles under them. Her face is a bit pale and I see wrinkles on it that I haven't seen before. There's no reassuring Mama smile. *Everyone is broken by this, not just me.*

I take a breath and shrug off Matty's embrace. "Mama, I'm so sorry I woke you." I walk over to her and smooth a strand of silver hair from her face. I fashion a smile on my face. "I kinda lost it." I realize I still have my Grey cup held to my breast and hold it out to her and she gently takes it and looks at it with tears in her eyes.

"Kinda?" I hear Matty give a small chuckle, and suddenly

Anger whispers to me, and I turn on Matty, stamping my foot and raising my voice, practically spitting at him. "Well, why not? Aren't you angry? How can you be so calm?"

I see him take a step back, but his eyes stay on me. I don't see any hurt or anger in them, just the warmth that has always been there, and now I can clearly see his love. He furrows his brows as he gazes at me standing ready to fight. Aaron stops in mid-sweep, and I see a glance pass between him and Matty.

This beautiful copper-skinned man sighs as he steps toward me slowly, as if I'm some wild animal he doesn't want to spook. "I told you. I don't let myself get angry since, I don't know, I was maybe twelve. I had a real bad time with my temper as a kid and it got me almost expelled and it cost me a few friends. So now I have to keep it under control." His voice is even but there is a sense of plea in it.

His stories surface in my mind, and I remember his description of a schoolyard fight with his ex-best friend. I soften. "I'm not mad at you, Matty. It's just….this waiting. Not knowing…My babies… I can't lose them like…." I feel my knees go loose, and I sink to the floor. I put my head in my hands and start to sob anew. Matty's big body folds down to the floor next to me, and he gathers me up and pulls me into his lap where I continue to cry, as he holds me close, kissing my hair.

And then there is a knock on the door that startles everyone.

The boy who rode up on the bicycle and knocked looks around the room with big eyes after Carisa invites him in. I recognize him. He works weekends down at one of the shops and always helps the older folk with loading their groceries. One time he even went home with one of the real old ladies and put all her foodstuffs away as directed and washed the dishes in her sink. She was so thankful, she tipped him fifty markers, and I remember she had said to Mama that he was going to grow up to be a good man. But for the life of me, as I sit cradled on the floor in Matty's lap, I can't recall his name.

Mama, a bit of pink now in her cheeks and her soft, everyday smile on her lips, has shifted into Mama-mode, and she is clucking over him. He makes eye contact with her and also with Aaron and Carisa, studiously avoiding looking at half-naked Matty and the odd general of the BPF who sits on the floor in a man's lap and has egg on her wall. In his hand is a large plain envelope.

"I was asked to deliver this to this address and to be sure it went to General Wallace." He glances around the room, and I know he is hoping he is wrong who that is.

I sigh and uncurl myself from Matty. Standing, I swipe at my eyes and my nose and straighten my shirt, glad I opted to put pants on after my shower. I shake my head and say, "I'm General Wallace." I make no excuses for anything.

He hands me the envelope, and I nod and see Aaron pull some markers from his wallet and tip the boy who moves quickly back to the door and I see, through the front window, him jump on his bike and ride away.

With Matty at my shoulder, I open the envelope and pull out a letter sized photograph. There is a moment of pause as we both stare.

I drop to my knees, the photograph fluttering away, and I vomit, placing more egg and toast on the floor beneath me, as I hear a roar of fury from the man I love as he flips the table onto its side, scattering the rest of the morning's repast.

Aaron's voice calls, "Matt! Not the...." The front window

shatters as a chair flies through it to land in the front yard causing the photograph to dance back into my vision.

There, sitting on an elegant sofa in a room with blue walls, is Rob Abernathy. My ex-mother-in-law sits primly next to him, clear pride written on her face. My daughter stands between his legs, smiling, her head tipped onto his cheek, and dark-haired Kik and sandy-haired Mac are happily settled, one on each of the monster's knees, laughing.

Also by Sarah Branson

A Merry Life: Book 1 Pirates of New Earth

Navigating the Storm: Book 2 Pirates of New Earth

Made in the USA
Middletown, DE
19 February 2023

25216730R00222